Regret to Inform You...

Derek Jarrett

Regret to Inform You...

Matador
9 Priory Business Park,
Wistow Road, Kibworth Beauchamp,
Leicestershire. LE8 0RX
Tel: 0116 279 2299
Email: books@troubador.co.uk
Web: www.troubador.co.uk/matador
Twitter: @matadorbooks

ISBN 978 1784623 524

British Library Cataloguing in Publication Data.
A catalogue record for this book is available from the British Library.

Printed and bound in the UK by TJ International, Padstow, Cornwall
Typeset in 11pt Aldine401 BT Roman by Troubador Publishing Ltd, Leicester, UK

Matador is an imprint of Troubador Publishing Ltd

There are over 100,000 World War One memorials in the UK.

*Perhaps there should be a memorial to those at home
who suffered for their loved ones fighting and dying abroad.*

It is to these millions that this book is dedicated.

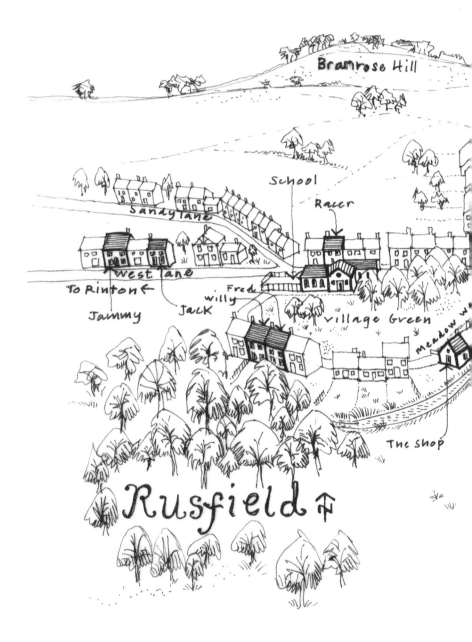

Bramrose Hill

School

Racer

Sandy Lane

West Lane

To Rinton ←

Jammy

Jack

Fred

Willy

Village Green

Meadow W

The Shop

Rusfield

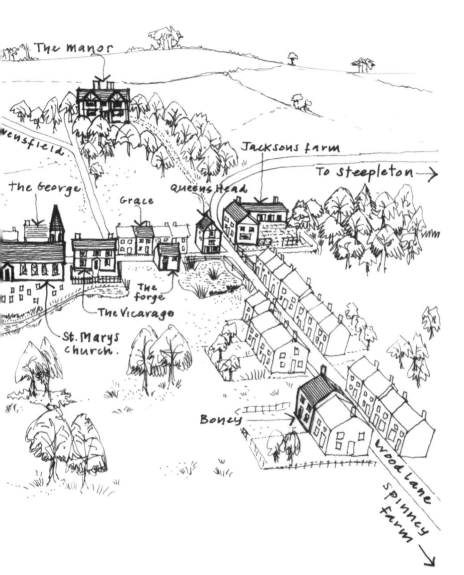

The manor

Wensfield

Jacksons farm

To steepleton →

the George

Grace

Queens Head

The forge

The Vicarage

St. Marys church.

Boney

Wood Lane

spinney farm →

'I will weep when you are weeping;
When you laugh, I'll laugh with you.
I will share your joy and sorrow
Till we've seen this journey through.'

- Richard Gillard, Hymn 'Brother, Sister'.

The Six Young Men

John Atkins (Jack)
James Carey (Jammy)
William Johnson (Willy)
Albert Jones (Boney)
Abraham Richards (Racer)
Frederick Smith (Fred)

Part One 1912
Part Two 1914 – 1919

PROLOGUE

Thursday, 15 January 1874

The pall of smoke rose slowly. Dark grey below, becoming ever paler until it was lost in the powder-blue sky. It gave no clue as to its origin, but a fire of great intensity must have been the cause. Whilst at first appearing becalmed, it provided the only movement on this windless and sweltering day.

The cause had to be a good distance away, for much closer was the lush green of trees stretching in every direction. So dense was this green that it could only be a tropical forest. No sound came from this forest, but perhaps the animals had been warned of the distant blaze and fled.

Nearer, the soaring trees gave way to land that had been cleared; a red carpet of soil, littered with occasional tree stumps and rocks. Whilst nothing save the gentle ascent of this pall of smoke was moving, and that only slowly, a closer look showed two signs of activity, but only just. On one of the tree stumps, a bird; grey-brown above, buffy-brown below and with a predator's beak. It was gazing as if with troubled eye, towards a larger being close to the ground. As eyes adjusted to the dazzling sunlight, a human figure, hardly crawling over the bare ground, would have been recognised. This figure was also in brown, but that uniform was filthy, blackened and torn. The man, for assuredly it was just that, edged forward, clawing his way onwards. The buzzard moved closer.

That movement saved the man: a soldier grappling to stay alive, a man whose actions were to hugely affect his son, at that time but a young child.

Part One
1912

ONE

Morning, Friday, 22 March

From the gentle, tree-covered slopes, the village was little different to others in this part of rural Suffolk; the small clusters of cottages, the soaring church spire and occasional human movement were unremarkable. As one got closer, it became apparent that many of the cottages were in need of repair: old thatch or broken tiled roofs and peeling paintwork. The narrow streets, where carts and horses vied to make the rutted impression, wove their way between the cottages. Given such an expansive landscape, it was surprising that the clusters of homes were so tightly packed: perhaps to protect each other from winter gales that occasionally swept up from the not too distant river.

Such was Rusfield, once a bustling scene, at least during the sowing and harvesting times when there had been employment for villagers wielding hoe, dibber and scythe. However, since many fields had been bought by a distant brewery, machines had taken over and many from generations of agricultural workers had been pressed further into a state of poverty.

To the west of the church could be seen the village school, a beacon of hope both when it was built thirty-five years earlier and now to the present generation. Families were large with many of the two-up, two-down cottages giving slim comfort to their large numbers. Some teenagers had learnt enough to move to one of the nearby towns where there were demands for builders and clerks; some to London where the urban sprawl gave opportunity, the workforce returning each Saturday afternoon. A few of the more ambitious, along with some who felt they had nothing to lose, had just migrated to Canada, two as far as New Zealand.

Apart from the church, few substantial buildings could be seen. The red-brick school and nearby schoolhouse, from which Peter Meadows and his wife would shortly be leaving, were partly obscured behind towering elm trees. Similarly, part hidden by the bare trees, was the decade-old Methodist chapel, which had replaced the former wooden structure. To the north of the village, and sensibly half-hidden by a dip in the hillside to catch the best hours of the sun, was the one large house, its mainly timbered walls and high, grey-stone chimneys clearly announcing a Tudor origin: the manor. To the south-east a substantial farmhouse and finally, a light-bricked, many-windowed and pleasant house near to the church: the vicarage.

The land around the church was owned by a Cambridge college, one of the reasons that make church history a fascinating story. St Mary's had stood since the eleventh century, its many additions and alterations almost hiding its Norman foundation. Coinciding with the final year of George II's reign, a priest was appointed to work among the people of Rusfield and four adjacent parishes, but a few years later he became poorly and the kindly bishop had removed the responsibility of the other four parishes from him: so it remained. The house was splendid in its fine Georgian style. With the realisation that parish priests might have large families, six bedrooms were included along with two studies and three living rooms.

The bedrooms had never been fully used, as the most productive incumbent had a mere three children and the current vicar, the Reverend Arthur Henry Windle and his wife, were childless. He had moved to be curate to the Reverend Charles Gulland twenty-one years previously, becoming its sole occupant when appointed as the vicar two years later. Any thought of moving to a grander church was counterbalanced by his unexpected feeling of comfort in working in this poor village. Undoubtedly, his delight in subsequently marrying the lovely, vivacious, much younger Eleanor had added greatly to this feeling of contentment. He could never stop counting his good fortune in taking a service at Wensfield, a village some four miles away, when he had first seen the beautiful Eleanor Brown. Whilst he later asked for God's forgiveness in having such feelings towards her in the midst of a morning service, he had been immediately enchanted by her looks, from her long black hair and her high cheekboned face to her elegant bearing. Such beauty, above all a gentleness, that reminded Arthur of a Vermeer painting he remembered from his student days.

On this Friday morning in late March, they were breakfasting in the room overlooking the attractively created patio in their large garden. The room was high ceilinged, light and comfortably furnished, as Eleanor, whilst thrifty, was a splendid homemaker.

'It is, of course, this evening that we'll be at the school hall for Peter's farewell. He really has achieved great things and I'm sure many of his old pupils will be there,' Eleanor ventured.

'Indeed,' her well-groomed, fair-haired husband replied, 'I hear there is to be something of a pleasant surprise for him, well deserved. After the shambles that I believe surrounded the former master, Peter has really moved things on. It's hard to find anyone who speaks ill of him and we'll be very fortunate if the new man achieves as much.'

'I need to go round to the school at five o'clock to help set things up when the other teachers are making sure that Peter's out of the way.' A slight sound from outside the room caused her to pause. 'Is that someone at the door?' she asked.

Arthur moved his plate to one side, stood up, revealing his full height of over six feet and moved into the elegant hallway. He returned a minute later carrying two letters.

'One for you, my dear, and one from the bishop's palace. I wonder what this is about.'

He sat down, took out his reading glasses, opened the letter using a spare knife from the table and read. A slightly quizzical look appeared on the face of this forty-four-year-old priest.

'What is it my dear? You look troubled?' Her husband passed Eleanor the letter which surprisingly asked, or rather told him, to see the bishop the following Thursday, just six days away. The precise hour should be agreed with the bishop's secretary although late morning was clearly suggested. A communication from the palace was not uncommon; what caused Arthur some puzzlement was that it was personally addressed and signed by the dean, rather than one of the many cathedral secretaries.

'Maybe,' suggested Eleanor, 'he's going to put forward a change for you, my dear. Certainly all that you've done here deserves recognition.'

'Would you like that?' repeating a question he had often asked her.

'I'm not sure. I know that with all the sadness you suffered in your early years here you might have once been pleased to move, but times change. I like the village. What of you?'

'I should only follow the best way of serving God. I'll just have to wait to see and find out what the bishop wants.'

TWO

Evening, Friday, 22 March

Rarely were the streets so alive with villagers, least of all an evening with a slight drizzle in the air. March had been a wet month and following on from an unusually snow-stricken winter, the weather was a constant point of discussion among the villagers; but not tonight, as other thoughts were uppermost in Rusfield. Glimmers of light showed as doors opened and people set out on the short journey to the school along one of several ill-lit and poorly-surfaced streets.

Coming out of one of the cottages in Meadow Way, the sprightly Judith Johnson looked back over her shoulder and called out to her son, 'Keep an eye on Ruby, Frank.' She knew that of her entire family, she and Ray worried most about dear Ruby. Some villagers called her simple, but her mother thought of her as innocent, sometimes lacking judgement for her own safety. Ruby was a girl who had always loved being held close, all right with her siblings but a worry to Judith now that her daughter was fast developing into a pretty, young woman.

As her neighbour emerged from next door, Judith commented to her, 'We shall miss him. He seems to have been here for ever.' Her own seven children, including Ruby, had all come under the sound instruction of the schoolmaster,

7

Peter Meadows. 'My kids always knew where they were with him.'

Liz Smith nodded in agreement as she joined Judith. 'Aye, you're right. I once thought he was harsh, but he was right.' Liz Smith had only the one child, of Fred's father she never spoke. The two neighbours took the short walk across the village green, quickly merging with the flow of villagers coming from Bury Way and Pond Street. There were many exchanges of cheerful greeting, all knew each other well. Approaching the well-lit school they went through the open double gate, along the short, stony path and entered the small, wood-panelled lobby opening into a well-lit room from which much chatter could be heard.

Major Sebastian de Maine, chairman of the school governing board, welcomed everyone. He was some sixty years old, slightly balding and wearing his customary thin-framed spectacles. 'Although what he really knows about the school and the children beats me,' commented Susannah Jones. 'He made sure his kids didn't come here, but went off to that posh school in Norwich.'

'Their loss,' responded her fair-haired and tall friend, Pauline Richards. 'They couldn't have done better than come here to find out about life and to set them up. Both of mine got good jobs when they left here.'

As they moved into the largest classroom, which also served the 130 children as a hall, they were surprised at the number of people there. The high room with beamed ceiling was painted a pale blue and displayed colourful pictures ranging from animals of the world to charts with handsome styles of writing, clearly examples for the children to copy. The early arrivals were sitting on chairs or ink-stained desks, the later ones standing near the back. The ever-elegant Olivia Atkins, attractive, almond-eyed and admired by all the bachelors and many other men in the village, smiled at the latest arrivals and moved nearer to the corner to give more space. A few

8

minutes later a hush descended as the schoolmaster, his wife and governors, all holding a position of some importance in the community, walked on to the improvised stage. A little clapping from someone near the front, a number suspected it to be one of the teachers, started more enthusiastic applause. Sebastian de Maine was smartly dressed with high collar, regimental tie and lightly-checked waistcoat and matching suit, although a close look showed the latter to be slightly worn. He held up a hand, an obvious call for order.

'Tonight, good people, we are gathered to thank the one who has given many years to our community. Our school opened in 1876 and of the intervening thirty-five years, our schoolmaster has been in charge for twenty-seven. He has ruled it well and that so many of you are here tonight is a measure of the high regard in which we hold him.' (Applause) 'He has made us proud of being able to send our children here.' (Slight guffaws were apparent at his use of the words 'our children').

Peter Meadows and his wife, Audrey, the only female occupant of the row of low chairs, looked a little embarrassed. The passing of years had treated them well. Peter had been appointed when he was an enthusiastic thirty-eight-year-old, and that enthusiasm, along with his charming smile and good looks, remained. His wife, who had done so much good in the village to support her husband, also retained both her health and attractive looks. They would be sorely missed as they moved to the West Country to be near their two children and three grandchildren. Now, the end of March, they would be settled in to their new home by Easter.

The clapping, joined by some cheers from the back of the hall, greeted the schoolmaster as he hesitantly rose from his chair, nodded and smiled. 'My many thanks to our school chairman, Major de Maine, and to all of you who have come along this evening. I am amazed to see so many here, thank you for coming. I remember my first visit to Rusfield when

I was appointed to this school. Is it possible that it's twenty-seven years ago? That was a special and proud moment. Any progress that we have made in that time has been due to our splendid staff.' He gave a special nod at Miss Rita Small, a lively and squat figure in the front row who had been at the school for all but two of his years. 'There are so many to thank, but I must make special mention of our vicar; you have been so supportive as has your dear wife since she came to the village.' He spoke clearly and swiftly, recalling some of the traumas that the school had been through, like the fire in two classrooms some eight years previously, and of many joyful times.

'Miss Small asked me earlier this evening what had been my proudest moment. There have been many, but let me remind you of a very special one that all of us share in feeling so proud. Remember that wonderful day in March 1908?' There were many nods. 'Our football team had been strong for the previous two or three years, but in the Michaelmas term of 1907 and the spring term of 1908, they reached amazing heights. It was on that glorious Friday evening, 20 March 1908, four years ago almost to the day, when they won the Three Counties cup.'

Great applause rang out, whilst the faces of six young men in the far corner of the crowded hall reddened in embarrassment. People turned to look at them and one or two standing near them spoke or mouthed their congratulations.

The schoolmaster held up a hand and the audience quietened again. 'It was a wonderful evening which I will never forget. I see six of them standing together now, though they've all grown a little since then! They were great friends then and it's good to see them together tonight. It was their behaviour as much as their skill of which I was so proud.' He looked very purposefully towards the young men who by now were even more flushed at the schoolmaster's words. 'As I'm sure we all know, one of them has gone on to achieve amazing success on the running track. Abraham Richards, we are delighted. When you were five you could race faster than the boys three years older and when you played in our football team you could easily outrun the opposition. Your friends, even the newspapers, rightly call you Racer Richards. It's well deserved now you're one of the three fastest quarter-mile runners in the country.'

There was prolonged applause before the retiring master concluded: 'There have been so many through the school of whom we can all be proud. It has been my joy to have given even a little help.' He sat down to much applause and the chanting, led by Willy Johnson, of "For He's a Jolly Good Fellow".

The chairman stood and called upon young Florrie Edwards and Robert Groves from class three who had been waiting at the side of the hall under the eagle eye of their parents. The children came forward with a long box, wrapped in colourful paper with green ribbon. As carefully rehearsed, they stopped just short of Peter Meadows and waited for the chairman to speak. 'To show our appreciation of our retiring schoolmaster, his many friends have collected for a present that we all hope will bring him much pleasure in his retirement.'

'Open it up,' someone cried out from the right side of the hall, a cry immediately taken up by others. Peter Meadows bent down, took the package from the children and laid it on the table put in place on the platform. The ribbon proved easy to untie and the wrapping removed. He lifted the top from the box and Peter Meadows let out an audible gasp. He carefully lifted out a telescope. He had difficulty in expressing his thanks and his wonder at such a gift.

'Remember,' Racer Richards said quietly to his neighbour, 'how he used to show us those pictures of the night sky and get us to name the planets and clusters of stars?'

'Aye, and everything in nature,' added Jammy Carey.

Miss Small quietly moved from her place to sit herself at the piano. She struck a chord and all stood as the national anthem was played. Some may not always have thought much about their relatively new monarch, but their loyalty to King and country was such that all joined heartily in singing. The well-rehearsed children at the front sang two verses, their parents less sure of the latter one, although those near the front of the audience easily heard a beautiful soprano voice. This was well supported by the small group of young men at the back of the hall; a fine baritone voice blending with the soprano and children. The Revd Arthur Windle thanked God for the retiring schoolmaster and pronounced a blessing. After the amen, a number of ladies hastily disappeared into the kitchen. Sandwiches and cakes soon appeared and cups of tea were collected from the serving hatch. Many gathered round Peter and Audrey Meadows and wished them well, including all six of the proudly remembered school team. He smiled at each of them. It was rightly said that Peter Meadows had a wonderful memory of each child that had passed through Rusfield School.

Eleanor had not been surprised to see her father, Charles Brown, in the audience; as she knew that he and Peter were good friends. 'Father, I didn't know you were coming. You're very welcome to stay the night at the vicarage.'

'No thank you, my dear,' replied the ruddy faced, fine-featured man. 'I enjoyed the walk here and I will enjoy the walk back to Wensfield. There's a good moon, so I will be fine. But, if you'll excuse me I'll just have a quick word with Peter. I'll miss him.' He moved over to speak with his good friend. After much chatting, the first people, mainly those with young children at home, left and the trickle became a greater movement.

'It was a lovely evening,' Eleanor said to her husband when they got back to the vicarage. 'So many will be forever grateful to Peter for all he has done for the school, and for leading the effort to set up the reading room.'

Their minds dwelled for a few moments on how Peter Meadows had persuaded Fred Jackson to give up one of

12

his unused barns to be equipped with whatever tables and chairs could be found and how Peter had personally bought, scrounged and begged for books to provide some kind of a place to read. Money had come from someone, known only to Peter. Books and newspapers were not things to be found in many homes in the village, but he had done remarkably well. They both knew that many of his pupils had been encouraged to use the reading room, which he hoped would become a habit on leaving school.

'Surely a night to remember,' smiled Eleanor, who had been Peter's major helper in setting up the reading room. She had done her best to ensure that some of the books might appeal to the younger females in the village, in spite of some early snide comments at her efforts. 'And mentioning the success of that football team was very kind with some of the lads being there. I remember Peter telling me how you used to support the team, Arthur. Of course, that was just before we met and I'm sorry I never got to see the school's great success on the football field. Altogether, a lovely evening.'

'Indeed, it was. Thank you dear, for all your preparation at the school,' smiled Arthur, 'you all made it a wonderful evening.'

They prepared for bed; the Revd Arthur Windle first retiring to his small dressing room, book-lined and less than tidy. He first jotted down notes of things that had occurred to him during the day for inclusion in the coming Sunday service: prayers must be given for God's protection of the brave young men that had just set off from Liverpool on their way to Canada. He thought about the newly appointed schoolmaster to take over from his friend Peter; then, his meeting the next evening attempting to improve the village street lighting, hoping that he could lead people round the usual disagreements that were notorious among the lighting board members. Finally, he reflected on the letter he had received that morning from the bishop's palace.

He knelt down in front of the simple wooden cross, one of the few gifts from his father who had brought it back from some foreign place, and prayed: 'Be with me God when I meet with the bishop. In truth you know that I would be sad to leave this village, but if you are speaking through the bishop to tell me to move on, may I fulfil that with determination and service to you. Your will, not mine be done. Amen.'

This tall, misleadingly austere-looking man of God crossed himself, got slowly to his feet, undressed and retired to bed; the moon cutting a narrow band of light across the bed. His arm went round his beloved Eleanor who turned towards him, gave her loving smile and kissed him. He was awake long after she had fallen asleep and, in spite of a joyful evening, he was a rather troubled man.

THREE

Evening, Friday, 22 March

The George, a small and sparsely furnished cottage, was of indeterminate age. One of three small public houses in Rusfield, it owed its offer of 'a room to sleep' to a badly written notice in the window for the unsuspecting traveller. In need of a fresh coat of paint, both inside and out, it still had its share of regular drinkers and being close to the school, Willy Johnson had suggested that the six friends pop in after the farewell event for the schoolmaster. Whether or not there was a legal age for drinking barely mattered to John Harrowell; he had a high regard for the six young lads who had brought glory to the village and in making an addition to his takings.

The room in which the six pulled up chairs around an unenthusiastic fire was draughty, gloomy and low ceilinged. The stocky and ever-cheerful Willy had always been the recognised leader of these lifelong friends, thus the natural captain of the school football team. Not renowned at school for being an academic, he had charm, tenacity and an ability to bring peace to arguments; everyone knew that once he set his mind on something, his terrier-like qualities generally won the day.

'It was good of old Meadowman to mention the team, if it hadn't been for his coaching we would never have made it,' Willy said as their full mugs of beers were passed around, just Albert Jones with lemonade. 'He doesn't seem to have changed since we left and that look of his tonight was just like the times he dished out punishments. Anyway, it's great being together again. Long time since that happened.'

They sat quietly for a moment, each recalling times shared in the past. 'Remember,' said Jammy Carey whose calloused hands revealed the heavy work of this muscular, well-tanned builder, 'how we used to meet in old Fatty Jackson's barn at Pond Corner, mess about and share what we thought were dirty jokes. It's a shame the others couldn't be here tonight. I know Tom and Copper are working in London and I guess the others just didn't get to hear about Meadowman's retirement or weren't interested.' He turned his stocky frame and looked at Fred Smith for he, along with the others, always felt for their friend's hard life. No father and Liz, his mother, taking in endless washing to raise enough money for the two of them and her own elderly and sick mother. At least with Fred working at Joe Bacon's smithy, the money situation had greatly improved. 'What have you been up to lately, Fred?'

'Not a lot, we've been going through a thin time with horse shoeing.' He glanced across at Willy for all knew that they were the very closest of friends. 'Willy is amazing, he knows so much about these things. Last Sunday we wandered across Bramrose Hill and good old Willy again tried to help me name some of the trees and plants that are just coming into bud, but best of all, and even I knew this from one of the school bird books, we saw a couple of buzzards circling high up. I thought they'd all been wiped out.'

'You're right,' chipped in Willy, his kind, weather-worn and strong features always evident. 'Let's hope they've come back for good. Since that bugger de Maine up at the big house imagines that even crows and jackdaws are a danger to his pheasants and shoots them, we'll have to keep an eye on him. Mind you, his son, Lionel, isn't much better. If he thinks he'll do anything about the buzzards I'll really sort him out. Lose my job up there, or not.' The others all knew that he meant just that. 'How's your job, Boney, going at the brewery?'

'All right,' his tall friend replied, 'it's only seasonal, but we're kept busy most of the time, 'specially when the harvest comes in. I'll be fine for a month or so although it's pretty boring at the moment cleaning all the machinery. A few weeks ago poor old Walter Mayling had his hand badly mashed up and I can't see him being able to work at such a job again. Not as bad as my dad's accident, but bad enough. They are not nice people to work for, but then a job's a job. But that's enough about me. You're the one who's becoming famous, Racer, how are things with you?'

The handsome, well-bronzed and charming Abraham Richards smiled in his usual modest way. 'Oh, I'm a very lucky one. It's healthy working on the farm and Mr Mansfield, my boss, lets me have time off to run which I can usually make up at weekends or in the summer evenings. He even took me in his car to a couple of races last year. It's all going very well, thank you.'

'So tell 'em Racer about your fastest time,' interjected the baby-faced, red-haired and normally quiet Jack Atkins. 'You know, when I came and watched.'

'Well, it was nothing special,' replied Racer. 'I managed 51.8 for the quarter mile in the season's last race in September last year and I certainly hope to beat that this year. The track last time was grass, but I'm up at Stamford Bridge in London in August and the track there is cinder and should be a lot faster. I hope to manage something around or just below 51 seconds.'

'Well,' said the ever-supportive Jack, 'you should be in the Olympics in the summer.'

'No chance of that, although I'd love to go to Stockholm. I hear that a couple of Americans have managed around 48 seconds for 400 metres and that's only a couple of yards shorter than what I do in three seconds more. That's some going. No Stockholm for me, although I'm determined to try for the team at the Olympics in four years.'

He raised himself slowly from his chair and the others watched as he poked the fire and put on an extra log. The immediate warmth from the burning logs replicated the warmth that each of them felt in their first get-together for all too long. Since knowing each other from a very young age, they had always rejoiced in each other's achievements, jealousy never seemed to rear its ugly head. Living so close to each other, their parents had always been friends, as had their grandparents. Willy, Boney and Abraham were cousins, a relationship much repeated in the tight network of village families. It was sometimes like sharing each other's parents as well as having one's own and when there was a family sadness that, too, was shared. They all knew that Jack's father, Edward Atkins, had been killed in a terrible thunderstorm and how all the community had given huge support to Olivia, his lovely widow.

The six went on to swap stories of their schooldays, recent family and village news, as although most lived at home still, work gave them little time to all meet up.

'Do you know,' chipped in Jammy Carey, 'I've sometimes felt a bit ashamed of some of the things we used to get up to.'

'Like what?' asked Racer.

'Well, like the time we moved old Grumpy Grout's privy.'

'I don't know about that one,' intervened Jack Atkins.

'Well,' went on Jammy who had first mentioned this old exploit, 'you remember old Grumpy whose cottage backed on to the pond? He always seemed a miserable old devil anyway, but I'd been ticked off by him for skimming some stones across the pond. I know it didn't involve you, Jack, but Fred, Boney and I decided we'd play a bit of a trick on him. At that time Grumpy's privy was a small shed in his rear garden that backed right on to the pond. We all knew that he went to The

Queens Head every night, so during the evening we slipped into his back garden and managed to lift the privy up and turn it right round, so the door almost hung over the pond. We then waited nearby. Eventually old Grumpy came home and, just as we knew he would, he walked down his garden to the privy. Of course, he couldn't understand what had happened as he obviously couldn't get inside it.'

'So what happened next?' asked Racer who had certainly not heard this one before.

'Well, he just went and pissed in the pond. A bit disappointing really,' answered Jammy. 'Poor old Grumpy.'

'Well, I never knew about that, though of course, I remember Grumpy Grout well enough. One thing I must tell you,' continued Racer, 'as I expect you know Mr Mansfield always has a party night just before Easter at Spinney Farm. He says it's his way of thanking everyone. It's always on the Wednesday before Easter. He says that as there aren't so many workers now that he's brought in more machinery, we can each take along three or four friends. So, how about it? It will be a good evening, anything up to fifty people.'

Jammy Carey knew he could not make the event as he would still be in Ilford working on a building site that had to be finished by the end of April, but the rest thought they could manage it and agreed on a seven o'clock meet up in The George.

'We can then all walk up to Spinney Farm,' added Racer. 'There will be plenty of beer, some girls if we're lucky. You've got a good voice, Boney, so we can rely on you for our sing-song.'

Other things they had done were recounted. Jammy Carey, who had spent much of the time since leaving school working away from the village, asked about the vicar's wife. 'I hadn't really seen her before. She is beautiful. Do you have to be a man of the cloth to get a wife like that?' There were smiles and laughs; Jammy's interest in girls had started well before

19

leaving school, although all of them had regularly swapped stories about village girls, tales often exaggerated. Before long their evening came to an end with warm handshakes as they left, either singly or with friends. All of them had jobs to go to the next day, even though it was a Saturday.

That they were now not able to meet together so regularly probably caused them to be a little out of practice in sharing each other's troubles: Fred, worrying about his overworked and sickly mother; Willy, of his beloved sister Ruby; and Boney Jones about his injured father who would probably never be able to work again. Most surprisingly, was a very worried Racer Richards who had recently been approached by an unknown, but obviously unpleasant character who offered him £5 to lose his next race, or face the consequences.

Racer's parents had been particularly kind to Jack's mother when her husband had been killed, so it was natural that the two boys had become great friends almost as soon as they could walk to each other's home. On leaving The George, Racer made certain that he and Jack set out together on the short walk home. A few minutes later these close friends were deep in conversation, Jack's normal, smiling face changing to a deep frown.

FOUR

Morning, Thursday, 28 March

The sky remained a leaden grey, the drizzle falling on the following Thursday morning as Arthur let himself out of the vicarage. He had taken particular care in dressing for the occasion; Eleanor had insisted on ironing his clerical shirt, frock coat and trousers and with his moustache neatly trimmed and his thick, fair hair suitably parted, she had said how proud she was of him as they parted with a kiss.

The thirty-mile journey to the bishop's palace in Canchester would take until mid-morning, so an early start was necessary. The old, rather battered Georgian clock in the hall was showing a few minutes to seven o'clock as he let himself out. He put up his umbrella, wishing he had chosen rather more suitable footwear, but galoshes would hardly be suitable wear to visit the bishop.

Although he was a well-known figure cycling around the village on pastoral visits, the state of the road to Steepleton and the continuing rain, made such a start inappropriate for his appointment. He was delighted to see that the bowler-hatted and full-bearded Sparky Carey, no one knew why this nickname, was outside with a pony and cart. He seemed able to get his hands on most things needed by villagers and, whatever doubt some may have had about his total honesty, his redeeming quality of kindness was a byword in Rusfield.

'Mornin' Rev'rend. Jump aboard. Glad ye 'ave an umbrella. As yer can see, I couldn't get a proper cover for me cart.' Arthur clambered aboard with his umbrella still up, noticing that the main part of the cart was full of logs for a later delivery. He held the black umbrella to give as much protection as possible to the two of them, but was glad of his black waterproof cape. The road near the pond was awash and there was a deeply-pitted stretch as they went past Fred Jackson's farm. Fred had told Arthur that whatever bricks and rubble he placed in the holes, they seemed to be swallowed up, but along Manor Lane the road improved a little.

Apart from the occasional curse from Sparky, toned down for the sake of his ecclesiastical passenger, few words were exchanged. The rain, fortunately now more gentle, was a strong deterrent to conversation and even as it grew lighter, the sky promised no real improvement. The journey to the station in Steepleton, a town of some 6,000, was four miles. Apart from passing an unrecognisable figure with a sack held over his head, they saw no one on this thirty-minute journey; much care was needed by Sparky as he kept the cart wheels clear of the deepest, water-filled ruts. Reaching the station forecourt, Arthur felt in his coat pocket and pulled out some coins.

'Nay. Nay, Your Rev'rend. You do plenty for nothing for us in the village, so you keep that. Safe journey.' With profuse thanks from Arthur and a slightly embarrassed acknowledgement from Sparky the two went their own ways, to very different activities.

Five minutes until the train was due; a local one which would carry him to Canchester. In spite of its interesting historic buildings, not least the cathedral and its adjacent buildings, Arthur rarely visited the city with just occasional shopping trips with Eleanor, mainly pre-Christmas, and infrequent attendance at concerts in the cathedral. His duties in the parish took up much time, quietly supporting parishioners and trying to improve life for those in Rusfield, although he would never have given claim to either.

Whilst he appeared unaware of the apparently contrasting sides of his personality, Eleanor knew all too well that many villagers saw him first as rather an austere parish priest, but ultimately a kind, generous and caring man. He remained strict to his interpretation of the Bible and how priests were expected to act, but was loving and generous in his understanding of people. It was the latter that had drawn this seemingly different couple together, when Arthur had all but given up hope of ever finding someone to share his life again, after the appalling death of Florence, his first wife. He never ceased to thank God for his beloved Eleanor, kind and beautiful in looks and spirit. He knew that it was her smile, her good sense and love that gave him strength. Her faith was much simpler than his, fine-tuning her life to the Sermon on the Mount. Not for her the ancient utterances of the Old Testament, often advocating revenge. Christ's simple words were the tenets of her Christianity; her vision of God was not easily compatible with ornate cathedrals, academic debates of complicated church teachings and church artefacts, but of Jesus on a hillside speaking to poor people from nearby villages. Arthur understood this driving force behind his wife's life, albeit that his own faith was built more on the Ten Commandments and canon law as much as Christ's teachings. But these differences in belief mattered little, indeed somehow they seemed to bring them closer together, for their love for each other, both spiritual and physical, was never in doubt. Both rejoiced in their deeply intimate relationship.

Passing through to the up-train platform, he was surprised to see one of his parishioners, one of around a dozen travellers waiting. Susannah Jones, a pleasant if rather careworn middle-aged woman, was doing her best to shake the rain off her umbrella. Arthur went to her, raised his hat and asked if she, too, was going to Canchester.

'Nay Reverend, just to Branton,' naming the small town two stops before his own.

'You must have been very proud when the schoolmaster spoke so well of the school team, I know Albert was an important player in that team. Where's he working now?' Arthur asked.

'Pity is he's now working at Bifields in Branton.' Arthur recalled that it was at the same brewery where Sidney, Susannah's husband, had met with his accident two years previously.

It seemed rather a trite question to ask how Sidney Jones was, but ask he must.

'Well, he can't work: getting a job when you've had your arm cut off makes that impossible. That's why I'm off to the brewery now, to see the buggers.'

Arthur gave a slight smile of what he hoped was encouragement and in no way an admonishment of her vocabulary. Indeed, the thought flashed through his mind that whilst he didn't approve of such words, Eleanor would have smiled and said, 'Well, she used the word because it was probably right.'

At that moment the train pulled in and it was natural that both should get into the same compartment. 'I've had this latest letter from them,' continued Susannah, 'saying that they're not prepared to give anything.'

'Why, what did you ask for?'

'Well, Albert, young though he be, spoke with the union man at Bifields, but a fat lot of good that was as the brewery does its best to keep the union quiet. Albert was even warned that if he made any more enquiries, his work might be found to be wanting and as there are lots of people looking for jobs, he might join them. I spoke to the schoolmaster and he kindly wrote a letter which I carefully copied out. It said it was the company's fault for not looking after their machines properly and they should give Sidney some money for losing his arm. Now, yesterday, I got this letter saying they had looked at things very thoroughly and it was all Sidney's fault; even going so far as to say that he might well have been drinking. Well, Reverend, as you may know, my Sidney hasn't touched a drop for years. Why, he even joined one of them temperance groups, as did Albert.'

'So, what are you going to do now?'

'I'm going straight in to Branton, go up to brewery and make sure I see the boss.' She passed the letter, which she'd been tightly clutching, to Arthur. He read the terse letter and passed it back.

'Well, Mrs Jones, do let me know how you get on, maybe I can do something to help.'

She smiled her thanks. For the rest of the journey they talked of village matters: street lighting, the state of roads and one or two family matters. Susannah Jones found herself able to talk very easily with her vicar, in a way that few others, apart from her very closest friends, encouraged. By now they were drawing in to Branton and Susannah Jones stood, brushed back a lock of her dark hair, thanked Arthur and left the carriage.

Arthur reflected on their conversation, regretting that he had not offered help before and making a mental note to call on the family in the next few days. He had been glad of their conversation, it had taken his mind off the impending meeting with the bishop and he found the rest of the journey much more worrying, although he criticised himself for his introspective thinking.

FIVE

Morning, Thursday, 28 March

The way up from Canchester station to the cathedral was steep, the twelfth-century planners had chosen the highest point to create a building to the glory of God. Arthur knew the short cut off to the left; a street, indeed rather more a wide alley that he loved. The cobbles edged with moss seemed ageless as did the centuries-old walls on either side, richly varying in reds and greys, chipped near ground level with signs of hand-pushed vehicles knocking against the sharper corners. To Arthur every stone breathed its great age.

Rounding the final corner his gaze fell upon the 800-year-old cathedral, a wonderful mixture of Norman, Perpendicular and late-Gothic styles, remodelled over the centuries by a succession of bishops as if each had vied with his predecessors to create an even more glorious structure. It soared into a compelling statement of God's might, revealing the wonders of architecture and man's power. Arthur had always loved such fine buildings, yet he wondered how many workmen had toiled and died in its construction.

Although he had not seen a great deal of his father in his own formative years, his father soldiering overseas and his own years at boarding school preventing a very close attachment, they shared certain passions. From his love for fine cathedrals and his experience in a modest rural church, Arthur sometimes confronted a dilemma: he found himself torn between serving the people in his own small village and a wish to be part of the priesthood in this great monument to God.

He approached the bishop's palace along a cobbled pathway. A truly illustrious house, built in the fifteenth century, it had been the home of many bishops; those who had extreme wealth from their large land-ownership to more humble men who had been servants of their people and cared little for earthly treasure. It had stood, and would continue to stand, whatever frailties or strengths bishops might demonstrate. He knew that the blue door, part hidden in the angles of two wings to the house, was his way in, remembering how he had first anxiously entered through that door in the autumn of 1891 when appointed to Rusfield. Only slightly less anxious this time, he again entered, into a surprisingly well-lit hall; late nineteenth-century windows had replaced much smaller ones. He was greeted by a priest, clearly a humble part of the hierarchy leading to the bishop.

'I am the Reverend Arthur Windle and have been summoned by the bishop. I have an appointment with My Lord the Bishop at eleven o'clock.'

The older man rose slowly to his feet, greeting Arthur with a kindly smile. 'Welcome. Please follow me,' leading him along a narrow corridor, wood-panelled and with a floor that was well worn yet which caught the eye with its rich glow. The clerk pushed open a large, heavily decorated door and signed for Arthur to enter. 'Please wait here, sir.'

Arthur looked around the room. The windows on one side which looked out on to a small courtyard were clearly of a relatively recent age, perhaps early last century. Arthur, thinking it best to remain standing, called the bishop to mind. A pleasant, rotund figure with well-kept beard came into his mind. Seeing a set of some dozen prints on the wall opposite to the window, he moved across the room for a closer look, but before he got there, the door opened and in walked a cleric whom he did not know: a man with sharp features, balding head and richly robed.

'Let me introduce myself. I am the Very Reverend Edgar Hartley Williamson, recently appointed dean of the cathedral.' Arthur smiled a greeting, and whilst he knew that a new dean had come to the cathedral, wondered about his presence now; was the matter of his own future of such importance that it warranted dean and bishop?

'His Lord, the Bishop, sends his regrets, but has started a severe cold which rules him out from seeing you. Please sit down.' He waved Arthur to one of the several chairs and settled himself at a distance which Arthur felt a little unnecessary. 'We haven't met previously. Please tell me a little about your background: your training for the church and appointment.'

Arthur felt rather as if he was being interviewed for a position in the church; maybe that was the intention of this meeting. 'Well, I went to Wycliffe Hall in Oxford which, as you know, provides an excellent training for the ministry. I qualified in 1891 and was first appointed as a curate to Rusfield, but as vicar when the Reverend Charles Gulland died two years later; I took his place and that is where I am now.'

'And, of course, it's really an accident of church history that you are vicar of a sole parish. Tell me, how many live in Rusfield?'

'Together with the many surrounding small farms and cottages I think,' replied Arthur, 'that at the last count there were just a few short of nine hundred. Thirty years ago there were, I believe, rather more, but since fewer men are now needed on the land, a number of families have moved to Steepleton or Canchester for work.' He could see that the dean was itching to move on.

'But let's get on. Tell me, how are things with you in Rusfield: the congregation, your church officers, your own well-being? Please speak freely.' The dean's tone was businesslike, something less than warm or inviting.

'Things are well at St Mary's. Many people need considerable help and most families are supportive to the church, although that support, as I'm sure you must know, is lacking in worldly wealth. Many families find it hard enough to feed adequately, as the villagers have long depended upon agricultural work. A number rely on the little that their womenfolk bring in by straw-plaiting, although the calls for that are much less now that the factory in Lupington imports most plait from abroad at cheaper prices.'

'Yes, yes. But do they attend Divine Worship? Do you have many communicants and young people undergoing the training to become members of our blessed church?' Somehow, it appeared to Arthur, that whilst the dean demanded much activity in Rusfield, he hardly expected positive answers from such a rural parish.

'The number of communicants,' replied Arthur, 'remains fairly constant and the number on major feast days is encouraging. What is really encouraging is the way in which families support one another during these hard times. You ask about church officers. We rejoice in the ones who faithfully fulfil such duties. I realise that all but the older members work long hours and have limited time or energy to expend on such duties.'

'You have told me enough of your parish for me to be able to write my report for My Lord the Bishop. Let us turn to you more personally.' Arthur noted the emphasis on his final word.

'I have now been parish priest for nineteen years and rejoice in having the good fortune to be at Rusfield. I am also fortunate in keeping good health.'

Arthur was about to elaborate a little, but raising his hand enough to suggest he had heard sufficient about Arthur himself, the Very Reverend Edgar Hartley Williamson interjected: 'And your wife, I believe you are married – and family. You have, I understand, a very desirable residence.'

'The vicarage is most pleasant. I am blessed with a lovely wife, Eleanor.'

'Your second wife, I believe,' said more in an accusatory than sympathetic tone. 'And children?' as if this was his intended question when he had asked of family.

'It is our only true sadness that we have not been blessed with children, but for me the love of my wife is rich compensation.'

'And your wife?' Arthur felt more and more as if he were thirty years younger being questioned by his headmaster.

'She, too, keeps well and gives me support in all I do. She visits many parishioners and has a wonderful way of listening to people and knowing the best way to respond. I treasure her in all that she does, just as I do in her being my wife.'

'She sounds an interesting person. I understand that her support extends to women gaining the vote; that she belongs to this new suffragette movement, even to sympathising with the Women's Social and Political Union. Is that the case?'

'Most Reverend, let me say that the suffrage movement is not new, it is at least forty years old and my wife does believe in equality in voting. She does have sympathy with the WSPU, but is less than certain about the ways in which it goes about its claims.'

'You mean,' cut in the dean, 'the group that is setting out to destroy our nation's harmony and well-being. They are saying that our church is wrong in that they see us supporting the government against such outrageous demands. Only recently they disrupted a service at Westminster Abbey and this very month over one hundred women were given hammers and instructed to smash windows in the very centre of London that caused over £5,000 of destruction.'

Arthur could see the dean bristling with anger and his face becoming redder, an anger undoubtedly seen by this newly appointed man in the cathedral as righteous. 'Is that what your wife wants?'

'Eleanor certainly believes that women should have the same voting rights as men, but she does not support anything which would harm anyone. To her, the sanctity of life is even more important than gaining voting rights.'

'You sound as if you agree with her,' uttered the dean, almost in disbelief.

Arthur, showing his anger less evidently than the dean at being questioned about his wife, replied slowly. 'I firmly believe that some of the things being done by the movement are wrong. I do not believe that this is the right time for voting rights to be given to women, even if that comes about in the future.'

'Have you told her this? Have you tried to dissuade her and show her it is wrong? Indeed, very much against our church.'

'Just as I know my wife's feelings and deep beliefs, she knows mine. As we agree on most things in life, so we disagree on some others. But one thing that we entirely agree upon is that we respect each other's views. Eleanor knows how I feel, but I know her views.'

'But as a priest, have you done all you can to reveal her mistaken beliefs?'

'I am a priest, and I may well be a poor one in much I do, but to Eleanor I am a husband above all else.'

There was an audible sigh from the Very Reverend Edgar Hartley Williamson, but for all his rank in the cathedral's hierarchy, he felt checked by the gentle force of this parish priest's words. 'My Lord, the Bishop, had suggested that as you have now been in your parish for over twenty years, the future way in which you could serve the church might be discussed. However,' he paused for a moment, 'I have taken up a great deal of your time so let us keep that conversation for another occasion.' He lent forward, placed his hands on the elaborate arms of his chair and stood.

Arthur realised that the dean was indicating that he go: to Arthur the feeling was mutual. With almost unseemly haste the dean stretched out his hand, briefly and weakly shook hands and ushered Arthur to the door. A terse, 'Thank you for coming, I know My Lord the Bishop will read with interest my summary of our time together.'

SIX

Afternoon , Thursday, 28 March

Leaving the bishop's palace, Arthur felt a mixture of disappointment and anger; disappointment at not meeting the bishop or having any further clue to his future, anger at the dean and his questioning about Eleanor. He wondered if it had always been the intention that the dean, perhaps a new hatchet man, should see him. Such things were not unknown in the intrigues of the church.

Distressed, even annoyed by his feelings of anger, Arthur checked his agitated stride, turned and hurried along the paved path to the main door on the west side of the cathedral. Apart from a lady arranging flowers and a family of three, probably visitors, the great building was empty. He gazed first at the wonderful fan-vaulted ceiling, remembering how he had felt overawed on his visit to King's when at the age of thirteen his father had walked him around Cambridge. Arthur had never understood why his father intended to set him on a highly academic course which, in his own mind, Arthur knew he would never achieve. His eyes moved on to the beauty above the altar, a series of stained-glass windows revealing the life journey of Christ from humble birth to the cross.

On one side was the smaller Beaufort Chapel to which he moved. Before its small but wonderfully clothed altar, he knelt, waited and gradually became consumed by the history and magnificence of the cathedral. He trembled at his own weakness in wanting a move to suit himself rather than his God. He waited, yet a certain emptiness caused him to feel that in some unexplained way God was further from him than when he knelt in his own church.

He left, retracing his steps to the beginning of the narrow market lane; its downward slope matching his recent declining regard for the meeting at the bishop's palace. Unlike his own feelings, the sky had cleared and a gentle sunshine lit up the street. Arthur purchased a newspaper from a young lad as he needed something other than the morning's meeting to occupy his thoughts. The next train was in twenty minutes, a slow one stopping at each station on its way to Rusfield. He determined to read his paper.

The main story revolved round the Women's Enfranchisement Bill being defeated in the House of Commons. Clearly the *Canchester Daily Times* applauded this result, although Arthur knew that Eleanor and her friends would accuse the government of downright trickery in gaining a victory. All were waiting to hear news of Captain Scott's attempt to reach the South Pole, but meanwhile, the newspaper gave details of Norwegian claims that Amundsen had reached it three weeks previously. Scott's disappointment made his own frustration at the meeting with the dean of little significance. He needed to pull himself together.

Reading on, he saw that plans were almost complete for the opening of the Olympics in Stockholm and his mind turned to Abraham Richards whom he knew hoped to run for Great Britain four years on. His musing was interrupted by the approaching train.

Once inside the carriage, he finished the newspaper all too quickly and found his thoughts returning to the morning's unexpected outcome. Arthur wondered if the bishop had told his new dean how to run the conversation and did the dean really mean that unless he stopped his wife being an active member of the suffragettes, he would certainly not get any form of promotion? It certainly seemed so. How would he put things to Eleanor when he got home? They had always been honest with their own views and whilst they had often discussed, indeed sometimes argued about each other's views, they always respected the other's opinion.

He was surprised how quickly the return journey was over. The sky further lightened and there were traces of blue above Steepleton station as he alighted from the train. It reminded him of one of his mother's many sayings and proverbs, 'Enough blue to make a sailor's pair of trousers'. He thought of his mother with great affection and wondered when she and his father would next travel up from Dorset to visit them.

He found himself really enjoying the hour-long walk back to the village. It did not matter if he messed up his shoes now, although he was careful to avoid the deepest potholes which were well over ankle-deep in water. He stopped to watch a hovering kestrel looking for an unsuspecting vole and giving a masterly display of aerial suspension; then his attention was caught by a much larger bird flying some distance to his right over Bramrose Hill - a buzzard. He was reminded of his student days at Wycliffe Hall when he cycled into the Oxfordshire countryside and enjoyed the things of nature. Arthur had never had any doubts that whilst magnificent buildings were created by men, albeit to the glory of God, birds and all nature could only have been created by God.

Getting to the edge of the village he walked across to give a friendly greeting to Mrs Cruise, one of the oldest parishioners. She was sitting in the doorway to her cottage, busy plaiting the last of the straw from the previous year's harvest. No doubt she needed all the light she could get, Arthur knew her eyesight was failing in her endeavours to gain a meagre income to add to her old age pension. How glad she must be that Lloyd George had introduced the pension; five shillings might not seem a lot, but he knew it made a huge difference to Mrs Cruise and others like her.

Rounding the final corner before he would reach home, he almost bumped in to one of the Reynolds' children. 'Hello,' said Arthur, 'where are you off to?' Although seeing one of the youngest of this family of ten children, he already knew the answer.

Tucking the bedroll even more tightly under her arm, Lily replied, 'Well, sir, it's my turn to sleep at Auntie Bertha's house this week.'

Arthur knew that the Reynolds' house, like most in the village with just two rooms downstairs and two up, could not possibly sleep all of the large and growing family and some of the children slept elsewhere. 'Take care,' Arthur called out, 'see you at Sunday school.'

Five minutes later, he was standing on the vicarage doorstep searching for his key when Eleanor opened the door. 'Arthur, my love, welcome back. You must be exhausted. I've got the kettle on.' She put her arms round him and they kissed. Arthur took off his mud-splattered shoes, hung up his hat, coat and cape, following Eleanor into the large kitchen. 'Now, Arthur, you sit down. I've made some teacakes so have one, or more if you like, with your tea.' He sat down in his favourite chair wondering how best to tell Eleanor all that had happened. He need not have worried, for how good she was at judging the best way to start a conversation. The soft blue eyes settled on Arthur, but she let him get well underway with his tea and teacake before prompting him to speak.

'So, how did you get on my love? How did you find the bishop?'

From telling his wife how surprised he was to find that his meeting had been with the dean, he moved on to what he now thought to be the real purpose of the summons to Canchester.

'It seemed to me that you should really have been there although, of course, I didn't know that until this morning.'

36

His wife gave a slightly puzzled look, but refrained from interrupting him. 'Well, it was as if his questions about my background and St Mary's were just a prelude to his real purpose: to launch into the fact that you supported the suffragettes.'

'He what?' In spite of her intended silence to listen to Arthur she couldn't help interjecting these words of surprise. He could sense her tone of disbelief.

'After I told him about the support you give to me in the parish, he said in a very direct way that he knew you supported the suffragettes. He leapt to the conclusion that you supported, indeed were actively involved in their more extreme activities.'

Arthur was finding it increasingly hard to relay to his vivacious wife all that had transpired at the bishop's palace, but neither he nor Eleanor ever stopped short of telling the truth. 'He really said all that, Arthur? Pray tell me what you said?'

He finished his cup of tea, a moment to collect his thoughts. 'I told him that you definitely supported the movement, but the sanctity of life was overwhelmingly important to you. In other words you would never knowingly cause harm to another. I told him I respected your views as you do mine. Believe it, or believe it not, he demanded to know whether I had used my position as a priest to dissuade you.'

He wondered how Eleanor would respond: disbelief, anger and if anger, to whom would that anger show? To the bishop? The dean? Even to himself? As had been the pattern in so much of their life together, he was surprised at her words.

'Poor Arthur! And you had gone wondering whether you were to be offered a bigger parish, whilst the whole plan seems to have been spying on me.' She stood up, moved across and lightly kissed his cheek. 'Thank you for saying what you did. I know we don't see eye to eye on votes for women, but we will always respect each other. I love you even more for saying that.'

Arthur relaxed as their love remained unaffected. 'Come on,' said Eleanor, 'it's not raining and it won't be dark for another hour. Let's take a walk along Church Stream.' Arthur nodded in delight.

Quickly dressed in warm coat and wellington boots, they left by the back door, walked to the end of the garden, through the small wooden gate and onto their own special path which came to the deep gully from which Church Stream emerged and crossed Bury Way beyond the churchyard. How many times had they walked together along this narrow path as it followed the shallow stream? It was slippery now and care needed to be taken. The trees, a mixture of oak, horse chestnut and elm still showed their unadorned winter wear.

Eleanor stopped and turned back to her husband, the path was too narrow here for them to walk alongside each other. 'I love this time of the year,' she said. 'Of course, it's lovely when all the leaves show themselves, but look at the patterns of the bare branches; that oak over there, amazing.' They stopped, too, a little further on and Arthur gently pulled a low branch even lower.

'Look, sticky buds. I remember as a child I once collected some, took them home and gave them to mother. Strange, I hadn't thought about that until just now.'

Eleanor ducked under a low, almost horizontal branch on which many children had swung, stretched out her hand and took Arthur's and guided him underneath. Like the many young lovers who had walked hand in hand along this stretch over many years, they rejoiced in each other's company. 'Damn the dean,' thought Arthur.

As if reading his thoughts, Eleanor returned to their earlier conversation. 'If the dean should ever question you again about my support for the suffragettes, suggest he and I meet. Perhaps I can persuade him to change his views. I just cannot believe that God plans for people to have different rights; surely he is a God of equality.' Quickly realising that she had, perhaps, unwisely returned to this theme, she pointed to some small yellow flowers on the nearby bank.

'Aconites or celandine, I can never remember which. I really ought to know.'

They wandered on a further half mile, stopping to look at some lonely violets, a few late snowdrops and a cluster of rooks' nests in the tall beech trees. 'I think we must turn back as it will be dark in thirty minutes or so.' Reluctantly at first, but then more eagerly gaining pace, they turned and retraced their steps along the same path. A pair of bickering mallards and a late-calling blackbird which flew angrily across their path were the only sounds. Now they held hands even on the narrower parts of the track. Arthur opened the gate and together they went in to the vicarage, took off their coats and wellington boots. It was as if each knew how the walk would end.

A few minutes later they were in their bedroom. Eleanor had slipped off her outer clothing. She held out her arms, Arthur crossed to her and they embraced. Their embracing became more passionate as each undressed the other. They stepped a shade apart and gazed at one other. Arthur could not believe how beautiful she was, she of how aroused he was. Arthur, a full foot taller, stooped and kissed her firm breasts and hardened nipples with much gentleness. She lowered one hand and held his manhood. They kissed again, almost fiercely. They fell, rather than being led by each other, on to the bed. In a moment Arthur was astride his love, she so ready to receive him. They were drawn together as magnets. The rhythm of their loving equal only to the way they understood the rhythm of each other's lives. In a single moment of joy, their lovemaking reached wonderful heights and they were spent. Their love for each other was immense: Arthur, unable to understand how he deserved such a beautiful and loving woman after all that he had done; Eleanor, with equal love, had one remaining thought going through her mind: God, maybe this time.

SEVEN

Morning, Wednesday, 3 April

A week later, the first Wednesday in April, sunrise was shown in Arthur's diary as six o'clock, but the sky suggested another overcast day. He had been up for almost an hour, for much needed his attention. Having lit his table lamp, he was planning three services: Maundy Thursday, Good Friday and Easter Day itself. He knew he could leave the choral parts in the hands of Rita Small and the choir which was blessed with some good voices, not least those of Eleanor and young Albert Jones. Encouraged by the school, Albert had been auditioned by the cathedral choir, but had felt that he belonged in Rusfield; his voice had easily changed from a boyhood soprano to a rich baritone.

Starting with a time of prayer, Arthur's thoughts were now fine-tuning the sermon for Good Friday. Rereading the story of Christ's suffering and death, he prayed that he could somehow convey this central tenet of the Christian faith to his congregation, which he knew would be considerable. The day before, a letter from his parents had announced they would call in on the Saturday. He knew that calling in meant a three or four-day stay and so some of his parishioner calls would have to wait until Charlotte and Hector Windle returned to Dorset. It would be good to see them.

Around the village, a few other lighted windows showed up. The Johnson family had long started their day, as Ruby needed to be up at the manor to light fires for the de Maine household and, whilst her brother, Willy, officially started work an hour later, he chose to walk with his young sister on these grey mornings. They had both got up as quietly as possible, but with Frank, Harry, Robert and David sharing Willy's room and Ruby sleeping alongside her mother and Rachel, it was almost impossible not to trip over someone or knock something over. Washing downstairs in the small scullery with water drawn the night before and dressing from already prepared clothes, Ruby and Willy were soon ready. After a hurried slice of bread with some of their mother's rich plum jam along with a mug of tea made from the ever-simmering water on the wood-burning stove, they reached for their outdoor coats and stepped outside into Meadow Way.

As they turned from Pond Street to face the slightly uphill ten minutes' walk to the manor, the sky began to lighten from its iron grey. Whilst not being able to see his face which was partly covered by a hood, they knew it was Racer setting out on the rather longer journey to Spinney Farm. As ever he was moving at a fast trot, not through any lateness, but to help keep his body finely tuned for the approaching running season. They exchanged waves.

The path, flanked by mainly bare hedges on either side, was wide and well worn. It led not only to the old manor, but eventually to Wensfield four miles away. Halfway up the slight hill, Willy took his sister's arm and whispered: 'Stop a moment; I want to show you something. Look over there, see the large oak tree?'

The ever-faithful Ruby followed his instruction, though her puzzled look showed that she had no idea what she should be seeing. 'It's hard to see now, but in the vee from the main trunk you should be able to see a dark shape.' After a few minutes Ruby was able to make this out. 'Well,' explained Willy, 'that's almost certainly the buzzard's nest, a big one made of sticks. If it's really come to stay it should be laying as many as four eggs in the next week or so: might even have already laid one or two.'

Ruby smiled at his words. 'You're so good at these things, Willy,' marvelling at her brother's knowledge.

'Well, I just try to keep my eyes open. Now don't ever go closer than we are now, but have a look each day on your way home. Keep an eye open for the adult bird sitting on its eggs and later feeding the young birds, but sadly, they probably won't all survive.'

They reached a fork in the path, taking the right one which led slightly downwards to the wooded dell where they could make out the high chimneys of the manor. The dark-haired Willy had approached this late sixteenth-century house from the same track on many occasions, but he never ceased to be enchanted by its appearance. To him it was perfect, rising seamlessly from the surrounding land, its stone walls almost growing out of the earth.

By now the sky had considerably lightened and there was promise of a better day. They reached the barred gate over which they climbed. Old Peter was under close orders to lock the slightly dilapidated wooden barrier at night to deter poachers from stealing any livestock, though such attempts were not always successful. From the gate, the way to the house became well defined, as vehicles needed a good surface before entering the road off to Steepleton.

'When is Master Lionel getting home?' Ruby rather suddenly asked, enquiring about the nineteen-year-old younger son of the de Maines.

A slight frown came to Willy's face; he had little time for someone whom he thought arrogant, rude and a little untrustworthy. Turning to his sister, he replied, 'Any time now he'll be back from Cambridge. I heard the major mentioning this to Florrie, but why do you want to know?'

'I just wondered. Nothing, really.' The interest of Ruby

rather puzzled Willy. He looked at her and realised how grown up she was now: pretty, if slightly overweight, with a sweet face. One part of him was pleased as her question suggested she was beginning to become interested in boys for, which he thought, it was about time. But the other half wished that the haughty Lionel had not been the first youth about whom his sister should pay attention.

The well-dressed track led towards the large, centuries-old oak door, above which the date of the original building was clearly shown, 1583, along with a family heraldic crest; it was inside that evidence of the repair work that was needed showed itself. Willy and Ruby had been surprised to see an upper room on the south side well lit and Peter confirmed the early rising of his master and mistress. Indeed, Florrie had been summoned to serve tea just before half past six, a most unusual occurrence. When Willy asked Peter if his master and mistress were leaving the house, his reply was that he knew of nothing to give rise to an early morning start. 'In any case,' went on the balding Peter, who certainly looked the elderly retainer that he had been for nearly fifty years, 'you know about the party over at Mister Mansfield's farm tonight? Well, it seems he has invited all of us there as well and so the major is providing all the beer and Elsie has already started some baking to take over there.'

'I didn't know that. That's something of a last minute arrangement, isn't it?' replied Willy. 'I'm already going, as Racer who works there, has been allowed to invite a few friends as well. Ruby, I expect you can go as well.'

'That's lovely, but I won't have time to get ready,' blushed Ruby.

'Well, that's no real problem,' added Peter. 'Mr Mansfield is letting everyone at Spinney Farm off at five o'clock so they have time to go home before the party. Bit of a surprise that the major is doing the same, although just recently it seems he does whatever he can to please Mr Mansfield.'

In their large bedroom which displayed a certain faded elegance, Isabella and Sebastian de Maine were deep in a conversation, their serious expressions reflecting more than a casual conversation. They sat facing each other, Isabella on the soft green covered chaise longue, her husband on an equally graceful, though well-worn stool.

'Seb, I know you want to keep the status quo, but some things just have to change. Times are different now and, in truth, have been since your father lost so much in the seventies.' Her husband sighed, finding it difficult to admit that anything needed to change. However, he knew his wife was right as was nearly always the case in financial matters, small or large.

'No one's to blame,' encouraged Isabella, 'but we were fortunate that Jack Mansfield loaned us enough to cover the cost of the new tractor. Without that we really would be in trouble with the bank. Such a kind man.'

'Indeed he is and I know he will keep things to himself. But what are you suggesting Isabella?'

'Well, at the moment there's no way we can increase the farm income except by raising the rents of the farm cottages or the four cottages in Meadow Way and I know you won't do that.'

'You're right. I know a lot of people around here see me as a Victorian-style landowner who is only interested in making money and shooting, but we have a responsibility. Our tenants can hardly get by anyway and I would like to increase their wages, not raise rents.'

The delicately-featured Isabella knew he was right in his understanding that villagers viewed him as reserved, even aloof, but she also knew he had a deep, if largely hidden sense of responsibility to his workers, indeed to the whole village. She knew how much these difficult financial times upset this strong feeling of responsibility, upon which his sense of pride was built. Both knew that much repair work was needed both to the inside and exterior of their home, but Isabella was too sensitive to raise this matter.

'Well, let's think of money going out,' she suggested. 'We really could manage without both Florrie and Elsie. Let's also think about some of the village things we support. It was a lovely idea of yours to send money to Peter for the village reading room, just as it is to provide the beer for tonight's party at Jack's farm, but these things do cost money and maybe we could ease up a little, at least for the time being. Perhaps wheat prices and prices of some of our other products will soon go up a little.'

The dapper Sebastian flinched at some of the points she had made, but deep down he knew that something needed to be done. 'I'm not sure about some of these things you mention,' responded her husband, 'but, I agree we need to think about them.'

'I know, my darling. And I love you the more for not wanting to hurt anyone. Another way of looking at things has to be about raising some money. Might we not be able to sell the parcel of land butting on to the Steepleton Road? The brewery could well be interested; they seem to be doing very well and wishing to extend all the time. What do you think?'

Sebastian pondered deeply before expressing any thoughts. 'It's hard to know which crops and animals produce the best return and I guess we may have gone on for too long just doing the same thing. Jack Mansfield is doing very well at Spinney Farm and when we were all at Sir Lancelot's place last Christmas, Jack and I were talking and he said he was carefully weighing up the benefits of moving more towards cereals. Let's see what advice we might get from Jack. Perhaps we could invite Mabel and him to dinner. But what really worries me,' he went on to say, 'is what of the future? I'm lucky in that I keep well, although this damned leg troubles me at times. We had both hoped that either young Ralph or Tobias would take over, but they both seem to be going in very different directions. I was really quite saddened to hear Ralph talking about going off to America to further his career in finance and Tobias has never really shown any interest in the farm.'

'All too true, which just leaves Lionel. Can you see him running the place?'

Sebastian stood up and wandered towards the leaded window overlooking the paved courtyard. 'Quite frankly, I can't,' he replied. 'He really worries me. In spite of the allowance we give him, that never seems to be adequate for each term. We don't know much about how he's doing at Cambridge, but if things are like the school reports we used to receive, he'll be wasting much of his time. So it's a difficult age he's at, but he seems very arrogant and thoughtless. I don't even like the way he treats our staff, Peter in particular.'

'Sadly, Seb, I worry about him, too. Maybe he will change when he's finished at Cambridge, but right now I don't hope for too much. However, let's give ourselves a little time to think about what we've been talking over. If we do, I'm sure the next year or so can bring worthwhile change.'

Her husband glanced at his fob watch on the dressing table. 'It's nearly eight o'clock and we've already been up for two hours.'

Smiling, Isabella added, 'We mustn't make a habit of being early risers, otherwise Peter and other staff will wonder what we are up to, and that won't do.' Sebastian, for all his reserve, stood up, walked over to his wife, laid his hands on her shoulders and gently kissed the top of her head.

EIGHT

Afternoon, Wednesday, 3 April

Arthur was pleasantly surprised to find that by late afternoon he had finished preparations for the Good Friday and Easter services. He had also selected prayers and readings for communion and a meditative service the next evening, in preparation for Good Friday. That lunchtime he had visited the Jones family in Wood Lane and learnt that Susannah Jones had talked her way into seeing the brewery manager who had reluctantly promised to consider her appeal for some compensation. Arthur made a note to call again in a week's time to see if any reply had been received.

Eleanor was upstairs helping Eliza Carey prepare the two largest spare bedrooms for the visit by Arthur's parents. His father, fastidious at best, always spoke of being a poor sleeper and Eleanor had already given them the main bathroom, with its recently installed gas water-heater. Colonel Hector Richard Windle expected his warm bath every morning.

Eliza normally came in for two mornings and one afternoon each week and whilst this did not include a Wednesday, she had responded to a plea for this extra help. Eleanor always felt apprehensive of the visits by Arthur's parents; whilst a little more warmth had crept into their relationship, particularly with Charlotte Windle, she had no idea of any remaining problem with the colonel.

Arthur needed to be in St Mary's vestry for a seven o'clock meeting with the churchwardens and three other parishioners to discuss arrangements for Empire Day on 24 May, Queen Victoria's birthday. Arthur thought this a slightly strange date, for when the celebration had started ten years previously, the Queen had already been dead for over a year. The occasion was always a landmark in the village: the children received extra geography lessons to realise the extent of the Empire and there was a half-day holiday for a church service for adults and children. With Arthur's strong feelings of Empire he would again lead zealous prayers for the King and the royal family, but he felt the evening's committee meeting was premature for an occasion well over a month away, not least as the focus should be reserved for the Holy Week services. This meeting should all go smoothly, Arthur thought to himself, but with George Cooper being one of the churchwardens, some minor disagreements might well emerge. Arthur found it sad that whilst the village community generally showed harmony and support towards one another, discord was not uncommon in the council of St Mary's. George Cooper had been a churchwarden for thirty-one years and seemed set on looking back to former times and how the church and everything about it had gone downhill. Not infrequently, he would refer to Arthur's predecessor, Reverend Charles Gulland, and the services he took, even though he had died twenty years previously.

With the clock showing five o'clock he realised there was time to make one pastoral visit before returning for supper and decided that he should call on the Smith family to see how the overworked Liz Smith was coping with her elderly and ailing mother, Martha. It was certainly not worth getting out his old bicycle, a gift from Mrs Grout when she moved away from the village following her husband's death. He left by the rear door and after walking through the churchyard, crossed the green and turned towards Meadow Way. He waved to Miss Rushton who was at the door of her small haberdashery shop near the corner of the green, one of the four village shops that provided essential needs. Arthur had never been able to find out her first name; indeed, many in the village wondered if she owned one.

He worried about Liz and her elderly mother Martha. Clearly Liz worked desperately hard and had been much relieved when young Fred got work at the smithy. Arthur guessed that Liz was around forty, but she appeared much older. Little was known about the family background as she had moved into Rusfield from some distance away, London had been rumoured, with her mother and baby Fred; reference had never been made to Fred's father. Fred had found school work a struggle, but had earned the respect of all by his gentle nature, good manners and his prowess on the football field.

Her small cottage was one in the row of four owned by the de Maine family and backed on to the village green. The front door was ajar. He knocked and immediately Liz called out her usual greeting: 'Come in, the door is open.' He had visited most cottages in the village, many of which were poorly furnished, but none as bleak as the Smith home. The floor was simply packed mud, uneven, even dangerous in places, on which stood three rickety upright chairs, a crudely-made table and two stools piled high with an assortment of rags, wools and a box of straw; the latter for Liz's well-intended but rare straw-plaiting endeavours. There was a large fireplace with cooking implements in the hearth, also hanging from hooks set into the blackened lintel, and a high pile of hefty logs. In one corner of the room, next to the stairs, there was a bed round which a curtain, made from an old blanket, was draped. Arthur knew this to be Fred's bed. A picture of the school team with Fred in the front row was the only adornment.

Liz appeared through the opening to the other downstairs

room, smiled and generously welcomed Arthur. She certainly looked an elderly lady, stooped shoulders, missing teeth and lank, greying hair. As she wiped her flowered though well-worn apron across her sweating face, Arthur realised she had been laundering in the back room. 'Please excuse the mess, Vicar.'

'I partly came to enquire after your mother, maybe even to pop upstairs to speak with her for a few minutes.'

'That's really kind of you, Vicar, but she has just dropped off to sleep. I know she would like to see you another time and I will, of course, tell her you kindly called.' He passed through to the back room which was full of washing, some hanging up to dry, more in the large sink. The bare, plastered walls were running with condensation and a further pile of washing rested by the large mangle in the corner.

'Looks as if you have plenty to keep you busy,' Arthur said.

She laughed. 'Yes, there is quite a lot to launder at the moment, but there aren't really many folks around here that can afford their washing to be done although I don't charge but a few pence. I'm lucky that I get a lot from Spinney Farm and Mrs de Maine kindly sends some down from the manor, but not so much recently.'

'So how are you Mrs Smith and tell me about your mother? I heard she is rather poorly at the moment.'

'Oh, I'm all right, as long as I'm kept busy with washing. I'm really very lucky and young Fred is a godsend. He's kept busy at the smithy working for old Joe, but when he gets home he'll start chopping up wood that he's collected, helping me hang up the washing, ironing and generally tidying up.' Looking around, Arthur could not imagine the latter activity took much of Fred's time, but he knew she received much other help from him.

'I'm afraid mother is not well at all. We managed to get the doctor in last week. Thank goodness for the good health fund. I manage to pay sixpence a week and it really does soon mount up. Anyway Doctor Spencer said that her lungs are really struggling and she doesn't help herself by not eating properly. In the kindest way, he explained that she wouldn't be with us for much longer. Still, she's fifty-six and had a pretty good life. I just don't want her to be in pain and the doctor gave me something which can help.'

'I'm sorry about that,' comforted Arthur. He reached across and lightly rested his hand on Liz's arm. 'You know that if you ever want me or Eleanor, just send Fred round to let us know.'

'Your Eleanor is the world's kindest. She popped in last week and helped me with folding some big things and then cooked some food for the three of us that she had brought along. She really is a saint.'

At that moment a slightly breathless Fred came in. He looked mildly flushed and gave Arthur a cheerful greeting. He went straight to his mother, put his arms gently round her, and kissed her. 'How is Gran?' Not every lad of Fred's age would put his arms round his mother, greet her with a kiss and immediately show his concern for his grandmother, thought Arthur. He really is a thoughtful son.

After their visitor had left, Fred went into the back room and saw the large heap of wet washing. He immediately set down his lunch-box, picked up the sheet which was on the top of the washing pile, shook it out well and folded it.

'I'll just go and see how mum is,' his mother called as she set off upstairs. 'You get yourself ready for the do at the farm tonight.'

But the ever-helpful Fred continued with shaking and folding the washed items, knowing it to be a sensible prelude to ironing. It wasn't too long before he had arranged all in a neat pile, which certainly made it look less overwhelming. He then took one item at a time, putting it through the mangle. It had been extremely kind of Mrs de Maine to suggest to Liz Smith some years ago that as the washing house at the manor had been equipped with a new mangle she would be pleased for Liz to have the old one. Having finished the mangling, Fred popped back into the front room, collected a large kettle of water that was on the hob, poured some into a bowl, added some cold and took off his grey shirt. Freshened up by his rather spartan wash, he took a lightly-striped shirt from one of the several shelves in the cupboard he had constructed next to his bed. He had ironed it the evening before and it certainly felt better than the one he had been wearing all day at the forge; the smell of horses was never far away from Fred. He slipped into his slightly-worn waistcoat and finally a grey and green jacket which Mr Wallace, one of the most regular customers at the forge, had given him a month previously. He felt properly dressed for the evening, one to which he was looking forward to sharing with his mates.

NINE

Afternoon, Wednesday, 3 April

Jack Atkins had cycled the four miles back from Steepleton six times a week for almost four years, but on this particular Wednesday he wanted to cover the distance with greater alacrity than usual. He counted himself fortunate to have got the job at Davis' bakery and was determined to make it work out well. Starting as a delivery boy he had collected yeast from Jarmins and then taken the fresh, rich smelling bread to restaurants in the lively market town. He now helped bake the bread, even managing it well on his own. Maybe, one day, he would own a bakery and with this dream growing stronger each year he worked hard to make it a reality. This cherubic-looking seventeen-year-old surprised his employers with his determination, just as he had surprised football opponents by being the school team's most prolific goal scorer.

Wednesday had been early closing day in Steepleton for as long as people could remember, but occasionally Mr Davis Junior, although he had long since enjoyed his sixtieth birthday, asked Jack to stay on a little later to give the bakery a 'welcome extra clean'; this Jack willingly did, but now he was keen to get back to Rusfield. The prospect of an evening with his mates at the farm party was most inviting, but first he wanted to spend some time in one of his favourite places.

A few minutes after the nearby clock at St Ethelbert's struck two o'clock, he took off his overall, washed his hands, donned his heavy coat, bade farewell to Mr Davis Junior and took out his originally blue bicycle. Jack had never lost his energy or fitness since his sporting days at school and enjoyed the slight challenge as he pedalled out of the town centre and up the slight hill past Pratchetts Machine Works. The four-mile route was so well known by Jack that his mind began to wander. It was along this road, though on the stretch through the wooded area near the junction to the manor, that his father, Edward, had met with his terrible end when less than thirty years old. Jack, unborn at the time of his father's death, had always wished he had known him. Having nearly finished ditching along the road, a sudden thunderstorm blew up and anxious to finish the work, unfinished labours brought in no pay, Edward Atkins had disregarded the danger posed by the nearby giant oak tree and his metal tools. Villagers had heard the thunder and remembered an exceptionally vivid flash of lightning. It was some two hours later that a passer-by, old Joe Groves, had come across the badly burned body of this young man. Whilst the detail of the tragedy was well known, Jack knew little about his father. Olivia, his beautiful widow, had always turned away from telling Jack much about him and this evasion was evident with other villagers. As a boy, Jack had been bewildered by this; later he had realised that it was out of respect for his mother's feelings.

When Jack was ten, his mother told him how she had come to the village. 'I was an only child and my parents owned a bookshop in Butcher Row in Coventry, not far from the bishop's palace. But one night the next-door furniture dealers caught fire that quickly spread to my father's bookshop. We all lived above the shop and I was the only one to survive. It was horrible and sometimes I can still see that great fire. I was eighteen and maybe it was because I was younger than your grandparents that I was able to climb out and escape. I stayed with my grandmother for a while, but I realised I had to look after myself. In a magazine I saw a job for a nanny at Spinney Farm where an elderly gentleman, Mr Herbert, lived with his son and his wife and two young children. I applied for the job and two months later moved to Rusfield. Well, that's how I came to live here. I've been very lucky because a lot of people have been very kind to me, just as they have to you.'

Jack remembered so well his mother telling him all this and after two years at the farm that she had married and moved into the cottage where she and Jack now lived. However, Olivia could not bring herself, either then or now, to say much about her time with Edward. Nor had she ever bemoaned the fact that in one night in Coventry she had lost both her parents, her home and her life had been transformed from a middle-class eighteen-year-old girl to being a penniless orphan. Jack had often placed flowers on his father's grave that showed the date of his father's death on the modest headstone: 23 October 1894. He had realised his mother must have been pregnant at the time of her husband's death as he was born the following April. Jack and his mother were very close and she had provided the strength to encourage him in his learning and had become the source of his own integrity and ambition. They had always done much together, talking about books, exploring the wonders of the countryside and sharing jokes, not least that he, along with most people who were baptised John, were expected to answer to the name of Jack. To Olivia, Jack was the centre of her world; having lost so much, he was so precious to her, but she could never be accused of mollycoddling him.

He had told his mother that he would go straight to the reading room for a couple of hours and now as he reached the edge of the village he turned left into Jackson's Farm, the home of the reading room. The door to the barn was open; Jack knew that one of Mr Jackson's workers padlocked it at dusk each day. Fred Jackson, rather unkindly referred to as

Fatty Jackson by Jack and his mates, was a generous man and just modestly said that he had always enjoyed reading. The roof had been repaired and walls made sound. Jack walked to the internal steps that led upwards to a floor opening, taking care as the light was mainly limited to the open door. Jack had noticed a bicycle leaning against the barn wall, but as that could have been left by any farm worker, he was still surprised to be made aware of slight movement in the area to which the stairs led, the reading room itself.

'Good afternoon, Mrs Windle,' Jack said as he greeted the vicar's wife with his captivating smile; his words said in such a way as to express genuine pleasure at seeing her.

'Good afternoon to you, Jack. Not the first time we've seen each other here; I know how much you enjoy reading. I'm here because we've been fortunate enough to be given a set of *Encyclopaedia Britannica*. I've only managed to bring the first five copies on my bicycle this time, but we'll soon have them all in place.'

'That's marvellous,' exclaimed Jack. 'I've seen them in Steepleton library, but I know they were always too expensive for Mr Meadows to buy them for our school.'

'They are, indeed, expensive, but this was a gift. You may know that Mr Herbert, who had Spinney Farm before Mr Mansfield bought it, moved to Canchester quite a few years ago. Well, he must have learnt about our reading room because in his will he made special mention that all his books should come here. This is an old edition, actually printed in 1860 when I expect he had them as a child.'

The red-haired Jack, whose grey eyes reflected his excitement, could not stop going over to the table where the thick, cloth-bound books lay. He touched them, they looked wonderful.

'So, is there anything in particular you are looking for, Jack, although I realise you know your way around well enough?'

'Well,' responded Jack in his quiet, modest tone, 'I want

to find out more about the kinds of grain that make the best bread. I know quite a bit already, but Mr Davis sometimes wonders what's best to buy from the mills around Steepleton. I recently read in a magazine how a lot of experiments have been going on with different kinds of wheat.'

'Well, you may be lucky although clearly these volumes are out of date in many ways, but at least bread should be in one of the volumes I've brought along. Jack, I want you to be one of the first to know that we have managed to find someone to be here every morning, except Sundays of course, for half an hour which means anyone will be able to borrow a book. The committee, and I know your mother is one of its hardest workers, decided a small charge should be made for this and the money go towards buying new books. Have a look at these rules. Do you think they are all right?'

'They look fine to me,' replied Jack as soon as he had read through them. 'It will be really good, although some of us will find it hard to get in at the right time to change books.'

'Well, we are trying out the idea from the start of May and will just have to see how things work out. But before I go Jack, let me ask how your mother is; I haven't seen her for a week or so?' Eleanor thought highly of Olivia Atkins and admired her for the way she had brought her son up on her own, encouraged him at school and, so she had heard, never missed being on the touchline when he had been playing school matches. She knew that Olivia's artistic skill with pen and ink drawings was well sought after by a number of children's book publishers.

'She's very well. Thank you for asking. Mother is really quite busy at the moment as she needs to get some illustrations finished.' He smiled, adding: 'There are so many drawings of lions and tigers around that it's quite frightening! But I do know she is always grateful for the way in which you and Mr Meadows set up this reading room. She was in here last week; something to do with looking up some shrubs that she didn't know. And thank you for bringing along these encyclopaedias, they're wonderful.'

They smiled at each other and Eleanor turned to the steps and descended. Jack thought to himself: Jammy's right. She is a pretty lady, nearly as pretty as my mother.

The vicar's wife always looked elegant, but never extravagantly dressed. Her skirt for cycling was slightly shorter than she would otherwise wear, its maroon colouring showing off well the cream blouse and medium-heavy fawn short topcoat. Her dark hair flowed freely, she generally refused to follow fashion and wear a hat. 'Just an idle fashion dictated by some male designer,' she had once declared to Arthur.

Now on his own, Jack turned eagerly to the new books and was soon reading about bread in its many forms and then turned to look up dough. He read solidly until he was suddenly aware of the church clock striking. There were in this upper part of the barn four windows which gave reasonable reading light and by going to one facing west he could just read the church clock: four-thirty. He carefully put all five volumes of the encyclopaedia on the shelf that Mrs Windle had cleared for them.

The sky was beginning to fade as he mounted his bicycle and rode the short distance to his home towards the far end of West Lane. Time to tell his mother about the new books, his meeting with Mrs Windle and then to get ready for the farm party to which he was greatly looking forward; and, before that, meeting up with his mates in The George for a quick drink.

Morning & Afternoon, Wednesday, 3 April

Abraham Richards, along with the rest of Jack Mansfield's workforce, had well finished the early sowing and were preparing to get the cattle and pigs out to the fields, although the recent spell of prolonged rain had set things back. Extra ditching had been necessary as a number of banks had collapsed with the seemingly incessant rain. But today saw a break from the usual work, as most were busy getting things ready for the Easter-week party. Somewhere around seventy could be expected and excitement at each of the three farms had increased as the event got closer.

During the past days, Hezekiah Freeman and Aubrey Watson, next-door neighbours and two of Jack Mansfield's older labourers had cleaned out the large timbered barn. Tall ladders had been used to get up high to clear cobwebs and bird and bat droppings although Abraham and Tommy Bruce, another fit young man, had carried out that duty. Soon after purchasing the farm, Mr Mansfield had the earth floor of the barn properly paved and the two older men had thoroughly washed it the previous day, carrying buckets of water in from the main farm pump and vigorously brushing until all traces of its recent use disappeared. They had then constructed a temporary stage using a motley selection of timbers although when Abraham jumped up and down on it, he found it safe enough. Now he and the rest were busy putting things in place.

'It's really good of Mr Mansfield to have this party,' commented Abraham to Tommy. 'I remember he organised something the first year I worked here, but that was just for those who worked for him.'

'Aye,' replied his mate, 'it's kind asking everyone over from the manor and Mr Jackson's farm. Should be a really good evening.'

'Let's get the seating sorted out first,' suggested Tommy. 'Mr Mansfield said we should do our best to have seating for seventy. Your suggestion, Racer, of using the wooden boxes from the store next door is a good one.'

Fifteen minutes later they had brought in enough boxes and allowing, as Tommy put it, 'Two bums per box,' they had enough for around forty. Next, they struggled in with several wide planks which they placed on upturned wooden barrels. 'That's enough for around sixty. Mr Mansfield said he wanted ten proper chairs for guests, so let's take the small cart from outside up to the store next and load them on.'

A short while later, Streaky Bacon and Dan Reynolds came in carrying an assortment of materials, with Dan announcing: 'These will do to cover the boxes and help keep splinters out of people's backsides.'

'That looks really good,' commented Racer. 'With the stage over there we know where the entertainers are going to be, so let's set up the chairs in the best position for the guests, keeping the middle for dancing.'

'Don't forget the tables we have to bring in for the drink and food, mugs and so on. I think they will all be best over in the corner furthest from the door,' added Tommy.

An hour later the barn was ready, lamps were brought in, some hung on previously fixed wall hooks and two buckets of water placed nearby. Doris Groves and Grace Reynolds, two young girls who worked in the large farmhouse, appeared carrying armfuls of bunting. 'We've been cutting out triangles and squares in as many coloured cloths as we could find,' said the pretty, dark-haired Doris, clearly aware of her good looks. Grace and Abraham gave each other a smile. They had been friends for years; their birthdays were only a month apart and the two had always vied for top place in the class. They saw each other less often now, but enjoyed exchanging news of families and what each was doing.

'Come on,' encouraged Abraham, 'let's see how long they are and then we can either hang them round the walls or fix them so they go from side to side.' They agreed that running them between opposite walls gave the best effect and this was soon done.

'I'll just run up to the house,' said Racer. 'Mr Mansfield asked me to let him know when everything was done.' He hurried up the short distance to the substantial Georgian farmhouse. The Mansfields' two daughters had married and moved away, but five domestic workers were maintained, not least to ensure the farm workers had proper meals. Within five minutes Abraham was back accompanied by the farmer. He was a well-built man in his mid-fifties, comfortably dressed in dark grey matching jacket, waistcoat and trousers, the latter embraced by tight-fitting calf-high boots.

He took a long look around and then his strong-looking face broke into a smile. 'It looks good, lads and ladies.' Doris and Grace immediately broke into blushes. 'You've all done well. Maybe just move those tables for the drinks and food a little forward. Tommy, go and find Peter and a couple of other lads and tell them they can start moving the ale and other drinks down here. Thanks to all of you. It's nearly midday so I don't see why everyone can't finish around two o'clock, go home and get ready for this evening.'

By fifteen minutes past two, the barn and yard were quiet. Abraham and Tommy, helped by two other strong youngsters, had negotiated the last items needed for the evening and all except Abraham had departed. He was just changing from his working clothes into more suitable attire for his next activity. He put on some lighter footwear which together with his loose-fitting top and leggings made him ready to run home, his working clothes in the backpack. Not wanting to miss any opportunity to improve his fitness for the new season, he set off along Wood Lane, away from the village for a mile, turned right to circumvent the most outlying farm cottages before turning north to approach Rusfield by way of Parkers Wood and the meadow. As he got to the village green, Miss Rushton briefly stopped cleaning the window of the haberdashery, smiled and called out, 'You're doing well, Racer. We're all proud of you.' He wondered how Miss Rushton's mother, who also lived above the shop, was faring as she had not been well of late. Abraham waved back, running between the towering, yet still bare elms around the green and sprinted the final hundred yards to his house at the church end of West Lane.

He had drawn off a bucket of water before setting out for work and fixed it to a wooden contraption which he had often used. In the seclusion of an outside shed he stripped. Then taking one of the ropes fixed to the bucket he pulled it slowly so the water ran over his fair hair and down his well-muscled body. Refreshed, he dried and prepared himself for the long-awaited farm party. He knew his parents would not be in for a couple of hours; he had always been grateful for the way they had supported him in schoolwork at which he excelled and his sport. Now, no one was prouder of his achievements on the athletics track.

Abraham had a younger brother, James, who worked with their father and although there were only four of them in the immediate family, the web of relations spread to several in the village. Boney Jones and Willy Johnson were his first cousins, as well as close friends. His grandfather had told Abraham when he was a small boy the story of Jeremiah Richards, from whom all the family were descended. His story went that this man had served as a private in the young Colonel Arthur Wellesley's army in South India well over a century earlier, returned to England and finding his wife had disappeared just walked until he came to a village where there was some work. That was Rusfield and from his marriage to a robust village lady, a large family had descended. Abraham promised himself that one day he would try to find out more about his ancestors.

Albert Jones had been delighted when he successfully bargained with his boss at the brewery that by working an extra Saturday afternoon he could store up a free half-day for a later occasion. At first Albert had thought the future afternoon off could be for watching a cricket match in Canchester, but when Racer mentioned the farm party he had gained permission to use it for this Wednesday afternoon. Leaving Bifields at one o'clock, he had caught the quarter to two train from Branton and by alternating between a fast walk and a long-striding trot had got home in well under an hour.

Albert and his family lived in Wood Lane, a short distance from the pond on the way to Spinney Farm. He did not enjoy the work at the brewery, but was grateful for it; almost the sole income for the family of seven. His feelings towards the brewery had taken an upward turn when his mother told him that the brewery boss had promised that some thought would be given towards compensation for his disabled father, but still no letter had arrived. His mother earned little more than a pittance with her straw-plaiting and irregular help at Spinney Farm. She was more than willing to work all hours of day or night, but little work was available. Then there were Albert's four young siblings to support: George, Henrietta, William and Florence.

The back door was open as his father had slipped down to the reading room to do a little tidying. His family admired him for always doing his best in domestic and voluntary village work in spite of the pain that still emanated from his arm stump. As he entered the cottage, Albert ducked; with his height of over six feet he had long grown accustomed to the low lintels and ceilings in the cottage. He, William and George used one room upstairs, his sisters sharing with his parents. Albert was liked by all for his ever-happy nature; he thought of himself as fortunate when he heard of so many sad life stories, but he harboured various ambitions. Maybe, when his younger siblings were old enough to go to work, he might follow the older lads who had set off to Canada. They had arrived there some months earlier and letters home had spoken of good work opportunities. He had even talked this over with his close cousins, Racer and Willy Johnson, but had sworn them to secrecy. It would all be at least seven years away since George, the youngest of his brothers, was still only six.

He went upstairs, changed into older clothes, collected an axe and a large sack from the shed he had recently constructed next to the privy at the end of the garden, crossed Wood Lane and took the narrow path to the wood a quarter of a mile away. There had been a lot of tree damage during the violent storm in February and he had already piled a good store of logs into the new shed. He took a smaller track, probably caused by a deer, and was soon at the fallen tree. As his considerable strength swung the axe, his mind turned towards the evening. The only sounds apart from the axe blows were the occasional sound of a friendly robin and the petulant squawk of a blackbird annoyed at the disturbance. Having chopped all the logs he would be able to carry in the sack, he set off back home. His thoughts now turned to getting ready for meeting up with his mates in The George and then the party up at Spinney Farm. He wondered which of the girls would be there, especially Doris Groves about whom he had heard several promising things.

ELEVEN

Evening, Wednesday, 3 April

At half past six Willy, Jack, Boney, Racer and Fred were nestled down in The George. 'Well, we are a smart looking lot,' laughed Willy as they gathered close to the fire for a little light and warmth. 'It should be an enjoyable evening.' As he was saying this, he noticed that Racer's normally cheerful face was wearing a troubled look. Ever quick to pick up nuances, he asked, 'How are things with you, Racer?'

Eyes turned to their friend whose fair hair and handsome looks had little changed since they had all been at school together, although his physique was now strongly muscled and bronzed. 'Well, I'm not sure where to start, but I've got something to tell you all. It's quite difficult really, but when I told Jack he persuaded me to tell you. He said it would remain a secret between us.'

The others nodded agreement, their interest immediate. A faint blush had come to Racer's face and he looked at Jack whose broad, friendly face signified support and encouragement. Thinking they were going to hear about Racer's plans for his season's running, their faces took on worried looks as he went on to tell them about the threat that had been made to him.

'You mean,' Boney said slowly and deliberately, 'that this man actually threatened you if you dared to win. Who is this wretch?'

'I've only heard him called Froggy, but I've seen him at several race meetings.'

'A strange name,' chipped in Willy. 'I'd call him something much stronger. So what does he look like?'

Racer screwed up his eyes as he thought for a moment. 'I would say he's about forty, medium height and slim. His face is pockmarked and he's balding.'

Together they talked this through, agreeing that Willy would put the absent Jammy Carey in the picture. Suddenly, realising the time had come for them to set out on the twenty-minute walk to Spinney Farm, Willy announced: 'All right then, we've agreed. I'm sure we can sort things out for Racer. Look, I've got to pick up Ruby, so I'll run ahead, collect her and catch you up.'

He was as good as his word and accompanied by the excited Ruby, soon caught them up. Racer had already thanked the others for their support and now, outside of Ruby's hearing, added his appreciation to Willy. It was a mild evening, the starlit sky promising a fine night. As the group turned the pond corner, Racer said: 'Some good news, lads. The vicar was talking to my father after last Sunday's service saying that someone, he wouldn't say who, has donated a set of cricket stumps, three bats and some other gear. You remember Mr Mansfield said we could use his lower meadow for playing, so it looks good. We'll all play, won't we?' he added, turning to the others.

'Of course,' replied Boney. 'It's time we had a Rusfield Cricket Club. So when do you think we can have a match?'

'Well, how about trying to get one against Wensfield over the August Bank Holiday? I'm sure we could get a good team together. You would be our star batsman, Boney,' he suggested. 'I remember you whacking the ball and breaking a school window!' The others laughed and talk was light-hearted as they strolled along Wood Lane, before turning into the broad track leading to the farm.

Other villagers were in front of them as they approached the well-lit barn, with more following. There was much chatting and laughter as they went in. 'It looks lovely,' announced a very happy Ruby. 'Look at all the bunting and decorations: and what a lot of people here.'

The barn certainly looked splendid for this joyfully anticipated occasion with Mr and Mrs Mansfield greeting all comers; everyone agreeing that it was delightful to be joined by friends from the manor and Jackson's farms. All had made great efforts to dress well. The small band was already playing; as the new arrivals came in it was, "The Boy I Love is Up in the Gallery". Sammy Hatfield on accordion and Bernie Thomas with fiddle had been joined by young Peter Jackson on his flute. The trio was gaily dressed for the occasion with brightly-coloured hats, each sporting a large feather. Jack Mansfield was telling his wife: 'I don't think anything like this has taken place in here before, old though the barn may be.'

Willy suddenly felt a sharp tug on his sleeve. 'Ruby love, what's the matter?' he asked his sister. 'What is it?'

'Willy, he's here. I was told he wasn't coming. I want to go home.'

'Who, Ruby? Who do you mean?'

'Master Lionel,' looking in the direction of the de Maine family group, at the same time trying to hide behind her brother.

'Well, what does it matter, Ruby?' He remembered how she had asked a few days previously when Lionel de Maine would be home from Cambridge. He realised that Ruby's feeling towards Lionel must be stronger than he had thought then and she obviously could not cope with the occasion. 'But Ruby, you can stay with us. You can't go home now and anyway we'll have a lot of fun here. I'll look after you. I promise.' He gently kissed the top of her head, but felt the grasp on his arm tighten. 'Look, there's Doris and Grace over there. Let's go over and see how they are.' He sensed that Ruby relaxed a little as they walked across the crowded floor to the two girls serving cakes and sandwiches. They all exchanged pleasantries with news of family and friends; this was just one of many conversations taking place where virtually all knew everyone else.

After time for everyone to have a drink, Jack Mansfield stepped on to the stage, smiled broadly and clapped his hands. A few guests clearly did not hear the first clapping of hands, but a large number of quietening hushes brought everyone to order, Willy noticing that Lionel was into at least his third ale.

'Good friends, my wife and I are greatly pleased to see you all. Thank you for joining in this celebration. I am particularly pleased to welcome Mrs and Major de Maine and Mrs and Mr Jackson. Our three farming estates have come together this evening so we can thank everyone for all the hard work you do.'

There were immediate and clearly sincere nods from the other two landowners, with a 'hear, hear' from Fred Jackson.

'We want it to be a really good evening with everybody enjoying themselves. We're very fortunate to have lots of entertainment planned and opportunities for joining in some singing and dancing. Do go over to the bar at any time: but let's now get on with the fun. Our compère this evening is,' turning to his farming friend in the front row, 'Mr Jackson. Over to you.' All joined in hearty applause as the tubby, ebullient farmer stepped on to the stage; he was to surprise the audience with his new role.

'My dear friends,' started the smiling Fred Jackson, dressed in a heavily-striped suit with a yellow waistcoat attempting to keep his paunch in place, 'we are very fortunate that Miss Small is kindly playing for us, just as we thank our extremely well-dressed trio of musicians, Sammy Hatfield, Bernie Thomas and my own son Peter on his flute. Let me thank the four strong men who somehow managed to bring the piano down from Mrs Mansfield's drawing room. She assures me that it's not her best one – or at least, isn't now! We are going to start with some songs for everyone; you know the songs; our musicians will play them and so let's sing.'

Rita Small, now sitting at the piano smiled, nodded at Sammy Hatfield the leader of the trio, and struck up the introduction. By the fourth note, all knew the tune and were ready as Fred Jackson, with raised arm, brought in everyone to "Daisy, Daisy". The singing was hearty and many started to sway in time to the song. Some of the verses were not so well known, but the chorus was joyfully repeated several times. "Any Old Iron", "Boiled Beef and Carrots" and "Daddy Wouldn't Buy Me a Bow-wow" all followed in like vein. Fred Jackson's conducting became increasingly frenzied as he both led and caught the spirit of the gathering. All joined in the applause, repeated when the conductor gave his thanks to the four musicians. They all beamed, the trio doffing their colourful hats.

'I would particularly thank the leading singers whose excellent voices just led us so well. We will be hearing two of them later on. But let's turn to the first of three solo acts: individual performances of brilliance. First, let me introduce someone you all know who has kindly carried his musical saw all the way from Sandy Lane to play for us. Ladies and gentlemen, Mr Robert Berry.'

It was an exaggeration to say that all knew this lightly-bearded and balding man who was only occasionally seen outside his garden which he tended with loving care. His crop of vegetables was always something to behold, but Jack Atkins who lived nearby had often thought that he looked a sad man, an appearance promoted by his downward-curving, straggly moustache. One idiosyncrasy that most villagers knew of Robert Berry was that he always had a Union Jack, now rather faded, flying in his garden. Village gossip was that he had once been in the army, but being over forty when he moved to the village no one was sure. He was not a man who talked about himself, indeed about much at all.

He came on to the platform, on which a stool had been placed, carrying the longest saw that even local woodcutter, Dan Reynolds, had ever seen. He gave a rueful smile, sat down and tightly gripped the saw between his knees with the serrated edge facing the now curious audience. In his right hand he held a long bow and with his extended left hand the saw handle, curving the blade into an s-bend. In an unexpectedly confident voice he announced that he was going to play part of Handel's *Largo*; the result was as unexpected as it was magical. By altering the bend in the saw he expertly changed the pitch and, to Rita Small's knowledgeable ear, he added vibrato by causing the hand holding the saw end to tremble. A great burst of applause rang out as he played the final note and in answer to robust shouts of 'more', he shuffled his position a little and, without announcing the title, played "Abide With Me". This time there was a standing ovation and Robert Berry smiled, left the stage, probably not to be seen again outside his garden for a long time.

'The next item,' announced by compère Fred Jackson, 'will astound all by its brilliance.' Young Tommy Bruce came on to some ribald cheers from his contemporaries and from a bucket he took three balls and started juggling. Very cleverly he kept the balls aloft whilst reaching into the bucket for a fourth. This was successful, but trying to gather a fifth all seemed to go awry and ended with a scattering of coloured balls. However, the audience was in a mood that whether success or failure came about, a round of applause followed. This encouraged Tommy to give a much more successful demonstration using a bowler hat, a walking stick and three lightweight hammers.

'Not sure whether I most liked the one that went wrong or the last one,' whispered Isabella de Maine with a smile to her husband. All wondered what was to follow.

'I have great pleasure in introducing our next performer who will give us a rendition of one of Rudyard Kipling's great poems. Ladies and gentlemen, Major de Maine.'

Many were surprised that it was the manor owner who now came on stage, a man considered by most to be aloof through rank and, as he was perceived by his behaviour, his birthright. Now he took centre stage, bowed, announcing: 'The poem "If", by Rudyard Kipling.' As he opened with the words, "If you can keep your head when all about you are losing theirs", Abraham, Jack, Willy, Fred and Albert all found themselves silently reciting it along with the major. No whisper, no cough, nothing interrupted the major's recitation as he delivered Kipling's words with great composure; at the end there were calls for more. This sixty-year-old with his strong military bearing stood, slightly embarrassed, and announced: 'Another great poet of our times is John Masefield who wrote *Sea Fever*.' Whilst it was unknown by the audience, they were enthralled by both the words of the sea's magic spell and by the major's tone. The applause rang out.

As he unassumingly bowed and stepped off the stage, Fred Jackson took his place, held up his hand and added his thanks to the three entertainers. He announced that there would be two more communal songs before a break to have glasses filled and food eaten. 'So, my friends,' he smilingly announced, 'Miss Small and our fabulous trio will now lead us in singing two songs: you all know "Where Did You Get That Hat?"; the second one is probably new to you, but I heard that Hezekiah Freeman has a good voice and I have persuaded him to join with me in leading the singing. We will lead the way. If you don't know, it's called "I'm Henery the Eighth I Am".' To further cheers and accompanying wonderment, Hezekiah stepped carefully on to the stage and joined Fred Jackson.

After the first song Miss Small gave the trio a nod and they played the chorus of the next through once. On a repeat, the duet sang together, well in tune it was agreed. 'Now, everyone join in after listening to the tune once more!' To increasingly raucous cheers, the four players struck up again and led by the two stage performers all joined in. After well-timed bows by Hezekiah and Fred Jackson, all were invited to a twenty-minute break.

At this announcement there was considerable movement with many moving towards the bar and food counter. There was much chatter about the evening's entertainment and expressions of surprise at the previously unrecognised talents of the quiet, older men: Robert Berry, Hezekiah Freeman and Major de Maine. All agreed that it was a wonderful evening with a lot more to look forward to in the second part.

TWELVE

Evening, Wednesday, 3 April

As the interval was announced, it was to Grace Reynolds that Abraham walked, appearing to stroll in a nonchalant way, but in truth in more determined vein. 'Hello Grace, how are you?' smiling in his delightful way at this most attractive girl with golden tresses falling gracefully to her shoulder and a smile to match his own.

'I'm very well, thank you Abraham. What a splendid evening with everyone enjoying themselves and how splendidly people are dressed.'

Whilst nicknamed Racer by most in the village, Grace had always liked the name Abraham and through all the years they had shared the same classes, she refused to use the nickname adopted by most when his athletic qualities had become so obvious.

'Indeed, they are,' agreed Racer. 'And Grace, I would just say what a lovely frock it is that you are wearing.'

'Thank you. That's very sweet of you. I'm glad you like it.' The slight blush lighting up her pretty face was of pleasure, not embarrassment. She had always thought of him as a dear friend vying to be top of the class at school, but taking as much pleasure in the other's success as their own.

'Grace, can I get you a drink?'

'Thank you. That would be lovely.' Most had already obtained their drinks or were in the queue for beer, so he was back within minutes, carrying two matching drinks. 'I know we see each other quite often Grace, but we're both so busy working for Mr and Mrs Mansfield that we don't seem to have time to talk with each other. How are you getting on?'

'Very well thank you, although I wish I had time to give mother more help with all of the children, but that's how it is with such a large family. Abraham, we've known each other almost all our lives and I know you can keep a secret.' He smiled reassurance, looking with fresh eyes at what a beautiful girl Grace had become. She was the oldest of ten children and the thought went through Racer's mind that it was a wonder she could always look so smart from such a crowded household.

Abraham led her to a quieter part of the barn where both could sit. 'Do tell me,' he said. 'You know I will keep everything to myself. I'm flattered that you should want to tell me.'

'You will be surprised,' she continued haltingly, 'that Mrs Mansfield has suggested I might like to become a teacher. Imagine that!' she added with a smile.

'It sounds a great idea,' Abraham replied. 'Tell me about it.'

'Well, she knows I did well at school and has seen me teaching the children in the Sunday school and was kind enough to say that I have a way with children.' She was thrilled to see that her old school friend was giving her his full attention. Some might laugh and accuse her of having ideas above her station, but she knew that Abraham would not be like that. 'She says that there is a college in Canchester where I could go and even indicated that she had made enquiries and that I could probably get a grant. If not, that I could carry on doing some work at the farmhouse and she and Mr Mansfield would pay my fees. Isn't that amazingly kind of them?'

Doris and Albert had come to sit on the straw-covered barn floor just a few feet away, but their conversation seemed as earnest as the one he and Grace were having. Nevertheless, Abraham kept his voice down when he said, 'I'm sure you'd make a great teacher.' He briefly and gently laid his hand on Grace's arm and was thrilled that she didn't move it away.

'That's sweet of you to say so, Abraham, and what about you? I know you are doing amazing things in running, but what about your work?' she asked, looking him steadfastly in the eye. 'I hear good reports,' she added with a smile.

'Very well, I think. Mr Mansfield is a really good boss. He's so up to date with what's happening in farming. I happened to go into his office the other day and I've never seen so many farming magazines.' Grace nodded, as Abraham realised, she would often go into his room to clean. 'He talks about moving more towards arable crops, saying that you must see what kind of farming gives the best financial return. Grace, you just said how kind Mrs Mansfield is to you, well, Mr Mansfield is like that, too. You'll never guess what?'

This time it was Grace who rested her hand on Abraham's arm as she encouragingly smiled for him to tell her. 'Well, he said that there's a course at Steepleton College in September about farm management for one and a half days a week and he wants me to go on it. He said that if I did well and worked really hard I would be able to help with managing the farm in three or four years.'

'That's wonderful, really wonderful. Oh Abraham, what an exciting future for both of us. How lucky we are.'

As they continued to lightly hold each other's hands, they looked over to the other side of the barn and saw that two men were arguing. One was Lionel de Maine, the other, Bernie Thomas, the evening's fiddle player, and that Lionel appeared the worst for his drink. His father quickly took his son's arm and without any hesitation led him, quite forcibly, out of the barn. He returned a few minutes later and briskly walked over to rejoin his wife who had linked up with Mr and Mrs Mansfield.

'My dear Major,' beamed Jack Mansfield, his bushy eyebrows moving slightly with his smile: 'your rendering of those two poems was splendid, just as everything about tonight is good. How fortunate we are to live in such a place. I know our village has a lot of people who find it hard enough to get by, but the kindness shown to us since we moved here is remarkable.'

'Amen to that,' added his elegant wife. 'I wish we could do more for everyone, but maybe this evening goes some way to thank them.'

Mrs de Maine quickly came in on the conversation: 'Mabel and Jack, we would love you to come over to dinner soon. It would be really nice to have a quiet dinner just for the four of us.' Sebastian de Maine inwardly thanked Isabella for her gentle way of following on from their conversation about seeking advice from Jack Mansfield.

'That's very kind of you. We would love to, wouldn't we Jack?' The following Thursday was happily agreed, but their conversation was interrupted by Fred Jackson asking everyone to take their places.

As Mabel and Jack Mansfield moved to their seats, she turned to her husband, nodded in the direction of Grace and Abraham, saying, 'What a splendid couple of youngsters they are.'

'Indeed,' replied her husband, 'and I'm so glad you agreed that I should talk to young Abraham about him playing a bigger role in the management of Spinney Farm. I'm not getting any younger and I can't think of a brighter young man than him and I'd bank my reputation on his integrity and loyalty.'

'I agree, but you'll be all right for a fair number of years yet, Jack,' she smilingly added. 'Do you think that young Grace and Abraham are becoming attached?'

'Mabel, what an old romantic you are! They're just old school friends and good company for each other this evening.' Mabel Mansfield smiled to herself, taking her husband's hand as they sat down for the next part of the evening.

Fred Jackson almost bounced on to the stage. 'I hope that you are all well fortified with liquid refreshment not to mention the splendid things provided by Mrs Mansfield and others. Thank you to them; let's give a big round of applause.

'Our entertainers have lavished their excellence upon you, now it's your turn. Time for some dancing and if you don't know the steps, don't worry as all will become plain. Ready for the "Gay Gordons"? Now we want everyone on the floor in pairs, so find a partner and then standing in those pairs, make a big circle.'

The younger men moved with considerable speed to find a partner, Abraham to Grace, Albert to Doris and Willy to his sister Ruby; the older men were a little more reluctant although Major de Maine and Mr Mansfield quickly helped make the circle with their wives. 'Now, I'm going to ask our musicians to play and we'll all join in,' announced the compère. 'I'll call out the instructions and don't worry if you get something wrong. Just try not to knock each other over!'

The quartet struck up and all joined in. After a few minutes all went well although as Willy remarked to his sister, 'It's just as well it's not too light in here to show up where I go wrong.'

'Oh Willy, you dance very well. It's really good fun. Where did Lionel go?'

'I really don't know,' replied Willy. 'Let's just enjoy the dancing.' And everyone did. There followed similar instruction for the "Military Two-Step" and whilst some of the footwork was not embraced by all, the result was greatly enjoyed. Abraham noticed that Albert and Doris Groves made off to the darkest corner of the barn where they sat together on the deep layer of straw.

After the dances, there followed much light-hearted talk with most apologising to partner for treading on toes. Folk found somewhere to sit with a few filling up their glasses. Fred Jackson took to the stage again and announced that by popular request all were invited to join in singing "Daisy, Daisy" again.

Whilst this twenty-year-old favourite was being sung with great gusto, few noticed that Eleanor Windle had moved from the guest seats.

There was little doubt why Albert and Doris had found one of the darker areas of the barn. Albert was wondering how far he could go when he realised someone was standing immediately in front of him. 'Albert, are you ready? It's nearly our turn.' He wondered if it was a knowing smile on Eleanor Windle's pretty face.

Fred Jackson called for silence. 'Two of our number have particularly fine voices. We are grateful to them for prompting the rest of us in the communal singing, but now you can enjoy them as soloists and then in a duet. It is my great pleasure, first to introduce Mrs Windle. Our vicar's wife needs no further introduction.'

Eleanor stepped on to the stage. Wearing a long crimson skirt with a lighter red blouse she was, indeed, a very attractive soloist. 'Dear friends,' Eleanor started, 'just two songs. The first is a poem recently set to music by Edward Elgar: "Dry Those Fair, Those Crystal Eyes".' Miss Small was the sole accompanist this time as the audience sat enraptured as Eleanor sang. She was known to have a beautiful voice as she was heard with the St Mary's choir, but tonight was different. Few present knew the song, but there was not a movement from her audience and some later admitted to shedding a tear.

Her second song, "I Dreamt that I Dwelt in Marble Halls" was known by some and as Major de Maine remarked to his wife, 'That was even more beautiful than the first, and that was lovely.' The applause was great as she gave a delightful, self-effacing curtsey and left the stage.

'Thank you,' said Fred Jackson who appeared slightly humbled by Eleanor's singing. 'Now we have another fine singer who may come as a big surprise to you: to sing firstly "Did You Not Hear My Lady" and then "Lead, Kindly Light": young Albert Jones.'

As the tall, broad-shouldered figure stepped on to the stage there were both cheers and gasps of surprise. 'Well,' whispered Abraham to Grace, 'I know he had a good voice at school and he sings in the church choir, but he has kept quiet about this. Let's hope it's all right.' He was later to admit that his cousin's light baritone voice was the finest he had ever heard. The audience responded with rapturous applause.

Eleanor joined Albert on the stage as the applause died down and quietly announced that they would sing two duets, hoping that everyone would join in the second. The first, "Love, Could I Only Tell Thee", was to be talked about for many days to come, the two voices blending beautifully. The second, "Land of Hope and Glory" with its patriotic words to Elgar's rich music was a triumphant finale.

As the two singers left the stage, they smiled at each other, both recalling the hours they had practised under the tutelage of Miss Small. 'So, to our very last item: another dance. Take your partners for a waltz.' Abraham again partnered Grace, Albert with Doris and, as Willy asked Elsie Groves to dance, he was delighted to see that his good friend, Fred, had taken Ruby on to the floor. Two waltzes followed to bring to a conclusion a memorable evening of entertainment in Rusfield. A flourish on the piano from Miss Small brought silence before everyone joined in the national anthem.

Many conversations, along with laughter and some with arms round another's shoulders, broke out. It had been agreed that workers from all three farms would come in at half past six the next morning to clear everything away; to do that now would have been an anticlimax to the evening. It continued a warm evening for early April and the moon gave good light as all the villagers walked to their homes. Albert was holding Doris' hand, their bodies often touching as they talked; Abraham and Grace walked together and when they reached Grace's cottage, Abraham, after rehearsing in his mind several times what he was going to say, said: 'Grace. It's been a perfect evening. I found out that the reason Mr Jackson knew the dances is that he and Mrs Jackson go to Steepleton on the first Friday of each month where there is dancing and a music hall at the Victoria Palace. I wondered if you would like to go?'

'That would be lovely, Abraham. Thank you. I will very much look forward to it. Thank you for seeing me home and sharing so much of the evening with me.' She smiled at Abraham who lent towards her and gave her a gentle, but quick kiss. They parted, no longer just old friends, but with sparks of love and admiration for each other.

When, a short while later, Albert bade goodnight to Doris their kisses were stronger as his arms encircled the willing Doris.

Eleanor Windle was the one person who did not walk home. Sparky Carey was waiting with the pony and trap a short distance from the barn and as Eleanor stepped into the small carriage, she thanked him saying: 'I could easily have walked home, but it is very kind of you to collect me. I'm sorry that your son, James, could not make the party tonight. Young Albert Jones explained that he is working away and won't be home until late tomorrow.' The drive was a short one and with the pony delighted to have an unexpected run out, they soon drew up outside the vicarage.

She pushed open the door and went in. As she hung her crimson shawl over the chair in the hall, Arthur came from the lounge to greet her with a kiss. 'I hope you had a good evening, my love. I'm sorry I couldn't join you; when I called on Mrs Rushton I thought it would be a short visit, but soon after I got there, Doctor Christopher arrived.'

'So, how are things?'

'He could do nothing for her. He sat with her whilst I stayed downstairs with her daughter. After a while he suggested Miss Rushton went upstairs. I followed her and we sat there quietly and after some thirty minutes she died. Miss Rushton asked me to pray with her and so we stayed together for a while.

She was, of course, very upset but did say that her mother had been in a lot of pain recently and so this evening had brought some relief. I've been to her shop often enough, but tonight I got to know what a sweet lady she really is. Apparently she has no near family, but said she has good friends in the village. I suspect most are customers whom she has got to know over the years and she may have very few, if any, close friends. We must keep a close eye on her.'

He knew that more than anyone else Eleanor would call, not just to express immediate sympathy, but would continue the contact. 'Incidentally, I discovered her Christian name. It's Violet, a pretty name and so apposite for this lovely lady. Of course, this all meant I missed the meeting earlier this evening in the vestry about Empire Day. On my way back from Miss Rushton I called in to apologise to George Cooper but as you can imagine, he wasn't pleased. It was far too late to get up to the party so when I got home an hour ago I had a bath and it seemed sensible to put on my nightwear. But amid the sadness of the evening, I heard some good news from Doctor Christopher. It appears likely that the hospital board will agree to a nurse coming to live in Rusfield; but tell me about your evening.'

'I'm so sorry for Miss Rushton; thank you for all the support you're giving her – and your news about having a village nurse is wonderful.' Eleanor went on to paint a most happy picture of the evening saying how some unexpected talents had become apparent, particularly Albert Jones' singing. 'I think I will just run a bath as well,' she said. 'With all the activity this evening and so many people there, the barn got really warm and the dancing was quite energetic.'

'I'll just draw off the water for you.' This was now an easy job since the gas water-heater had been installed.

When Eleanor emerged to have her bath, Arthur went across the landing into his dressing room, or little sanctuary, as he sometimes called it. He sat quietly, his thoughts moving over many village events and villagers. He then knelt before the unadorned cross, and prayed: 'Oh God, I know that the soul of Mrs Rushton is safely with you. Help us all to give comfort to her daughter in her sad times. Be also with Martha Smith in her hour of need and may her daughter receive help and feel support at this time. There are so many in our village that have great worries and needs. Give me the strength and wisdom to do what I can do to help.' He paused for a while before continuing: 'God forgive me for all my sins; I have so totally failed in my duty as a humble priest. Memory of my sin lays heavy on my heart.' He crossed himself, slowly rose, turned out the lamp and went to check that doors were locked, candles and lamps extinguished.

A single candle was burning near the bedside. Eleanor was sitting in bed and on seeing her husband come in, opened her arms to him. He walked across, climbed on to the bed and they held each other close. 'My darling,' were Eleanor's only words as she gently came out of his arms, leant forward and drew her nightdress over her head, dropping it on the floor beside the bed. She lay back with that wondrous smile that Arthur knew and loved so well. He pulled off his night attire and lay next to her. They kissed with increasing passion, tongues touching and hands feeling each other's body. Arthur raised his head, moved down and kissed her breasts, nipples brown and erect. His tongue and lips moved downwards and he seemingly kissed every curve and part of her body. As he lingered lower, Eleanor gave a gentle gasp and her legs moved slightly apart. She had never felt such love. She reached down and gently lifted his head, 'Now let me kiss you.' She touched and kissed Arthur's body, stopping for a while as she reached his very manhood which was so ready to consummate their love.

It was an hour later that Arthur extinguished the candle. As he came back in to the bed, Eleanor's arms enveloped him; they kissed and lay together, exhausted by their lovemaking, rejoicing in it.

THIRTEEN

Thursday, 4 & Friday, 5 April

Peter Woods could never believe his good fortune in becoming a postman. He had always wanted an open-air job and realised how well life had turned out; his weekly wage packet of £1 6s 4d was enough for his modest needs. When attending Steepleton Board School he had known his academic record was easily surpassed by other boys leaving school, nor was it just an academic shortcoming that made progress unlikely, more against him was being blind in his left eye.

Even at the age of twenty-one he occasionally reflected on how he and his younger brother, Walter, had gone out to look for birds' eggs. They had a good collection, but at the age of ten Peter did not have a jackdaw's egg. Jackdaws tend to build their nests in old chimneys, but such structures were outside the scope of even the adventurous Wood brothers. Then Peter had spotted one as it returned with sticks to a substantial elm tree on the edge of the town. Eggs might be there.

The nest was high and after a fifteen-minute hard climb he made it to the nest and saw four pale blue eggs with their blackish-brown markings. He realised that he needed both hands free to climb down and did the only possible thing, placing the egg in his mouth which was a preferred option to his trouser pocket where it would almost certainly break. Still eight feet from the ground, he missed his footing and in trying to catch a branch only succeeded in catching his left eye on another protruding one; the egg breaking in his mouth. Visits to the doctor and to the small hospital in Steepleton failed to save his eye; he could still taste the egg.

When he left school nearly three years later, Peter had come to terms with his impairment and obtained a job as a messenger boy, but was now a fully-fledged postman. Smartly dressed in his blue uniform, proudly wearing his peaked cap, he was a well-known figure cycling the four miles from Steepleton to Rusfield. His cheery disposition was a major reason for people happily waving as he rode past, but he also thought it had much to do with delivered letters usually carrying good news. There soon built up a warm relationship between villagers and this tall, lean young man with ginger hair hidden under his cap.

On this Thursday morning, he entered the village and dropped off a letter to Mr Jackson at the farm, the red metal carrier at the front of his bicycle lightly piled with post. It had been sorted into a number of small postal sacks, each one for a different part of the village. On the way to Rusfield, he would deliver post to the few farms and isolated houses on the left-hand side of the road, delivering to the other side on his return.

This morning after delivering one letter to Miss Small, he continued along Wood Lane to the farm where Mr and Mrs Mansfield were regular recipients of mail. He managed to squeeze the small parcel through their letter box, noting that it was yet another one from a London company called Gamages and bearing a red stamp. As he cycled back towards the main part of the village he saw Mr Mansfield talking to his fellow farmer outside one of Mr Jackson's barns. He waved to them and both gave a cheery return greeting.

On to the houses in Pond Street, but apart from one for the smithy's house, there was nothing until he reached the vicarage. He pulled out a letter addressed to Mrs E. Windle, The Vicarage, Rusfield. It had the usual red one-penny stamp which bore the image of the new king. Since ending his interest in birds' eggs, he had taken up stamp collecting. If he delivered a letter bearing a stamp unknown to him, relatively unusual in Rusfield, he would not hesitate to knock and politely ask if he might have the stamp on his next visit. He had been delighted that just recently there had been letters with Canadian stamps, an exciting addition to his collection. He now slipped the letter through the brass letter box in the dark blue vicarage door and went on his way. The rest of that morning's round was uneventful and his mind turned to a four-day holiday.

At the moment the letter came through the letter box, Eleanor was passing through the hall having come downstairs from checking that everything was ready for their guests in two days. She picked up the pale cream envelope, noting that it bore a Canchester postmark, passed through to the writing room, picked up the letter opener from the bureau top and slit the envelope open. She unfolded the boldly handwritten letter and read the Canchester address. Under the heading, "Votes for Women, The Women's Social and Political Union", she read:

Dear Mrs Windle,

I am taking the liberty of writing to you since I understand you are rightly sympathetic to the great Suffrage Movement. No doubt you have heard of increasing action being taken in our determination to gain our rights. On Friday 24th May there is a meeting of all interested women at the George Room, 25 Bowker Street, Canchester. The meeting will start at 7.00pm sharp.

I am delighted to say that Mary Sophia Allen who has been imprisoned three times, twice bravely going on hunger strike, for supporting our movement will be the speaker.

I have pleasure inviting you to participate in the meeting; please make yourself known to me on your arrival.

Yours sincerely,
Amelia Payne-Croft

A variety of feelings came to Eleanor as she reread the letter. She was pleased at the association with women's rights, yet uncertain of her feeling towards the tone of militant action. Since she and Arthur had first fallen in love, she had kept to their vow of being open and honest. She would not have difficulty in showing Arthur the letter, but knew that it would cause him concern at a time when he had much on his mind with all that Holy Week promoted as well as his parents visiting. She decided it would be best not to tell Arthur until after his parents' visit. She returned the letter to its envelope, took it upstairs and placed it with other correspondence in her dressing room.

Good Friday dawned clear and bright. It would be a quiet day in Rusfield as many in the village would attend one of the Good Friday services. Arthur would lead both an hour-long service late morning and a period of reflection before the cross in the late afternoon. There had been a modest-sized congregation at the watch service in the two hours leading to midnight the previous evening. Children were generally not expected to play out of doors on Good Friday, although Eleanor had expressed the view to Arthur that she did not really think God would mind.

Eleanor, still with the previous day's letter in her thoughts, set out after an early lunch on the short distance to Jackson's Farm where she had been invited for a cup of tea with Henrietta and Fred Jackson. Eleanor realised that Arthur must be weary with all the church services and made it easy for him to stay behind in the vicarage: 'You have a rest, dear; there are still Sunday's services and you won't get much rest time with your parents here.'

Arthur was most grateful for his wife's thoughtfulness. Complete with a glass, jug of cool water and a report on the World Missionary Conference which had been held in Edinburgh almost six months previously, he went in to the large conservatory and settled into his favourite chair. After something less than two pages, his mind turned away from the report and his own thoughts took over. He realised, not for the first time, that he was uncertain about his own ministry. He wondered if the villagers received anything worthwhile from his sermons for as he had looked down on the pews, with faces he knew so well, were there any that looked really caught up by his words? He doubted whether anything his sermons included made any difference to their lives.

He stretched out to take a drink, still wondering about his calling. He was sure his faith was firmly placed, but did God actually mean him to be living his years out in Rusfield. He wondered how disappointed he, and perhaps Eleanor, was that his visit to Canchester Cathedral had not brought about an offer of a move.

He closed his eyes so that he could reflect more deeply on his life. There had never been a single moment when he had felt God's call, no moment on a road to Damascus as Paul had known, rather a gradual stutter towards entering the church. He remembered the village near Aldershot where it all began, a smart house suitable for a young army officer, wife and child. His father was often away, but he could clearly remember one occasion when great excitement had abounded on his father's homecoming; he would have been five or six at the time. Of course, his mother was always around, loving and gentle, but then had come the time when he was sent off to Longchase Grange School. He could recall the building, a rambling country house, cold and somehow unfriendly. He had sometimes slipped in to the quietness of the small, wood-panelled chapel and found peace there; the dark and rather eerie corners of the old building became less frightening, although he still stayed away from them.

There had been George Berman, who had been a good friend, and together they had comforted each other when things went wrong or bullying had reached out to one or other of them. He remembered one Saturday afternoon when he had found George in tears, but refusing to say what was wrong. However, a few days later his friend had suddenly come out with a story which Arthur at first could not understand. George said that after the whole school had been on a run the previous Saturday and he had been the last to leave the cold and sombre washing room, Mr Elders, the mathematics' master, on supervision duty that day, had come in. He had smiled and had offered to rub George's back dry. His friend had been surprised, but not inclined to contradict a teacher. Having dried his back, the master commented on what a fine body George had. He reached down and rubbed his stomach saying that was still a little wet. In his friend's own words, the next thing George knew was that Mr Elders was touching his willy. Arthur asked his friend what he did. He tearfully replied that he had cried out, picked up his clothes and run out of the changing room. George was too upset to say any more and two days later, term ended. George did not return to school for the summer term and Arthur never heard from him again. There was a thought in his mind that God would protect someone as hurt as his closest friend. Arthur was saddened by the loss of his friend, but delighted, though puzzled, that Mr Elders had also failed to appear for the new term.

He went on to Monkswood, a larger school, when he was thirteen and settled in quite well. He still loved the holidays and spent as much time as he could with his mother who now usually declined the opportunity to accompany her husband on his overseas tours to South Africa, Egypt, Ireland and India, where he was based for three years. Then the time had come for Arthur to sit the entrance examination for Oxford; he failed, as he knew he would. His father was by then a lieutenant colonel and very much wanted his son to follow his own footsteps into the army, as he had his own father. Arthur had always felt uncomfortable at this idea and whilst his eyesight may not have been sufficient cause for rejection from the county regiment, this was the reason he gave to his father. Arthur had then to think of an alternative path to follow.

He remained uncertain about his career, but increasingly felt the appeal of going in to the church. He had thought that every priest must have no doubts in their own personal faith, but perhaps that was not so. He believed in God and felt this in his heart, but remained uncertain of some of the church's teachings, but maybe that was just a matter of searching after that truth. He respected the ordered form of the church, its official hierarchy and learnt, from his father, a love of great church buildings and liturgy. He loved great cathedrals, but not the high orders of service or the Oxford Movement which struck no inner chord for him. Quite close to Oxford was an Anglican seminary, Wycliffe Hall, established less than twenty years earlier. Arthur applied for entry and commenced his studies for the training of clergy there in 1888.

Arthur came to as a shadow hovered over him. 'I'm so glad you had a good rest, Arthur. You deserve it after all your recent activity,' said Eleanor as she placed a cup of tea on the table beside her husband. 'Now, you enjoy your tea. I just need to check one or two small things and then we are ready for your parents' visit tomorrow. It will be lovely to see them. I will be ready to join you in a few minutes for the time of reflection before the cross.'

As she went out of the room she smiled to herself at the thought of what her father-in-law would say if he ever learnt about the letter she had received the previous day.

FOURTEEN

Saturday, 6 April

'Come on, Arthur. It is your parents who are staying, not royalty,' Eleanor laughingly commented to her husband when she saw him unnecessarily tidying the bookshelf on their main landing.

'Sorry, my love. It's just a silly habit. I love mother coming, but I always feel anxious about father.' He had often wondered why this should be; always feeling close to his mother, able to share his hopes and doubts with her, but quite different with his father. Family friends and acquaintances sometimes spoke of Colonel Hector Richard Windle in revered tones, alluding to his bravery and outstanding courage. Arthur knew how as a young officer, his father had escaped from a ferocious tribe in the Gold Coast, that his colleagues had been killed, but he alone had struggled and managed to escape. However, Arthur thought to himself, I am over forty now and must stop feeling intimidated by him.

His parents arrived promptly at three o'clock, dismounting from the modest carriage in which Sparky Carey had collected them from Steepleton station. Arthur and his mother's hug was a genuine welcome of affection, the colonel's light kiss on Eleanor's cheek rather less. Son and father shook hands, mother and daughter-in-law warmly embraced.

Twenty minutes later and the four were sitting in the conservatory with tea served by Eliza Carey who had come in to carry out a few extra duties. As talk continued about the journey from Dorset, mutual friends and family news, Eleanor looked at her husband and again thought how he had taken the strong, good looks from his father, yet the more gentle nature of his mother. Colonel Windle still bore an upright six-foot frame, little spare weight and Eleanor could well imagine Arthur looking like this some twenty-five years on, although she hoped with less harsh lines souring his face. Arthur had inherited his father's very fair hair although his father's had now taken on an almost silver appearance.

The afternoon and early evening passed by with an amicable exchange of news until Eleanor announced it was time to change for dinner to be served at seven-thirty.

'Your parents seem well, although perhaps your father looks a little more frail than last time we saw him,' Eleanor remarked as her husband laced up the back of her green floral frock. Going downstairs, Eleanor and Arthur were almost immediately followed by the older couple. After each had enjoyed a glass of the colonel's favourite sherry, they were soon seated round the large, well laid out oak table, where dinner was served; conversation moved on quite easily.

'So, Colonel Windle,' began Eleanor, who had never wished to give any offence by using any other title, 'I'm sure you are still as busy as ever. Are you involved in any new projects?'

'Well, yes, actually I am. You may have heard of the Territorial Force which is made up of volunteers and linked with its local regiment, in our case the Dorsets.' The colonel, although sitting and enjoying the game pie, seemed to grow an inch or two as he launched into his reply: 'They are a support force to our regular army in case of serious problems. I was asked to give assistance to those running this Territorial Force when they are carrying out military exercises, mainly on Salisbury Plain. I thought my army days were over when I retired back in '06, but it seems there is still a role for me to play.'

'And I'm sure you play it very well,' interjected Arthur. 'I think a similar group has been formed in Steepleton.'

The colonel placed his cutlery on his plate in order to give more weight to his words by using his hands. 'Glad to hear it. Many of us have been aware for the past ten years or so that Germany has been building up its forces and I'm glad to say that some of the far-sighted government politicians have realised that we have to be prepared.'

'But surely,' Eleanor said, 'no one is really anticipating fighting between our countries? After all the King and the Kaiser are cousins.'

'Maybe,' spoke the colonel with increasing hand gestures, 'but we just have to be prepared. None of us wants any more wars, but the best way forward is to make sure that any potential enemy realises it would be easily defeated. The Territorial Force is just a reserve in case our regular army has to leave our shores.'

Charlotte Windle carefully levered the conversation away from wars to less contentious issues. She knew all too well that her son felt as strongly as her husband about maintaining the strength of Britain and its Empire, but felt this might not be a view shared by Eleanor.

After a choice of desserts followed by coffee, Charlotte asked if she might be excused as tiredness was setting in after their long journey. Goodnights were said and she left, followed five minutes later by her husband to his room.

'Well, thank you darling,' said Arthur giving Eleanor a kiss. 'That was a good start to their visit. A pleasant enough evening, let's just hope the rest of their stay is as peaceful.'

'Indeed it was,' commented Eleanor. 'But Arthur, was it just my imagination that there seemed something of a distance between your parents? I know they have never demonstrated much in the way of feelings towards each other; that simply doesn't appear to be your father's way, but they really didn't seem to communicate with each other at all today; but it's probably just my imagination. Anyway, I must go to thank Eliza for all the help she's given tonight, and pay her. She really is a treasure. She will have done most of the clearing up and we can finish anything else in the morning.'

A few minutes later, Arthur extinguished the downstairs' lights and went up to his sanctuary. He knelt down before the cross given by his father, crossed himself and prayed: 'Dear Father, I thank you for all that you have given to me. I pray for my parents, that any space between them may be filled with love; that you will lead me as I take the Easter Day service. May the great joy of the resurrected Lord shine through the service and through any words you place in my mind. May all the people of our village learn more of your love. Forgive me for my sin. You know the most inner secrets of my life, forgive me. And Lord, I thank you for the love of Eleanor. Amen.'

FIFTEEN

Morning & Afternoon, Easter Day, 7 April

As she walked along Pond Street towards St Mary's with six younger members of the family, Grace may have thought it a happy coincidence that Abraham was approaching from the opposite direction. In truth, he had told his parents as they left for St Mary's that he would catch them up, and then dawdled until he saw Grace coming from the opposite direction.

'A happy Easter, Abraham,' welcomed Grace as they met at the church gate.

'And a very happy Easter to all of you,' a smiling Abraham said to the family. 'It's lovely to see you again, Grace. I expect you're taking a Sunday school class, but I wonder if I could speak with you afterwards?'

'Of course, the children can walk home with father; we can see each other then.'

She led the Reynolds flock into the church where Frederick Richards, Abraham's father, was welcoming people in his usual charming way. The church quickly filled up, children sitting near the front wearing their Sunday clothes, quite different to their everyday wear. Eleanor, together with Arthur's parents took their places and the congregation moved closer together to create spaces at the end of pews for last-minute arrivals. Rita Small had begun playing the organ some time earlier, but on the hour the music changed and the choir processed in, followed by Arthur who climbed the six steps to the pulpit.

Arthur later felt that it had been a joyful service for Easter Day with well-loved hymns and readings, but he was, as ever, less sure about his sermon. For all the spiritual nature of a church service, Arthur sometimes felt like an actor; he had to give a good performance. But he knew one essential question that separated him from an actor: had the people felt God's presence?

After the service there were many conversations between villagers. Eleanor sat in a corner pew with her words of comfort being graciously received by Violet Rushton. Abraham was waiting near the lychgate for Grace and after her siblings had set out for home, they chatted easily with many smiles. He asked Grace if she would walk out with him the following day, perhaps towards Bramrose Hill where Willy had mentioned a nesting buzzard. Knowing she would be busy helping with domestic duties in the morning, Grace suggested meeting at three o'clock to which Abraham happily agreed. Arthur was busy shaking hands, wishing everyone a blessed and happy Easter.

The sun had cut through the clouds and although far from providing other than early spring warmth, it added to the general feeling of a contented community. It was left to George Cooper to bring a cloud to the occasion. 'Vicar,' started the old and seemingly joyless churchwarden as he approached Arthur at the church door: 'I don't know why you never have that great hymn, "Forty Days Thy Seer Of Old". It was one the Reverend Gulland always had and we miss it.'

Before Arthur could think of an appropriate response, he was aware of another within hearing distance. Frederick Richards, with a gracious smile at the churchwarden said, 'George, it's twenty years since the Reverend Gulland left us and it was always a hymn I, for one, couldn't really understand.

Vicar, it was a grand service and good that so many shared it. Thank you.'

With mumbled words that fortunately neither could catch, George Cooper walked off, no doubt thinking of other things that, in his mind, had changed for the worse. Arthur smiled at Abraham's father and thanked him for coming to the rescue. 'I just saw Abraham briefly, you must be very proud of your son's running feats.'

'Thank you, Vicar,' replied Frederick. 'Yes, his mother and I are, indeed, proud of him. He's set his heart on running better and faster, but I also think he's doing well on Mr Mansfield's farm.'

Arthur appreciated Frederick Richards' intervention and hoped that this kindly and thoughtful man reflected the dominant mood in the village towards the morning service. As all too often, his mind turned to George Cooper for whom nothing that Arthur attempted seemed right.

Sunday lunch passed well. Eliza had prepared vegetables the day before when getting things ready for the Saturday evening. The roast lamb exuded a mouth-watering aroma from the kitchen and by half past one, all were enjoying the meal. The colonel complimented Eleanor on the repast, adding that he would be taking a rest in the afternoon. Charlotte Windle casually announced that from where she had been sitting in St Mary's, she had noticed some wall inscriptions which she would like to look at more closely.

She graciously declined either Arthur's or Eleanor's offer to accompany her. 'Wrap up well. The sun will soon lose all its warmth and the church is a cold place,' suggested Eleanor. Having donned a warm coat, Charlotte walked across to the church, stopping to look at some of the spring flowers which were emerging. As two figures came from the village-green side of the churchyard, Charlotte stopped.

'How nice to see you, Mrs Windle,' said Olivia Atkins with a broad smile.

Jack, who was with his mother, added his own greetings. 'Are you staying for several days?' he asked, polite and charming as Charlotte remembered him from previous visits to Rusfield. The three of them chatted for a while, Charlotte being delighted to hear about the progress of the reading room with Jack speaking enthusiastically of how much it offered him, and briefly of his work in the Steepleton bakery.

When Jack excused himself for a few minutes, Olivia knew that the subject for his attention would be her husband's grave. She knew of Jack's unspoken, but obviously strong feelings towards the man he had never known. Charlotte Windle and Olivia chatted on until he reappeared.

'It's always nice to catch up with village news,' said Charlotte Windle as mother and son finally prepared to move off. 'It's nearly a year since I was here last and the village seems to move on well. It's been lovely talking with you both and I wish you every continuing success with the reading room. And Jack, I'm glad to hear your work is going well.'

As Olivia and Jack moved on, Charlotte lifted the latch and pushed opened the heavy seventeenth-century door. She entered and in spite of its dimness, spent many minutes looking at various wall plaques before returning to the churchyard and reading some of the headstones. The recurring names borne on these weather-worn stones revealed how some families had lived in Rusfield for centuries, many still having descendants in this small, proud if poor village.

SIXTEEN

Afternoon, Monday, 8 April

Robert Berry took off his cap and resting one foot on his fork, delved into his pocket and withdrew a well-worn grey handkerchief. As he mopped his brow, he knew this must be one of the warmest Easter Mondays in his memory, apart from those when he had been in India and South Africa with the Tigers. He had enjoyed his time abroad, especially the comradeship in the Leicestershire Regiment, but the futile waste of life he had seen in what became known as the Boer War had sickened him and he had been glad to return to civilian life. It was really chance that he had settled in Rusfield, as an old comrade had once lived in the village and mentioned it to Robert.

He thought back to Wednesday night when he had, perhaps foolishly, been persuaded by Fred Jackson to perform at the farm party although, surprisingly, he had rather enjoyed it. Still, back to the digging; he remembered his grandfather saying that any vegetable patch should be dug over before Easter Monday had passed. There was hardly a breath of wind to disturb the Union Jack flying high in the garden, which he flew as a tribute to comrades who had fallen in fighting for their country. He looked towards Bramrose Hill, rising half a mile away, where he could see four figures in pairs, separated by a good distance, walking towards each other along one of the lower paths to the hills.

Whilst Robert could not make out faces, Arthur and his mother were one of these pairs, enjoying a leisurely stroll. The colonel was having his normal afternoon nap whilst Eleanor was taking the opportunity to call on Violet Rushton and then, if there was time, to see the poor, overworked Liz Smith who would almost certainly be laundering. Easter Monday provided no holiday for her nor, indeed, many others in the village; the loss of a day's pay could not be afforded.

In any case, Eleanor knew well that Arthur's mother looked forward to some time just with her son, as she was always concerned how he was faring. 'Eleanor is as lovely and sweet as ever,' she was saying as they stopped to look around at the fields which were becoming greener by the day. 'I really see her as the daughter I never had. Sadly, I do realise that your father is less than gracious to her, which is so wrong because she makes us both so very welcome.'

'I am very fortunate, Mother, and I don't understand why father never unbends to dear Eleanor. I realise his upbringing and army experience have helped create a certain aloofness, but I know she becomes worried about the lack of warmth between them; it's just something neither of us understands.'

His mother put an arm round her son of whom she thought so highly. 'It's a complicated and long story, Arthur, and I'm not too sure myself. But, perhaps, I should say something, if only to explain that in no way is it her fault. It really began when Florence died.'

'But that was hardly Eleanor's fault,' Arthur burst in.

'I know dear, but your father was so pleased when you married Florence. Her father being a brigadier made it a perfect match as far as your father was concerned. Truth to tell, at the time I was uncertain. I knew that the relationship between you and Florence had been largely engineered. I hope unkindness isn't my natural way, but I realised that she, too, had had a very narrow upbringing, probably more so than you, dear. Florence was by no means an unkind girl, but I always saw her as rather cold and unyielding. Of course, I hoped and prayed you would both be happy; your father was over the moon with delight. Then came the appalling accident and it was certain that in your father's mind no one, but no one could fill Florence's shoes.'

Arthur had always realised part of what his mother had just tried to explain. Yes, he thought, his marriage to the dark-haired, slim and not physically unattractive Florence, only nineteen when they married, could be seen as one of convenience. He had always blamed himself for the lack of warmth in their relationship, but she had often resisted what he thought was a moment of love. But then had come the great tragedy. He remembered how excited Florence had been with the suggestion by friends from her Aldershot days of going to Paris, visiting the Louvre and other great art galleries. In fact, it was the 18 October, the day after their first wedding anniversary, that she had been collected from the vicarage, taken to Steepleton station and on to London to meet with the others. She was very excited and he could still hardly believe the terrible chance that had caused her death.

Having stayed in the French city for three nights, on their last morning Florence did some shopping on her own and arranged to meet her friends near to the Gare Montparnasse, to leave Paris for the return. At that moment an express running between Granville and Paris had overrun its stopping buffer, ripped across a large section of the station concourse, through a thick wall and plummeted over thirty-feet below at exactly the time Florence and her friends were walking by. Her friends were greatly shocked, but only slightly injured. No one in the train was killed; Florence alone died, instantly.

Many tried to give him comfort, but he felt that he had

failed her by not bringing enough love to their union and was in a state of terrible despair for a long time. For several months, Charlotte had come to live with him in the vicarage, fearful that he might commit injury to himself. Community roles had been reversed and it was caring parishioners who brought comfort to their priest; the bond between Arthur and the people of Rusfield became ever stronger.

He came to, finding that he and his mother had walked on without him realising it. Approaching them along this grassy track was another couple. Arthur smiled; it was Abraham who spoke the first words, 'Good afternoon Mrs Windle, good afternoon Vicar. Mrs Windle, you probably don't know my friend, please allow me to introduce Miss Grace Reynolds.'

Grace smiled and said how nice it was to meet. 'It's such a beautiful day that Abraham suggested a walk. We are on our way to see if we can spot a buzzard's nest that a friend has told us about. I hope you are having a pleasant walk.'

They chatted together for a few minutes, Charlotte thinking what a fine couple the two made. As they parted, she turned to her son and smiled: 'What a beautiful couple, so handsome and so much in love.'

'But Mother, I don't think they are more than friends.'

'Arthur, are you blind? They may have talked very politely with us, but they only had eyes for each other.' Her eyes twinkled even more as she added: 'It rather reminds me of you and Eleanor when you first met and, I'm delighted to say, things don't seem to have changed!' Arthur could think of nothing to say, but blushed and turning to look back he saw that the young people were now hand in hand and very close to each other as they walked on.

Words were unnecessary, but Arthur knew her thoughts followed on from their previous conversation. After a while she spoke: 'Arthur, I may have said more than I should have done about Florence, but I just want you to know how much I rejoice in you and Eleanor having found each other. I thank

God for that and would that the feeling was shared by your father.' It suddenly struck Arthur that whilst he remembered his mother occasionally using a pet name, often Hec, when addressing his father, he could not remember this happening either on this visit or the previous one; indeed, they hardly talked directly to one another at all.

He would often wonder later whether what he addressed next encroached too much on his mother's privacy: 'Mother, is everything all right between you and father? He looks well, but is there anything I should know?'

'Arthur, things are just as they have been between us for some time. Have no fears, but there is one thing I would say to you: all your life, you have heard people talk about the bravery of your father when he was in the Gold Coast, how he and a small number from his battalion were ordered to settle a tribal dispute that looked as if it might develop into open warfare. We know things did not turn out well and all, bar your father, were killed; that he showed great fortitude in escaping as he was badly injured and literally crawled to safety. It was purely good fortune that another group of men had put down on the nearby coast and gone inland to look for water and found your father. But, Arthur, that was nearly forty years ago and life has moved on. You must not allow that incident to so affect you that, at times, you seem to stand in great awe of him. Like the rest of us, he has weaknesses as well.'

Arthur reached for his mother's hand, took it and they walked on together. 'And Arthur, it was remarkable that Grace mentioned that she and Abraham hoped to see a buzzard today.'

'Indeed, it would be grand to see buzzards settling in this area.'

'No, Arthur, I didn't mean that. You see, it was said by one of the soldiers who rescued your father that it was the movement of a bird towards him that caught their attention, otherwise they might never have spotted your father and saved him. It was said that bird was a buzzard, albeit different to this one. Perhaps a buzzard is a sign of good fortune.'

They completed their walk as the sun became lower over Rusfield; never had mother and son felt so close to one another.

SEVENTEEN

Morning & Afternoon, Tuesday, 9 April

'We are being collected just before three o'clock this afternoon,' Charlotte Windle quietly reminded Eleanor as she was pouring coffee at the breakfast table. Eleanor had set up breakfast in the conservatory and whilst the garden had not moved on too far from its winter clothing, primroses, daffodils and early tulips were in full colour.

The colonel was busy looking at birds feeding on the nuts that Arthur had put outside earlier. 'I see greenfinches, chaffinches and goldfinches; do you get any bullfinches? A favourite of mine.'

'Very rarely,' replied Arthur. 'I keep a list of birds I've seen in the garden and bullfinches are on it, but I've only seen them on a few occasions.' He turned to his mother: 'You know you and father are very welcome to stay on.'

His mother smiled sweetly: 'Thank you all the same, but we must leave this afternoon. There is one thing I would ask.'

'And what is that?' offered Eleanor in encouraging tone.

'Well, yesterday when I happened to meet Olivia Atkins and her son, Jack, I was hearing about your new reading room. It sounded extremely interesting and I wondered whether I might be able to have a look. Would that be possible?'

'Of course it would,' Eleanor quickly replied. 'It may not be open, but I have a key. Why don't you and I go along later this morning leaving Arthur and his father a chance for a good chat?'

'That would be lovely, dear,' replied Charlotte.

Arthur realised that he had hardly been on his own with his father since he had arrived on Saturday. 'We can sit in here Father. I'd like to hear more about the work you are doing with the Territorials. It sounds really interesting.'

The sun was still shining, although a little more breeze had come up, when Eleanor and Charlotte left the vicarage just before eleven o'clock. The two men chatted on current affairs for a time before Arthur asked how the Territorial Force had started. His father drew himself up in his chair and explained. 'Just a few politicians realise that whilst we still need imperial forces to maintain the Empire, there is always a possible threat from Europe. So four years ago, the Force was set up to give men a chance to join the army on a part-time basis. The men train at weekends and evenings. In Dorset it all seems to have gone very well.'

'So what is your role in all this, Father?'

'Well, some of the men have no idea of what they are taking on when they join us; most don't even have the ability to march properly. Arrangements have to be made to get them fitter, enable them to drill properly and know about weapons and my work is to seek out the right people to train the men and make sure the training is going well. Then there are weekend camps which I've organised in some of the wilder parts of Salisbury Plain much of which is owned by the army.'

Arthur could see his father's growing enthusiasm when he asked, 'And you get plenty of men volunteering for this?'

'Certainly,' came the immediate reply. 'Of course, it's not the same as being a professional soldier, but plenty of young men want to serve their country and do something worthwhile. Our country and the Empire are facing real dangers which seem to escape the prime minister and all his cronies, but we must be ready.'

'Well done, Father. Incidentally I see you are wearing your old regimental tie and I noticed Major de Maine from the village with a matching one at church on Sunday. Did you ever come across him? He would be about your age, I imagine.'

'De Maine, no, the name doesn't mean anything to me,' responded his father, 'but as he was only a major it would hardly be surprising if I don't remember him, even if our paths did cross. But changing subjects, I wondered whether you still see anything of Eleanor's parents. Not a man I particularly want to know, although I found his wife pleasant enough.'

Arthur knew that his father could never really accept that his son had married the daughter of a butcher; that had been made clear when they met at the wedding. On the contrary, Arthur had always liked Eleanor's parents for their modesty and charm and greatly admired his father-in-law for his depth of learning which, Arthur knew, was all self-taught. It was a quality that he had passed on to his daughter.

'Oh, yes. We often walk over to Wensfield to join them for lunch,' replied Arthur. 'But Mr Brown has been saddened by the departure of his good friend, Peter Meadows, who has just left our school. They shared many interests, particularly in the night sky and would often walk the four miles to each other's house on clear nights when there was plenty to see.'

His father came out with a whiplash response, 'Can't see much interest in that. Only time I wanted to know about the night sky was when we were in remote parts of India and Afghanistan and relied on the stars for night-time guidance.'

Tactfully, Arthur was just about to suggest a walk round the garden, when Eleanor and Charlotte came into the conservatory. 'It was absolutely wonderful, Arthur. Eleanor and the other volunteers have done a marvellous job. You must all be very pleased with it. I must tell people about it in our village, but now I must finish the packing.'

After a buffet lunch of cold meats and salad, final preparations for departure were made. Sparky was as ever on time and cases soon loaded. Farewells were said and Charlotte Windle gave profuse thanks to their hosts, the colonel a rather briefer, 'Thank you.' All had passed well Arthur was thinking, when his father's final comment came as unexpectedly, as unintentionally close to their stay ending in disaster.

'I hope the train from Steepleton proves reliable as we need plenty of time for the change-over to Waterloo station. When we were on our way up there was a large number of women across the front of that station waving banners and shouting about that bloody suffragette movement. They all need their arses slapped.'

Arthur looked at Eleanor. Her cheeks had reddened and Arthur thought for a moment she was about to say something. He loved her and admired her all the more for remaining silent. Sparky cracked his whip, without touching the pony, and his parents were driven away.

'I'm so sorry, darling, for that. My father always expresses his own views without thinking how others might be upset.' He was then surprised to see that Eleanor was smiling and then collapsing into laughter.

'What is it my love?'

'I was just thinking of your father trying to slap my arse! He wouldn't live to see another day.' Arthur knew that he certainly would not have wanted to have been in his father's shoes. He put his arms round his still laughing wife and together they went indoors. They had the rest of the afternoon and the whole of the evening to themselves.

EIGHTEEN

Morning & Afternoon, Monday, 27 May

The children proudly began their parade from the church hall, crossing Bury Way and stepping up the slight bank on to the green. The sun shone and teenagers, parents, friends and other enthusiastic villagers clapped their approval as eight-year-old Rachel Reynolds, smiling broadly in her May Queen dress, led the way.

'How splendid all the children look,' remarked Jammy Carey to his great friend, Willy Johnson, as the children surged on to the grass which had received the Whitsuntide parade for more years than anyone could remember.

'Children's day, indeed,' Olivia Atkins said to Pauline and Fred Richards. They were standing under one of the great elms with its new summer foliage providing a welcome shade on this unusually warm morning in late May.

'And I see,' added Pauline, 'that many are keeping up with our tradition of wearing their new clothes. They all look splendid and there seem more children than ever.'

Arthur Windle, standing nearby, quietly reflected on this old custom of buying new clothes to wear for Whitsuntide, although he knew that for many Rusfield families this meant that a child was wearing clothes handed down from an older sibling. He turned to Eleanor: 'We can all be proud of the children and their parents who obviously do everything they can to turn them out well dressed for this special day. But looking round it seems a little strange, and certainly sad, that Mrs Cruise isn't here this time. She always brought her little stool along and sat with her back to this very tree. I expect there will be a big number at her funeral tomorrow.'

'Indeed,' Eleanor replied, 'Mrs Cooper was saying that the two of them used to straw-plait together when they were both young; taking it in turns as to whose home they worked in and she was really upset at losing her dear friend. She must have been a good age.'

'When I last called,' replied Arthur, 'I dared to ask her just that. She told me that she wasn't quite sure, but old Fred Piper told me she was at least seventy-five. So I think we have to settle with that for tomorrow. It will certainly keep Alfred, Fred and Jack Groves busy with the bells in the morning; hopefully all three can manage to get away from work.'

Even as they were talking about one of the oldest Rusfield inhabitants, the children moved into a well-rehearsed, large group with the youngest helped by Rita Small. On their teacher's signal they sang the first of three songs. After the clapping from all sides of the green, some younger children danced around the maypole which Fred and Abraham Richards had erected earlier in the morning. As soon as that finished a few novelty races were organised by Mr David Watts, the new master at the school.

Just as the church bell sounded out its twelve peals, parents joined their children telling them how well they had sung, danced and raced. Picnic baskets were opened up and families enjoyed the beautiful day. Willy Johnson drew Jammy Carey apart. 'That was really good. It doesn't seem long since we were all parading on to the green for Whitsuntide. Do you remember?' Jammy nodded. 'Long time since you've been in the village, Jammy. Been busy?'

'I can't believe it was Easter the last time I was home:

nearly two months ago. Busy, you ask. You're right,' replied the muscular Jammy. 'The number of houses we're putting up near Ilford is amazing; it never seems to stop. Anyway, how are you Willy, and the rest of our mates?'

He knew by the seriousness of Willy's face that something was not quite right and listened in amazement as Willy told him about their friend Racer's problem with being instructed to lose his next race.

'That's awful,' he replied. 'Poor old Racer. Do the others know?' Willy went on to say how they had heard from Racer about the threat when they met before the farm party.

'Yes, I'm sorry I couldn't manage it. Anyway, I'm sure we can sort things out. When is his next race?'

'It's towards the end of June, Saturday the twenty-second. It's a really big race, the most important one he's been in so far. It can't be a great distance from where you're working, at the Crystal Palace. He's excited about it and says there are some really good runners. There's no way he will do anything other than try to win, whatever anyone says or does. But what can we do?'

As one or two families packed the few remains of their picnics, Willy and Jammy continued talking. After prolonged exchanges they agreed the best way to overcome the threat to Racer.

'So when are you off back to Ilford?' Willy asked.

'Early, I need to catch the seven-fifteen from Steepleton. In fact, I really ought to go for the six-forty. What you've told me Willy, is a worry, but I'm sure what we've planned will put it right. You'll tell the others what we've agreed, won't you? I probably won't be able to get home before the race, but if anything unexpected crops up I can always write you a note.'

'Yes, I'll explain everything to the others,' promised his ever-reliable friend.

'Anything else been happening? How's your family, Willy?'

'Well, I'm worried, and I know mum is too, about Ruby.'

'Ruby? But what's wrong? Is she unwell or something? She's always such a sweet girl.'

'Well,' replied a sombre-faced Willy, 'I know she finds things quite difficult at times, but she's really being quite odd about some things recently.'

'What kind of things?' asked Jammy, sympathetic as always.

'Well, she always used to like working up at the manor, but for the past couple of months she seems to have become frightened of things. Last week she asked me if I could help her find work somewhere else. I think some of the other girls may be bullying and offloading some of their work on her. I will just have to keep a close eye on things and maybe speak with Florrie and Elsie. But don't worry, I'll sort things out.'

They parted, both pondering over the problems discussed but, as ever, delighted to have met and spent time together.

NINETEEN

Morning & Afternoon, Tuesday, 28 May

'Sixty-six, sixty-seven, sixty-eight,' counted Fred Richards, smiling encouragement but becoming increasingly worried by the puffing from the heavily-bearded Jack Groves. 'We're nearly there.' At seventy-five they stopped, with even the rugged Fred Richards dropping his head for a moment and catching his breath. Of the six bells just three had been rung to mark the departure of Rose Cruise, in unison with no attempted change ringing. Fred, as the most experienced of the three, had rung the treble; Alfred Reynolds, number three bell; and Jack Groves, the tenor. The trio each let go of their woollen sally and allowed the ropes to hang free.

'I don't know who thought of it, but it's a great idea ringing the funeral bell once for every year of the person's life and Mrs Cruise was a dear lady. I know I shouldn't say it, but hopefully not too many people will live far beyond her age.' The younger two men smiled at Jack's words.

In the stone-walled ringing chamber, the men took their jackets from the nearby coat hooks and from the cold and cheerless chamber in the tower these close friends carefully descended the stone steps, each worn in the centre by centuries of bell-ringers. The three exited from the tower by the narrow, stud-encrusted wooden door and went round to the porch through which they joined the congregation for the funeral of one of Rusfield's oldest inhabitants. Because of her age, Rose Cruise was one who had given permanency to the community and it would seem strange passing her cottage without seeing her sitting in the doorway. There, on her high-backed chair, holding under her left armpit a bundle of dampened straw from which she would pull out the individual lengths, moistening them with her tongue to keep them pliable and then plaiting them into the required size. She had borne the unpleasant and often painful scarring at the right side of her mouth, the trademark of most straw-plaiters. She was always dressed in black, the common colour for most of Rusfield's older ladies. Protecting her dress she had a dark blue cover over her lap against which the straws showed up well. Only the oldest inhabitants could recall her husband who had died in a farming accident nearly half a century earlier.

Whilst Major de Maine read from *Corinthians*, Arthur was pleased to see that St Mary's was full. He had felt it inappropriate to question the theological meaning of a "send-off", but knew that a full church was a suitable expression of how highly Rose Cruise was regarded. After the burial next to where her husband had been laid many years earlier, Arthur tried to speak, albeit briefly, with each person as they moved across to the green where the ladies, he was not always sure who this wonderful band of ladies were, had prepared cakes and sandwiches along with cups of tea. All had been set up near to Violet Rushton's shop so that hot water was readily available.

Some mourners had drifted away, but small groups of villagers were still chatting whilst Olivia Atkins, Pauline Richards and Eliza Carey led the way in clearing the plates and cups from the wake. Liz Smith had got the washing up well underway in Violet Rushton's scullery when she passed that task over to Ruth Groves, apologising for leaving before all was done; but other helpers knew that she needed to get back to check that her mother was as comfortable as possible. Fred Richards had commandeered two helpers to move the four trestle-tables back to their resting place in the church vestry.

'It was a good service, remembering an elderly villager for whom many clearly had a high regard. Thank you for your thoughtful words. We are, indeed, only a brief speck in the history of this earth and it is no bad thing for all of us to be reminded of our frailty and transitory place in time.'

Arthur was faintly surprised, but grateful to hear Major de Maine's words. He had found himself in one of the small groups left on the green, which included the de Maines and Mr and Mrs Mansfield, whose friendship seemed to have grown since the farm party in early April.

'Indeed, Vicar,' concurred Jack Mansfield. 'I would add my thanks as I would for two other village matters.'

'Thank you, but what are these other matters to which you refer?' asked Arthur, slightly bewildered.

'Well, firstly, the extra street lights which are now in place around Pond Corner and at the other end of the village near Sandy Lane. They really will make a difference when we move into winter.'

Arthur blushed slightly as he gently held up a hand as if any further words would embarrass him. 'Thanks for the lights should go to the entire lighting committee and more than anyone else we should thank Fred Richards who persuaded one or two who questioned the cost involved.' Referring then to the young Methodist minister who had just taken up residence in the manse, Arthur added: 'It has also been wonderful having the Reverend Reggie Gregg on the committee; he, too, has a persuasive nature.'

The major smiled and turning to his friend said, 'Jack, you mentioned two things for which we should thank the vicar. I see he is too modest to ask about the second, so I will.'

'I refer,' replied the well-built farmer, 'to our new village nurse. I was chatting to her earlier and she is delighted to be in Rusfield. Undoubtedly, she will be a great asset to the community.' He turned to Arthur and added, 'Thank you for that.'

'But really,' replied Arthur, 'I had very little to do with that either. There has been a move in many parts of the country to provide more immediate medical help. I simply raised this with Sir Lancelot Prestwish, whom I knew was chairman of several hospital groups and has a big say in such matters.'

'That's as may be,' responded the major, 'but you got things moving. As we are four miles from Steepleton and do not have a telegraph office in the village, we are helpless in an emergency. The nurse will be on hand to help.'

'And she seems a very good person: really down-to-earth,' interjected Mabel Mansfield. 'She was telling me that she was at the Mildmay Memorial Hospital in North London, which trains many nurses, and was happy there, but had always hoped to work in the country. Let us hope Rusfield suits her.' Turning to the de Maines, she added, 'You will come back with us for tea, won't you? Tommy Bruce can drive you home later.' Farewells were exchanged and the four friends walked off towards West Lane where a smart carriage with a patient pair of greys awaited them.

'They really are most pleasant people,' said Eleanor to her husband as the quartet went out of earshot. 'When I first met the major I thought he was aloof and didn't really want to have much to do with other villagers, but I was very wrong, as first impressions often are.'

'My love, that sounds just like me, yet I never seem to learn. But did you know that it's the major who has made a cottage available for Nurse Hazlett, virtually rent free. I think he probably owns all four of those cottages over in Meadow Way, where the Smiths and the two Johnson families live.'

'I think you're right, Arthur. Judith Johnson said as much to me a while ago and added how fortunate she is with the low rent. Of course, the end cottage had been empty since old

Aubrey Rayfield died back in February and just after Easter Willy Johnson was doing some roof repairs and painting the inside of the cottage. Nurse Hazlett remarked how clean and light it was inside.'

As Eleanor spoke she moved on a little before saying, 'Arthur, it's still pleasant enough to go for a short walk along Church Stream. It will give us the chance just to talk through my dilemma.' She took her husband's hand, smiled and they crossed the green and narrow track near Miss Rushton's shop, moving on to the well-trodden path that led alongside the small, sparkling stream.

'It's as well the ground is firm after all the recent dry weather,' she remarked, looking down at her dainty shoes. 'Well, my love, I've told you everything and yet I still don't really know what to do. How about you being the parish priest and advising me?'

'You're teasing, darling. When you told me after my parents had returned home about getting that letter from Mrs Payne-Croft, I felt things would be difficult for you. I understand your dilemma.'

'You are right, Arthur. Yes, I was pleased to be recognised as a person supporting women's right to vote and I was happy to go to the meeting last Friday. It was good to know that there are many others who feel the same. I agreed with the speaker that strong action is needed to show the government that we mean to change the law and I can support such things as chaining oneself to railings, but her passion seemed to tip over into a dangerous obsession.'

'From what you've told me, Eleanor, it was extremely brave of you to speak out as you did. When you mentioned all the glares you got, I felt almost frightened for you.'

'Well,' replied Eleanor recalling the evening all too clearly, 'I hope I didn't leave anyone in doubt that I supported the movement, but that I would not embark on anything that might injure or cause great distress to anyone. I felt I had to say something. I think I was rather silly to do that, but it just came out.'

Gently squeezing her hand, Arthur said, 'You know I don't agree with the present suffrage movement, though I think there will be a time when everyone has the vote. I just don't believe that time is now. We both know each other's feelings well enough, but it certainly wasn't silly for you to speak out. It was brave of you.'

'Arthur, I love you for not opposing my view; most husbands aren't like you. It's wonderful that we can disagree, but still respect what the other thinks and does.' Her clasp of his hand tightened, causing him to stop. Eleanor stood on tiptoe and kissed him. 'I think you've really solved my dilemma. Thank you. Come on, it's time we turned round. I really do fancy a nice cup of tea. Race you home!'

As she gained three paces, Eleanor stopped, turned, smiled and said, 'I think it not comely that our parish priest be seen running.'

TWENTY

Saturday, 22 June

'At least it isn't raining this morning, but it is so grey, as if the weather has gone into mourning since old Mrs Cruise's funeral,' Robert Berry commented to Sammy Hatfield, good friends since they had played at the farm party. Indeed, there had barely been a day without rain. The roads and footpaths were awash and no one could remember the stream by the vicarage being so high. The village green squelched with water and the fields of wheat and barley were like paddy fields.

The pond had overflowed into parts of Wood Lane and Pond Street, making it an irresistible pathway for the children fortunate enough to live at the east end of the village. Mr Watts had told the children to bring a spare pair of shoes, his newness as master making him unaware that many of the scholars only had one pair. After a gentle word from Arthur he sensibly relented in his advice and now many children padded round their classrooms barefoot or in stockinged feet.

Peter Woods' light postal delivery on this unusually dry morning had included two for the vicarage and it was an hour later that Eleanor and Arthur, returning from a visit to Liz Smith, collected the letters from the hall. The first bore a Canadian stamp; Eleanor wondered whether Peter would be asking for it on his next visit. It was from Fred Bamford who had emigrated two years previously. 'It's good to see that young Fred is getting on well. I'm sure his parents are very proud of him,' Arthur said. 'This other letter is from the bishop's palace, so I can't imagine it will be very exciting.' He slit the typed envelope open, drew out the single sheet, read and looked aghast.

'What is it darling?' asked Eleanor. 'Not bad news, I hope.'

'I can't really believe what I'm reading. It's from the dean. I hardly dare show it to you.' A deep frown accompanied the letter as he passed it to Eleanor.

My dear Reverend Windle,

I regret that rather longer has elapsed between our meeting and this letter, but I have been particularly busy since taking up my appointment as dean. Following our conversation I made a written report to the bishop and he has instructed me to write to you.

This important matter concerns your wife's activities with the Suffrage Movement which is clearly against the well-being of the nation and of the church. I was at least pleased to learn that you did not support your wife's activities, but was alarmed you felt unable to press your views upon her. I hardly need to mention the group's outrages that have been directed against the church, causing much damage and distress.

I trust that you will have now prevailed upon your wife to abandon such a wanton and criminal course. The bishop agrees with me that when we learn of such a change, we may continue our discussion regarding your future within our beloved church.

Arthur sat quietly whilst Eleanor read. She read it through again and, to Arthur's surprise, broke into laughter. 'What a man! How can anyone, least of all one who calls himself a man of God, write like that? Suppose we invite him to the vicarage so he and I can have a proper debate. Would that not be a good idea, Arthur?'

Arthur could not help giving a rueful smile. 'Eleanor, my dear, I don't think it would be a good idea at all; the poor man would never be the same again. Let's just ignore it.'

'I agree, Arthur. He seems a very embittered man. Maybe one day our paths will cross, but I agree with you, just ignore it.'

The unrelenting rain promoted many worries. The children at the Sunday school, almost all in the village, were looking forward to their annual fun day. Abraham Richards and his friends were eagerly anticipating the big athletics event at the Crystal Palace although with all the rain, Abraham was relieved to know that the grass track had been replaced by a cinder one. The clash of the Sunday school treat and athletics meeting was deeply felt by at least two villagers; Grace would love to have seen Abraham race and he would have been happy to help with the children on their special day.

Three days earlier Abraham, Tommy Bruce, Streaky Bacon and Dan Reynolds had excitedly gathered round a silver and blue motor car which appeared in the forecourt of Spinney Farm. 'Well lads, what do you think?' asked Jack Mansfield, giving them a broad smile and the silver bonnet of his latest acquisition a loving pat.

'It's amazing, sir,' gasped Tommy. 'Where did you get it from? It's beautiful.'

'It's a new model, a Phoenix, and it has a powerful 11.9 horsepower engine. As you know, Mrs Mansfield and I went away last weekend. Well,' continued the farmer, 'we visited friends in Cambridge and they drove us down to Letchworth. You've probably heard about it; it's been built in the latest fashion of a garden city. Well, there's a small factory there producing these and the owner gave me a drive: I took over and that was that! Coming home and knowing there was so much mud and water lying on the village roads, I took the longer way in through Applewick, but it's still got a lot of muddy splash marks. I'm going to drive it into the green barn. Dan, would you fill up some buckets and give me a hand washing it down, please?'

Two hours later while Abraham was stripping down an old harrow, a job that the steady rain did allow, Mr Mansfield came in. 'Abraham, a word with you. I know that on Saturday you've got a really important race. I would like to see it and I suggest that I drive you to the track. It's only seventy miles. What time does the meeting start?'

'Well, the meeting starts at two o'clock and mine is the fourth event, which would make it around a quarter to three. But sir, are you sure? It's really so kind of you and I would love it,' answered the rather startled Abraham. 'I was going with my parents, but they had already promised to help with the Sunday school treat. Anyway, I'm hoping to run next month at the Great Stadium on the other side of London, so they are going to that.'

'Well. That's settled then. You be here for eight o'clock. I can get Doris to put something together for us, but make sure you are wearing something warm and let's hope it's a dry day. That would certainly make a change.'

Later that evening he bumped into Willie Johnson and told him about his good fortune.

'Well, that's wonderful,' responded his friend. 'But you take care. You know that we're all coming. Jammy is going straight there from Ilford and Boney, Jack, Fred and I are all leaving here together. We're not sure how long it will take, but don't worry; we'll be there in good time.' With a smile he added a parting comment: 'And you had better win!'

'Don't expect too much,' replied Racer, 'there will be some really strong competition.'

Saturday came round, a rare dry day. Jack Mansfield drove well and while the road had some residual water lying on it, the conditions improved as they approached Colchester. From time to time, Mr Mansfield pulled to the side of the road to consult his map, but pointing out to Abraham the route, his young passenger was soon able to advise the way to take. Most of the roads were clear, but at Braintree there was a market and fair which half-blocked the main thoroughfare. Market stall owners, buyers, horses, carts and just a few motor cars made that part of the journey slow and Jack Mansfield needed to drive carefully. Later, Abraham found it especially thrilling when they went through the Blackwall Tunnel; it was difficult to believe they were passing under the river.

As they reached Lewisham there was a great buzz of activity, the number of motor vehicles increased and suddenly they were confronted with a tram coming towards them. Both realised that the tram tracks defined its route, but there seemed little agreement among other motorised vehicles as to which side of the road was the right one. A stubborn horse had come to a standstill with its load of hay, the anxious driver thoughtlessly stopping on the tram tracks, but amid the general cacophony of noise the carter gave his horse a stronger prod and it finally moved on.

A short while later, Abraham realised they were nearing their destination. They found the athletics track quite easily and both were dazzled by the impressive edifice which Abraham realised was rightly called the Crystal Palace. As they neared the track, Abraham could see it was built round a concrete construction which he realised was a cycle track. There were banked seats on all sides with people sitting and enjoying this first day of sunshine for several weeks. On one side of the track, which he could see was either gravel or cinder, Abraham saw a long, low wooden building which was clearly the major viewing place for spectators. Jack Mansfield drove towards a grassed area where a good number of motor cars and a large omnibus were parked.

'That was absolutely amazing, Mr Mansfield. Thank you

so much,' Abraham said as he eased himself out of the car, glad to stretch his legs.

'I've got you here and now I wish you all the very best for your race. But if you open the trunk you'll see a food hamper which Doris put together. Let's enjoy that first.'

Doris had certainly done well and they enjoyed an excellent picnic, although Abraham ate very modestly. He had seen a chalked sign on a large board with an arrow pointing towards a low brick-built construction, clearly stating "Competitors". He had also seen Willy, Fred, Jack and Boney hovering near the building and was sure that Jammy would not be far away. He tried to think optimistically as he bade Mr Mansfield a brief farewell and clutching his much worn backpack, its most vital contents being his running vest, shorts and spiked track shoes, strode over towards the changing room. Within the shadow of the overhanging, ridged roof he was confronted by a balding man whose pockmarked face wore a sneering look: Froggy.

TWENTY-ONE

Afternoon, Saturday, 22 June

'So,' the wretched forty-year-old man spat out, 'you're still running then; that's a bit of a surprise. I've got your twenty-five quid and...'

As he spoke he felt a sharp tap on his shoulder and turning round saw the husky Jammy. 'You can keep your money, mate. The man you're talking to is going to win today.'

Froggy turned back towards Racer and was just about to say something when he realised that four other menacing figures completed the circle round him. 'Eh, what's going on? Who the hell are you lot?'

Jabbing the pockfaced Froggy with his forefinger, Boney, the tallest of the group, said, 'Unlike you we go for fair play, we don't like people who make unpleasant and stupid threats.'

Even under his ill-shaven features, the man seemed to pale and his shoulders drop a little. Boney and Jammy each took a short step forward, now sandwiching the man between them. 'If I were you, I'd crawl back to wherever you came from.'

'And', added Jammy to his friend's words, 'don't ever threaten anyone else.' Resting his hand on Racer's shoulder he added, 'If my friend here ever tells me you've been anywhere near him keep a close watch over your shoulder. We know where you live, so now go.' Boney took a slight step back, just room enough for the man to hurriedly slip out of the tight pack and, with just a quick look back, scamper away and disappear from sight.

'I don't think you'll see him again, Racer,' commented Boney. 'But Jammy, how do you know where he lives?'

'Well, to tell you the truth I don't, but in the case of dealing with cheats it's no bad thing to play them at their own game.'

Racer, still looking nonplussed, turned to his friends. 'I had no idea what you had dreamt up, only that you told me you would deal with that wretched man. I can never thank you enough. You really looked a menacing bunch and I'm not surprised he was frightened off. Fred, I would never have thought you could look so threatening.'

The slightly-built Fred smiled. 'Well, I must say I have been practising in front of the mirror at the smithy.'

'Well, you were all marvellous,' chipped in Willy. 'I'm sure Froggy won't come near us again. Racer, it's all up to you now, so just get out there and run like the wind.'

With more heartfelt thanks to his friends, Racer turned, picked up his backpack and hurried off as he saw runners for the first event going on to the track. As he entered the building, he was confronted by clusters of young men, some fully changed and waiting for their call, others chatting with a confidence that Racer could not feel and a few sitting alone with their private thoughts. He moved towards the white card showing his event and, placing his backpack on the slatted bench was delighted to be greeted by another runner.

'Why, it's Abraham, isn't it?' asked a muscular young man whose hair was even fairer than Abraham's. 'We raced against each other last year in Cambridge, you remember?'

'Of course,' replied Abraham, with a warm smile for greeting. 'It's James, isn't it? How are you?'

'Fine, thank you; so we're running for different teams today. I count as a Londoner as I've lived in Ealing since I started working in my father's business. Well, the track looks good in spite of all the rain. Do you remember that track last time we raced? It was one of those with such tight bends that we actually had to slow down if we were on the inside.'

As the two young men opened their bags and changed, they chatted. Abraham recalled how he had been narrowly forced by James into second place, but felt his own fitness and running tactics had much improved since then. Changing into his shorts and running vest, Abraham slipped on a pair of old trousers and a warm jumper which he would leave by the side of the track minutes before the start.

'Runners for the 440 yards, over here,' called the bespectacled official. Racer had not recognised any of the other six athletes, but James had told him to be especially aware of one, a swarthy man who, according to James, was likely to go off at a cracking pace.

All the athletes had friends and supporters in the crowd, but a particularly loud explosion of sound came from his five faithful friends who were as near to the finish as they could get. He modestly raised his hand to acknowledge this support. Abraham and his three teammates wore short lengths of blue material pinned to their running tops, the London runners, similar-sized red markers. He followed his group, placing trousers and jumper in a neat pile and put on his running spikes, a present from Mr Meadows, his old master at school, and his wife. 'I won't always be there to watch you,' Peter Meadows had said to his former pupil, 'but every time you put them on remember I'm supporting you.' Abraham remembered the exact words as he walked towards the starting line.

He picked up a small trowel from the box of tools by the side of the track and walked to the white line which ran straight across the track. He had drawn the small card bearing number five which meant he was towards the middle of the eight runners. He knew it was clearly an advantage to be on the inside of the track, so his start was essential. With the toe of his left running shoe as close to the line as possible, he made a mark to know where to carefully scoop out a small hole with the trowel for his right foot. Like the others, he knew the track circuit was nearly 500 yards round so the starting holes would be no risk to them.

'Get to your places,' called a grey-haired steward wearing a smart if rather worn green and purple striped blazer. The runners were pleased that a starting gun was to be used; a whistle occasionally produced a rather muted signal, creating confusion. Abraham went to his mark and took up his crouching position which he had adopted halfway through the previous athletics season. With the extra push that the starting hole gave him, he had a favoured start. He knew that he had trained hard and felt in good form, but the start and the final fifty yards were vital.

'Get to your marks,' called the starter, standing on a foot-high wooden platform just in front of the starting line. Abraham, left toe to the line, right spiked shoe in his starting hole, settled in to a comfortable position and lightly wriggled his shoulders, as much to relax his mind as his body.

'Get yourselves set,' came the instruction. Abraham made a final upper body adjustment, pushed his right toes more firmly into the starting hole, erased the other runners from his sight and set his whole mind on the cinder track spreading ahead. He was determined to get on the inside as soon as possible, but would prefer another runner to lead the way for the first 300 yards.

The crack of the gun caused spectators to flinch, the runners to fly forward. Eight athletes… a confused surge of colours in an increasingly jagged line as the first thirty yards were covered in what to spectators seemed no time at all. The cutting in towards the inside of the track, a slight jousting between two runners with one almost falling, picking up his stride again, but a couple of vital yards lost. Almost single file now as the first curve was reached, with the three front runners striving desperately to get into the best position;

two now emerging in the lead and at least three runners suddenly too far behind to threaten the leaders. No difficulty in picking out Racer in his emerald green running vest. Now in second place to a white-topped London athlete with a fair-haired runner almost on Racer's shoulder. The race down the straight towards the final curve showed an increase in pace and a growing distance between the first three and the rest of the field. As Willy said later, 'Racer, I never thought I'd say this of you, but your running was something of beauty.' In sight of the blue finishing tape, Racer's stride appeared to lengthen slightly and his feet barely to touch the cinders. To the shoulder of the leader and then in a glorious final sprint, Racer drew level, passed so easily that with each stride he drew further ahead. Breasting the tape, Racer was clearly five or six yards in front, with the London runner and James fighting for second place.

Whether or not they were allowed on to the track, led by Fred the five friends came running to Racer. 'That was amazing,' Jammy burst out. 'I've never seen anything like it.' The others gave out their praise as Racer stood, hands on hips and smiled.

'Thanks,' he said.

As he spoke, the fair-haired James came to Racer and generously shook his hand. 'You came past me like a steam engine and I couldn't keep up. I wonder what your time was?' Racer was soon to learn he had been recorded with 50.6 seconds; two seconds faster than his previous best time at the end of the 1911 season. He couldn't believe it.

'I guess old Froggy is miles away by now,' smiled the ever-supportive Jack. 'Come on Racer, here's your clothes, don't get cold. I can see you sweating, nearly as much as we are from watching you!'

Racer's departure to change was delayed for a few minutes as Mr Mansfield joined the group. 'That was a wonderful run, Abraham, and your time which I just heard is a tremendous start to the season. Well done, indeed. Now, as your good friends have said, go and change. I'm sorry I can't take you all home in my motor; Abraham, I suggest that you and I leave as soon as you are ready. We can be home by mid evening and I'm sure your parents and brother will be dying to know how you got on.' Abraham hoped that Grace would, as well.

TWENTY-TWO

Late Afternoon & Evening, Saturday, 22 June

Many pedestrians, but few vehicles, were to be seen as Jack Mansfield undertook the return drive. When they had left Braintree a few miles behind, he surprised Abraham by suggesting that they stop for a quick celebratory drink. 'Let's pull in here; this looks a good place.'

Jack Mansfield turned off the road on to the rough forecourt to the inn, advertised as The Royal Oak. It was clearly an old inn and as they went into the low-ceilinged room, both were surprised at the number of people already drinking. In addition to a group of cyclists, apparent by their smart cycling gear, there were half a dozen walkers clearly enjoying a drink after a warm ramble.

The overweight, but jovial publican soon provided both drinks. 'Well,' said the older man, lifting his glass, 'let's drink to your continuing success on the track. You'll make Rusfield famous yet.' Realising that more talk along these lines would further embarrass the young man, Jack Mansfield changed the topic of conversation. 'Abraham, there are two things I would mention to you although I would ask that the first remains confidential between us.' He picked up his half empty glass and took a long drink. He replaced it on the rather heavily-chipped table, Abraham greatly wondering what he was going to be told.

Jack Mansfield's handsome face broke into a warm smile, 'I happen to think you can make a great future in farming. I hope you stay with me at Spinney Farm, but you must, of course, always feel free to move on if better opportunities come about. So it's up to me to provide real opportunity, and here's the confidential part. You may have realised that Major de Maine is finding Manor Farm something of a handful and he and his wife would like more time to themselves. You will understand, Abraham, that I can't go in to all the details but to cut a long story short, Major de Maine and I have come to an agreement whereby the lands from the two farms are to merge under one management; essentially we are combining the two farms and turning more land into arable. I still like to think I've got a number of years for active work, but Mrs Mansfield is also keen we share more time together. She would like to explore parts of Europe, especially France and Italy. I must say I would, too. Abraham, if everything goes well for you, there will be the opportunity for you to take over more of the management of the single farm and, in time, major decisions. As I say, please keep this to yourself. So, what do you think?'

To say that Abraham was dumbstruck was less than the truth. He sat silently for a moment, and then took Mr Mansfield's lead by finishing his drink. 'Sir, what you have just told me is the most exciting thing I have ever heard. You can be certain that I won't let you or the major down in any way.' His excitement almost overcame him.

Mr Mansfield held up his hand, 'Come on, Abraham, it's time we moved on.' The rest of the drive in the glorious early evening sun was soon undertaken and Abraham, who had almost slipped into a light doze, was surprised when he realised they were back in Rusfield. A few minutes later, Jack Mansfield pulled up in West Lane outside the Richards' house. Abraham was profuse in his thanks, but his kind boss just said that it had been his pleasure and how wonderfully well the young runner had done.

As Abraham opened the front door he called out, but no answer came. He looked into the kitchen and the rear garden, but no. Going into the street in front of the house he immediately heard shouts, better described as cries of delight and excitement; it must be something on the green. Leaving his backpack in the kitchen, he crossed the narrow lane and passed the school; the noise becoming louder.

He was surprised to see what looked like half the village population on the green, most taking part in a great game of rounders. Dozens of children were taking part in the big game; many more in other attractions: skipping, throwing and catching balls, climbing favourite trees or swinging on the ropes which hung from an old elm tree. Others were rolling around in less well-defined, but exciting activities. He then spotted his mother, sitting on a log under one of the great elm trees, chatting to Rita Small, the schoolteacher.

She smiled as her son approached. 'Oh Abraham, lovely to see you. How did you get on?'

'But where's father? I'd rather tell you both together.' Abraham and his mother had lovingly teased one another for as long as either could remember and he had deliberately put on a solemn look which she took as a harbinger of disappointing news. She turned to one of her many nephews, eight-year-old David Johnson, Willy's brother: 'David, please run over and ask Uncle Fred to come over here as Abraham's just arrived.' In a flash the young lad had delivered the message and Abraham's father and younger brother trotted over, eager to hear the news.

'Well, son, how did you get on? I'm sure you did your best and that's the important thing.' All eyes were now on Abraham as he maintained his solemn look. But he couldn't keep it up for a moment longer and broke in to a broad smile, 'Well, actually I won and I did my fastest time ever, 50.6 seconds.'

Abraham was lost in the midst of all three throwing their arms round him and congratulating him. 'I'm so proud of you, son. You deserve to do well and the whole village will be proud of you,' said his mother; a tear appearing on her cheek.

'What's happening here?' Abraham asked

It was Fred Richards who explained. 'Well, all the Sunday school children had a marvellous time at Mr Jackson's farm, but when they came back they were so excited that the older ones, encouraged by Doris and Grace, organised a game of rounders. You can see Eleanor Windle batting at the moment. Everyone seems to have joined in.'

'I'm so glad they had a good time,' said Abraham. 'Father, you mentioned Doris and Grace, but where are they?'

'I don't know about Doris, but Grace has just taken your young cousin, George Jones, to Mary Johnson's house as he cut his knee when he was swinging from a tree once too often.'

'I think I'll just go over and see if he is all right then,' Abraham replied with exceptional casualness.

His mother smiled: 'Yes, Grace might need your help.'

He hurried across the stretch of the green to the end cottage in Meadow Way and sure enough young George was sitting on the doorstep with Grace putting a light bandage round his knee.

'Now that will be all right,' smiled Grace at the stubbornly brave young lad who had fought hard not to cry when he saw blood running down to his shoe. Grace suddenly caught a glimpse of the slight shadow cast over her and turned.

'Why, Abraham! I didn't know you were back. We've had a wonderful time today, haven't we George?' she smiled gently, patting her patient on the shoulder. 'But how did you get on?'

'Well, Grace. I managed to win.' He was just about to add a little more of the afternoon's events when he found she had thrown her arms round him and with her feet almost off the ground, kissed him. 'Oh Abraham, that's marvellous. I'm so, so pleased. Everyone will be so proud of you.'

Abraham glanced round, overjoyed at Grace's kiss, but a little anxious that other people might be around; only young

George, and he was already scampering back to the green after thanking his emergency nurse.

The sun was now quite low, but seemingly reluctant to set on the village. The air remained warm and calm. Parents and children were leaving the green even as Grace and Abraham returned from Meadow Way. They were holding hands, Grace remembering the kiss with joy, Abraham with wonder. Hand in hand they walked to the field. The sun dipped lower; the young couple were joyously happy. That night, children slept deep from their tiring and exciting day, most adults with contentment. Word about Racer's win had spread quickly and all were proud of this fine young man's feat. It had been a good day for Rusfield.

TWENTY-THREE

Wednesday, 31 July

July also dealt a hand of almost incessant rain. On this last day of the month, Arthur and Eleanor were looking out of their kitchen window from which they could see the water from Church Stream almost lapping into their garden. 'There must be a problem further along the stream,' Eleanor said, tucking herself comfortably and lovingly into her husband's cradled arms. 'It must be around five-feet deep in the gully and, surely, that can only be the result of blockage somewhere along the flow. It was good of Fred Richards and Joe Bacon to put up some fencing round the deepest part and I hear that Mr Watts has been telling the children to keep well away.'

Major de Maine had read that the eruption of a volcano in Alaska was a likely cause of the exceptionally bad summer, but he found little support in any of the Rusfield pubs. 'Tosh,' retorted Bernie Thomas over his favourite pint, ''tis just bad luck.' Churchwarden George Cooper wondered if it was God's answer to so many changes at St Mary's, but had the good sense to keep this thought to himself.

The main calls on Nurse Betty Hazlett, who had settled in to the village very happily, were little to do with the weather; but with the elderly, and the spate of births extending several large families even further. Yet as the rain beat down, one village topic surpassed the weather: Abraham Richards' next race.

As the couple turned away from the dismal scene through the kitchen window, Eleanor suggested a second cup of breakfast coffee. Family, church, village and all manner of other thoughts and ideas were often talked through over their extended breakfast time. 'After all,' Eleanor had once said, 'that leaves the nights for other activities.'

Arthur passed a cup to Eleanor and said, 'Good idea, my love. One or two things I'd be glad of your thoughts about.'

'You mean, not just about the big race next Monday!' smiled Eleanor.

'Well, let's start with that. The whole village has got so excited about Abraham's big race and the Bank Holiday makes it a really big athletics meeting with all the best British runners taking part. Abraham, of course, was invited because of his victories at the Crystal Palace and then Twickenham. He's such a fine young man and remains so self-effacing; I'm sure his modesty is inherited from Fred and Pauline Richards. You know that Jack Mansfield and Fred Jackson have kindly organised two charabancs from Steepleton to the Stamford Bridge stadium, which means that there's room for at least sixty people. Well, I happened to see Fred yesterday and he told me there are just a few spaces left and did we want to reserve two. What do you think, my love?'

Eleanor put her coffee down and with a mock serious look replied, 'Well, I think that for the sake of the church it's something the vicar and his wife should be seen to support, don't you?' She broke into a glowing smile before adding, 'Of course I want to go. It's going to be a splendid day out, whatever the weather, although I was glad to hear that both the charabancs have emergency covers that can be pulled over. I heard from Mabel Mansfield that everyone would have to get to Steepleton by nine o'clock to catch the charabancs as the transport company regards the road out to Rusfield being too bad to use in view of all the rain. But we can do what most others are doing, walk into Steepleton.'

'That's wonderful. I'm seeing Fred in St Mary's later on today. Did you know that Abraham was actually mentioned in *The Daily Telegraph* after last Saturday's win?'

'Indeed, Major de Maine showed me the piece. It even said that Abraham should have been running for Britain in the Olympic Games which have just finished. And did I tell you,' added Eleanor, 'that I'd met a very, very excited Grace. Apparently she, Doris Groves and Albert Jones all went with Abraham to Twickenham. I think that Grace and Abraham are not the only young lovebirds we have in the village; it seems that Doris and Albert are often with one another.'

'Your mention of Albert reminds me that he told me he was particularly proud to see Abraham running in a green top, the same colour as the shirts their great school team had worn; I thought that was a lovely touch.' Their conversation was interrupted by a heavy knock on the vicarage door. They both stood, crossed the kitchen, went through the dining room and into the hall. Arthur opened the door.

'Good morning, sir.' There was the smartly dressed Peter Woods holding out two letters. 'Forgive me for not just putting the letters through your door, but I wondered if I could ask a favour?' He looked at Eleanor, one of his favourite villagers.

'Of course, Peter. How can we help?' she responded with her dazzling smile.

'Well, Mrs. Windle, I told you once I collect stamps and I couldn't help noticing the one on this letter.'

'But', replied Eleanor holding the two letters passed to her and looking more at the one that appeared to interest Peter, 'it's the same stamp as on all letters.'

'Not really, ma'am,' Peter hurriedly said. 'If you look very carefully you can see that the design round the king's head has changed.' He excitedly placed the second letter alongside before explaining: 'This is the penny stamp since the coronation, but if you look at your letter, can you see the difference?'

Eleanor and Arthur looked more closely. 'Well done. I see what you mean.' Peter smiled.

'Just wait a minute, Peter.' Eleanor took her letter and disappeared inside for a moment. She returned carrying the empty envelope. 'Here you are, Peter; you are most welcome to it. I must say you have very keen eyes.'

Peter blushed, 'Thank you very much. You are most kind.'

'Take care Peter,' added Arthur as the young postman turned to leave, 'and do let us know the next time any of the stamps change. It's really interesting. Thank you.'

Arthur closed the door and returned to the kitchen. He could see that Eleanor was worried after reading her letter. 'What is it, Eleanor?'

She passed the letter to Arthur and he realised why it had caused his beloved Eleanor concern. 'I see it's about another suffrage meeting in Steepleton.'

'I'm surprised that they have even sent me another invitation,' she said, giving a faint smile. 'I won't be going; I cannot support actions that endanger people or cause them real harm. And I mean it.' Firmness had come into her voice with this last comment, a tone that Arthur had heard many times and respected.

'And,' continued Eleanor, 'they have been carrying out more and more dangerous stunts. Three pillar boxes in Steepleton were recently set on fire and I read in the *Steepleton Mercury* that Amelia Payne-Croft, she's the one who sends these invitations, had said they needed a martyr to publicise their demands. Then last week Mabel Mansfield told me that a lady just released from prison had the idea of becoming that martyr and had thrown herself down a thirty-foot-high iron staircase near Parliament. Fortunately she landed on some wire netting, but she did have severe spinal injuries. No, I can't support that kind of thing.'

Arthur wrapped his arms round Eleanor. 'I know what you do will be right and I love you for that. Now this other letter is from my parents.' A look as worried as had been Eleanor's when reading her letter, appeared. He passed the letter to her who, as perceptive as ever, waited a few moments after reading it before saying: 'I understand why you are worried, my love. Your mother just doesn't mention how your father is and has signed it as if he doesn't exist.'

'It's just as we thought when we went down to Dorset and, indeed, when they last came here. Maybe mother is angry at the way father often treats you and how he regards your parents. Certainly something has happened between them, or am I imagining it?'

This time Eleanor embraced her husband before saying: 'No, I'm afraid it seems so, Arthur.'

Peter was still thinking about his newly acquired stamp as he cycled past the pond and along the slight incline of Wood Lane: a solitary letter for Mr S. Jones. Peter knocked on the door which was immediately opened by young George. 'Thank you, Mr Peter,' the youngest in the family said as he took the letter.

Peter knew most of the village children by now and, with a cheery wave to George, remounted his bicycle. Continuing along the rutted lane, his round ended with a most welcome cup of tea at Spinney Farm where Grace Reynolds kindly invited him into the scullery. Peter had heard how she and Abraham were courting and he reflected on how lucky the star athlete was. The two exchanged village news, particularly about Abraham's last and forthcoming race. Then on to his cycle for the four miles back to Steepleton.

During the afternoon Arthur decided to make a number of pastoral visits, deciding to first visit old Martha Smith. How she managed to hang on to life was a mystery, to some a miracle, but Eleanor thought that perhaps the best blessing would have been if she had quietly passed away. He also wanted to call on Violet Rushton, still deeply grieving for her mother, and spend a little time with the very elderly Ruth Watkins. Before leaving the vicarage he went into the kitchen where Eleanor and Eliza Carey were both immersed in making jam, the fruit given by Robert Berry and the products bound for the early autumn sale at the church. 'I'm just off to make a few visits. I especially want to see dear Martha Smith.'

'Please give her and Liz my best wishes. Liz seemed her ever-usual self when I popped in last week, although how her mother appears cheerful when she has so much pain, I can't imagine,' said Eleanor as she kissed her husband on the cheek.

'And please, Vicar, give her my best wishes, too,' added Eliza. Arthur had comfortably grown used to being called "Vicar" by most of the villagers. It had been "Sir" or "Your Reverend" when he had come to Rusfield and he had felt ill at ease and distant from the villagers when these titles had been used.

He sat with Martha Smith for a good while; when Liz had called out for him to come in, she told him her mother was awake as she had taken up a mug of tea ten minutes previously. After a little exchange of pleasantries and village news, the bedridden lady asked Arthur to read to her. She pointed to the nearby ledge, Arthur noting her pathetically thin and wrinkled arm. Arthur was faintly surprised to see a bound collection of works by Sir Walter Scott.

'I love that book,' gasped the old lady. 'I don't know where it first came from, but my mother gave it to me. I know it so well 'cos it taught me to read. Will you read me "The Lady of the Lake"? Leave out the first part and go straight in to the chase. I love that.'

He turned to the hundred-year-old poem and began to read. Martha listened intently, with a slight smile on her lips, as Arthur read of the stag chase. By the time of the eighth verse, a glance at Martha revealed her with eyes closed; the rasping breaths suggesting she was now asleep. Arthur quietly closed the book, knelt by her bed and silently offered a prayer for this fine, elderly lady, and then tiptoed down the bare, dark staircase.

On entering the back room he found Liz struggling with folding large sheets; he offered his help which she gratefully accepted. After warmly expressing her gratitude, she told Arthur how much her mother loved his visits. 'And the times your lovely wife comes. It all does her a power of good.'

Arthur walked along the short stretch of Meadow Way, finding Violet Rushton moving some jars, mainly of sweets, prior to wiping down the shelves in her shop. 'Oh, do come in, Vicar,' greeted the shop owner. Arthur immediately told her he had come to see her rather than make a purchase, although when he did leave he had purchased some of his favourite liquorice allsorts. As he later told Eleanor, he had found her much brighter than previously, for while talk about her mother remained the main topic, this appeared to be joyful recollections of her life.

After his final call on ninety-three-year-old Ruth Watkins, he returned to the vicarage where Eleanor immediately offered a cup of tea. 'Let's go through to the conservatory, as the sun, though rather watery at the moment, is out,' he suggested.

Eleanor listened eagerly as Arthur told her of his visits and she had just embarked upon news learnt from Eliza Carey, when a loud knock at the door interrupted their conversation for the second time that day. 'Wonder who it can be at this time? Certainly not Peter wanting to show us more about stamps,' said Eleanor.

'I'll see,' replied Arthur moving rapidly through the lounge and hall to the front door. He opened it and standing there with the biggest smile he thought he had ever seen, was Susannah Jones together with her husband, Sidney, holding a letter in his one hand. The clearly delighted lady let out a shout of delight and threw her arms round the astonished Arthur, a shout bringing Eleanor rushing to the door to find a lady, whom at first she could not identify so buried was her head in his chest, embracing her husband.

'Oh, Vicar, and Mrs Windle, do please forgive me, but I can never, never thank you enough.' Susannah had stepped back slightly, her cheeks aglow, still with a big smile.

'What is it, Susannah?' asked Eleanor. 'What has happened?'

'Oh, it's quite amazing. Sidney, show the vicar the letter.' Sidney, never a man of many words, excitedly passed the typewritten letter to Arthur. He read it, passed it quickly to Eleanor and turning to the couple invited them in.

'No thank you, Vicar. We want to go and tell our cousins the good news. Fancy, the brewery giving us fifty pounds and it was all because of you writing that letter.'

'This really is wonderful,' replied Eleanor. 'Sidney, you so deserve this because you have really suffered by losing your arm and your job. What will you do now, if you don't mind me asking?'

'Well,' replied Sidney, 'it's a lot of money, more than I could have earned in a long time at the brewery. We didn't think we would get anything and I can't thank you enough either, Vicar.' Arthur modestly acknowledged the compliment with a nod, thinking of how he had invoked the support of the de Maines, particularly of Isabella who, in turn, had contacted her brother, Sir Lancelot Prestwish. The pressure on the brewery owners had obviously paid dividends.

'Anyway,' continued the excited Sidney Jones, 'while we didn't think the brewery would give us anything, we had still dreamt of what we might do. I expect you know that Mr Somerville is thinking of selling his butchery since Charlotte his wife died. We don't know how much it would cost to buy the shop, but maybe we could manage it.'

'And,' went on Susannah with equal excitement, 'two of our children will soon be leaving school and they could help us; maybe Albert would be interested as well.' More congratulations and thanks were shared before they excused themselves, holding hands and with Susannah clasping the letter.

'What marvellous news for them,' Eleanor said as Arthur closed the door. 'It was good of you to help so much.'

'And the others, too,' replied Arthur. 'There's no doubt about it that Sir Lancelot had the most to do with it.'

The couple spent the rest of the evening in the lounge, contentedly reading. It wasn't too long before Eleanor announced that she would retire for the night. 'You follow when you're ready, darling,' giving Arthur a light kiss on his head.

Arthur only read for a further few minutes before putting out lights and going up to his small, book-lined dressing room. His thoughts and his prayers blended to a conversation with his God. He felt close to his Maker.

'Thank you, God, for all your gracious gifts. Thank you for Eleanor and her love, for our home and our friends in the village. Thank you for the happiness given to Susannah and Sidney Jones. I remember the Smith family; give comfort to mother and daughter, to Ruby Watkins and to Violet Rushton. May all in the village with worries be comforted and give me the strength to do what I can to help them. I ask that my parents may be helped to overcome any difficulty between them. Forgive me, Father, for all my sins, especially for the harm I have caused others.'

He stayed kneeling for a few minutes thinking of the good things that had happened that day and then listening. He quietly stood, moved to the bathroom, changed into his night clothes and a little while later joined Eleanor in their bed. They had much over which to rejoice and show their love for each other.

TWENTY-FOUR

Sunday, 4 August

The Sunday of the August Bank Holiday surprised everyone, a fourth successive fine day. The morning service was a joyous occasion with a large congregation. Ever since the well-remembered village party in April, all had wanted to hear again, others for the first time, the singing of Eleanor Windle and Albert Jones. This morning they delighted everyone with Frederick Jerome's beautiful duet for soprano and baritone, "Thy Will be Done". 'It was as if two angels were singing God's praise,' Judith Johnson remarked to her husband on their way home. 'Indeed,' replied Raymond, 'they have such lovely voices. 'Specially a surprise hearing young Albert.'

Not spoken out loud at matins, but silently prayed by many, had been the hope that young Abraham would do well the next day and after the service much talk was of the race and the excitement of so many who were to have the day out at Stamford Bridge. 'It's going to be tremendous,' smiled the unusually relaxed Fred Smith. 'I'm looking forward to it so much. I hear that we're gathering near the pond at quarter to eight, so that we've got plenty of time to walk down to Steepleton for the charabanc.'

'That's right,' replied Willy. 'But we don't have to walk

right into town as the charabanc company is quite happy to meet us at Pratchetts, which will save us half a mile.'

Eleanor and Albert had been surrounded by many friends congratulating them on their wonderful singing, but as others moved away, Grace turned to Eleanor. 'Mrs Windle, can I talk with you sometime? I realise now isn't convenient for you, but I just wondered if I could, sometime.'

'Of course, Grace, but only if you call me Eleanor. Mrs Windle makes me feel so old and there's only a few years difference in our ages. Well, maybe slightly more than a few,' added Eleanor. 'At least tell me what it's about. For such a beautiful morning, you look worried. If I can help, of course I will.'

'Well, it's nothing too serious, but when I was in Steepleton library last week I couldn't help hearing two ladies talking and your name came up... Eleanor,' she hesitatingly added.

'Really? I hope they didn't say anything too awful about me,' she smiled.

'Of course not. How could they, about you! No, they were talking about a meeting of women who support voting rights and your name was mentioned. One of them said that you had been at a meeting.'

'That's right,' replied Eleanor, 'but why do you mention this?'

'Well, I've thought a lot about the suffragettes ever since I read a newspaper article. I think everyone should be able to vote and I wondered whether you thought I should join them. I know I would be too young to vote, but I think it's something important for all of us.' She had become a little breathless as she rushed out her feelings and her face was made all the more attractive with its pink glow.

'Well, you must come round to tea sometime and we can talk it all over. Tomorrow, when we will have an opportunity to chat, we must arrange a time. Perhaps next weekend or one evening if you wish.'

As Eleanor moved away, her place next to Grace was taken by Abraham. 'Grace, I just wanted to say that I'm sorry there won't be time to go for a walk this afternoon, although I would have loved that. You know how James Bagshott, the fellow I've raced against a couple of times, has invited me to stay tonight at his home in Ealing. It's good because Jack Atkins is coming as well and really kind of James as it means we won't be rushed if anything goes wrong. So we're catching the quarter to four train from Steepleton which means we shouldn't get to his house too late.'

Grace smiled, 'Of course, and you must not allow anything to go wrong. Keep your rushing for the race.' She reached out and held his hand.

'Thank you, Grace. And I want to say, how gorgeous you look today.' He added, a little hesitatingly, 'You always do, but that is a particularly beautiful frock. I love the colours.'

'Thank you Abraham. I'm glad you like *this* frock.' Abraham noticed how Grace put a particular emphasis on the word "this". He also noticed her face embracing a broad smile.

'Grace, am I missing something? I just wanted to say how I liked this frock, but you made it sound as if I almost didn't like what you usually wear.'

'Not at all. You are very kind about what I wear, but I just remember a time when that wasn't so.' Her smile became broader.

'Grace, I'm sorry, but I don't remember that.'

'I know you don't. It was at the party several years ago when we were celebrating leaving school. I spent hours making a lovely green and orange frock for the occasion, just for you, and you never noticed. You were just mucking about with the boys.' She reached out and took his hand and gave him a light kiss on his cheek. 'I've still got the frock so maybe I should wear it. Trouble is I don't think it would fit.'

Abraham looked at her glorious figure. 'I don't think it

would,' he blushed. They were the last to leave the church grounds.

The sun continued to spread its warmth over the conversations about the great outing the next day.

TWENTY-FIVE

Morning & Afternoon, Monday, 5 August

'It feels like Moses leading the children of Israel to the Promised Land,' Eleanor laughingly remarked to Olivia Atkins as they walked along the road out of Rusfield on a gorgeous summer morning.

'Except,' smiled Olivia, 'that Abraham's friends are leading the way for the charabanc in Steepleton. The Promised Land must be Stamford Bridge.'

At the front, led by the quick striding Willy Johnson, were Albert Jones, James Carey and Fred Smith. They were slightly outnumbered by the young lasses who were with them: Willy's sister Ruby, Doris and Elsie Groves, Judith Edwards and Grace Reynolds who could hardly believe that her new sweetheart, Abraham, was the centre of everyone's thoughts. Boney and Doris were walking hand in hand.

The sixty who had set out from near the pond were well strung out. Sammy Hatfield and Bernie Thomas along with Robert Berry had accepted the alternative mode of transport to Steepleton as Sparky Carey, as usual, had come up trumps with a pony and trap. Old Peter Groves had turned his hand from general worker at the de Maines to driving the farm's enthusiastic Gallop, a willing seven-year-old driving pony which was thriving in the excitement. The major and his wife had set off with Peter, along with young Tommy Bruce who had sprained an ankle the previous day, but was determined not to miss his fellow worker's great day.

Willy had been delighted to see that Ruby and his good friend Fred were walking together. 'But Fred,' remarked Ruby, 'you seem to be worried about something. Is it your Gran? I know she is really poorly.'

'It's partly that,' responded the ever pale-faced Fred, 'but there's one or two other things as well. I don't want to spoil this special day so let's talk about you, Ruby.'

'Well, it's been much nicer at the manor since Lionel went off. No one seems to like him, not even his parents very much.' She paused. 'Oh, Miss Hazlett and the Reverend Gregg. I didn't see you catching up with us.' She turned to Betty Hazlett, the village nurse, and to the Methodist minister, both of whom had been around long enough for most villagers to get to know them. Betty had never been so happy; the manse occupant finding it harder to settle in, but both had found themselves caught up in the village excitement and joined the London pilgrimage.

'I didn't know you were coming up to London with us,' continued Ruby.

The squat, orderly, middle-aged and ever-optimistic nurse smiled. 'Well, truth to tell I just couldn't miss out on such an occasion. It's all very exciting.' Turning to Ruby she asked: 'Do you often walk to Steepleton?'

'Not very often, but sometimes if I need something special, like at Christmas and then...' She stopped in mid-sentence and stride. She almost bounced in the air pointing over to her left and calling out: 'Look over there everyone. Willy, come quickly.' She excitedly called out to her brother who was just a few yards ahead.

'What on earth is it, Ruby?' As she began to speak he followed her pointing hand and immediately saw it. 'Well done, Ruby. You're right, it is a buzzard.' In a moment their friends and others were grouped round. 'Look,' pointed out Willy. 'Look near that short post on the other side of the field and you'll see the brown bird sitting on a tree stump. Can you see its pale necklace of feathers catching the sunlight?' Everyone looked and gradually all saw it.

'It's beautiful,' agreed Eleanor, whose group had now arrived, first wondering what the excitement had been about. 'Well done, Ruby. Thank you.'

Blushing from the praise being heaped on her, Ruby responded: 'Well, I think it's a lucky sign and means the day is going to be even better.'

At that moment there were calls of "move over" and the two pony-drawn traps approached from behind. Both vehicles pulled up and conversations broke out between those in the carriages and those on foot. It must have been the movement of the two vehicles that caused the buzzard to take off, magnificently flying across the barley field towards them before veering to its left, then wheeling above the trees and disappearing beyond the nearby wood. Some thirty minutes later, everyone was relieved to see the two brown and orange charabancs waiting outside Pratchetts. There were cheers and a hastening pace became evident.

Slight, but good-natured jostling to sit with particular friends ensued, but it did not take long for everyone to find a seat on one or other of the charabancs. The long vehicles, with highly polished chrome round their extensive bonnets, had been well prepared for the occasion. Access into the vehicles was easy as each row of wooden seats had its own side door, although some villagers had to squeeze up to fit everyone in. 'Makes it all the more friendly,' Nurse Hazlett remarked to Violet Rushton; they had become good friends which had helped the haberdashery owner overcome her grief at the loss of her mother.

Straw hats and bonnets were quite plentiful although flat caps were most in evidence. Sitting behind Jack Mansfield who was wearing a straw hat, Rita Small wondered if it had been made from straw plaited in Rusfield. 'Mind you,' she whispered to her teaching colleague, Priscilla Picton, 'I prefer my bonnet which at least won't blow off.' Union Jacks and some home-made banners appeared among passengers and Albert Jones had a large one which he needed help to display: *"Come on Racer; all Rusfield is running with you"*.

At the rear of the first vehicle Ruby and Fred were engrossed in conversation as were Doris and Boney. Eleanor, a few rows in front, turned to Arthur and remarked: 'I see that romance is flourishing in this fine weather. It's lovely to see the young people together.' Arthur could not think of a suitable reply and just smiled. Not for the first time that morning, he wished he had listened to her advice more carefully about what he should wear; it was already warmer than he had expected.

Conversation and scenery vied for the travellers' interest, the former generally winning. After passing close to Colchester, Sammy Hatfield remarked that a stop would be in order. This was a view shared by a growing number, a need not felt by the younger passengers, but one which reached Jack Mansfield. He moved forward and had a whispered conversation with Fred Jackson. It was agreed they stop at Braintree where Charlie Border, the driver, knew there were some public lavatories. 'If it had just been for us lads we could have stopped near any one of the trees or hedges,' Sammy remarked to Bernie Thomas, 'but it's nice having some of the lasses aboard.' He noticed that his friend, too, had cast an eye in the direction of Doris and Grace.

Jack Mansfield and Abraham had thought Braintree busy with its Saturday market when they had been held up six weeks previously, but it was nothing compared to the scene that greeted them now. Not only was there a market, but accompanying fair stalls spread down the main street.

Charlie Border pulled to a halt, his colleague, Cyril Hemsley, following suit, just before the main market stall area.

He spoke in a booming voice: 'It's best if those who need to, get out now. You'll find the public lavatories in the main square, about a hundred yards on. Then, if you continue straight on you'll find both coaches waiting just beyond the square. We'll meet up in twenty minutes.' He leapt out and trotted to the other charabanc to make a similar announcement.

Doors of both charabancs opened and passengers spilled out. There was a general movement forward, although it was noticeable that some moved on more quickly than others. Frederick Abrahams smiled at his wife saying, 'I would think everyone for miles around now knows why we're stopping. Not, perhaps, the most subtle announcement.' It was not long before all were plunged into the midst of a great variety of market and fair stalls.

Fred found Willy by his side. The well-set and kindly Willy touched his friend on the elbow and in a gentle voice said to Fred: 'Forgive me for mentioning it, but Ruby said that you were worried about something. Is it something you want to talk over? With all this crowd and noise no one else will be able to hear us.'

Willy, above all his friends, was the one for whom Fred had the greatest respect. His mind flashed back to times at school, and often since, when Willy had talked things through with him, advised him and even saved him from unintended trouble spots. 'Thank you, Willy, it might help.' They walked on quietly for a few paces. 'You see I had quite an argument with mother last evening. I know she gets tired, but what she said was really too much. I hate arguments,' added the gentle Fred.

Willy's mind turned to the amiable and hard-working Liz Smith, wondering what she could have said that had caused an argument between normally loving mother and son; it must have been something exceptional.

'It's a bit difficult to explain really,' Fred said, his cheeks colouring up a little. 'As you know, except for me, mother and gran have always been on their own. I think I have an Auntie Mary, my mum's sister, but I've never met her and I don't even know where she lives. I know mum and gran moved from London before I was born, but no one ever mentions anything about my dad. Well, some time ago I did ask mother and she just smiled and let it pass. I've pressed her more, even asked gran, but she just went quiet. The most I ever got was: "Well, that can wait until you're a bit older." As I've got older I've really wanted to know. You see, I've always remembered a story that Miss Picton told us at school.'

Willy thought he would gently interrupt. 'She was a great storyteller, but which story do you mean, Fred?'

'Well, it was one she told us about a family that lived in a wood and how they woke up one morning to find a baby on their doorstep. It was supposed to have been left by a fairy and it all ended happily, but I think I may have been left on my mother's doorstep when she lived in London and she thinks it better that I don't know, because that would mean she isn't really my mother. But I love her very much, and gran too; I just want to know the truth, Willy.'

After a few minutes Willy, as deep thinking as he was tactful and kind, spoke: 'Fred, I don't know, but I do understand why you want to know about your father. It's hard for me to say anything, but I can only suggest you tell your mother how much you love her, that you don't want to quarrel, but you hope she will tell you about your father – one day. Do you remember Copper?'

'I do, he was about the best full back the school team ever had. Poor old Copper!'

'That's right,' agreed Willy. 'He had a mother and father who were always knocking him about, arguing with each other. I remember how Copper and his little sister, Louise, often came to school in tears and sometimes came round to our house late in the evening because their parents were in The Queens Head. They were awful to Copper, no wonder he

153

went off to London as soon as he left school. What I do know is that Copper and Louise had no one to love them, except each other.'

He found Fred gently nodding. 'I suppose if you look at it like that I'm lucky, at least compared to poor Copper. Thanks Willy. I knew you would help.'

By now they had moved beyond the main crowds and could see the two charabancs waiting. Some were already clambering aboard and in five minutes all were ready to move on. Passengers were drawn more away from conversations as they came to the built-up areas showing signs to Romford, Ilford and Leyton; on through part of the city of London where the road went past magnificent buildings, then squalid streets of desperately poor homes. The juxtaposition of wealth and poverty caused Eleanor to turn to Arthur, gently raise her eyebrows and sigh. Arthur knew her thoughts and could only agree about such an unequal society. Into the old King's Road with its elegant shops, an open area of grass and trees which had survived the general rush to build, and then a first sight of Stamford Bridge. 'Is this impressive stadium where Abraham is really going to race?' Grace wondered.

TWENTY-SIX

Monday, 5 August

As Abraham and Jack entered the turning off Kings Road and saw the high wall carrying a large sign announcing "Stamford Bridge Stadium", the young athlete felt his anxiety twisting into a tight knot in his stomach. Jack's presence was a tremendous support, his natural optimism and sense of humour proving a timely antidote to Abraham's anxiety.

It had been a great help staying in Ealing with his running friend, James Bagshott, who had told Abraham that his own running days were past. 'Abraham, you've got huge potential and you're so young. You must do everything you can to succeed on the track.'

James lived in a large house in Blondin Avenue where his parents, Judith and Grenville Bagshott, were delighted to host the two Rusfield men. The whole family which included Patricia, James' sister, had decided that they would go to watch the athletics. Jack was delighted to know that eighteen-year-old Patricia would be there; she was certainly a very pretty auburn-haired young lady.

The journey from Rusfield had taken nearly three hours, as trains on a Sunday were not plentiful, but it had been fun. Then a short walk took them to the row of substantial late-Victorian semi-detached houses. Having settled into a high-ceilinged upstairs bedroom, Abraham and Jack joined the family for a most pleasant evening meal. Talk, not surprisingly, was much about the forthcoming race, but when she noticed Abraham's rather tense look, Judith Bagshott lightly kicked her husband's ankle and diverted the conversation.

'I don't expect you know why this is called Blondin Avenue do you?' she asked.

Both Rusfield lads shook their heads although a smile came on to Jack's face. 'Well, no I don't, but I do remember once reading a book about great feats and there was a man called Blondin. Didn't he walk across Niagara Falls?'

'Well done, Jack,' she replied. Carefully bringing her daughter into the conversation she added, 'Patricia will tell you all about him and why our avenue got its name.' She encouraged her with a delightful smile.

'Well, I do know quite a lot about the man, but I don't want to bore you. There was this Frenchman who became known as Charles Blondin who went to America and did some amazing trapeze and other acrobatic feats. Anyway, he had this idea of walking across Niagara Falls on a tightrope which was around 350 yards long. Can you imagine that? Oh, it makes me feel funny just to think about it.'

'That's just amazing: thank you,' uttered Jack as enthusiastic as he was well-mannered. 'That's just hard to believe. But why is your avenue named after him?'

'Well,' cut in Grenville Bagshott, 'a few years ago this road like other newly built ones needed a name and apparently Blondin came to England and lived and died in Ealing, although I don't think this avenue is where he lived. The next road is called Niagara Avenue.'

'But Patricia, how did you know all about this?' asked Jack.

'Well,' replied this slightly blushing daughter of the house, 'at school we all had to find out about the street where we lived and I was just lucky to live in one that turned out to have such an interesting name.'

That night Abraham slept well and the whole household was thrilled to see a brilliant sky with penetrating sunshine when they shared breakfast together. With promises of meeting up after the race, James walked as far as Northfields and Little Ealing station with them. Jack's small bag contrasted with Abraham's much larger one carrying all his athletics gear which he guarded with great care. Six stations took them to Earls Court where they changed to go the few stops to Walham Green; then a short walk to the athletics stadium, which they knew was also used by a football team. Families carrying bags, the occasional policeman, a newspaper vendor and group of smart infantry soldiers all added to the increasing bustle. Not quite knowing what to do, unusual for the normally calm Abraham, Jack took over. He spotted an open gate with, just beyond, a green metal turnstile by which a straw-hatted official stood next to a sign: *"Officials and Competitors"*. They made towards this.

'Official or competitor?'

'Competitor,' replied Abraham.

'And trainer,' added the ever-smiling Jack.

Once inside, the size of the stadium was even more impressive. The centre area was clearly a football pitch whilst round it ran the red-coloured cinder track. Abraham stopped. 'Do you see that, Jack? The track's marked in lanes.' Jack could immediately see what had caught his friend's attention.

'But why?' asked the puzzled Jack.

'Because it makes it fairer. You have to run in the lane you're given which means you can't cut in front of each other, much fairer. And you can see the short lines going the other way in the lanes; well that's so we start in what is called a stagger and then everyone runs the same distance. I wonder if we can go and have a close look. I see a couple of runners are already practising on the bends.'

They turned away from the track and spotted a door for competitors. Jack said, with a broad smile, that he would temporarily abandon his duties as trainer and find a drink and somewhere to sit. 'You just get ready although I'm sure it's too early for that yet. The programme the official gave us says your race is at a quarter to two. So plenty of time.' He gave Abraham a shoulder pat and wished him every success. 'Let me know if there's anything you want. I'll keep an eye open for you: just wave.'

Out of the corner of his eye, Jack saw a large green flag being waved and caught the sound of shouts which he suddenly realised were intended for him. Turning, he spotted Boney and Jammy waving and calling to him, so he trotted towards the holders of the green and white banner: not only Boney and Jammy, but a great crowd from Rusfield. So they had arrived safely.

When Abraham passed through the competitors' door he was surprised to see so many people around, the majority of who were obviously athletes. He knew the stadium had been built some thirty years earlier and it certainly contrasted with some of the places he had previously raced. In the early days he had often changed in no more than a wooden hut, occasionally in the open. He knew the running track was reputed to be the best in the land and his friend James, who had raced here twice, told him it was the fastest track he had known.

The large wall clock and each area had its own, showed half past twelve. The first race, the one mile, was scheduled for one o'clock so those athletes would already be changed and warming up. Abraham was determined to run faster than he had ever managed before and prove that the track was the best in the country, but he knew he should try to relax. Too early to change, so having checked all was ready, he sat, closed his eyes, not in prayer, although that may have been a good idea, but to relax. He took in deep breaths and found that he was already losing some of his early anxiety.

He opened his eyes and found he was looking up at a tall, military figure smiling down at him. 'You must be Abraham

Richards,' grinned the newcomer, some ten years older than the Rusfield runner. He shook Abraham's hand and introduced himself. 'I'm Wyndham Halswelle. I see we are drawn next to each other on the inside lanes. I heard how you won at Crystal Palace, so I'll need to watch out.'

Abraham was thrilled, although that feeling was mixed with a return of some anxiety. He knew about Lieutenant Wyndham Halswelle who had won the quarter mile in the Olympics four years previously.

'Sir,' said the ever-polite, but never obsequious Abraham. 'It's a great pleasure to meet you, I've heard so much about you.'

'Most of which,' responded the dark-haired and heavily-moustached athlete, 'will have been of some time back. I thought I had stopped serious running in 1908, but decided to make a final effort this year. Oh, and please call me Wyndham. Perhaps not a Christian name I would have chosen, but we can't always be responsible for our parents' choices,' he added in an engaging tone. 'But, have you ever run in lanes before?' The young runner was quick to say that this would be something new.

'Well, you do have to get used to it, although it's not as difficult as you might think, you must stay in your own lane and that needs care when you go round the bends. Look, bring your spikes and we'll go to have a look and practise a little on one of the bends, just so you get used to it.'

Together, having picked up their spikes, they returned the way they had come in and walked through a small picket gate which abutted the track. Abraham followed as he was led to the nearest bend. Donning their spikes, they jogged along the straight leading into a bend, a second time picking up the speed. 'Look Abraham, I'll stand on this bend and watch you don't step over the tramline. You know you are running on the inside which is, of course, the sharpest bend.'

When Abraham had walked back from the bend by some

ten yards, Wyndham gave a shout. Abraham broke into a fast stride so that by the bend he was almost at maximum speed. Three more test runs and he felt confident.

'That was well done, Abraham. It's not as hard as it seems, is it? You'll be fine.'

'Thank you so much, I'm really grateful. I know I would have been really worried without that practice; you are most kind.' They walked back towards the changing room. Abraham hardly able to believe he was chatting with an Olympic champion; his wildest dreams were coming true. 'But Wyndham,' he started with some hesitation, 'why didn't you run in Stockholm? Britain could certainly have done with you.'

'Truth to tell, I decided I'd had enough after the London fiasco four years ago. You know the story well I expect.' Indeed, Abraham well knew the story: how the twenty-five-year-old Lieutenant in the Highland Infantry had been favourite for the Olympic quarter mile, but his main challengers, all Americans, appeared to have pre-planned to stop him. One of them blocked the Scot, running diagonally in front of him, forcing him to the edge of the track and using his elbow to prevent any overtaking, a tactic which was often used in America. The offender was disqualified and the race rerun two days later. When it came to the rerun, lanes were marked to prevent a repeat of these tactics, but the other American runners refused to participate and so Wyndham had been the only runner in the final.

'Having a walkover in an Olympic final was nothing of which to be particularly proud, so after a couple more races I decided to quit running.' He smiled. 'However, as I'm based in England this year I decided to have a few last races.'

They were soon joined by other athletes; all introducing themselves to each other. Abraham was almost overwhelmed by the other competitors. In addition to Wyndham, there was the current Scottish champion, Alastair McGrath, and Richard Rickard, the swarthy Londoner whom Abraham had beaten at Crystal Palace and, above all the six-foot American, Carroll Haff, whose Kansas drawl delighted Abraham. Abraham had had no idea that one of the recent Olympic finalists would be in his race. He could only hope that his plan for a fast start and then to closely tail the front runner until committing himself to a final all-out effort, would succeed.

The athletes' conversation drew to a halt as the runners for the second event, the 100 yards, were called. Abraham and his fellow competitors had already put on running shorts and vests, running spikes checked and all were ready. In a short while the official that had greeted Jack and Abraham over an hour earlier appeared and called for the runners. He checked the eight against his list and led them to the open door leading to the track. All were slightly dazzled by the brilliant sunshine and their eyes took a moment to adjust. When they did, Abraham was amazed to see so many people. 'How many people do you think there are here?' asked Abraham.

'Nearly forty thousand, I believe,' replied the official. Abraham felt he needed to pinch himself to be certain all this was really happening. Roars from the crowd greeted the runners; prizes for the previous race having been given out. Abraham glanced around and suddenly picked out the large green and white banner being brandished from the front row of the stand nearest to the finishing line. The official spoke to them, advised them that he would lead them to their individual starting mark and give clear instructions for the start. 'And don't, whatever you do, start before the pistol sounds and keep in the lanes. I'm sure you gentlemen will make it a good race.'

They had walked out to the track in lane order, Abraham leading the way. The official stopped and referring to his papers said: 'Richards, this is your mark.' Abraham watched as the other seven runners were taken to their starting marks. Running vests were all in different colours so the athletes could easily be recognised. Abraham's green was, of course, instantly known by the Rusfield contingent.

'But,' said Fred as the athletes went to their marks, 'it's not fair. Abraham is last; he's got further to run than the rest.' Several murmured in angry agreement.

Grace turned to Fred: 'No Fred, it's all fair. Although it must have been a surprise to Abraham when he found out about the lanes, he did recently explain it all to me. You see, the further you are away from the inside lane the further you would have to run, so to make it the same for everyone the runner on the outside starts in front. But don't worry, it really is fair.' She was not sure whether Fred and, indeed some others understood, but they nodded in sagely fashion. If a girl could understand it, then they were not going to say otherwise. Six of the eight runners used the trowels available from the trackside to make a foot grip.

'Get to your marks.' Abraham, along with the other five who had made a mark, crouched lower. He went through his much practised procedure: right spiked shoe gripping hard, into a relaxed position, shoulders given the customary loosening movement and a final wiggle of the left foot so it was just a fraction short of the starting line.

'Get yourselves set,' the official called out. Abraham couldn't help seeing the other seven runners stretching out in front of him, something he had never experienced before; an upper body adjustment, followed by a push of his right toes into the starting hole to give greater leverage and total concentration on the track ahead. His mind focused on a fast start, the thought of when to make the final sprint to the finishing tape could be erased from his mind for the moment. The lull to the final instruction seemed endless. The huge crowd was silent. All eyes were on the runners, Abraham being the sole objective of the sixty Rusfield villagers. Their hopes hung on the next minute.

As always the crack of the gun surprised the crowd, Abraham seemed to make a very fast start. Few in the crowd understood the second gun sound, but the runners did and knew what it meant. 'What's going on,' was the question asked by thousands.

Arthur knew and turning to those around him explained: 'It must be someone has fouled, probably started too early.' A few moments later he added, 'I don't like the look of this,' as the starter walked up to Abraham and the runner next to him. 'Don't say they are going to be disqualified.' The groans of despair from those surrounding the vicar were numerous. It was only later that they learnt from Abraham exactly what had happened.

'I was nearest to the starter. When he said "Get yourselves set," like all the others I was ready. After what seemed a terrible time gap, the gun falsely clicked and then the shot rang out. At first the starter said that two of us were disqualified for starting before the gun, but in fact only Wyndham next to me and I had heard the faint click which we just thought must be the start. So we were just a moment ahead of the others and clearly that's not fair. The starter did not understand until Wyndham explained. He's such an experienced runner that he knew. So we weren't disqualified, but went back to the start.'

Indeed, after a few minutes to collect their thoughts and for the starter to reload his pistol, the same procedure was repeated, each athlete going through his much rehearsed drill again. The gap between "To your marks" and the crack of the pistol again seemed huge, but Abraham knew he must not start before the pistol sounded; another offence might well mean disqualification. The Rusfield supporters waited in silent agony.

Only the smallest fraction of a second separated Abraham's start from the rest. He seemed to then fly towards the first bend. It seemed impossible to reduce the gap between himself and Wyndham in the next lane, but reduce it he must. Over the second hundred yards he felt himself gaining on three runners, but as they entered the final bend, the crowd found it impossible to judge who was ahead.

'Who's winning?' screamed Jammy. 'It's not like last time when you could see who was ahead.'

'You will in a moment,' replied the quietly-spoken Jack.

As they came out of the final bend and entered the straight, three coloured vests were ahead: the American's red, white and blue; the blue and white of Wyndham's Scottish shirt and, wondrously, the green of Abraham and Rusfield. Lanes four, two and one neck and neck: the American, perhaps, a few inches ahead. The roars must have been heard miles away as each cheered on their own favourite, but as Willy said later, 'I reckon our cheers and roars were the greatest.'

Thirty, twenty, ten, five yards to go and still too close to call. Just short of the line Wyndham seemed to lose a few inches to the others; almost touching the tape it seemed that Abraham threw himself forward. He had won.

If disbelief, wonder and sheer joy could be measured, the scale of each coming from the Rusfield crowd would have reached record heights. At first they were uncertain, this was too much to expect, yet here were other runners going to Abraham who had sunk to his knees, congratulating him. Grace was weeping. Pauline, Frederick and James Richards were in tears as were so many. 'Wonderful, wonderful.' Willy echoed the words of so many. Never, never could a village people have been united in such pure delight.

Half an hour went by before they saw Abraham walking towards them, carrying his bag and the broadest smile ever seen. The first words spoken were his. 'Thank you everyone. You made all the difference.' The congratulations were too many to record; others joined the joyful Rusfield group. Wyndham, who had already given Abraham the biggest hug he had ever received from a fellow runner, went on to congratulate his parents. The Bagshott family added their praise, giving Jack time to ask the pretty Patricia if he might write to her about anything else he could find out regarding Charles Blondin. With a happy smile, she agreed.

Two more races had been watched whilst Abraham had taken a bath and changed, but it had been agreed that the return journey should be made as soon as he joined them. 'It's quite a long journey and we don't want to be too late home.' The journey was one of the happiest that had ever been made. The cheers, the talk, the sense of pure celebration were boundless. Everyone wanted to sit next to Abraham, Rusfield's champion.

The two coach drivers shared in the celebration and agreed to drive right back to Rusfield and they arrived by seven o'clock. There were more people near the pond waiting for news. It was a long and very happy evening.

Nine o'clock found the six close friends in the untidy, cramped rear garden of The George. The usually morose landlord, John Harrowell, had surprised them by buying each a drink. It was the usually retiring Fred who expressed the feelings of all by simply saying: 'To the best runner in the world. Thank you Racer, it was amazing to see your green running vest in front at the end.'

Abraham gave his usual modest smile. 'Well, I wasn't at all sure that I was in front. Thank you all for coming.'

Willy put his glass on the rough-hewn chair that served as a table. 'Racer, what was your time? We were so delighted you won that we forgot to ask.'

'Well, thanks to the other runners who really pushed me, I managed 48.4 seconds which is much better than I've ever done before. The track today helped. But enough about speeds, it's my turn to buy you a drink; without your support I'd never have won.'

He disappeared inside and a few minutes later reappeared with a tray of five ales and an apple juice. He passed them round. As soon as they all had their glasses, Boney turned to Abraham and asked: 'Racer, where are the next Olympics?'

'Well, it's to be in Berlin.'

'You'll be there,' put in Jammy, 'and we'll be there to cheer you on to victory.'

'Oh I don't know,' smiled Abraham, '1916 is a long way off and a lot could happen between now and then.'

Part Two
1914-1919

.

TWENTY-SEVEN

Thursday, 27 August 1914

'Get yer friggin' head down, you stupid coppernob. And put yer 'at on. I don't want yer friggin' brains scattered all over me.'

The shove on his shoulder forced Jack's face into the dry ground. He had only taken his cap off for a moment. The sun was unbearably hot and he could feel the sweat running down his back as the heavy material of his uniform ill-matched the August weather.

'Sorry, Sarge,' half-smiled the ever-agreeable Jack, more concerned about upsetting the harsh, steely-glaring Sergeant Burgess than endangering his own life. He gave a final mop of his brow before replacing his rough-edged cap which he felt to be wearing a furrow into his forehead; it smelt with sustained sweat. Jack patted his rifle.

He looked out on the momentarily peaceful scene which reminded him of the Salisbury Plain where his fortnight's training had taken place. However, his mind rapidly returned to reality, as it did for the other 200 men barely hidden by the slight dip in the summer-burnt grassland. Less than a mile away, well positioned on a heavily wooded hillside was the enemy. To Jack's left were three mobile guns, each behind a limber and six horses. The horses, like the men, had struggled with the guns since the failure to hold the Mons-Condé Canal line. By nightfall on Monday, 25 August, II Corps, including 700 men from the 2nd Battalion Suffolk Regiment who had been brought over from Ireland, were in retreat.

Now the forgiving and gentle horses were casually eating the unappetising, but welcome grass. When Jack and Fred had joined the retreating troops they had been as shocked to see the state of the horses as they had the main body of men. A frail looking grey had an angry wound on its left hind with dried blood down to its rear fetlock. Fred's natural inclination was to ignore his own tiredness and give a little comfort to the horse, but he dared not risk the bellowing of his sergeant.

Jack knew that to their left were some larger calibre howitzers; their deafening noise from earlier in the day still ringing in his ears. Now, there was also a brief lull in the onslaught from the German guns. The main force had struggled the thirty miles from Mons; they were filthy, bedraggled and fighting hard to keep up their spirits. The fighting was not going as Jack and the others, who had signed up with adventure and excitement running through their bodies, had expected.

The first serious fighting on the previous Monday had been before Jack and Fred had joined the main body of men. Could that really only be three days ago? he wondered. I was in Southampton then! Now they were part of the force attempting to hold up the powerful German advance until even more support arrived, but Jack and Fred together with Racer and Boney, hopefully not far away, really had no idea what was intended next.

Enemy guns started up again and peace was shattered by a shell only forty yards from where they lay, throwing up a shower of earth. 'Keep yourself as close to the ground as you can, Fred,' urged the ever-encouraging Jack. 'They can't seem to get their range quite right, so we'll be all right.' His words were more comforting than were his thoughts. The nearby lighter British guns answered back; all knew that the quick-firing 4.5-inch howitzer was a weapon feared by the Germans. It was the much heavier guns of the enemy that the British lacked.

The minutes crept on, each one marked by the appalling sound of guns from both sides. Jack was suddenly aware of a movement to his left. Turning, he saw an officer crouching but moving rapidly towards Sergeant Burgess. A hurried conversation and the officer scurried on towards a larger band of men 200 yards to the right. Trailing just behind was a private trying to keep up with him.

The men round Jack and Fred heard the orders coming from Bellowing Burgess; Jack preferred not to pay attention to the names some had given their sergeant. 'Listen, you bleeders. The officer thinks we're 'aving too easy a time, so we're moving on. It seems the lovely commander has decided that we can't go on retreating. There's a village about a mile away and we're to make our way to this 'ere Caudrey and dig in. We're at last going to make a stand and not give in to these friggin' Krauts. So get yerselves ready, make yerselves beautiful and be ready to move when I tell yer. It'll be in the next thirty minutes. Don't 'ang about when I give the order.'

There was nothing to do, but wait. Jack had once heard how in the moments of drowning the whole of life passed before the victim. He did not know about this, but in the minutes of waiting for Bellowing Burgess's order, the events that had moved him from Rusfield to this remote part of northern France ran through his mind.

It had been five months earlier that the six of them had been together in The George. Jammy Carey's building work had taken him to the mansion of Sir Lancelot Prestwish on the edge of Steepleton, so he now lived at home and was able to meet up with his mates more regularly. It was Jammy who had seen a poster in Steepleton, inviting young men to join the Territorial Army. 'Sounds great,' he had told the others.

'They meet every Tuesday in their headquarters near the town centre, seven-thirty for two hours.'

'What do they do there?' queried the more cautious Fred.

'Well, they teach you army drill, reading maps, loading and unloading a rifle and they even have manoeuvres up on the Steepleton side of Bramrose Hill.'

'And what about shooting?' asked Boney.

'Well,' replied Jammy, reaching for his drink, 'Frank, a mate of mine, says that after a few weeks training, you go out to the shooting range near Broston. He'll soon get his uniform. Well, what do you think?' He turned towards Willy, as always the one who led the way. The others knew he was thinking things through, his chin resting on his left hand providing the clue. Indeed, they were all thinking about Jammy's news.

Village activities were still enjoyed, but the monthly meetings provided a new dimension to their lives. Racer had established himself as the fastest quarter mile runner in the country; the others went to watch him when they could and in the hot summer they had greatly enjoyed the village cricket club, with Boney and Willy excelling. The six had been delighted that they had joined the Terriers; the Tuesday evenings could not come round quickly enough with the six trying to meet near the pond and walking in to Steepleton. They rapidly learnt basic military skills with the monthly manoeuvre in the expanding company of Steepleton Terriers being one of the highlights.

On the very day that war was declared, they had met as usual at the pond. The previous day's Bank Holiday had been much quieter than usual, in spite of dancing and the children's sports on the village green. The troubles in Europe had cast a blanket of anxiety over the whole of the country and Rusfield, along with the whole nation, was filled with a passionate sense of righteousness and patriotism. The six young men responded to the cry for justice with enthusiasm and excitement. Now, talk took on an excited, yet increasingly serious tone. There was only one topic at the Territorial Army HQ: it was about when the men should volunteer.

Two days later, on Thursday, 6 August, Jack had worked a little later than normal at the bakery enabling him to meet up with Boney when the brewery worker came into Steepleton on the six-thirty from Branton. In turn, they met with Racer and Fred who had walked in from Rusfield and the four strode down Broad Street to the impressive town hall, which had been built on the wealth of Steepleton business, in Queen Victoria's reign. They were amazed to see a queue stretching over a hundred yards. There was much banter, talk of the excitement of war, of having a crack at the Huns and the anticipation of going abroad for the first time.

A huge poster under a Union Jack greeted them as they went in to the large hall. It called for volunteers with a graphic illustration of an evil looking soldier, spiked helmet and uniform which was clearly that of a German. The enemy was, as Jammy said, 'Getting a well-deserved kick up the arse' by the proud British soldier in the poster. Jack was not alone in being moved when he saw it.

Mention of being a Terrier gave immediate access to the recruitment officer's interest. 'Name? Age? Are you sure about that? Address? Occupation?' Answering with excited nods, a document was thrust at Jack which he was told to sign.

'Over there,' ordered the fiery, heavily-moustached recruiting officer. He had moved across the room to where, armed with tape measure, a younger man was assessing each recruit. All seemed to satisfy the needs of the moment, although Fred later told Willy that his weight had almost proved a problem. 'Only eight stone and six pounds,' remarked the officer who had been consulted by his subordinate doing the weighing. 'I suggest you eat a bit more my lad. But you'll do.'

So, the four became members of the 2nd Battalion of the Suffolk Regiment. Jammy and Willy had similarly enrolled in the Suffolks at the Territorial Army headquarters where queues had been even longer. Parents and loved ones were upset, some hurt, to hear that the young men were to report to the Steepleton base on the Saturday morning; suddenly life for the families was changing. Yet the overwhelming feelings were of excitement and pride; excitement on the part of the young men, pride felt by the families that their men were standing up for Britain and the Empire.

It was Sparky Carey and his cart that took them from Rusfield with a large gathering of villagers waving farewell. A number of Union Jacks had suddenly appeared, most home-made, to be waved by the children. Arthur Windle went from man to man, shaking hands with each and giving a blessing. As he stopped and talked with Jack, the last of the six great friends, Arthur wished that he, too, was going with them. For the rest of his life, Abraham would remember his departing kiss from Grace; it caused a momentary doubt of what he was about to undertake.

In Steepleton there was a further health check, signing on and receipt of a basic food ration for the journey, then on to Paddington and Warminster. At each station a growing number of men, mainly young, joined them until there was little room left on the western-bound train. The reception at Warminster was swamped with large numbers of men each carrying bag, backpack or holiday case. The rough and tumble of over 1,000 men being moved in to regimental groups was clearly a challenge for the uniformed men, involving nearly one hundred of the Suffolks; the six Rusfield men managed to stay together.

Some London lads found Salisbury Plain frighteningly different to their home area, but to Jack it was not so different to his beloved Rusfield countryside; the emptiness and silence were just on a grander scale. The training immediately got underway and they were kept frenetically busy; the long marches each day carrying heavy packs were exhausting.

Blisters became hardened skin and muscles toughened. Fred found the going harder than the other five, but their encouragement and his own determination got him through. After two weeks training they were adjudged ready to move on: Saturday, 22 August. It was a two-day march to Southampton and Jack was glad that his daily cycling from Rusfield to Steepleton had helped keep him fit. Most of the march was along roads, with the large contingent often having to move into the side as many vehicles were transferring provisions to the docks. The roads became more crowded as they got closer to their immediate destination.

Coming in sight of the great estuary, the number of ships amazed Jack. The whole place was alive with activity which at first seemed chaotic, yet must clearly have had a purpose. The vessel to which they were ordered was a passenger ship that had been taken out of a side dock just when its life expectancy had been thought to be over. Every square yard of the deck found men sitting and resting, most enjoying a welcome smoke.

Together again and along with some 2,000 others, the Rusfield six had embarked at nine o'clock on the Sunday evening. There were clearly many regular soldiers on board, their confidence and general know-how ill matched by the bewilderment and uncertainty of the recent volunteers. There was an all-round smartening up when a general, unnamed but recognised by his elaborate uniform, came on board. Anchors were lifted and the ship, without too much hesitation, got underway an hour after midnight; less than three weeks after war had been declared.

For Jack and his mates this was the first time they had been on a boat and all were glad the sea was smooth that night. The approach to the French port was slow due to the mass of ships and small boats that littered the port of Le Havre; it was late morning by the time they arrived at the French dockside. Directed to the nearby station, the men were relieved to learn that the next stage of their journey was by train. Word soon spread that their destination was Mons where they were to support a large contingent of regular soldiers who were struggling to delay the Germans on their advance through that part of northern France. The train journey was hot and most men had to stand, but it was preferable to marching. On arrival at the important railway junction at Cambrai, the troops were ordered out, given more equipment and ordered to line up ready to march. The distance to Mons was well under fifty miles and would have to be accomplished within two days, but this was never to be fully completed. Already a retreat from Mons was underway and it became increasingly uncertain where Jack and the new arrival of men would link up with the regular force.

Early on the second day of marching, Jack thought a thunderstorm was about to break the long, hot spell of weather.

'That's thunder, isn't it?' Willy asked Jack who was marching on his left.

'Funny thunder I'd call it. More like guns,' replied his mate.

It was mainly gunfire, but not entirely, that brought Jack out of his daydreaming. 'Get up yer idle buggers. I said be ready when I ordered. You've rested long enough. Up on yer feet.' It had only been ten minutes rest so perhaps one's life, or at least much of it, could run before you when you were drowning. Jack jumped to his feet, picking up cap and rifle. His immediate thought was not of the next march, wherever that might be to, but the bloody fleas. He seemed to be itching all over as if the tormenting creatures, resting in the seams of his underclothes, had also heard the call to move.

TWENTY-EIGHT

8 – 27 August 1914

Olivia Atkins was heartbroken. She was determined not to show her distress; somehow she must keep up the single appearance of pride in Jack going off to war. She was not alone in such feelings among the villagers waving off the six eighteen and nineteen-year-old lads; but maybe her grief cut deeper. Thoughts of her parents dying in the Coventry shop fire two decades earlier and of her husband being killed by lightning, ripped through her mind; to her, Jack was everything. Her love for him was overwhelming, but she hoped she had never smothered him, rather to encourage him to build his own life. How well he had done at school and then to work his way up in the bakery and now… Her sense of foreboding was almost overwhelming.

She looked around at the large number of friends gathered by the pond. Not only the parents, but the entire families of Abraham, Albert, Jammy, Willy and Fred's mother were there; the younger children laughing and waving their flags and messages of good luck. The crowd extended beyond relatives, for these six young men who had brought distinction to their school and village some six years previously, were again flying the flag for Rusfield. Some had wanted to accompany their sons to Steepleton, but it had been felt that the collective act of being together at the farewell in Rusfield was right.

Olivia turned and put her arms round Liz Smith, for both were losing their only child; there were tears in the eyes of both. 'I don't know what I'll do without him,' Liz said plaintively to her friend. 'He used to be a real handful, but now he's wonderful the way he helps me out and mother will miss him terribly. He will be all right, won't he?' In truth Olivia could only give a faint smile. Her fears exactly, but she must show a strength of the kind that she knew her beloved son would want.

'Liz, you must come round and have a cup of tea later this morning and whenever you feel down you must always feel able to call on me. We need to be able to comfort each other.' They looked an ill-matched pair; the stylish and beautiful Olivia, as well dressed as always, and the haggard, poorly clothed and prematurely aging Liz. But their likeness in feelings was greater than any superficial differences. Liz cuffed away her tears, smiled and moved quietly on.

As Olivia turned away from the distressed Liz, she almost bumped into one who was certainly not able to control her tears: Grace was sobbing. She kept trying to stop and replace her forlorn look with her usual gentle smile, but it was too hard. Olivia moved over to her, knowing that the departure of Abraham was heart-rending. Olivia knew that to Grace, now at the same age as when she had lost her parents, Abraham's departure to the unknown was unbearable. Both these young people had been carving out their own careers, together so much was promised; two fine young people deeply in love.

'Grace, it's lovely to see you albeit on such an occasion as this. We must try to give strength to each other. How proud you must feel of Abraham, just as I do of Jack. Tell me, how is the teaching going?'

She hoped the question might take Grace away from their shared sadness. It was as if Grace realised this brave attempt of Olivia's to move on and she managed a smile. 'It's going well, I love it. It's such a happy school in Wensfield and the children are so agreeable. As you know, I only started there in April, but the time has flown by.'

Although Olivia knew the answer to her next question, but keen to keep the conversation going for a little longer, she asked: 'But Wensfield must be nearly four miles away; how do you manage that?'

'Well, I've been using a bicycle which my dad got for me. It's fine in this weather and only takes me just over half an hour. I really quite like it although the track is a little rough in places.'

Olivia knew part of the track well. 'But, in the winter when it's dark; surely you can't bicycle then?'

Grace smiled. 'Well, Mrs Windle's parents, Mr and Mrs Brown, have said they have a spare room and I can stay there during the week. It's a most generous offer and I think that's what I will do. They are such nice people, not surprising when I think what a lovely lady Mrs Windle is.'

'Indeed,' said Olivia, thinking of her dear friend Eleanor. 'I'm really glad the teaching is going so well.'

'Yes,' replied Grace, 'it was so kind of Mr and Mrs Mansfield giving me the opportunity to train; now it's up to me.'

Even as Grace and Olivia were trying to console each other, so Eleanor and Arthur Windle were talking with Jammy's mother, Eliza Carey. Left without her husband, who had driven the six lads in to Steepleton, she too was anxious for the future. 'It's strange really,' said the beanpole-thin Eliza. 'Just to think that James had been away for nearly three years, then got work at Sir Lancelot's place near Steepleton so he could come back home and now he's off again. Mind you, we are proud of him as I'm sure we all are.'

And it was pride and excitement that were the overriding feelings of the villagers as, a few at a time, they dispersed and returned to more mundane tasks. The feelings of anxiety and even fear among the loved ones of the six men, who would now have reached Steepleton, was exceeded by the number of other villagers who simply glowed with pride.

It was the same sense of pride, albeit with a nagging feeling of deep anxiety for Jack and his mates that had settled upon Reverend Arthur Windle. Two weeks on from the departure of the young men, he had learnt from Eleanor, whose depth of village knowledge never ceased to astound him, that five more villagers had signed up, and that two of Abraham's colleagues at Spinney Farm, Tommy Bruce and Bob Bacon, were thinking about it. How that would leave Jack Mansfield at Spinney Farm, Arthur could not imagine: not least for harvesting. He could only hope the new machinery would cope.

Overwhelmingly, Arthur knew it was right that villagers were responding to the call to arms. His belief in the country's pre-eminence among nations and the rightness of the Empire, which had brought stability to a quarter of the world, was the basis of this strongly-held view and he knew his father would be sharing the same sentiment. He had made sure the service on the day after the lads' departure had included prayers for the young men and the theme had been one of the whole village pledging support to King and country. It was good that St Mary's had been full as he led everyone in the common cause of Christian right. The chosen hymns well reflected the nation's spirit of the time.

More recently, he was grateful to Major de Maine who had offered to talk to villagers on the coming Thursday, 27 August. He recalled his conversation with the owner of the manor. 'Vicar, I believe it is important that everyone understands just what is at stake and how we must all pull hard together. I have a suggestion to make.'

'So, Major, what do you have in mind? Please tell me.'

The major replaced his cup on the table and bristled with quiet excitement. 'Well, I have made a large map of Europe; actually it's taken me quite a long time. One of the problems is that not too many people in the village seem to have a clear idea of where the different countries are, nor on which side they are all on. With the help of this map I can explain what the situation is all about and how it is that our country, as well as France and the whole Empire, is threatened by the enemy. If people understand this I am sure it will make a difference. I see one newspaper said that the war will be over by Christmas, but I don't believe that at all.'

'I agree with you, Major. It's important we each do what we can at this time.' Arthur thanked the major and it was agreed the meeting be organised for the next Thursday. After talking about the little news that was coming through from France and Belgium, the Major departed for his stroll back to the manor.

Arthur knew that Eleanor was helping at the reading room as some new books had been donated and shelves needed reorganising. Jack Mansfield had kindly organised for a newspaper to be placed in there each day which Peter brought in from Steepleton along with the post. The newspaper was the main source of news from Europe and was avidly read by a number of villagers.

With Eleanor out for an hour or so, it was a good time for Arthur to catch up on some reading. He was much troubled by the degree to which he should use the pulpit to encourage the men to volunteer. His natural feeling was to make strong appeals, but certainly Eleanor had spoken out against this. 'Arthur,' she said in her ever-loving, but nonetheless determined style, 'God has to be neutral in wartime. Surely his love goes towards the men who are in danger on either side. We are not living in Old Testament times, so please think carefully before you start preaching for volunteers. And didn't you tell me that our Member of Parliament is soon coming to the village to do just that?'

Arthur did not quite know what to do, but he was certainly going to ponder Eleanor's words. In the meantime he knew that his latest copy of the *Church Times* waited his attention. Picking it up from his untidy desk, Arthur read the Bishop of Durham's emotional statement to the county's light infantry about the "holiness of patriotism". How far should he use the pulpit for rallying the people? Arthur wondered.

Certainly the Archbishop of Canterbury was stopping well short of urging priests to preach in such a way, but the Archdeacon of Westminster's latest sermon made the contrary viewpoint: 'I have tried to make it clear that recruiting appeals from the pulpit is intended to stimulate hearers to become eager amateur recruiting sergeants.' To the women in a congregation he appealed: 'Send your men today to join our glorious army.'

Arthur reflected on all the views. He decided on a compromise. Once a month he produced a four-page leaflet which contained St Mary's news of weddings, funerals, a little about the wider church and sometimes an editorial. He would use this. Copies would be printed in Steepleton and delivered to the villagers who contributed the necessary one penny, about half of the village, and then he would place a few copies in St Mary's and the reading room. He sat quietly, prayed for guidance and wrote: *No one living has ever seen, or is likely to see again, such a tremendous and widespread war which has burst upon us like a thunderstorm. Men of the right age must come forward to serve their King and country and act like true men. Women can help by their hands and hearts, and children, too, can do their part, for all can pray – pray as you have never done before. On Wednesday evenings and Thursday afternoons special prayers will be offered. A list of Rusfield men who have gone to the Front will be displayed in the church porch and they must be accompanied by our prayers.*

TWENTY-NINE

September - November 1914

> The Vicarage,
> Rusfield.
> September 1914

My Dearest Parents,

Thank you for your letter. Eleanor and I are so sorry to learn that you have not been well, father. We send our love and hope that your recovery is progressing well.

We are certainly very fortunate in keeping in good health, although of course, all is overshadowed by war news, which seems very mixed. I am sure we have all been shocked by the growing number of casualties that are reported in the newspapers. I can only hope that Lord Kitchener's appeal for more troops will be answered quickly.

There is also mixed news from Rusfield. Whilst some enthusiastic young men volunteered at the very beginning of the war, numbers have become a little disappointing. Next month, Sir Humphrey Watkinson, our MP, is addressing villagers and I can only hope that his words will bring forth fruit. We are hoping that most villagers will attend, especially as a patriotic concert is preceding his address.

In the meantime I am pleased to say that support is

being given to the Prince of Wales War Fund. Our parish council met in late August and adopted this plan and so far £12/5/6 has been donated. We are also donating the harvest loaf from our harvest festival to the Belgian refugees who have escaped the atrocities of the German army and since been taken in by the kind people of Steepleton.

The really good news is that the families of all our men in France and Belgium have now received letters. All write of how well things are going, remain optimistic about victory and keep well. Eleanor joins with me in sending our love.

Your devoted son, Arthur.

Arrangements for the evening were in full flow. Many remembered the previous concerts that had taken place in Fred Jackson's barn, but something completely different had to be planned for the Member of Parliament's visit. This time, the theme was patriotic and in every way supportive to the war effort; the concert would last for three-quarters of an hour followed by Sir Humphrey Watkinson's speech.

Hezekiah Freeman and Aubrey Watson, next-door neighbours and labourers for Jack Mansfield, had spent the whole day making sure the barn was spick and span. Many Union Jacks and three hastily made French Tricolours were brought in by Doris and her younger sister Elsie, who now shared the domestic work at Spinney Farm. These decorations where then hung on the wall behind the stage. It was left to Fred Jackson to bring in and fix the pièce de résistance: the newly produced poster of Lord Kitchener staring forth and stating: "Your Country Needs You".

Sir Humphrey arrived at the vicarage, transported by his own driver. He was accompanied by Lieutenant James Smart, linked to the Steepleton Territorial Army, who was acting as recorder for volunteers. Arthur gave a brief outline of the concert.

'For myself,' spoke Sir Humphrey in a forceful, but not unattractive way, 'I will briefly review the war situation and stress the absolute need for an immediate response to our leader's appeal. We must have several hundred thousand more men and that, almost immediately. Whilst our men have been performing valiantly and gaining some victories, it has to be said that the Kaiser has many more troops than we first realised. We need more men.' The last statement was delivered with such passion, a feeling shared by Arthur, that he sincerely hoped the evening's response would match the occasion.

Pleasantries were exchanged and Arthur found himself warming to Sir Humphrey who, whilst well distanced from them, seemed caring and thoughtful of his electorate. Eleanor had a pleasant conversation with the young lieutenant who expressed delight when he realised the connection between the village and his Terriers. 'That group from the village were good lads. They were so keen, bright and whilst they enjoyed themselves, they treated the occasions seriously enough.'

'Well, they are all somewhere at the Front now,' said Eleanor. 'We have heard from them and they all seem well. They will be very much in our thoughts tonight, as they always are,' she added.

'Of course, one was Racer Richards the famous runner, wasn't he? If any volunteers come forward who are anything like him and his mates, the evening will be worthwhile. Let's hope so.'

The barn was full for the occasion; excitement and an eager anticipation for performers and the visiting Member of Parliament were very evident. Yet as she looked around, Eleanor saw some worried looks. Poor Liz Smith looked more haggard than ever and even Olivia seemed to have lost something of her normal sparkle. Other parents wondered how their loved ones might be influenced by the evening event.

The concert was well received; there was much delight

as everyone knew the performers. All joined in the well sung and strongly patriotic songs, but it was the school choir that brought the audience to its feet with "The Marseillaise", "The British Grenadiers", "God bless the Prince of Wales" and "Red, White and Blue". The children were very smartly turned out, enjoyed the singing and joined in clapping when the efforts of Rita Small were singled out for special thanks by the vicar.

Sir Humphrey spoke well. He had obviously given the speech on a number of occasions; it was well rehearsed and gained by not needing notes. He spoke of the war's progress in Europe and his concluding remarks were delivered with particular passion as he explained why Britain had entered the war: 'We declared war in the great cause of international truth and honour, of friendship to France and of justice to Belgium. It is on behalf of the smaller nations that we are spending our blood and our money. Let Rusfield men prove that you possess moral backbone and are ready to stand up and help us as Christian soldiers in the cause of right against wrong. Let us sing together "Onward, Christian soldiers".'

The well-rehearsed Rita Small struck up the tune, and the first verse to Arthur Sullivan's great music was followed by the even more boisterous singing of the national anthem. A burst of spontaneous applause then burst forth for Sir Humphrey, just a few quietly lacking enthusiasm.

After all the excitement of the evening, Eleanor and Arthur were weary when they got back to the vicarage. The villagers had been slow to depart, not least as the number of men gathering round Lieutenant Smart was many; enough for Sir Humphrey to look pleased.

'So how many signed up?' Eleanor asked her husband as they collapsed into armchairs back at the vicarage.

'I heard it was fifteen with quite a few more enquiries. Anyway, Sir Humphrey seemed well pleased.'

'I saw that Richard Gadsell and Peter Frisby were there. Did they join up? They must be well approaching forty.'

'I think so, dear. So did the Rowe brothers: I saw both Ruby and Florence Rowe in tears at the thought of their husbands going away. What desperate times they are. I felt Sir Humphrey did very well, didn't you dear?' he asked.

Eleanor paused for a moment before replying. 'Bearing in mind that his job was to get volunteers he did well. For me he was too jingoistic, but I suppose that was necessary. However, I was very wrong in one important way; he was much more approachable than I had expected. Anyway, my dear, I'm going upstairs and straight to bed, otherwise I think I will fall asleep in this chair.'

Arthur stood up, kissed his wife and, as she turned to go out of the lounge, he moved towards putting out the downstairs' lamps and making sure all was safely locked up. A few minutes later he, too, went upstairs, going in to his small dressing room. He reflected on the evening's meeting, trying to measure its success; it was so important that the numbers of volunteers increased. He was too old to volunteer, but was there anything more he could be doing for the war effort? He felt all too powerless as he tried to visualise what the young men at the Front were going through.

He quietly stood, went over to his cross, crossed himself and hung his head in thought. 'Dear God, may I hear your voice clearly so that I know what I should do. Forgive me for my sins, especially those I have wronged. May the results of this evening's meeting be right in your sight; be with those young men from the village who are fighting at the Front. May they know of your presence.' He kept his head bowed in silence waiting to hear God speak to him.

Autumn moved on in the village, the streets and gardens became covered in falling leaves, the days shorter and the mornings cooler. News from the Rusfield men at the Front was quickly spread and the list in St Mary's porch of Rusfield men grew to thirty-one. Village pride grew with this increase, but some wondered why other able men had not volunteered. News from the daily newspaper lodged at the reading room became eagerly digested with the unpronounceable name of Ypres replacing those of Marne, Antwerp, Aisne and Flanders and the British casualties covered more and more pages. On a visit to Steepleton, Arthur and Eleanor called in at the library and read The Steepleton Times. Within were listed the names of eight men from surrounding villages who had, as the paper stated, made the final sacrifice. Their thoughts turned to the many young men from Rusfield who were somewhere in Flanders or France.

As they both read the local news-sheet, Arthur's eye alerted on a small paragraph which he immediately pointed out to Eleanor. As she finished reading, she turned and said: 'Well I'm pleased to see that Payne-Croft woman has officially announced that all the actions discussed by the local suffrage movement have been suspended. After all, it's important that the whole movement maintains as much support as it can and it certainly won't get much sympathy now, if it doesn't lie low.'

'But doesn't that rather disappoint you, Eleanor? I know how strongly you feel about obtaining votes for women.'

'There will come a time when this awful war is over and we can return to our rightful claims. My view of women's equality rights won't have changed.' Arthur nodded; he knew of his wife's determined thinking and did not mistake Eleanor's quietness on the subject for a change of thinking.

The first Friday morning in November was a most pleasant one. Whilst Eleanor and Arthur had gratefully accepted the lift in to Steepleton with Sparky Carey, they had opted to walk the return. Their shopping was light and the hour-long walk on such a fine morning had great appeal. The trees were enjoying the last of their autumn colours and the beeches and elms were particularly fine after the wet summer days. They were suddenly aware of someone approaching from behind and turning round saw that it was Peter Woods who drew up alongside them.

'Have you much post for the village this morning, Peter?' Eleanor asked the young man as he rested on his bicycle.

'Not too much, Mrs Windle. It shouldn't take me very long.'

'And how is the stamp collecting going? Have you managed to get any new or interesting ones recently?' asked Arthur.

'Well, there have been some fairly recently. There was a new one for me on one of the letters from Canada. Mrs Gilbert kindly let me have that. Then there are the new ones from the soldiers in France. They don't have stamps, but army envelopes. However, I decided they should be part of my collection. After all they are instead of stamps, aren't they?' he added with a broad smile. 'But I must be on my way. Goodbye for now.' He pedalled off towards Rusfield.

Eleanor and Arthur continued on their way, but as they passed the small road leading to the manor and came in view of Rusfield, they saw much activity. Now they could see a number of khaki uniforms, horses, with children and adults on the green next to the pond. The stride of Arthur and Eleanor became more determined as there was obviously something unusual taking place to cause such a crowd on a normally quiet Friday morning.

THIRTY

November 1914

'So what is going on?' Eleanor asked the excited Eliza Carey as she and Arthur reached Lower Green opposite to the pond.

'Well, isn't it lovely to see all these brave soldiers? They've come to water their horses.' There were a dozen soldiers, who were now surrounded by twice that number of villagers; children were much in evidence as this Friday was part of a four-day holiday in the school term. The children were having a wonderful time. Florrie Edwards and Robert Groves had already persuaded two of the men to lift them up on to the horses which were standing very contentedly at the water's edge. Villagers were crowding round, plying the men with questions; more were arriving each moment.

Gwendolyn Edwards came out of her cottage with her neighbour, Lillian Reynolds, who had joined forces to find enough mugs of steaming tea. Rachel Fielding walked from The Queens Head with another tray, this one of freshly baked scones. The men seemed very pleased to chat even as they were enjoying their unexpected refreshment, breaking off only to give another child a turn on the back of his horse.

Robert Berry who had seen many cavalry groups in his time, was thrilled that he had been taking a stroll round the village when, to his delight, he had seen the soldiers. 'So,' he knowledgeably said, 'I can see you're all from the 1st King Edward Horses Regiment, but what are you doing here?' he asked a fine-featured soldier, one of the youngest in the group.

'Well sir,' he responded with much charm, 'our captain is anxious that both we and the horses keep fit. We've been training over the other side of that hill,' he added, pointing towards Bramrose Hill. 'So we just came out this morning and coming across your village we guessed there must be somewhere we could water the horses.' He nodded towards the half-eaten scone and added, 'We clearly chose well. Everyone is so kind.'

Arthur had found himself by the captain, an older man with a neat moustache and sideburns whom Arthur judged to be in his mid-thirties. 'Let me say how much we welcome you to the village.'

The captain continued to stroke the mane of his fine dappled mare as he replied to Arthur: 'Your people have been so kind and I would ask you to pass on our thanks to everyone. We'll look back on our stop here with much pleasure.' He then spoke quietly to his men and the last of the children were helped down from their horses. 'Now,' called out the captain, 'we want to thank all of you for your kindness. You're wonderful people. Now men, ready.' Everyone joined in saying farewell, with many a thank you and best wishes as the men quickly got on to order. As they were ready to ride off the sergeant led three hearty cheers which rang round the green; tears were in some of the villagers' eyes. For many this was their first real contact with the war. The villagers waved, the men replaced their hats and rode off towards Steepleton.

Some stayed chatting, there was plenty to talk about. Peter Woods had seen the soldiers coming towards the village and made a slight adjustment to his delivery round, ending with the few houses at the far end of Sandy Lane. Now bicycling back up the hill, he slowed down outside the village butchers. 'This I must not forget!' he thought to himself. How much smarter the shop looked since Susannah and Sidney Jones had taken over. Everyone hoped that things were going well for the couple after the anxieties of Sidney's unemployment for several years. As Peter went in, accompanied by the satisfying jingle of the fixed bell, he was pleased to see one of his village favourites in the shop: Olivia Atkins, looking as pretty as ever, Peter thought.

'Good morning, Mrs Atkins, good morning, Mr Jones,' Peter said as he came into the shop. Shopkeeper and customer replies were equally cordial.

'Susannah is just cutting up some bacon on the smaller slicer in the rear room, Peter. So what can I get for you?'

Peter looked along the display. 'Mum asked me to get four lamb chops and a few pork sausages, please.' After paying, and wishing both a good day, he was just about to leave the shop when Olivia spoke to him.

'Oh Peter, I don't suppose there was any post for me this morning was there?'

'There was a letter, Mrs Atkins. I don't think it was from Jack as it looked too official for that. I hope that was all right,' he added encouragingly. 'I must be off now. Thank you.'

Why Olivia felt a spasm of anxiety she did not know. Perhaps it was from Jack for sometimes letters were put in different envelopes after the censors had looked at them. She only had to wait a few moments before Susannah appeared with the wrapped bacon and she was on her way. She found herself hurrying and was glad she did not meet anyone who might hold her up. She pushed open the front door and immediately saw the letter: a buff-coloured envelope which certainly looked official. Now, with trembling fingers she ran her nail along the envelope seam and pulled out the single sheet.

From the War Office notifying the injury of:

(No) 204483   (Rank) *Private*

(Name)   *John Atkins*

(Regiment)   *2nd Battalion Suffolk Regiment*

Which occurred   *place not stated*

On the   *30th October 1914*

The report is to the effect that he is in a field hospital

You will be kept further informed

Olivia's world moved, the walls tilted and moved again. She half stumbled, then grasped the back of the nearby chair. She sank into it, read and reread again and again the brief communication. *Notifying the injury... in a field hospital.* But what injury? Was he still alive? And the letter... dated 30 October. A whole week ago; so what had happened since? She sat slumped, a shell of her normal self. 'Oh God, I don't want anyone to be hurt, no one to be killed... but not Jack. Please God, not Jack.' Her mind was numbed, her thoughts twisting the same few words round and round. The tears flowed, she wiped them away; she must do something, but what? Liz Smith. What was it she had said to Liz? 'Whenever you feel down you must always feel able to call on me – and I'll do the same.' She must find Liz; she must share this awful news with her. Clutching the letter, she stumbled to the open door, pulled herself upright and set out. There was no need to take the road to Liz's cottage as that way she might meet someone; she could not bear that thought, so she cut across the green. The bonfire from the previous evening's rather muted Guy Fawkes celebration still smouldered. Some had wanted to cancel the event, but Olivia had agreed with those who believed that the children should be given the few enjoyable things that were still possible. No one seemed to be around as she reached the row of cottages... thank goodness the heavily scratched green door of Liz's cottage was open. She knocked, but went straight in. Passing in to the back room there was

Liz, her right hand guiding the mangle round, piles of dried washing on the nearest table top, a basket of unwashed linen by the door.

Liz was suddenly aware of the movement; she saw Olivia and immediately stopped her activity. 'Olivia, what is it?' Before Olivia could speak her friend knew there was bad news; the tear-stained face, the grey pallor said it all. 'Oh Olivia,' she said as she threw her arms round her friend, embracing her for she knew not what; just love.

'Oh Liz. Jack's been hurt. It may be worse. I got this letter,' still grasping it even in the embrace.

It was Liz who now proved the strength in this friendship. 'Let me see, love. You sit down,' but Olivia stayed standing, rooted to the spot in the anguish of the moment. Liz wiped her damp sleeve across her sweating face, and stumbled through the meaning of the few words. 'I'm so sorry, but Olivia, it may not be too bad. Surely, if it was really bad news you would have heard by now. It may not be too serious.'

But Olivia, always a realist, would never have said words of such comfort when they were not certain, but she was grateful for them now. They were silent for a few moments; they held each other's hand. They talked lovingly of their sons for they shared the awful ache beyond which Olivia could see no hopeful sign. Yet, thirty minutes later when Olivia hugged Liz again and left the cottage, she knew that although anxious times lay immediately ahead, she must wait for further news.

Jack had always been one of the most well-liked young men in the village and the news of his injury and, worse still, how serious it might be, rapidly spread round Rusfield. Arthur, who was particularly anxious, was the first to call on Olivia; Eleanor and many other friends visited her in the next few days. The village waited with her.

To Olivia the following days were endless. Each morning found her waiting for Peter. He, like all in the village, knew that she waited for a further letter: to announce grief or relief. He willed that he might have such an encouraging letter in his postbag, but the weekend passed and the early days of the following week: still nothing. The belief that company was a solace became accepted and realised by Olivia as she waited. Eleanor, who was busy with autumn pruning in the vicarage garden on the Monday, was aware of more people calling in at the church than was normal; she knew why.

By the Wednesday Olivia was despairing of hearing any news, ever. It was the following day that Peter arrived in the village earlier than normal. He had been pedalling hard, changing the order of his round so that he started at the far end of the village. He carried not one letter for Olivia, but two: both in formal buff-coloured envelopes. He was no believer, but came closer to God on that bicycle ride than he had ever felt before, praying for the right content of the letters. Past the vicarage, the school, the schoolhouse and, as he slowed down, he was not surprised that Olivia was again cleaning her front-room windows. She turned as she heard the bicycle brakes applied and the slight sound of the tyres coming to a stop on the road.

'Good morning, Mrs Atkins. I have two letters for you. I hope they have good news for you.' He wanted to stay, he wanted to know what was in the letters, but he respected his role - just to deliver. He cycled off to undertake the rest of his round.

With shaking hands Olivia took the two letters, both in their formal covers. She pushed open the door, into the front room and sat down. She placed the one on her lap and then slit open the other which was written in a hand she did not recognise.

The document, in different writing to the envelope, was in a scribbled hand: *Dear Mrs Atkins, I spect you are woryd about Jack. He is all rite. I was with him wen the shell exploded and bits came everywere. One peece got stuck in Jacks sholder and anuther in his leg. He was unconshus and went to the hospital. I went to see him yesterday and he is all rite. He says he is going to rite to you soon. I am all rite to. Love from Fred.*

It was the most wonderful letter that Olivia had ever received. She knew Fred had recently written to Liz, but that was probably his first letter ever. His writing portrayed the effort, but it conveyed the most marvellous news of all: Jack was injured, but was all right.

She turned quickly to the second letter. It was a pre-printed form which allowed the writer to cross out some statements and write in others. But wonder of wonders it was signed by Jack. Dated four days ago it must have caught up with Fred's letter written a day or two previously. Olivia read: *I have been admitted into hospital and I am going on well. Proper letter to follow at first opportunity.* Then followed Jack's signature. Olivia felt light-headed with relief. She realised she was smiling: the first time for days. She found herself kissing both letters. She must go to tell Liz and then Arthur. Soon, the whole village rejoiced for mother and son, but the loved ones of thirty-eight other Rusfield men quietly trembled a little more, hoped and prayed.

THIRTY-ONE

January 1915

The driving snow was as daggers, piercing and ever reducing the temperature of their bodies. The whiteness covered everything and, as Abraham looked out, the war-torn landscape looked momentarily peaceful. The land near this village of Givenchy-lès-la-Bassée was flat. The few trees threw their arms into the air as if in desperation; the snow-filled dips in the landscape caused by the endless bombardment of shells barely showed.

In the trench it was mercilessly cold and though a welcome change from the incessant rain of late December, the cold numbed the mind. Whatever top was spread over the trench, the wind-driven snow found its way through and the boards along the bottom of the trenches had long since disappeared into the filthy mess created by the stomping feet of the freezing men.

26 January. Almost unaware of the endless days that stretched out with dates becoming meaningless, this was the one that Abraham could remember: his mother's birthday. He tried to focus on his family for a moment; a foreign place. It would be winter in Rusfield too, but hopefully all were safe there. He thought of the letters received just after Christmas, now safe in his tunic pocket. All had seemed to be well. Grace

197

had just finished at Wensfield for the Christmas holiday and her letter was warm, loving and had given him a huge lift. His parents were fine, although his mother's anxiety crept between the lines.

'You finished now then, Richards? You lucky bugger. Off to paradise for a bit.' Sergeant Frisk gave him a friendly push. The final one of the twelve-day stretch in the trench, but Abraham felt almost too numb to think about the four-mile move behind the lines. They had at least held the Germans up in their westward assault; now there was talk of an allied offensive. His mind turned back to the disaster a month earlier. He still could not believe that attempts had not been made to destroy the heavily barbed wired barriers before their advance. Wire-cutters and mattresses as a way of cutting through or scaling the German defences had been a total failure. Scarred deep into his mind was how he had been one to attempt an advance which had been easily held up by machine guns. All had been made worse by the unbelievably muddy fields which had reduced the fastest advance to a slow walk. The men were cut down as falling skittles. The fields of dead and horrendously wounded men would always be with him. How he had survived and got back, he would never know.

For the past twelve days, enemy bombardment had been spasmodic, though news had been carried along the lines that fifty men in a not too distant trench had received a direct hit and all had been killed or dreadfully wounded. The job for Abraham and the rest had been to stay put, to prevent any German advance and wait for the reinforcements. How often they had been told of new forces arriving; where did they get to?

Now to collect his few belongings, wait for the command and move back quickly, hoping the snow would keep falling to cover their movements. They had been told of a part-surviving barn a couple of hundred yards back where the men from the scattered trenches would assemble and then move back the four miles to a village. He had to move slowly along the ditch as there were men all the way; those replacing the ones about to leave had increased the numbers. All were trying to keep out of the yellow slime. Some had cut little shelves into the side where they could sit, though uncomfortably, at least keeping their feet a little drier. Abraham had smiled when it had been suggested to him by Evans that he should make an "arse-hole".

A few other men were already on the move. Jones, the voice from Rhondda, Wilson the joke teller, and Smithers who seemed unable to control his shaking limbs, yet had proved among the bravest when he stopped, stooped down and gathered up a wounded man. Abraham seemed to have known them all his life. The sergeant barked at them, yet at a strangely quietened level: 'Remember, keep your heads down, weave from side to side and run like hell to the barn. Richards, you lead the way, you're supposed to be able to move fast.' Up the few steps, out of the trench, strange clambering out from this side, wait a moment for the men behind and move, move. Even as they started out, the snow lessened: encouragement enough to hurry. A light covering made running easy, a snow-filled hole and they were into the white wilderness above their knees. Abraham hoped he was moving in the right direction. He had taken a bearing before leaving the trench and believed he was keeping a straight line, but the uneven terrain made calculations difficult.

He grimaced with relief as the outline of their targeted barn showed up. He could see two other lines of men coming in from the left. Into the black barn where men were packed, most cramming together under the part where the beamed roof strangely remained intact.

'We'll give it two minutes,' commanded the officer Abraham knew as Lieutenant Brownsmith, as he had often inspected the trench. Fresh faced and fair haired, he looked no more than twenty. Yet, thought Abraham, he seemed capable.

'If any group is not here in that time, they'll have to find their own way. We're a sitting target for any stray shell.'

They lined up ready to move off. Rifles, ammunition, grenades and a bevy of other necessary items were heavy, but the incentive was greater. Abraham found himself alongside Smithers, whose shaking seemed to have stopped. How he wished he was with his village mates. They had started in France together, but had then been placed with different groups. He had seen Willy just before the fiasco near Wytschaete, or Whitesheets as the men called it, and Jack and Fred shortly before that, but their hopes of remaining together had long been snatched away. After the first mile, the movement became a little slower as not all men were in great physical shape. Indeed, Abraham had been shocked when he first joined them to see how pale, thin and pinch-faced some looked.

Coming round a small wood, they were suddenly on a road: a crossroads and a large group of people; not military, but civilians. As Abraham passed this pitiful group of men, women and children, some with small carts either carrying babies or piled high with unknown goods, he realised they were refugees. Escaping from the ever-changing battle line, their worst fears had been realised as either German or British army had come in to their peaceful village. The innocents caught in a war of which they had no part. Army vehicles going eastwards drove round the refugees who were too weary to leave the road.

Ten more minutes and two farms were passed, then a growing number of cottages and a small market square. They had reached their "paradise", as Sergeant Frisk had called it. Hardly that, thought Abraham, but seemingly peaceful, even the guns which had started up again were less threatening. They may not be out of all danger, but the days here, five they were promised, would be something of an idyll.

The village, its name unknown by the exhausted men,

was virtually deserted. Its inhabitants, almost all employed on the land, had found their peace disturbed by the retreating German army in one of the few allied successes. Most had been forced out, but the few villagers who remained were pleased to see the British. In ones and twos, men were lodged with them, greater numbers in the few large buildings. The two administrative buildings, proud ones from affluent times, were taken over by much larger numbers; Abraham was one of these.

In the high, late nineteenth-century hall, clearly the place for public meetings, he found himself one of around a hundred men. Abraham, who was appalled to realise how filthy he was, queued patiently for one of the few washbasins; the water becoming immediately blackened. A partial quick strip was possible, but Abraham would have given much for a few minutes under his home-made shower back in Rusfield. Feeling a little better, he moved in to the adjacent room to eat. The food was most welcome, splendidly cooked meat for the first time for days, dry and hot. It was good. He was just getting up from his resting place when a familiar voice caused him to look up with startled joy. 'Why, it's Abraham, isn't it?'

And there stood his good friend, James, whom he had last seen in the summer of 1913 when Abraham had been running in London, but much better remembered as his host in Ealing the year earlier. For a few minutes rank was forgotten. 'James, my dear friend, how wonderful to see you. I won't ask you what you're doing here as it's probably much the same as me. How are you?'

'I'm fine,' replied James. 'Well, what a place to meet. I've only just arrived; indeed I only came over from England five days ago. It seems my platoon is being sent ahead to bolster those already there to hold up any German advance. But what about you?'

Abraham told his story, modestly making his last few months on French soil sound easy ones. He said nothing of the terrible dangers he had faced and little of the awful losses that had occurred. James would learn of that all too quickly. From talk of the present, they inevitably turned to past times shared. They had time to talk, clearly they would be in this temporary sanctuary until both were ordered to the front.

'So, how different to that time you came and stayed with us in Ealing. I've told so many people about that amazing weekend when you won at Stamford Bridge. Who could forget it?'

Abraham took on his usual embarrassed look and turned the conversation. 'Your parents were so kind in looking after Jack and me. You wouldn't know, but Jack was injured. After a while in hospital he was sent home to Rusfield and later returned to France. I don't know where he is now.'

'Surprise for you, Abraham. But I did know. Indeed I probably know more than you.'

'But how's that?' asked the puzzled Abraham. 'I know about his injuries and recovery, because both Grace and mother told me about that in letters. But you?'

'Ah,' smiled his friend. 'Put it all down to my sister. I don't know if you realised that after your visit to us in Ealing, Patricia and Jack corresponded about their shared interest in Blondin, the trapeze artist, but letters became more frequent and Patricia was often mooning over Jack. Several times they had hoped to meet up, but father thought she was rather young for that and, in any case, Ealing and Rusfield aren't exactly next to each other.'

'So what happened then?'

'Well, Jack's mother knew all about the fondness that had developed between them, and when Jack was injured, she wrote to Patricia albeit that she waited until she knew Jack would recover. She must be a special kind of lady.'

'She is, indeed,' agreed Abraham, rejoicing in news of his great friend.

'Well, mother and Patricia made the journey to Rusfield.

They stayed with your vicar, the Reverend and Mrs Windle, is that right?' Abraham nodded. 'They stayed there for three days and, of course, Jack and Patricia spent a lot of time together. When I was home on leave from training in Yorkshire, mother told me how everyone in Rusfield had been so kind. She wrote recently that Patricia was hugely upset when she recently learnt that Jack has been sent back here. But I suppose everyone back home is the same when that happens?'

They talked deep into the night. Two young men moved from the peace of England into this embattled France, but for a short while transported to more peaceful times. But both knew that this was something of a fantasy; that soon they would be at war again.

THIRTY-TWO

January- April 1915

It was a cold January in Rusfield too, but the icy dagger that cut deepest into the villagers was not of the weather, but news of a death in Flanders.

Sparky Carey sometimes drank at The Queens Head, as his credit at The George occasionally ran short. He had stomped through the ankle-deep snow along Pond Street to the best managed of the three drinking houses in the village and was not surprised to find George Edwards to be the sole drinker. Served with his favourite ale, Sparky sat next to his fellow villager who was sensibly close to the fire. 'Spose you've heard the bad news?' began George, putting his drink down on the adjacent table.

'What's that then?' asked Sparky, anxious to sip his first pint.

'Well, Rachel was just telling me that young Charlie Chambers has been killed.' He saw that Sparky looked momentarily puzzled. 'You remember, he was always known as Copper. The Chambers lived in Sandy Lane; always a bad couple.'

'Oh yes, I remember. The parents knocked their children about; young Copper and his sister, Louise. A nice lad was Copper, a friend of our son; a good footballer though it looked as if a breath of wind could blow 'im over. So what happened?'

'Well, I'd forgotten that Rachel here,' the landlady had joined the two drinkers, 'is a cousin of Susannah Chambers.'

'A cousin, but not a friend,' interrupted the mildly flirtatious Rachel Fielding. 'Couldn't abide her, she was so unkind to her kids and her husband was even worse. I was glad when they left the village and only heard a bit about them from time to time.'

George seemed mildly disgruntled that the telling of the news had been taken out of his hands; chipping in as soon as he could. 'Well, Rachel was saying that the kids moved to London.' With the inside of her angled arm the landlady had a way of gently easing up her ample bosom; it was one of several attractions to The Queens Head.

'And,' interrupted Rachel, 'I heard from Louise from time to time. This morning I got a letter from her telling me that Charlie was dead. Seems he was in that place called Flanders; terrible thing this war.'

The two drinkers nodded sagely. So the first person from the village was dead. Sparky knew James would be upset, indeed, so was he for he remembered this lad who went through life protecting his young sister. 'And, I'm afraid,' said George breaking the long pause in conversation, 'he won't be the last. We know that Jack Atkins came close to losing his life, so who next?'

They only had a week until further bad news reached the village.

Peter Woods was thrilled. In the emergency that gripped the postal services there was an immediate shortage of deliverers to outlying parts around Steepleton. The telegraph office was next to the post office where Peter reported each morning, but he was as surprised, as he was pleased, when asked to deliver telegrams as well as the post. He readily agreed to the two conditions: that telegrams be given priority and that these along with urgent letters might well need delivering at times other than during his normal round. A friend asked him why he was doing this and Peter found it hard to explain; he just felt he owed it to the people in Rusfield.

He had pedalled furiously out of Steepleton and made fast time to Rusfield. Small patches of snow remained in the protection of hedges, but the road was clear as he bicycled toward the village for the second time on this Wednesday in early February. He had picked up four letters that had come in too late for his morning delivery, but it was the buff envelope, heavily marked "Immediate delivery", that was his main mission. He knew that military deaths and injuries were sometimes conveyed in letters, sometimes by telegram. The one addressed to Mrs R. Rowe was an urgent letter.

By now he knew most of the villagers. Old Mrs Rowe, whose husband Peter had never known, lived in Sandy Lane. He knew that her two sons, Ernest and Aubrey, had joined up a few months earlier; this letter was to Ernest's wife, Ruby, in Meadow Way. Turning into Bury Way, he was spotted by Arthur Windle who knew there could only be one reason for Peter passing through the village in the early afternoon. Into Meadow Way, Peter passed Miss Rushton's shop and then pulled up at the second cottage. The orders from the post and telegram office were clear: in the case of an urgent communication, he must knock.

Knock he did. This was the part of his work he hated, yet he had a strong feeling that it was something in the war effort which he could do. He was relieved that it was Mrs Florence Rowe who answered the door. As soon as she saw Peter, she paled.

'Yes, Peter?' she asked with trembling voice.

'I have a letter for the other Mrs Rowe.' He handed it over. Her look and weak voice only partly disguised her response; Peter could only guess. She quickly shut the door. He remounted his bicycle and rode back round the green; his thoughts dwelling on the scene inside the house. What news, what sadness?

As he turned into Pond Street he saw the Reverend Arthur Windle standing in front of the vicarage and he pulled to a halt. 'Peter, I imagine you were delivering a letter of the kind that no one wants to receive. I don't know whether you feel able to tell me to whom it was addressed?'

Peter considered for a moment, but he could not imagine any reason why not. The Reverend Windle was a fine man, a kind man whose reason for wanting to know could only be a good one.

'Sir, it was for Mrs Rowe, the Mrs Rowe who lives in Meadow Way.' Arthur nodded.

'Peter, I have a high regard for you and what you do. I know it's not an easy job and you clearly care about people. We are all in the midst of very sad times and there's not much any of us can do, but sometimes it may help if I know who needs support: from me, from my wife, relatives or friends in the village. None of us wants to interfere, just to help in these bad times. Do you understand what I'm saying, Peter?'

Peter did. 'Yes sir. I want to help as much as I can.'

'Well,' replied Arthur, 'if you have any of these terrible letters or telegrams to deliver in the village, it may help if I know as soon as possible. I leave it with you to think about.'

As Arthur went back into the warmth of his house, he wondered if he was right. Was he guilty of prying into matters that were not his concern? He had thought long before speaking to Peter Woods; Eleanor had voiced her gentle support for what her husband intended. 'You may be able to help Arthur. I know you are only doing it for the right reasons.'

By the next day, the news of Private Ernest Rowe's death in Flanders was known throughout the village. He, like Copper Chambers, had grown up in the village and been to the school. That the most recent death was of a man whose home was still in the village, brought an added thrust; leaving a widow and a month-old son a still deeper grief.

Arthur Windle knew he had been largely responsible for supporting the war effort by organising the meeting addressed by Sir Humphrey; if that had not happened, would poor Ruby Rowe now be grieving and her young son fatherless?

As the winter was gently transformed into an early spring, more bad news followed: three men wounded. When Tommy Bruce returned home to recover from a fractured ankle, his parents and friends were surprised that he was loathe to tell them about his time in France, dismissing questions with the words: 'Not much. You just get on with things.' His parents were further surprised that he appeared anxious to get back to the war, whilst Tommy just pondered on his feeling of guilt at leaving his mates to carry on while he was back home.

'The trouble,' Arthur Windle commented to Eleanor over the breakfast table, 'is that amid all the bad news everyone wants to support the young men and the whole war effort, but there doesn't seem anything we can do to help.'

Whether an answer to a prayer or simple coincidence, Eleanor felt the latter, a response came the next day – and from an unexpected source, indeed, from two.

Neither Violet Rushton nor Robert Berry had ever been to the vicarage, but mid-morning both appeared on the doorstep. It was Eleanor who answered the knock. 'Sorry to disturb you ma'am,' said the usually reclusive Robert Berry, 'but we wondered if we could speak with the Vicar for a few minutes?'

He looked mildly embarrassed, yet determined. Violet Rushton just smiled, adding, 'And you too, of course, Eleanor.'

Eleanor, surprised, even puzzled, was quick to respond. 'Of course, come in. Arthur is in his study, I'll give him a call.' She led them into the light, restful lounge and beckoned them to sit. Violet Rushton sat on the edge of an upright leather armchair, her colleague remained standing.

A few minutes later Arthur appeared. After warm greetings, the four sat. 'Now, how can I help?' asked Arthur turning to the unexpected duo. 'Please.' The two looked at each other and, surprisingly to Arthur, it was Robert Berry who spoke. He was usually to be found in his large garden, although Arthur had noted his occasional attendance at St Mary's when prayers and meditations were announced for the men abroad.

'Well, Miss Rushton and I have been talking. I called in at her shop a month or so ago and we got to talking about how we could help the men who are away. It wasn't too long after quite a lot of people had sent parcels to their men and Miss Rushton here got to saying that it was a shame if that only happened at Christmas. Maybe the rest of us could do something. Anyway, Miss Rushton came round to my house last week and we talked things through a bit. We thought we might be able to help.'

Arthur's interest was certainly aroused at his unexpected visitor's enthusiasm for an idea that obviously mattered to him. Eleanor smiled and murmured her encouragement. Looking at Violet Rushton, Eleanor did not want her left out of the conversation. 'So, Violet, please tell us your thoughts.'

'Well, as Mr Berry said, we got talking about the Christmas parcels and we thought why not organise the sending of parcels, food, cigarettes and a few warm things on a more regular basis? Why not encourage everyone in the village to contribute? We could all give something. How many men are there from the village that are away fighting now, Vicar?'

'When I looked at the list in the porch on Monday it was fifty-one, but it's growing all the time.'

'Well, we could try to send a parcel to everyone, say, once every three months. We could ask people to give what they can, it needn't cost a lot of money as some could sew or knit things. I've got my store at the back of the shop and can make space for things to be kept there, so people could bring things along at any time. Then, when the time comes round we could find people to make up the parcels ready to send.'

'It certainly sounds a wonderful idea,' Arthur enthusiastically replied. 'I know how much the men welcomed their Christmas parcels.'

'I also think,' added Eleanor, 'it's about them knowing they are in people's minds. It must be terribly lonely as well as dangerous wherever they are and just to know that people are thinking about them probably means a lot.'

'I'm sure that's true,' interjected Robert Berry, 'but there's something else we need to remember. The families of some of the men are very poor; I was talking to one lady whose son is in France, and she happened to say how difficult things had been made worse, since a soldier's pay isn't very much and little came her way. Some can't afford parcels on their own.'

Eleanor wondered whether their visitor, whose thoughtfulness was revealing a caring side of which she had not been aware, was thinking of Liz Smith who scraped together a living by hard laundry work and must miss Fred's earnings at the smithy.

The four went on gathering ideas and were surprised when they heard the hall clock strike twelve. They could all see the idea becoming a growing activity in the village, although just how much, they could not have imagined.

As the couple left the vicarage after warm goodbyes, Arthur turned to his wife. 'I'm not surprised at Violet Rushton, she has always seemed a caring person, but I wouldn't easily have placed Robert Berry in the same mould. I know some find him not only reclusive, but rather brusque.'

'Ah, Arthur. You've seen how he always has the Union Jack flying in his garden and we've heard he served in the army. Obviously, he has a great feeling for our men overseas; knows what that must be like and wants to do something practical about it. Bless them both.'

THIRTY-THREE

Saturday, 10 April 1915

The excitement opposite the pond was reminiscent of the time, five months earlier, when the children had been allowed to mount the soldiers' horses. 'It's as well it's a Saturday,' remarked Gwendolyn Edwards to Rachel Fielding from The Queens Head. 'The children would hate to miss this.'

The source of excitement was a red and green omnibus parked in the gravelled area between John Francis' shop and Gwendolyn's cottage. It was only half past eight on this grey April morning, but a crowd had already gathered. Twelve-year-old Lily Reynolds had been the first to spot it, when at first light she had been up as it was her birthday. Now there were at least thirty gathered round the impressive, shining omnibus, hooded but open-sided. Rachel Fielding had often wondered how her smartly dressed neighbour, John Francis, made a living from his shop. There never seemed much to buy there with few customers although some went into his back room where he doubled up as a barber.

When he had been in The Queens Head a week earlier and told Rachel how he had bought a bus and was going to provide a regular service to Steepleton, she thought the drinks she had served him had whetted his well-known ability to exaggerate. She realised now that he must have driven it into his large

211

barn running alongside his shop several days previously; she had seen him bustling between cottage and barn on several recent occasions; often wearing overalls. It was also Lily who had first spotted the name on this brightly painted vehicle: "The Rusfield Rocket".

'So what are you planning, John?' asked the elderly Joe Bacon from the forge opposite. 'It looks very smart and somehow you've managed to keep it a secret.'

'Ay,' replied the robust, proud owner of the village's first omnibus. 'It's time folks were able to get in to Steepleton without having to walk or bicycle. I plan to drive in every morning, except Sundays, and return about two hours later. I may think about an afternoon run as well. Anyway, I'm going in on an introductory ride at eleven o'clock this morning. I can take twenty-one passengers so we'll see who wants to go.'

Children rushed home to ask parents to take them into town and plans for the morning were changed. There would be no shortage of passengers.

Arthur and Eleanor quickly heard about "The Rusfield Rocket" when an animated Eliza Carey came in to do a morning's cleaning. She could hardly contain her excitement. 'Won't it be wonderful if we can easily get into Steepleton?'

'Indeed it will,' smiled Eleanor. 'We must be one of the few villages where there isn't easy transport, so what Mr Francis is promising is excellent news.'

Arthur had heard his wife talking and came into the kitchen to see who had called; he had forgotten it might be Eliza. 'Good morning Eliza.' He turned to his wife, 'I heard you mention John Francis' name, is he all right?' He was quickly brought up to date with the news by the excited Eliza.

'That is excellent,' he smiled, 'I wish the new "Rusfield Rocket" every success. It's long been needed and since the county authority gave us a proper road into Steepleton last year, it really is about time.'

'And,' added Eleanor, 'it's time we had some good news.

Nurse Hazlett told me yesterday that over twenty children now have measles and young George Jones is really quite ill.' She turned to Eliza, 'Will you please help me with putting up the curtains in the guest bedroom? I've been meaning to do the job for the last few days.'

'And I must take another look at my sermon for tomorrow,' interjected Arthur.

But neither replacing the bedroom curtains nor the next day's sermon were to be completed on that day. The knock at the door took both Arthur and Eleanor through the hall.

'Peter, how are you?' Eleanor smiled her greeting to the young man, who was becoming an increasingly important figure in the village; regrettably, sometimes for heartbreaking reasons.

Arthur saw the young man bearing a telegram. 'Oh Peter, more bad news! Who are you taking this telegram to?'

'It's for you, sir.'

'Oh, I see. Well thank you; perhaps an urgent note from the bishop.'

'Goodbye, Peter. Go carefully,' added Eleanor, realising how much Arthur wondered at the telegram's content. She closed the door.

Arthur hurriedly opened the telegram: *Your father is ill. Please come urgently. Love Mother.*

He passed it to Eleanor. 'Arthur, I'm sorry,' offered Eleanor, putting her arm round her husband. 'We know he's not been well for a while and clearly your mother wouldn't have sent this unless it's really urgent. We must get down to Dorset as soon as possible.'

'Indeed,' agreed Arthur. 'Poor mother, she will be so worried. There will be regular trains today, but tomorrow will be much harder; Sunday ones are few and far between. I'll have to get word to Fred Richards and he'll make the best arrangements he can for tomorrow's service. Maybe he can get the Reverend Herbert Mainwaring in from Steepleton. I'm so fortunate having Fred as a churchwarden.'

'And while you're dealing with that I'll have a word with Eliza and see if Sparky can conjure up some transport to take us to the station.' She smiled and gave Arthur a gentle kiss. 'I don't think the "Rusfield Rocket" would be a good idea on this occasion; we don't want everyone to know and add their well-meaning words before we set out.'

Arthur nodded. As Eleanor left to seek out Eliza, he went into his study and took down the green Bradshaw railway guide. There were two trains that could get them to Sherborne and it should not be too difficult to find a cab to take them the further three miles to his parents' house. He hurried along to the Richards' cottage.

'I'm so sorry,' sympathised the kindly churchwarden. 'You must get away as quickly as you can. I'll get word to the Reverend Mainwaring and I'm sure he will help out if he can. In any case we shall manage and I know everyone will be thinking of you and your family. Just leave it to me.'

The thought went through Arthur's mind of how much he was reminded of Abraham when talking with Fred Richards, his father. By the time he got back to the vicarage, Eleanor was busy packing. 'Sparky will be round here in half an hour. I think we need to take enough clothes for several days.'

Sparky, resourceful as ever, got them to Steepleton in good time with only a thirty minute wait for a train into London and they then made good time to Waterloo station. They were amazed at the vast crowds of soldiers, many with tearful loved ones; whether greeting or bidding farewell was hard to know. The awful thought went through Arthur's mind and, as likely as not through Eleanor's, as to how many of the young men soon to cross the Channel, would never return. How many would soon have their lives completely changed?

There followed an hour's wait and the two and a half hour journey to Sherborne. By the time they alighted at that station, the light had faded and a slight drizzle was falling.

'Good evening sir, madam, are you looking for a cab?'

Arthur was delighted, spoke his thanks and gave his parents' address. The driver set out on the Yeovil road, turning off after a mile to the small village where Charlotte and Colonel Hector Windle had lived since his retirement ten years previously. Wrapped in their thoughts, neither paid much attention to the journey and within twenty minutes the cab pulled up outside the eighteenth-century former farmhouse with its five acres of well-tended garden and woodland. The driver took the two cases along the cobbled drive and Arthur, having thanked and paid him, knocked at the door.

Within a few moments the door opened to reveal Charlotte Windle, as always elegantly dressed. 'Oh Arthur, how wonderful to see you.' She threw her arms round him. 'And Eleanor, how kind of you to come so quickly. Come in. It's warmest in the kitchen. I didn't dare dream of you coming today.' Her close embrace of Eleanor expressed as much warmth as to her son. They followed her into the much warmer and well-lit kitchen. Charlotte, her gaunt face breaking into a smile which Arthur knew and loved so well, stepped forward and, in turn, kissed both he and Eleanor. 'Oh, thank you for coming. Arthur, your father is very ill, sometimes barely conscious in between his long spells of sleep.'

The three sat in comfortable, well-worn chairs arranged around the open fire. 'So, Mother; tell us about father and then perhaps I can go up to see him.'

'As you know, he has not been well for many months, suffering from a shortage of breath and becoming increasingly tired. He hated that because he has been so vigorous all his life. Doctor Randall told me your father is suffering from a cardiovascular disease; I remember his own father's death and wonder if the problem is hereditary. As I told you in one of my letters, just before Christmas the doctor prescribed tablets, but told me that your father's heart was failing.' She momentarily paused in describing the deterioration in her husband's health. 'Two weeks ago, he had a particularly bad night and when Doctor Randall came in the next day he told me there was really nothing more he could do, his heart was rapidly failing. Doctor Randall arranged for me to have a nurse call twice a day and she is very supportive. Your father seems to drift in and out of consciousness, although I'm not always sure whether it is more a case of drowsiness.'

Arthur stood up, walked the few steps to his mother, leant down and lovingly placed an arm round her. 'I'm sure you are doing everything possible and if pain can be kept at bay that's the main thing. Eleanor and I can stay here as long as you like; we just hope that will help.'

'Of course it will; bless you both for coming. I suppose this is the time that everyone has to face. Now would you like to go up to see him; he's in the main bedroom. You must both be starving,' and turning to Eleanor, added: 'perhaps you would kindly help me get something simple to eat?' Eleanor willingly agreed, feeling that Arthur should see his father alone. She realised how distressed her mother-in-law was in telling them about her husband's illness, but could not help noticing a slight remoteness in her words. Thinking back over the years, Eleanor could not remember Colonel Windle always being referred to as "your father"; surely Arthur's mother used to slip a pet name in from time to time?

Twenty minutes later, Arthur came back into the kitchen with a worried expression. 'I sat with father, just holding his hand. We spoke only very briefly, but he knew I was there.' He turned to his mother: 'Father asked me if you had told me something and I said that you had described how poorly he was. I wasn't sure he understood. Then he drifted back to sleep.'

Eleanor was the first to realise that Arthur's mother was crying, silently but with shoulders shuddering. She went over to Charlotte whom she had always loved and put her arm round her. 'There's really nothing that I can say that's of much comfort, but know that Arthur and I care for you deeply and will do anything and everything we can at this sad time.'

Charlotte looked up, took a lace handkerchief from out of the sleeve of her green dress and wiped her eyes. 'Thank you, dear. I know you mean that and I really appreciate it.' She turned to face her son, 'Arthur. It was not your father who failed to understand what you said; rather that you didn't understand what he was saying. He asked you if I had told you about something; that's what is troubling him.' She sighed and stemmed her tears. 'You must both be very tired so we should all have this little supper and go to bed. But there is something that I have promised your father, albeit with some reluctance, to tell you. It's complicated and something that I shall find hard to say, but I promised him. Furthermore it's something that I feel you should know, but let us leave it until the morning.'

Arthur realised his mother was determined not to divulge anything further that night. Soon they kissed each other goodnight, Eleanor insisting that she be called if there were any worries in the night. Both she and Arthur wondered what it was that Charlotte Windle would tell them in the morning.

THIRTY-FOUR

Sunday, 11 April 1915

Apart from the rain lashing against their bedroom window, Arthur and Eleanor heard no sound during the night. No one slept well and by a quarter to eight the threesome were sitting down to a breakfast for which they had no real appetite.

'So what time does the nurse come in?' asked Arthur.

'Well, as it's Sunday she will come in just once today, probably within the next half-hour.'

There was tacit agreement that they wait until her departure before Charlotte Windle revealed what she had promised her husband. Arthur was relieved when Nurse Higgins left just before nine o'clock, having performed her duties in an efficient manner. They busied themselves clearing away the breakfast table, their minds on other things. After talking about her garden, Arthur's mother turned as the last plate was put away.

'My dears, hard though it is, it's time for me to tell you what I have promised your father. Shall we stay in here or go through to the lounge?'

'Let's stay in here, Mother. It's warm and comfortable.'

'What I have to say is by far the most disagreeable thing of which I have ever spoken. I would be reluctant to break my promise to your father, Arthur, but that I would do if I didn't feel you deserved to know the truth. You are a wonderful son and deserve to know this part of our family history, awful though it is. Whilst telling you I shall probably break down, but please don't worry or say anything. Simply let me get this out of the way although I realise that for both of you, things will never be quite the same again.'

Eleanor and Arthur acknowledged that they had been asked not to interrupt, so they simply smiled their encouragement. Charlotte went across to a kitchen drawer and extracted a green folder. 'This contains the full story. Arthur, I leave you to decide how much of it you pass on to dear Eleanor although having seen you so close for six years or more I can guess the answer to that.' She clasped the folder tightly, resting it on her lap. 'This contains the full and awful facts that I'm passing to you; I think it best you read it privately. However, I must first explain how this came into existence.' Eleanor noticed the tremble in her voice, a tear appear and a slight movement of the shoulders which prefaced a determined effort to continue.

'The whole saga goes back many, many years and I'm still not sure why your father told me what had been a secret with him for nearly forty years. When I asked him, he said that he did not want to die without telling me. I think it was more that he had begun to feel poorly at that time and did not want to die without forgiveness. It was only when he realised he was confronted with the inevitability of dying that his conscience got the better of him. I wish he had never told me; that I had been allowed to die in ignorance. If he was hoping for my forgiveness I have never been able to bring myself to grant that. Arthur, maybe you can help me to know how to forgive, I would love that. But let me continue.

'You may remember that we came up to Rusfield three years ago. As always it was lovely to share that Easter in your friendly village, but in other ways it was an awful time. You see, it was about two months before coming to see you that your father had first felt unwell and the doctor had hinted at a heart problem.'

Eleanor thought back to that visit and recalled how she had felt a distance, a gulf between Arthur's parents.

'I didn't want to worry you with the news of his heart condition, and certainly couldn't bring myself to tell you what I had so recently heard, although at first he only told me half the story. Whatever his reason for telling me, it was about what happened only a few years after we were married, when you were just a young boy. Arthur, you and I, friends, army colleagues and many others know the event of forty years ago when as a young officer your father was the only one to escape from a group of ferocious natives in a village in the Gold Coast.'

She paused; clearly this was a moment about which she had warned her listeners. Both Arthur and Eleanor wanted to comfort her, but again refrained from interrupting.

'In a few words, what we have believed for forty years was so far short of the truth that in reality it was the most awful lie any of us could ever hear. Yes, some of the story was true, but the part missed out is what I find unforgiveable. You must be wondering why and how things are recorded in this folder. Well, his experience made him aware of army bureaucracy and he knew some record would have been made of what happened on that day in January 1874. Whilst he had retired from the army, he still had important connections and made a visit to Aldershot. The record office there made available the report he had in mind. In fact, this was a record of the story he had told after he recovered from his injuries; with the additional record of the army officer who had found him when he had collapsed. Indeed, that captain was leading a small number of men to carry a message to your father when they came across him. If that had not happened your father would not have survived.

'Copies of your father's report and the brief notes of that captain are in this folder. What surprised, indeed really frightened your father was a third document. I don't know all the details of what was happening over forty years ago in that part of Africa, but I do know that there was a war going on with the Ashanti people; it was an important possession of the British. As always, lots of innocent people suffered, but a few months later peace treaties were signed between the Ashanti and the British. Some of the terms imposed by the British were harsh, but they conceded a few fairly unimportant points. One of these was that the British would deal with any of their officers who had needlessly brought suffering to the local people. Some kind of tribunal was set up in Accra and local witnesses made statements. One of these concerned your father and a copy of it is in this folder. Of course, the British had no intention of acting on the tribunal findings and I doubt if anything was done other than record witness statements.

'It's a statement signed by two tribesmen that reveal the events that were kept hidden from us; it's what your father eventually told me about. He admitted it was all true. I still can't really understand why he told me everything so many years later. Do you think it might have been his conscience, Arthur?'

Arthur was clearly thinking hard what to say and Eleanor was glad he offered no quick answer. What, indeed, could he say?

'Mother, of course what Eleanor and I have heard from you is distressing. We don't yet know what happened, but it is clearly something that has had a terrible effect upon you. It sounds likely that the events have been on father's mind for years, so perhaps it is about a feeling of guilt. Maybe he does not want to die with a secret still on his conscience. I don't know. Let me read the documents and, perhaps, we can all share in knowing what we should do.' He got up, walked two short paces to his mother, bent down and kissed her. The tears were streaming down her face.

It was Eleanor who spoke. 'I hope you won't think I'm interfering in something between both of you, but as Arthur said, I am so sorry that you are being caused so much grief. Why don't you and I go and look round your lovely garden? This will give Arthur time to read everything. How does that sound?'

Eleanor's suggestion was immediately accepted; Charlotte kissed Arthur and arm in arm with her daughter-in-law walked from the kitchen through the conservatory and into the garden.

As Arthur lifted up the flap of the folder he wondered just what he would find. Yes, three separate documents, none more than a few pages. He flattened out the one entitled: *In the words of Lieutenant Hector Richard Windle: 30th March 1874.* The names of the two recorders of the statement and a further witness were given along with name of regiment, previous service and other military details.

On 31st December 1873 I was stationed near Bekwai along with a large contingent of troops recently transported from London. At a briefing I learnt that 2,500 of our men together with several thousand West Indian and African troops were to advance towards Kumasi, the Ashanti stronghold. There were also smaller habitations where law and order was to be brought to bear, hopefully by peaceful means. I was in the force to move eastwards and deal with some small villages.

After a two day march we set up camp by a river. Major Flatman formed us into five groups, each to deal with specific villages. It was the first time I had led men on such an important mission.

The first settlement was peaceful. It was then a long march mainly through forest, although later we crossed a large area which had been cleared and previously farmed. One of the guides had spoken of Akrowbi as a primitive village occupied by two hundred natives. At around 11.00 hours on 6th January 1874 we were on a slight rise from which we could see smoke; I assumed this to be Akrowbi.

We advanced until we were close. In an open area cut into the jungle I could see a number of crude huts with around sixty natives including women and children. We must have been seen, because suddenly a spear plunged into the ground just in front of us. My guide told me this was the way the natives would indicate we had been seen, that now we should go forward and speak with the village leader. I ordered my sergeant and two men to accompany me as I went forward, the rest giving us cover. The chieftain came forward and raised his hand, but then everything changed. Two of the men with me fell, I could see the spears in their bodies; there was a great commotion as a horde of natives descended upon the men who were giving cover. I raced to the nearest trees to find myself with my sergeant and one other. We opened fire, but the numbers against us were overwhelming. My sergeant fell and I retreated. Only then did I realise I was wounded, blood was flowing freely from my upper arm. All I could see were bodies of men and some natives going from one wounded soldier to another and spearing them. I could barely lift my gun, so opposition was impossible.

I waited through that day but could see none of my men, I am sure they must all have been killed. That night I moved away from the village in the direction that we had advanced. My arm was increasingly painful and I had difficulty in walking. I have only a vague memory of the time from then until finding myself in hospital. I believe that was the middle of February.

This is an honest statement which I give freely and willingly.

Arthur sat back and placed the document alongside the others. Yes, this was what he knew of his father over forty years ago, a story he had learnt when a child. A story that had made him proud and, he thought now, revere his father. So what of the other documents? He picked up the second one, much briefer: a statement by Captain Bertram Oliver Pickering dated 20 January 1874. Arthur realised this second document was recorded just under a week after his father had been brought back severely injured:

On the 10th January I was ordered by Major Greensmith to convey messages to two groups that had not returned, including that of Lieutenant Windle. We were to provide any necessary backup.

I organised 20 men and with 3 guides and carriers we set out, a march of five days.

It was very hot and regular rests were necessary. After much forest we came to a cleared area probably by natives for farming. It was barren with just tree stumps and rocks. I ordered a ten minute break.

My sergeant suddenly pointed to a bird flying low. Probably a quarter mile away. It landed on a tree stump and as I looked I saw a slight movement nearby.

With two men I went to investigate. I realised it was a wounded soldier, unconscious but still breathing.

We poured water over him; there was little else we could immediately do.

In relays we conveyed him back to base, arriving on 20th January. He was admitted to hospital.

It was later I learnt this was Lieutenant Windle.

This confirmed the story Arthur knew so well, there was nothing that should have caused his mother undue distress so many years after the event. He picked up the third document dated 19 September 1874, with names of recorders, a witness to the proceedings and the two members of the Ashanti people who gave evidence. It was clearly a combination of what the two had said but in the translator's words.

Our village is Akrowbi. The people are good and peaceful. Many of our men were away hunting. Women were repairing two huts. We were skinning animals. Suddenly we saw many soldiers. Their guns were pointing at us. Three of the soldiers, one with white hair was their chief, came forward. Kwaku our chief went to greet them. Two of our young men went with him. As they got nearer, the young men raised their spears in greeting, but suddenly the white haired soldier shouted. The guns made big noises and the three men all fell. The guns went on firing and many were killed. The women and children ran into their huts. We hid. We watched the white haired chieftain give orders. He and other soldiers took the branches for repairing the hut roofs, held them in the fire and set the huts alight. As the children and women came out to escape the fires the soldiers shot them. There was much screaming and fire. One of the huts near the edge set fire to some nearby trees, it was the dry season. All the people except the soldiers and the two of us were dead. We were very frightened, we should have tried to stop it but just watched. The fire had been seen by our many men who were hunting. The soldiers were resting and later there was sudden noise as our men came out of the trees and attacked the soldiers. There was very much fighting and many were killed. Soon most were dead. We saw the white haired chieftain and one other run into the trees. They were chased by Yoofi. We do not know what happened to them.

We stayed hidden and later searched. Soldiers and our people were all dead except two young children who were injured. We each picked one up and carried them to another village a long way. There was much smoke and some trees were burning. After a long time we got to the village.

Horror at the enormity of what he had read descended upon Arthur. How much had the interpreter and the recorder fairly translated the witnesses' stories into a record? Yet his

225

mother said that his father admitted to everything in the document. Across the bottom of the third page were written three comments in a different hand, the writing clear, but the signature indecipherable. This addition to the report was dated 10 November 1874. Anxiously, Arthur tried to understand these comments:

> Captain Windle indicated it was totally untrue and was to deflect attention from the natives' barbaric behaviour.
> No further action to be taken.
> File.

Arthur involuntarily dropped the document alongside the others. This was a terrible nightmare. It may have been forty years ago, but Arthur could see it happening: the screaming children and women, the pointless killing, the burning. On the first occasion that his father had led men on such a mission, had he panicked? That seemed to have started the senseless slaughter. He felt sick, the sickness turned to anger. Anger at what his father had done, anger at how he was now causing misery to his wife, how he had built his life, his army career on such a terrible lie. How could anyone talk of forgiveness?

Where was God in all this? What did God tell him about forgiveness; was it for him to forgive and what of his mother? He waited and prayed, but could hear nothing. Each of his forty-seven years had been torn away. Yet he still believed there was a God, somewhere. 'Oh God, help my unbelief. Bring comfort to my mother. I know it is alone for you to forgive, yet help me to forgive my father for all the years of this secret. You alone know that I, too, am guilty of sinning.'

Arthur turned as the door opened. Eleanor was shocked at her husband's face; she could see misery and despair. He stood and went towards his mother. They flung their arms round each other and cried. Eleanor had never seen her beloved Arthur in such a distressed state even though he had borne so much sad news in his life and she shuddered at what she still had to learn. A sense of great pain lay upon the house. A little later, Eleanor read the papers and shared the pain with the others; no words could be found to speak their thoughts.

An hour later, Arthur went upstairs. His father, his hair sparse and white, was asleep. How could this old, dying man have carried out such an atrocity over forty years ago? How much grief had he caused his wife since telling her; did he really believe that confessing to her would remove his guilt? Arthur sat on a small chair in the corner of the bedroom. His head sank into his hands.

He just did not know how to comfort his beloved mother. As he paused in the hope that God would speak to him, some other words from a confessional prayer came to him: 'Almighty God, to whom all hearts are open, all desires known and from whom no secrets are hidden'. Perhaps God had always known of his father's dreadful act and had forgiven him. But what of his own secrets, was he not as guilty as his father; surely everyone has secrets?

Later that day Arthur's mother quietly fed her husband some warm soup, but he could manage only a little. Arthur and Eleanor sat with her. The next day the doctor visited Colonel Windle; he had now fallen into a deep sleep from which he could not be roused. That night he died.

THIRTY-FIVE

April 1915

News of the death of the vicar's father reached Rusfield through Arthur's letter to Frederick Richards, who had enabled St Mary's to continue with minimum disruption. Whether through age, illness or war, death brought a united sympathy from the villagers.

Charlotte Windle clearly needed time away from all the unhappiness of her home. The funeral took place in the small village church four days after Colonel Windle died; the large gathering of friends swollen by many army dignitaries. One of his father's contemporaries had sought Arthur out and offered to render a eulogy, but Arthur, knowing full well what would be said, graciously declined.

Eleanor and Arthur were worried about Charlotte's health; she was dreadfully pale and listless, so unlike her normal self. The day after the funeral, the old farmhouse was closed down and accompanied by six cases, Eleanor, Arthur and his mother left the house. After all that had happened, the Rusfield vicarage was wonderfully welcoming. On the hall table were many cards of sympathy and the rooms were full of flowers. Eliza Carey had received much help from Olivia Atkins in preparing for their homecoming.

For Robert Berry and Violet Rushton, the vicar's departure

to Dorset had created a dilemma. 'What do you think we should do?' asked the old soldier. 'It would seem to be insensitive to go ahead with the parcel project without the vicar and his wife, but I don't think they would want it delayed.'

'Let's wait a few days. Maybe they will stay with Mrs Windle for several weeks, maybe not.'

When word came that the couple were returning, Robert was delighted as were many others; not only churchgoers had missed the vicarage residents. It was after the Sunday service that Robert, with some hesitation, approached Arthur and asked if he felt able to meet. Remembering his mother's recent advice, Arthur concurred; he would get on with life even though his mind was not without some turmoil. It was agreed they meet on the following Wednesday. Many offered words of sympathy, but it was Olivia Atkins who was the first to speak with Arthur's mother: 'Mrs Windle, all of us are so saddened by your husband's passing. We all want you to know how much we are thinking of you. Please feel very welcome here in Rusfield.' Charlotte Windle stepped forward and kissed the attractive widow on her cheek, tears in her eyes.

Three days later, Violet Rushton, Robert Berry, Eleanor and Arthur shared tea and biscuits in the vicarage conservatory. The quartet knew rumours of the parcel project had already swept round the village. Eleanor had been surprised when going into the butchers, she heard Susannah Jones talking about the plan as if it were a fait accompli. 'Our boys need all the things we can send them,' she heard Susannah saying to Rita Small. 'We make up parcels for Albert, but I'm not sure all the lads do so well.'

'So when are we going to hear more about it? I was talking with the headmaster and he said he would encourage the children to do what they could.'

When Eleanor got home she told Arthur of the conversation. 'Arthur dear, the four of us meet tomorrow and I think we should get things started. And Arthur, there's one other thing.

This idea came from Violet Rushton and Robert Berry and it's important that villagers know that. We'll give them all the support we can, but let's remember that,' she smiled. Arthur nodded; he was wise enough to know that Eleanor's advice should be closely regarded.

It had been Violet Rushton who suggested that David Watts, the master at the school, be included in their council and the others had happily agreed; he had proved himself an enthusiastic member of the community as well as a sound headmaster. Maybe not the charisma of his predecessor but, as Eleanor reminded Arthur, 'He's only been here three years.'

After protracted and sometimes tetchy deliberations with the church council, the street lighting committee and coal club, Arthur found everything about the meeting refreshing. The purpose was clear and the determination of the five participants united. It was one group that did not need official appointments, but Robert Berry slipped in to being unofficial chairman. He was positive, resourceful and his kindness was well shown when he said, 'Vicar, I wonder if your mother would kindly help? I'm sure she would be an asset.' His growing friendship with Violet Rushton had caused them to work together to clear the rear part of her shop to store items.

They agreed that the following Sunday would be the best day to announce the plan. 'After all,' Robert Berry quietly mentioned, 'it's the Sunday nearest to St George's Day, so when could be more appropriate?' The others agreed, but it was at Eleanor's later suggestion that Arthur should read some verses from St Matthew, which she believed encapsulated the Christian message and spoke about the need for action with the parcels. David Watts readily agreed to speak to the children about the plan the day after the Sunday service.

The Sunday dawned bright and this may have encouraged the large congregation. Arthur felt villagers expected something to be said about the scheme. The hymns expressed patriotism and God's care and the prayers were directed to

God keeping watch over the men who were away, although Eleanor wondered how that matched with Ruby Rowe's feelings at having recently lost her husband.

From the pulpit, Arthur announced that he was deviating from the lectionary and read: *"For I was hungry and you gave me food, I was thirsty and you gave me drink, I was a stranger and you welcomed me, I was naked and you clothed me, I was sick and you visited me, I was in prison and you came to me. And when did we see you a stranger and welcome you, or naked and clothe you? And when did we see you sick or in prison and visit you?"* When he moved on to explain the idea for everyone to have the opportunity to give to the men away fighting, he heard murmurs of approval, something he could not remember during any other sermon he had preached in over twenty years at St Mary's.

The excitement and determination to make the scheme work could be heard through the eager conversations after the service and Robert Berry and Violet Rushton smiled at each other as they felt the plan taking off. It was over half an hour after the end of the service that Arthur and Eleanor finally got back to the vicarage.

'Well that started well,' announced Eleanor. 'It was a good service, Arthur. Thank you,' she added with a kiss on his cheek. 'I have some cold meats and cheese all ready for lunch, so it will only be a few minutes.'

But the lunch was not to be eaten for several hours as they were interrupted by a sharp, twice repeated knock at the door. Hurrying to the door, Arthur saw fourteen-year-old Harry Johnson on the doorstep. 'Yes, Harry, what is it?'

'Please sir, mother says will you come quickly to Mrs Smith. She's very ill.'

It was a summons that would not have surprised Arthur any time over the past two years. How the elderly, bedridden parishioner had clung on to life many could hardly imagine. 'I'll come with you, my love,' Eleanor immediately said. 'Harry, please run and tell your mother that we will be there in just a few minutes.' Arthur dashed upstairs, gathered two printed papers and returned to his wife in the hall. Together they left for Meadow Way, where they found Liz Smith's front door open; on entering they found next-door neighbour, Judith Johnson, waiting for them to arrive.

'Nurse is upstairs; I'll pop up and tell Liz you are here.' Eleanor had always realised what a capable lady this mother of eight children was, not least shown by her care for Ruby and the way she had brought up a strong lad with Willy's character. Judith soon reappeared, beckoning to Arthur to go up. Eleanor judged it appropriate to stay downstairs for, apart from anything else, she knew from many visits that the old lady's small room allowed little space for visitors.

The comforting, though grave Nurse Betty Hazlett turned to Arthur: 'She is very weak, Vicar. Bless her; I don't think she will be with us for very long at all.'

Arthur turned and gently touched Liz's arm; tears rolling down her careworn face, a desperate sadness had overtaken her features. 'Oh, Vicar, I think she really is leaving us this time. I wish young Fred was here; they love each other so much.'

Arthur thought of this cruel side of war: a separation that kept Fred from where he would want to be. He remembered all the times he had sat in this room and read to old Mrs Smith, often wondering what her early life had been like. He knew how much daughter and mother cared for each other amid all their hardships and how they had seen Fred go off to war with a shared fear in their hearts. He knelt by the bed and held the old lady's hand. Spoken prayers struck him as slightly meaningless at this time. He could only wish her to pass away painlessly. But, perhaps, through the haze of approaching death, Martha Smith could still hear as he quietly spoke the words of the twenty-third Psalm. Then he remembered her love of Walter Scott and spoke a little from his schoolboy memories. He suddenly realised all sign of a pulse had stopped; he turned and nodded to Betty Hazlett. She understood, leant down and confirmed her lack of pulse. Liz Smith, too, understood. She wiped away her tears, took a deep breath, bent down, gently placed her hands on her mother's shoulders and kissed her forehead. Never was a deeper love more evident.

'Vicar, will you just say that psalm again and then lead us with the Lord's Prayer.'

A little while later Arthur Windle and Nurse Hazlett went downstairs. The nurse spoke to Eleanor and Judith: 'Liz wants a few minutes alone with her mother. Her mother's death may have been long in coming, but the sadness and grief will be as strong as ever. Perhaps Fred will be able to come home for a while.'

Arriving at school the next day, the children already knew about the parcels for the troops' scheme. After lining up in their four classes, they went into the largest classroom, which doubled up as the hall, where they saw the large sheet on which Miss Small had painted: "Send help to our brave men", alongside a painting of a soldier. When the headmaster announced that they were all to be involved, excitement abounded and after he explained and the tasks were allocated, the normal silence following an assembly was broken with a happy buzz. Even the sternest teacher would have allowed this change from the normal routine: certainly Mr Watts, Miss Small, Miss Picton and Miss Jackson did.

The previous day, another name had been added to the list in St Mary's porch, making fifty-two altogether. Each name was written on two slips of paper, one given to a young child, the other to a senior pupil. Each soldier would then receive a picture with just a sentence from the younger one and a proper letter from the other. A perfectly handwritten letter would be expected from the top class; Rita Small told them, 'Nearly all the men came here, so you can tell them which class you are in, what you have been doing and what you like best about school.' The younger children were told to draw a picture of the school or, if they wanted to, of the village pond or green. A few asked to draw pictures of their families, requiring help to write the names below the carefully drawn figures. As Miss Mary Jackson went round to see what her children were doing she stopped at Ruth Chapman's desk. 'What a lovely picture of your family, Ruth. Have you got the right number?'

'Yes Miss, fourteen.'

'But you told me last week that you had seven brothers and three sisters. So with you and your mother and father that makes thirteen, doesn't it?'

'No Miss, 'cos mummy had a baby yesterday, but I don't know what to call him.'

The older children had an additional task, as they had to copy a letter which would be delivered to every home in the village encouraging support for the soldiers.

The response was remarkable. The next day children arrived with handkerchiefs, socks, small towels, sugar, tea, hairbrushes and combs. Within a week there were tins of meat and sardines, soap, jam, shirts and underclothes. Not all the clothes were new, but they were all beautifully clean and carefully ironed. Somerville's the ironmongers and Harry Groves the confectioners and grocers, found their sales rising steeply. If Violet Rushton knew things were being purchased from her store for the soldiers she deducted twenty per cent from the cost. More trips were made to Steepleton to get a greater variety of items; the "Rusfield Rocket" was more popular than ever. Arthur became worried that some families might be denying themselves much needed products, but Eleanor reassured him by saying that villagers were happy to make sacrifices.

Pauline Richards and the headmaster's wife, Rosie Watts, formed a group that met in a small room at the school to knit socks, gloves and scarves. 'They'll be needing them in the really cold weather,' Pauline had mentioned; enough to start off the group. Some of the older girls in the school spent time unpicking second-hand woollens that were brought along and rolling them into neat balls. Something that was clearly needed for the men was cigarettes. A few pennies were enough for ten and it was agreed that a packet had to go in each parcel. A weekly family penny became the unofficial rule and the number of packets that could be afforded grew. A carton of fifty packets unexpectedly arrived at Miss Rushton's shop, but she would never relay the source. Eleanor learnt of this gift the day after Jack Mansfield had called in to see her husband about tidying up the churchyard.

Violet Rushton's store space became filled. She and Robert Berry, along with half a dozen older children spent time organising things into piles of similar items. By the end of the fourth week, Violet and Robert agreed that the time had come to organise the goods into piles for the individual parcels. Already three more parcels were needed, making fifty-five. Meanwhile, Ruth Chapman had written in the fourteenth member of her family: Reginald. All were satisfied.

Some had realised that the cost of posting the parcels, although some wartime concessions had come in, would amount to a goodly sum. It was here that young postman, Peter Woods, had worked hard. Living and based in Steepleton, he had called at shops in the town virtually begging for money. Together with a collection among all the postal and telegraph workers, enough was raised and it was Major de Maine who had made enquiries about the correct addressing system. A week later, Sparky Carey's pony and cart, together with Violet Rushton and Robert Berry, left the village for Steepleton with all the addressed parcels. By this time Violet Rushton's store already had a few donations for next time.

Whilst Eleanor was clearing up after a little cooking late that evening, Arthur went upstairs to his small room. He read again the verses from St Matthew that had inspired the food parcels, then went to the cross, knelt and prayed: 'Bless all those who are faced with danger in this terrible time of war. Guide me to do your will at all times, forgiving me for my many sins.' He was silent for several moments before adding 'Amen'.

As they retired to bed that evening, tired but happy at how well the parcels project had gone, Eleanor and Arthur rejoiced in the second good news of the day. In the morning, Peter had delivered a letter to Arthur from Mary Smith that she would come down to visit her sister. In the wake of Liz's sadness at losing her mother, Arthur had managed to get Liz to agree that he should contact her sister. The address was nine years old, but clearly it was the right one.

'I know we're tired darling, but not too tired are you?' Arthur and Eleanor clasped each other in delight. Their lovemaking was as passionate as ever.

THIRTY-SIX

September 1915

'No one seems to have any bloody idea what we're doing here,' Albert Jones muttered to Jammy Carey. 'We just seem to go on waiting.'

Jammy, a little more thoughtfully, replied: 'Seeing all the extra troops arriving, I guess we're going to mount a big assault.' From the trench they could still see bodies lying out in front of them, stuffed dolls tossed aside; others had already been buried. They looked on the ill-kept graveyard which had once been called countryside. Further on they had seen men hanging on the tangles of barbed wire, killed even as they tried to cut through in the attempted advance five days earlier. There had been two gaps where engineers had cut through, preceding the race to overrun the enemy trench, but before they had got a dozen yards the Bergmann machine guns had sliced through them. Their bodies were beyond reclaim until any later advance.

The two Rusfield men had hardly been separated since arriving in France a year earlier, but after the first four months had only occasionally heard word of any of their other village mates. Boney had thought that as all were with the Suffolks they would stay together. 'But,' as Jammy had said, 'war's not like that. It's not organised, it happens, it's bloody chaos.'

After Le Cateau, came the fighting near Ypres, then the cold of Wytschaete, Givenchy and Bellewaerde. Names heard without meaning, without making sense. Words that did make sense were cold, rain, gunfire, mud, rats, "go now" and expletives which deserved no translation. Now for their night job, it was their turn, twenty of them for tonight's shift. Boney knew that when he had first come to this desperate place, he had heard the name Loos. He just couldn't believe that men were lying uncared for and unburied. Maybe he had volunteered, for some form of a burial must be given.

Three nights ago they had started. In groups of four they set off for where they had seen the bodies lying. Sergeant Crosbie was their leader and a Welshman who volunteered the name Taffy, the fourth.

'Is this what we really expected when we volunteered at Steepleton: undertakers?' muttered Jammy.

'Five minutes,' the sergeant now warned.

Faces charcoal blackened, gloved hands, filthy, flea-ridden and desperately tired, Boney suggested they were well dressed for the job. 'It smells right too. I suppose it was right us using the gas, but we might have made sure the wind was blowing the right way.'

'Either that,' interjected Taffy in a lilting accent, 'or made sure the gas masks fitted properly. I didn't know whether to suffocate in the mask or take it off and be gassed.'

'OK, up the ladder and over. Keep close to the ground. There's a little light from the sky so we should be able to see what we're doing, just hope the bloody Germans can't.' The same words each night. This strangely equipped quartet had noted the instruction of their sergeant: to go towards a cluster of bodies thirty yards ahead, slightly to their left.

Christ, the ground was rough to crawl along. How important the extra strappings round the knees. Boulders that had been thrown up by shells, potholes and heaps of stones. Still, their crawling bodies might be further hidden by the very obstacles they crawled round. Both Jammy and Boney had realised on their first night of this macabre job – was it three nights or a lifetime ago? – that the Sergeant had uncanny sight. Asked why, this east Londoner had replied: 'Stepney is famous for its carrot fields!'

The secret, if there was one, was to keep so low to the ground you felt more like burrowing through it. 'Keep yer arse down,' their leader reminded them before they set out. 'You don't want a bullet there or you might let out a give-away noise!'

No talk now, eerily quiet. The slightest noise was dangerous with the German trenches no more than two hundred yards away. They would have lookouts, as they knew that the British might well mount an assault before long; unless they were commanded to go forward first. The four knew of the endless barbed wire draped in every direction, a fearsome deterrent to men from both armies. So many times in the past few months, Boney and Jammy had moved forward, only to be repelled and end up back in their starting place. Boney had smiled when he saw his mate write on a piece of paper left in the trench they were leaving in order to attack, 'Don't worry, I'll be back!' How right he had been.

Three bodies here, all touching. How many days had they been here, or was it weeks? They all knew the drill. Boney moved to the upper part of the unknown soldier's body, felt round his neck, fingers touched the all-important disc. 'Get that, whatever else,' they had been told. This one may have slipped over the man's head, but don't risk that. Parts of bodies had been known to become disengaged. A quick snip of the cutters and it was free. A fumble and into the bag that he had round his neck. Make sure it was safe. He knew that somewhere there were loved ones who at least deserved to know that their man was dead.

To his left there was a shallow dip; judging by the loose soil in the bottom it was the result of a shell. From his bag,

Boney pulled a hand trowel. He had seen people back home using such a tool for planting seedlings; what a sickening role it was now playing. As soundlessly as possible, he scooped out a further few inches. Taffy and Jammy were extending the same shallow, each from their side. Sweat poured down their faces. Soon, each felt a touch; Sergeant Crosbie indicating that it was enough. Each pulled or gently pushed a body into the extended shallow. The corpses lay side by side.

Jammy tried to remove from his mind the thoughts that came crowding in. Who were these men? Who were their loved ones? Had they wives, sweethearts, children? Why the hell had they died? A different thought for each shovelful or armful of soil scraped in from the side of the hole to cover the body. The arm was better; less noise. A slight sound, just a snort, from the sergeant. Enough to tell them that they had done all they could to give these three men a burial. Now for the next ones. For two hours they continued, by which time some thirty had been given a crude departure, leaving just a collection of discs. Jammy and Boney knew there were other men nearby who were matching their own work. No disc removal must be made before a check that the body was dead. Stories abounded of men who had been found alive many days after lying out in the sun, without water, just fortitude.

No sound from the Germans tonight. They had found the same the two previous nights. 'Do you think,' Boney had asked his friend, 'that the Germans know we're out here and what we're doing? That just the other side of the wire they are doing the same?' Could there be such a regard for the enemy burying the dead when there was no hesitation in killing them the next day?

The crawl back to their trench seemed twice the distance as their outward one. Maybe it was, maybe they had strayed further, maybe they were just exhausted. Jammy never believed the story that one man had so lost his sense of direction that when he had finally made it back to his trench he found it was full of Germans. Jammy often wondered at the many extraordinary stories that wove their way along the trenches until he found himself in such vile conditions that it was only by listening to and telling such stories that sanity could be retained.

As they neared their trench it was as if the Germans knew that the men's gruesome, yet caring mission had been accomplished, or was it that they were preparing to make an attack? Neither Jammy, nor Boney were ever to know. The noise was tremendous; for once, the men setting the range of Big Bertha, their heavy howitzer, had got it right: but terribly wrong for Boney who had just regained the trench and for Jammy, Taffy and Sergeant Crosbie who were about to follow. The shell landed only yards away throwing a mighty cascade of earth and rocks into the dawn sky. Men were tossed into the air, limbs torn asunder, bodies buried. Men killed, others severely injured.

THIRTY-SEVEN

November 1915 - February 1916

As winter first stepped on and then crushed the mild autumn, two features were revealed in Rusfield: fear for absent loved ones and attempts to carry on normally. 'We have to keep things normal for the children's sake,' Rita Small said to her colleagues after school on the last Friday in November. 'They don't understand all the worries their parents have and we don't want them to think about them.' David Watts and Mary Jackson nodded. 'Our Christmas nativity performance and carol service must go ahead.'

'I'll take the costumes home next weekend and see that they are still all right,' added young Mary.

'And I'll look the music out and make sure the instruments are in working order. I seem to remember young David Johnson treating the big drum last Christmas like a wood-chopping exercise,' smiled Rita.

The teachers would have found many supporters. Arthur was determined the traditional Christmas services should go ahead, including carol singing round the village. Violet Rushton and Harry Groves had ordered in Christmas cards, Rachel Fielding planned to put up decorations in The Queens Head and her brother, Samuel, would follow suit at The Ark.

In the vicarage a similar conversation was taking place. 'We must carry on,' Arthur offered to Eleanor, 'especially for the children's sake.'

'And not only for them,' she replied. 'We know it's dreadful for so many, but somehow we must all keep going.'

'Indeed, my dearest. Poor Eliza looks sadder each day she comes in. She told me this morning that Susannah Jones went round to see her yesterday. They know Albert and James were together in early August and neither has received any letter since.'

'I wonder if Sir Lancelot has got anywhere. After Eliza told us about James, it was a good idea of yours to speak with the de Maines and ask them to raise it with Isabella's brother,' said Eleanor referring to Sir Lancelot Prestwish for whom James Carey had been working when he joined up. Arthur had thought that the great landowner with his contacts in high office might be able to obtain news and he knew Sir Lancelot had spoken with the local Member of Parliament, Sir Humphrey Watkinson.

'Eleanor, let me ask you something, please? Along with other clergy in the diocese, I am getting more and more directives from the bishop's palace, many of them emanating from the dean.'

'Ah yes,' Eleanor could not help interjecting with a smile, 'my great admirer, the Very Reverend Edgar Hartley Williamson. I wonder if he's still busy trying to stop women's rights? But sorry, my love, I shouldn't interrupt.'

'This latest directive causes me much thought. Let me read the beginning to you: *As the war continues, we must pray more earnestly for victory.* Eleanor, I fully understand why we should pray for those who suffer, but for the war? Can we be sure God is on our side? I imagine there are many Germans also praying for victory. I just wonder that as war is such an evil event, brought about by men, that God will have no part of it.'

Eleanor realised how troubled her beloved Arthur was. She had always seen his faith as strong and she did not see that in any way different now. 'Arthur, I not only understand what you say, but I agree. Perhaps, we all have our own picture of God and as you know my view is a simple one. It's the Jesus who delivered the Sermon on the Mount; that tells me about God. To me, war is so far removed from God that I cannot include him in what is happening on the battlefields. Let's pray for those who suffer and our own strength to support and show love, but I can't expect God to aid our guns more than the German ones.' She lightly kissed him; Arthur felt a shade less troubled.

But, in spite of deep fears and anxieties many positive things were happening in the village. The third batch of parcels for the troops had been despatched. The response had not only continued, but additions had been made. It was one of the large Reynolds family that first thought of sending hard-boiled eggs; led by Lily and Alfred, each of Grace's siblings proudly bore a large brown egg from home. 'Our chickens have been very kind,' announced six-year-old Alfred dashing up to Mary Jackson in the school play yard. 'We've made them hard so they will be all right.'

'Not if you drop them, it won't,' Lily, his pretty twelve-year-old sister, added.

How much she reminds me of Grace, thought her teacher: she's going to be another beauty. The boys will run after her just like they did Grace when she was with us.

The hard-boiled egg addition was taken a stage further when Florrie Edwards wrote her name and a message on her egg. 'Is that a good idea, Florrie?' her teacher asked.

'Well Miss, no one's going to eat the shell so I think it's nice.' Many copied her idea, with the sender's address included; maybe, thought Florrie, she would get a reply.

It was Mary Jackson, as supportive of the Methodist chapel as she was to the school, who had led another venture which soon became known as the "Methodist Jam Mission". On a walk across Bramrose Hill, Mary had noticed how well the blackberries were ripening. After chapel the next Sunday she suggested to fellow Methodists, Eliza Carey, Betty Hazlett and Rachel Fielding, that if they collected enough blackberries they could make a nice preserve to send to their men. By September the abundant crop was ripe and the following Saturday morning, nine stalwart Methodist ladies set out from the village and spent three hours filling up bags, pots and other containers with berries. The afternoon found the ladies in the kitchen at The Queens Head where the fruits were prepared, cooked and made into jam.

'So that's fifty-one jars,' announced Rachel. 'I did check in the church porch and there are seventy-three men. I'm sure we can make some more, so there's a jar for everyone. How about next Saturday?' All the ladies agreed to meet again and complete their labours.

When Violet Rushton and Robert Berry heard about these latest efforts they were thrilled. 'That's wonderful. We will just need to pack everything more thoroughly.'

However, none of this changed the agonies for the loved ones. Peter Woods knew well that Albert Jones and James Carey's parents were desperate for letters and each day willed that he would have one to deliver. As the end of the year grew near, news from the war continued to be mixed. Sebastian de Maine explained to his wife: 'The government will be trying to make things appear better than they really are. As you know, I was with Jack Mansfield yesterday and when we looked at *The Telegraph* we just couldn't believe the number of casualties.'

'I know,' agreed Isabella. 'It's been a terrible blow now that poor Robert Bacon has been killed. He was so young and it's such a short while ago that he started working for Jack Mansfield. I don't think poor old Joe at the smithy will ever recover. Since he lost his wife a few years ago, young Robert has meant everything to him. Then there's Richard Wincombe coming back home having lost his leg and poor Ruby, so worried about her brother Willy. If anything happens to him it would be terrible for her. But I do know how hard Lancelot is working to find out about young James Carey.'

'We can only hope your brother can find out something to help the family,' her husband replied.

It was from an unexpected source that news came. After Christmas and the New Year had passed, the sharp frost covered the hedgerows and trees for days on end and it was on one of the coldest mornings that Peter Woods, as ever without a heavy coat, pedalled his familiar route. He had noticed a neatly addressed letter to Mr and Mrs S. Jones of Wood Lane, but it was likely they would be at their shop; he would make that his first stop. As he opened the butchers shop door he was pleased there were no customers; just Susannah and Sidney Jones making up some packets of sausages. They looked up as the bell sounded.

'Good morning,' Peter spoke cheerfully. 'I have a letter, so I thought it best to bring it to you here.' Packets were put down, almost dropped, hands wiped on aprons. Susannah visibly paled, her husband hardly less so.

'I hope it's good news.' He always felt this was a mindless comment, yet felt he had to say something. He longed to know the content but, as always, gave a polite goodbye and left to continue his round.

'Oh Sidney, what is it? I don't know the writing. You open it.' Sidney had a slender knife to hand, slit open the envelope and drew out a single sheet of paper; it revealed a precise hand. Under an address showing a Sheffield Hospital, they read:

Dear Mr and Mrs Jones,

I am writing to you as your son Albert has asked me to. He hopes this letter finds you well. Albert is all right but he can not write as his hand is heavily bandaged. He was wounded, but cannot remember what happened. We are not sure when that was. He came here three weeks ago from a hospital in France, but we did not know his name as he did not have any identification with him. Five days ago he started to remember things and since then is really getting better. He remembered his name and two days ago his address and all about you, so I said I would write.

He is much better now and will be all right and I expect he will soon come home. He is having the bandages off his hand tomorrow and will write to you himself. He sends his love to you.

Yours sincerely, Marjorie Robinson

'Oh Sidney, he will be all right, won't he?'

'Of course he will, my love. I know how worried you were that the news would be really bad, I felt just the same. What a kind lady to write.'

'We must write back to her quickly, Sidney. We can give the letter to Peter tomorrow. Oh, isn't it wonderful to think that Albert is going to write. He must be getting better if he can do that, mustn't he? And this lady says he will be home soon.'

Albert's letter arrived three days later. He did not know how he had ended up in Sheffield, but he was proud of a scar on his forehead which added to his good looks. The doctor had ordered one more week in hospital, but he was up and walking. He would probably then have a further month's leave. 'It's quite a way for getting a month at home,' he ended. It was in the first week of February that he came home, slimmer although he had never been overweight, his forehead scar apparent, but fading; altogether looking better than his parents had imagined possible. They soon realised Albert did not want to talk about his time in France.

It was two evenings later when Doris Groves was with them that Albert opened out a little. 'You asked me about how I had been injured. Well, I'm afraid I wasn't looking what I was doing and got too near an exploding German shell,' he said rather lightly. Unfortunately, they could not give any answers to Albert's pleas for news about his mate.

'Jammy and I were together,' he explained to them. 'I know we were on our way back to our trench.' He paused and a distant gaze appeared for some moments. 'The next thing I knew was that I was in that hospital. I couldn't believe that nearly four months had gone by. It's really odd. They told me I had made things difficult as I must have disobeyed orders and taken off my identification disc. I don't remember doing that.'

Albert's story of the little he could remember took quite a time to tell. He was hesitant, unlike the direct and no-nonsense son whom they had known. Susannah was surprised, though delighted, to find him holding her hand. She was pleased that Doris and he had quickly shown how close they still were to each other. Susannah had always thought Doris to be a little brazen, but she was a happy, open girl and clearly she and Albert were fond of each other.

'Albert, I think it would be nice if you went round to see Mr and Mrs Carey. Eliza Carey came in to the shop as soon as she knew we had received that lovely letter from your nurse, but I know it simply made it worse for her, not knowing anything about Jammy.' Albert's heart sank, this was something he knew he should do, but had fought shy of doing. His mother was right.

THIRTY-EIGHT

February – March 1916

When Arthur had spoken with Isabella and Sebastian de Maine about Jammy Carey in late November, he had no idea of the chain of command he would set in progress. It happened that a week later, the de Maines went to dinner at Isabella's brother's grand house just outside Steepleton. Sir Lancelot Prestwish was, in fact, little better off than the de Maines, but having inherited the fine Georgian house and its surrounding three hundred acres, he gave a grand pretence of wealth. He also had the caring nature of the past three generations and when his sister raised the matter of Jammy, he immediately knew to whom she referred. His brow became more and more lined as he paid attention to Isabella telling him what she knew of the young Rusfield man.

'I remember him well; a strong lad who was working on some additional building here. He always seemed to be working harder than most. Sometimes I would see one or more of the others taking a few minutes off, probably smoking, but not him. But, perhaps, the time since his parents heard from him is not so strange for it must be hard to get letters home. Maybe it's not bad news, but if I can help find out anything I certainly will.'

He was as good as his word and a few weeks later met up

with local Member of Parliament, Sir Humphrey Watkinson. They were old friends and whilst their meeting had nothing to do with the war, time was easily found by Sir Lancelot to speak about the young soldier. The well-whiskered and elderly parliamentary member listened in his attentive manner. He may well have been getting on in years, but his grasp of matters and speed with which he saw solutions or ways to move forward had not declined.

'Well, it being the Suffolks helps, because I know quite a few of the senior officers of our local regiment. I believe Lieutenant Colonel Lewis is involved there and he's a good friend. I'll try to get to speak with Lewis although he's almost certainly abroad; but leave it with me.'

Sir Humphrey's name carried much weight and a communication was rapidly passed down the line to reach Lieutenant Colonel Lewis. Enquiries were made, reports filed and even in the midst of the continuous battle at the front, some weeks later word came back to England.

On reaching Sir Humphrey Watkinson, he spoke with Sir Lancelot who decided to telegraph his brother-in- law saying that he would drive out the following Friday to convey the news from France. Immediately Peter delivered the telegram to the manor on the Thursday, Sebastian discussed the meeting with Isabella.

'Seb, since it was Arthur Windle who first raised the whole worry about young Carey, I think you should invite him along tomorrow. I also wonder whether you should invite the lad's parents as well.'

'I think that would be going a little too far at this stage. We don't know what the news is, but I suspect it is not good. Let's see what Arthur Windle thinks, he's such a sensible and sensitive man and I will respect his view.'

At one o'clock the next day, a coach pulled by a splendid piebald drew up outside the de Maine's home. Sebastian and Isabella were at the door to greet her brother. Brother and sister were close and after a fond kiss, she took his coat (the services of a butler had been dispensed with a year earlier) and led him into the attractive, if slightly faded lounge. Arthur Windle was standing near to the roaring fire.

'Sir Lancelot,' began Arthur, 'it is extremely kind of you to come today.'

A wave of the baronet's hand accompanied by a generous smile at Arthur, brushed aside such an expression of gratitude. 'These are terrible times for the men away fighting, but no less so for their loved ones back here. We must do what we can.' Sebastian de Maine's offer of drinks was also brushed aside and the three men drew their chairs closer to the fire.

'Let me say straight away that it is bad news, very sad indeed. Two things are very clear. Lieutenant Colonel Lewis has gone to considerable pains to put together the report in spite of the terrible conflict raging and all the resulting chaos. Perhaps, I shouldn't say so, but no one seems to know exactly where everybody is, nor what is happening, but I'm sure the report details are as accurate as makes no difference.

'Young Carey and some twenty other members of the Suffolks were in the front line near Loos. Around 30 September, or at least within a week from that date, Private Carey was involved in some form of night activity. It seems that in a great blaze of gunfire the trench to which he and others were in was destroyed in a direct hit. In confidence, I read that whilst some casualties were taken to a nearby dressing station, some poor men were completely annihilated. No identification, no way of knowing which men were lost for ever is available. Sadly, the certainty with which loved ones can be given information is often out of the question. In Private Carey's case the official language is "missing, presumed dead". Sadly, I am assured that there is no doubt, no hope.'

There was a stunned silence. None of these men, not even the battle-hardened Major de Maine knew what to say. It was Arthur Windle who quietly and eventually said, 'Let us just have a moment of silent prayer for Eliza and Sparky Carey, that somehow they may be comforted in the days ahead.' The fire crackled and a log rolled forward in the silence.

It was Arthur Windle who went to see the parents to deliver the awful news they had been dreading. He asked Eleanor to go with him, as she was so close to Eliza and still not really knowing what to say, they knocked at the door of the small cottage. Sparky, who opened it, realised in a moment they were bearers of bad news; he called his wife and gestured for their sombre visitors to enter.

They sat down and having warned them to brace themselves for bad news, Arthur told them as much as he felt able. The moment when both parents stood, threw their arms round each other and howled in despair created an awful tableau, a bridge of misery, to remain with Eleanor and Arthur for ever. The parents' weeping would last for a long time; the grief and agonising loss for the rest of their lives.

It was ten days later that Peter delivered a letter which, when shown to him the following day, Arthur appreciated the sensitive nature of words:

> I deeply regret to inform you that your son Pte. J.A. Carey, No. 62732 of this Company was killed in action at the end of September. Death was instantaneous and without any suffering. I further regret that this letter reaches you so long after the sadness, but it has taken much time to establish all the circumstances.
>
> The Company was preparing for an attack and a small group of men, including your son, volunteered for a night action. The action was successful, but on their return an enemy shell made a direct hit.
>
> It was impossible to get his remains away and he lies in a soldier's grave where he fell.
>
> I and the CO and all the Company deeply sympathise

with you in your loss. Your son always did his duty and now has given his life for his country. We all honour him, and I trust you will feel some consolation in remembering this.

His effects will reach you in due course.

In true sympathy, James Bentley (Capt.).

THIRTY-NINE

March 1916

Albert Jones was devastated to learn of Jammy's death. His mind swam as he was prompted to remember how the two of them, in company with Taffy and the sergeant, had left the trench to carry out their gruesome night duty; but then his mind went blank. His lifelong mate had been killed, but fortune had smiled on him. Yet, when he read the letter passed to him by Jammy's mother, he almost wished he, too, had died.

His health gradually improved, his hand now restored to full use thanks to Nurse Hazlett. Each morning she bicycled from Meadow Way to Wood Lane, turning down the patient's suggestion that he should walk to her house. He felt stronger, yet his mind remained in turmoil. As he sat in the kitchen with the village nurse, he was surprised to find he could talk more easily with her than with his parents. She chattered about small village happenings and told him of her work before moving to Rusfield. It was into the second week of treatment that he realised he should be feeling happier in his mind. Was it the death of Jammy or the thought of returning to France? Yet part of him wanted to return.

'Nurse, I really am grateful to you for your kindness in helping me with my hand. You've done wonders for me. Now I can easily pick things up and the pain has disappeared.'

'I'm so glad,' the kindly nurse replied. 'I think that physical injuries are probably the easiest to get better.'

'How do you mean?'

'Well, you've really been through the mill and that must have an effect. I mean, I hope you begin to feel better in yourself?' Strangely, or so it seemed to him, Albert felt he wanted to talk about things and their time together that morning was longer than the usual half hour. When she left, he reflected on their conversation and wondered why he was so depressed. Perhaps it would be easier when he got back to France and could play his part again.

How could he feel low when the adorable Doris was so near? His mind dwelt on the day before. They had walked hand in hand across the lower level of Bramrose Hill when the sky had suddenly released a torrential downpour and they had run to an unused barn. As they sheltered, their ardour erupted and within a few minutes they were lying with clothes hopelessly disarranged. Their touches, their kisses, their words were passionate. Doris said afterwards that she did not know how she had the strength to push him away when nothing protected them from consummating their love. Yet each had given the other a beautiful and loving climax. 'My darling Albert, it would have spoilt everything if I'd become pregnant. It won't be long before this terrible war is over and when you are back I promise you, I will be yours. No one else will ever know me as you have just known me.' He clung on to Doris with the tremors of war momentarily cast aside. Doris wondered how she could bear him going away; it would be so long before they could be together again.

He would have dreamt on, but his pensiveness was broken by a sharp knock at the door. He sprang to his feet, opened the door and gasped in amazement: 'Racer! What the devil are you doing here? God, it's good to see you.' The cousins and long-standing friends embraced, stepped back, laughed and shook hands again. 'I can't believe it.'

Abraham did not seem to have changed at all. 'I got home yesterday evening for ten days' leave, so I came round as soon as I could. I'm sorry you've had such an awful time, but you look better than I thought you would. It's terrible about Jammy, isn't it? Poor Jammy. I'm going to see Mr and Mrs Carey tomorrow. That won't really help, but it's all I can do.'

'Oh, they will be pleased to see you. They've taken things very hard of course, but are struggling to get back to normal. Mrs Carey has thrown herself into helping with the parcels for sending off to France and dear old Sparky is giving more help to people than ever.'

Turning to news of friends, Boney said: 'I was talking to Mrs Atkins recently and she told me how Jack was always mentioning Patricia in his letters. Indeed she has written to Jack's mother several times.'

'She's a fine girl,' Racer reminisced. 'Indeed they are a splendid family. They were so kind to Jack and me when they let us stay with them before the big race. I met up with James, that's Patricia's brother,' he went on to tell his friend.

'Talking of girls, Racer; how is the lovely Grace?'

'I'm sure she's fine. She doesn't actually know I'm home; you don't always get advance notice of leave and with me it was just a case of "go now". So I'm going over to Wensfield later this afternoon and give her a surprise by calling at the school to meet her. I hope she'll be pleased to see me.'

Neither volunteered much about their time in France except light-hearted incidents and some of the people they had met. To both of them the great thing was not the conversation, but being together again. They walked round to The Queens Head for a drink; maybe The George held too many memories. It was while they were there that Boney remembered something.

'Racer, did you hear about your running friend?'

'Who's that?'

'That army runner you just beat when we all went up to Stamford Bridge.'

'You mean Captain Wyndham Halswelle. What about him?'

'I'm afraid he was killed last year. I'm surprised you haven't heard,' Boney went on, seeing how the news upset his friend. 'He was something of a hero, I believe.'

'He would be. He was a really great man. I shall never forget his kindness when he took me on to the track and showed me how to run in lanes. If he hadn't, I would never have won. How did you get to hear about him?'

'Well, it's really quite strange. I've never had anything to do with Major de Maine, indeed I always thought of him as a little stand-offish, but soon after I came home from the hospital I got a note from him inviting me up to the manor. When I got there we sat in their lounge and had a wonderful tea. I saw a different major that day. I asked him about his time in the army and he told me how he had served in South Africa and Egypt and then he mentioned your racing friend. Apparently the major was something of an athlete in his youth and this interest caused him to look at an athletics magazine when he had been in the Steepleton library. That's where he read about the athlete's death. The article said how he had been killed trying to rescue another officer, even though he was badly injured himself.'

'What a terrible loss,' replied Racer, 'such a good man.' He paused for a moment, obviously deeply upset; his mind returning to the occasion they had met over three years previously. 'So why do you think you were asked up to the manor?'

'Well, the major said that as he was too old to join up, at least he would do what he could. Apparently he had invited Jack Atkins when he was recovering from injury, so perhaps you'll get an invitation, too. And something else: last week I popped in to the reading room, how good it looks, but best of all, Miss Small was in there with some of the oldest children from the school. It was lovely to see her again. Anyway, she allowed me to talk with some of the children and said I could call in at the school anytime. Maybe we could go in together, Racer?'

'That would be wonderful.' Racer turned and looked at the clock over the bar. 'Well, I must go; otherwise mother will never forgive me for being late for lunch. I'm sure she's over-feeding me, so it's just as well I'm not racing at the moment. How long before you think you'll be going back?'

'I expect I'll hear something in about a week. Let's see if we can meet up again tomorrow. Maybe a walk over Bramrose Hill?'

'That sounds a great idea. Let's do that.'

They shook hands, clasped each other and went their own way. The same old Racer, Albert thought, but Racer reflected on a nervousness he had seen in Boney and how his hands had shaken when holding his drink. His deeply-etched face added years to his twenty-year-old cousin and lifelong friend.

FORTY

March 1916

With the sun making a weak attempt to break through the
grey cloud cover, the pony and trap with Sparky Carey and
Reverend Arthur Windle passed through the open wrought-
iron gates leading to Richford House. Just past two-thirty;
Sparky had been as punctual as ever. As he had said to Eliza,
'It's time I started doing something to help. James would
expect that from me.' Eliza had nodded to her husband in
numbed agreement. She had heard that time was a healer,
but felt the loss was becoming greater. As the two had set
out on the five-mile drive to Richford House, Sparky asked
Arthur Windle about the great house: 'I know they've made
the place into a hospital for troops, but why are you going
there, sir?'

'Well, to be honest Sparky, I don't know much about it
myself. I do know it's the home of Lord and Lady Davison,
but converted in to a war hospital. A few days ago I received a
letter from the bishop asking me if I would visit.'

Arthur realised that Sparky would have given anything
to be visiting his son, however badly wounded; and, in
truth, Arthur had mixed feelings about making this visit. He
wondered how the men would regard a visitor, but if it did
help then he was glad to go. Eleanor had offered to come with

him, but he had declined as he thought this was hardly the activity for a woman.

A final left-hand curve in the drive and there stood a magnificent country house, beautiful in its light-coloured stonework: built to entertain royalty. There was a variety of activity in front of the house: three ambulance wagons were parked, two carts from which large crates were being unloaded and three soldiers, one on crutches, were making their way towards the side of the house. As Sparky pulled up he said he would tether the pony and go for a little walk.

An uncertain Arthur clambered out of the trap and walked up the impressive stone steps leading to the massive wooden doors, one of which was slightly ajar. He pushed open the right-hand one, entered and stepped into the magnificent entrance hall. He was immediately aware of a smartly-dressed nurse sitting at a table. She looked up, generously smiled: 'Can I help you sir?'

'My name is Windle, the Reverend Arthur Windle, and I have received a letter confirming that I could visit this afternoon.'

Nurse Blendle, her breast badge bore her name, consulted a list. 'Welcome, sir. I will call for Sister.' She picked up a small, brass bell and gave it a sharp ring. The sound resonated round the large hall and within two minutes a severe looking lady with a bright blue cape over her white under-uniform, quickly approached.

'Good afternoon, sir. You must be the Reverend Windle. Thank you for coming. I'm Sister Carmichael. We have over 300 men here, all with bad injuries, some very severe indeed. Sadly, this war is causing injuries the like of which we have never seen before. Dr Howard, the senior doctor here, believes the men can be helped by people visiting; for them to realise they haven't been forgotten and, that however terrible their disfigurements may be, visitors will share time with them. Thank you for coming, but be warned; what you will see may shock you.'

She led him up the marble staircase, still embellished by exotic ferns once set in place by Lady Davison. As they approached the door to what Arthur imagined had been a hall for large parties, they were greeted by a smell: not unpleasant, but strong. There was a steady sound of activity: murmurs, cries of pain and the sound of trolleys being moved across the wooden floor. Entering the room decorated with lavish ceiling paintings and walls marked with light panels where Arthur realised paintings had once hung, he saw four lines of beds, perhaps sixty in total. Nurses busied themselves attending to the men's needs.

'I'll stay with you, but please stop and talk to any of the men. As you may feel able to come again, I think it's best to look around generally and become acquainted with the overall situation.' Arthur nodded; he felt unable to suggest any alternative.

'In this part, the patients have a variety of injuries, most are severe, but some are being repaired and are on the way to recovery. Further on you will see the really acute cases, where sadly some will never recover.' This forty-year-old woman gave a half smile and Arthur could feel her exuding compassion and obvious competence. He could only hope the men would not see him as a curious spectator.

As he approached the first bed, he could see little more than a swathe of bandages with a slight gap allowing the patient to see with one eye and to feed. Arthur quietly sat on a wicker chair squeezed in between beds. He realised the man was looking at him, but whether with welcome, suspicion or fear the bandages disguised. Struggling to know what to say, he introduced himself and asked the soldier's name.

'Private Arthur Whelby, sir,' a croaking Scottish voice spoke with difficulty.

'Ah, my name, too, is Arthur. But you sound as if you come from much further north than I do. How long have you been here, Arthur?'

'Since October.' The man spoke with great difficulty and being unable to move his lips made words hard to understand. Arthur asked about the man's home and finding he came from Glasgow, they exchanged a few words about the Scottish city; Arthur doing virtually all the speaking, the patient weakly nodding. As the one-sided conversation continued, the man's single word answers began to fade and Arthur felt it time to move on.

'I can't imagine my visit helped him,' Arthur volunteered to Sister Carmichael as they moved away. 'What is wrong with him?'

'You might be surprised, but he will have been pleased to see you. His face has suffered much disfigurement. The gun he was loading exploded, greatly damaging the upper part of his body. The left side of his face has been blown away, he lost one eye and a section of his jaw is missing. The pain from the burning must have been terrible. The hospital is very fortunate in that Dr Gillies, who has visited many times, is wonderful within the new field of reconstructive surgery and is building up one side of Private Whelby's face. His face must be kept covered for fear of infection. His wife came to see him last week which did him much good. For a long time, he begged us not to allow her to visit as he didn't want to be seen by a loved one, but in the end he was persuaded.'

Arthur moved on to another heavily-bandaged man wearing a pair of goggles. 'So,' asked Arthur, 'please tell me about that man?'

'This is Corporal Peter Adams, a Londoner. He's making quite a good recovery although I'm afraid the damage to his lungs will be permanent. He came here some four months ago having been gassed. The gas shell caused severe burning of the skin, particularly his face and his hands. He not only suffered severe burning, but had breathed in some gas. The goggles seem to reduce the distress to his eyes which are so inflamed.'

Arthur walked over to the goggled man, smiled and briefly

introduced himself, grateful that he knew the soldier's name. He was greeted by an attempted smile, sat down, reached out and held the man's hand. Their limited conversation was made through the massive wheezing and breathing difficulty of Corporal Adams. He came from Romford, an area slightly known by Arthur and the conversation was about that part of London. As Arthur made to move on, the patient spoke his most words: 'Sir, thank you for coming. Will you please say a prayer for me?' Arthur, surprised, leant nearer, closed his eyes and spoke the Lord's Prayer. The occasional gasp told Arthur that the gassed man was joining in.

The next bed that Arthur stopped at, although he would liked to have stopped at more, was of a man with pipes running from his arm, a leg and his lower stomach. A conversation ensued, but was brief due to the man's restlessness and obvious pain; after a few minutes Arthur felt the sister touch his arm to lead him on.

'I'm afraid that Private Bellamy will not survive; I don't know how he has hung on for so long.'

'So what is wrong with the poor man,' returned Arthur.

'He is suffering a terrible infection. Apparently, he was badly wounded and left lying in the open, half covered by the earth blown from a shell explosion. We know now that so static is the war area that the soil has become terribly contaminated. As you can see we are trying to drain off the infection, but this is only a temporary respite. He is such a lovely man.' Arthur realised that one of the many smells in the ward was rotting flesh.

From the far corner, came the sound of continuous shouting. 'It's fucking hell; just fucking hell.' The words were then lost in a miscellany of cries and unclear words that Arthur thought were probably other expletives. He went over to the youthful man who looked angrily at him: 'Fuck you mate; it's all right for you.'

Arthur was at a loss to know what to do or say. 'Tell me what the matter is if you want to.'

'I didn't know what they were doing, but they had cut off my fucking leg. It was all right before, but then they just fucking took it and I used to be a footballer.'

Arthur had no idea what to say or do; any words might further antagonise the poor man. Ashamed afterwards for his poor response, Arthur simply muttered, 'God bless you,' and moved back towards the sister.

'I didn't know what to say,' he confessed.

'None of us does. Poor Private Bland is suffering so much, mentally even more than physically and we understand his feelings. He came to us with advanced gangrene, but strangely not much pain and we wondered if his leg had lost all feeling. He would have died within days, so an amputation was the only hope, but we just don't know how to help his rage. In fact, the amputation went as well as one might hope and he may make a good recovery and with a prosthetic limb may walk again. What will happen to his injured mind I just don't know. Reverend, are you all right to go on?' Arthur felt uncertain, but nodded in a way that he hoped looked confident.

'We'll go into the next ward which is isolated from the rest. As you will realise, the twelve men have only just come to us. Their condition is grim, but when we have cleaned things up, they will all be a little better.' Sister Carmichael opened a door and led the way down a short, but well-lit corridor. As she opened the next door, leading to the old dining room, the smell hit Arthur.

'This,' said the sister, 'will at first seem as close to hell as you will ever get and we won't stay long. The men have a variety of injuries, some are almost certainly not life threatening and may soon move on to another hospital, rather more like a nursing home.'

Arthur had been surprised at the orderliness and air of tranquillity which he had seen, but this ward was totally different: most of the men totally unkempt, bandages were filthy. Nurses were at several beds washing the men regardless of screams and shouts of abuse. It took four nurses to hold one man down whilst a fifth did the best she could to wash him. Arthur's eye went to two men at the far end who looked altogether different; washing them had already occurred.

'They arrived by boat at Harwich early today and were driven here. They were filthy, their heads and bodies crawling with lice and goodness knows what else. As you can see it's hard for the nurses to get any vestige of order, but they will. For the moment we have an open mind about what's best for them.' She gently took Arthur's arm and led him back to the corridor. From there they walked across a room full of crates of many sizes. 'Our most recent stores, which have just been delivered.' Arthur recalled the vehicle he had seen at the front of the house.

'So, Your Reverend, I think you've seen enough for one visit. I hope it hasn't proved too shocking for you?'

Arthur pondered for a moment as to how to reply. 'It is indeed shocking; shocking that men should suffer so much and shocking that you and all the medical staff have to deal with man's inhumanity to man. I've heard enough about the war, seen the terrible casualty figures, but understood so little. Sister, what you are doing is truly wonderful, God's work indeed.' He saw a slightly quizzical look on her face.

After leaving the hospital and clambering into the trap, he gave Sparky a brief account of what he had seen, his final words to Sister Carmichael coming back to him. "God's work," he had said. He wondered at these words; if God was able to work through the nurses to heal and comfort, why did the same God allow the men to be injured and maimed in the first place? Did his words make sense; to him, never mind to Sister Carmichael? It was a troubled man who returned to Rusfield; troubled by what he had seen at the hospital, but much more by the relationship between God and suffering. How could they coexist in the same world?

The hospital visit affected him in another way. Having

thanked Sparky as he was dropped off at the vicarage, he was lovingly welcomed by Eleanor. After a quick wash and warm up from the cool drive in the open trap, Eleanor brought in cups of tea.

'Well Arthur, how did you find the visit? Not all pleasant I imagine.' Arthur told his wife of some of the men he had seen and the work performed by the nurses.

Eleanor's eyes twinkled: 'And do you still think it's a place for only men to visit; not really suitable for me and others of my sex?'

Arthur pondered for a moment. 'Eleanor, like so many other times, I was wrong. I did find it hard although I am glad I went. However, there must have been over fifty nurses and they are coping with horrendous problems. I admire them so much. No, it certainly showed me that women are more than equal to men on this one. I'm sorry I suggested you didn't come.'

'From what you have said there will be other occasions. Maybe we can find other people that might go. I'm sure the Mansfields, the Jacksons and the de Maines would go if they knew it helped the men. We could also ask Nurse Hazlett and Olivia Atkins. Let's see if we can organise a rota.'

Arthur smiled. How fortunate he was to have such a wonderful wife. He had little doubt as to which of the two of them the wounded soldiers would prefer to see.

'But we must both get ready for our next appointments,' Eleanor reminded her husband. 'The choral group is really going quite well; there are nearly twenty of us now and everyone is very enthusiastic. And guess what, Arthur? Young Albert Jones is joining us tonight. It seems an age since the two of us last sang together. Sad that he is back off to France in a couple of days; he still seems far from recovered.'

They shared a kiss before leaving the vicarage: Eleanor to the church; Arthur to the meeting of the Village Coal Club to see how the accounts were faring after such a cold winter. In the midst of this terrible war both activities seemed trivial, but it was all they could do.

FORTY-ONE

1915 - April 1916

Private Fred Smith was confused, unwell and deeply depressed. After a chance meeting had promised better things for him, the war had got worse and since Jack Atkins had been injured and returned to England nearly a year and a half ago, he had not seen any of his Rusfield mates. After fierce fighting around Givenchy, the small, beleaguered platoon, of which Fred was part, had retreated to await orders. The pain in his head still screamed at him as the guns had never ceased firing, but then came a brief respite. While resting near a heavily scarred village, a small group of Dragoon Guards had appeared at the nearby crossroads and Fred's eyes lit up when he saw their fine horses. When the men dismounted, leaving the horses to search for grass on the lightly snow-covered ground, he edged over to a fine-looking grey which turned and looked at him, recognised by the blacksmith's former apprentice as a welcoming look. It gave a gentle snort and nuzzled Fred.

'You seem to have made a good friend there.' Fred was caught unawares, turned and saw a moustached and smartly-attired major. He immediately came to attention and saluted.

'His name is Caesar. He's a fine beast isn't he?' the smiling officer said, giving the horse a couple of pats.

'Yes sir, a wonderful horse.' Whilst Fred was wary of

officers, talk of horses immediately dispelled that worry. He was suddenly back at Joe Bacon's forge, enquiring after a horse brought in for his attention.

'You seem to like horses, do you know much about them?' Shyly, Fred explained his work at the forge. The major was surprised at the conversation, but later reflected upon it as one of the few moments when rank was cast aside in a happy interlude in a terrible war.

Major Richard Carpenter sketched out something of Caesar's war. 'We got together when I came over with our regiment and were at Mons; lucky to escape free of injury. But now the army spends most of its time in trenches, our duties have changed.' He looked at Fred; this pale-faced private reminded him of young Peter who had been one of the stable boys on his father's estate in Leicestershire. 'I can see you easily bond with a horse; do you know enough to help heal wounds and cope with equine illnesses?'

Fred was not too sure about the equine part, but knowing it had to do with making horses better, he honestly answered: 'Yes.'

'Well, we are based in a camp about two miles from here. We carry out reconnaissance work, but for the past two months we have also provided a centre for injured horses; let's call it a horse hospital. Some carry serious wounds, others are exhausted and need their strength building up. So many are needed: pulling ambulances, supply wagons and the growing numbers of heavy artillery; they've become real war machines. You seem as if you could be useful to our force.'

Fred could hardly believe what he was hearing. The major went across to the fair-haired, young commander of Fred's platoon and asked, but in such a way as to expect agreement, that Fred be transferred to his command. Twenty-one-year-old Lieutenant Roseberry-Jones was surprised, for Private Smith had not displayed any qualities warranting such a request. 'Well sir, I'm happy to agree with your request,' he meekly replied.

Fifteen minutes later the Guards mounted their horses. 'Private Smith, you'll see the direction that we are heading. Make for that clump of trees and only a short distance on you will find our encampment.' So it was that some forty minutes later Fred reached the camp where he hoped his war would take a better turn.

It was an area which he judged to be ten times as big as the village green. On two sides stone walls marked the boundary, the rest surrounded by a wire fence. 'Bloody hard knocking those posts in,' Fred heard a hefty corporal say later. There were two large red-tiled barns near the centre which Fred thought must have been the reason for choosing this place, but he later saw another reason: a small stream running across one corner. Fred quickly learnt that Caesar's major commanded the whole activity.

He found himself under the immediate command of Sergeant Hughes who later told his new recruit that he had worked on a farm near Newbury for breeding race horses. 'Different sort of job, Smith, but at least I'm still with animals. I reckon they're more reliable than men.'

'Sergeant, what do you want me to do now?' asked the ever-willing Fred.

'Well, there don't seem much of you, but get some bales of this newly delivered hay into that left-hand barn and spread some around. I think there might be a frost tonight, so we'll have as many horses inside as possible. Oh, one other thing, you'll see there are some horses already in the one barn. They're in a pretty bad way and we need to keep a special eye on them.'

Fred could see that the opening into the paddock, used by many vehicles, was muddy with rutted wheel and horse tracks, most filled with water. Two days later he was to be ordered to move some posts and wire to create a more passable entrance. With the help of two privates, whom Fred found it hard to understand, ten bales were moved into the barn. The slight, but tough Choppy, a Liverpudlian, told Fred that a few years earlier he had been laying the foundations for a new building at Aintree race track when the owners had given him full-time work. This had brought him in to contact with horses. 'I loved them.'

Fred could see around fifty horses and he and Choppy were ordered to move three quarters into the barn for the night. 'Then see if there's room for the rest,' Sergeant Hughes ordered.

'Anyway,' explained Choppy, 'we open the door around midnight and then if anymore want to come in that's all right. You'll find a few decide to go out for a drink.'

Fred found his two new mates friendly. 'We're glad to have you with us,' said Baffer between gasps when moving the bales. 'There's plenty for Choppy and me to do, but sometimes we get a bit of help from one or two who come over from "next door", but most of the time it's just us.'

This was the first time since Jack had left that there seemed a chance to have any real mates; he knew people had rarely sought him out to be a friend. When he had started at the village school he found himself left out of other games and some poked fun at him as learning to read and write seemed more difficult for him than most, hard though he tried. Then in the third year he had found himself sitting next to Willy Johnson and from then on he always had a mate; they both loved nature and football. All bullying ceased.

Fred had already learnt that the nearby farmhouse provided quarters for the major and Sergeant Hughes. There was also a tall Glaswegian whose job Fred assumed, later confirmed, to be the major's batman and his messenger with the rest of the Dragoon Guards encamped a quarter of a mile away, referred to by Choppy and Baffer as "next door".

Fred's work was just completed in daylight and Choppy went off to collect food from the HQ. It was basic, but filling thought Fred. 'Good grub,' he commented to the other two:

it was more substantial than his mother could often provide. He wondered how she and his gran were getting on. He desperately hoped he would get some leave so he could see her at least one more time; hope that so far had led to nothing. He was very grateful to Jack's mother as he had received a lovely letter from Olivia Atkins thanking him for his note telling her that Jack was recovering well. It was the first letter he had ever received, but thereafter she wrote to him every two or three months. He had also received two letters from the vicar and one from Major de Maine.

In answer to his question about sleeping quarters, Choppy pointed out that each barn had a raised platform and by being there they could keep an eye on the horses. 'As it's yer first night Fred, you and I will be in this barn and Baffer in t'other.'

They saw Sergeant Hughes once more that evening. 'I've just had a look at the poorest horses and there's a couple that might not see out the night, but make sure you keep a special eye on them. Chopton, you and Smith take it in three-hour shifts to stay awake and get down regularly taking a look at the really sick ones. Smith, with all this hay around take care with your light.' Fred nodded. What a lucky thing it was that he had befriended Caesar. Bedding down with the horses was fine; he could think of no better place to sleep.

The night passed quickly enough after Choppy had taken him on a round of the eight sick horses. Fred could see that five were being nursed for really bad wounds, two from shell explosions, one shot in its hind quarters and two, the sickest of the group, from an undiagnosed sickness. Both were unreasonably thin, yet had grossly distended stomachs. Fred could see a fluid coming from their noses which on closer examination gave out a foul smell. They were further alarmed when the one, a piebald, gave off slight tremors. 'Apparently they had been together moving howitzers up to the front and then almost collapsed,' explained Choppy. 'They really had to be encouraged to get this far and steadily worsened. When the major came in yesterday he said if they don't quickly get better we'll have to put them down.' Fred shuddered as he heard this, but his mind went to some of the terrible human casualties he had seen who had been allowed to go on suffering without any hope of such an ending.

On two further checks that night he ensured that water was easily available and did his best to check their heartbeat. Joe Bacon had been a good teacher and shown Fred that by placing his hand on the left side of the chest, just under the elbow, he could feel the heartbeat. The piebald and its sick companion appeared no better and heart rates were irregular.

The next day he fully understood when the sergeant told them the two would have to be put down. When the other horses were out in the field enjoying the freshly spread hay on a morning of rare winter sunshine, the sergeant, Choppy and Fred went in to the barn. Meanwhile, Baffer and two men who had come over from "next door" had pulled a low cart into the area where the sick horses lay. They had also tethered two fit horses ready to pull the cart on the final journey for the piebald and its companion. Fred had seen horses put down before, but could barely look as the sergeant took out his revolver and placed the nozzle against the piebald's forehead. As the shot resounded round the barn, the horse gave an involuntary shudder. This final act was repeated with the other creature. Fred could see the sadness of the sergeant burdened with the death of creatures that should have been enjoying their work in peaceful villages and countryside.

The sergeant came over to Fred. 'Yes, it is the worst thing that I ever have to do. What a bloody world it is; these two fine creatures are the most innocent of all victims of the war. They don't deserve this; at least we volunteered for it, it's our job.' He turned to the other men. 'Now let's get the rest done.'

'They take the body about 500 yards from here, where a ditch has been prepared,' Baffer explained to Fred. The operation was repeated for the second corpse when the cart returned an hour later. Sergeant Hughes and Choppy got on with checking all the horses, placing a yellow band round the tail to show the check had been done. Meanwhile Fred and Choppy got on with "shit shovel duty", clearing the plentiful supply of dung in the barn into barrows, which they then carted over to prepared pits.

With the war almost totally static, the small band of men continued to care for more horses although, as Baffer said, 'Sadly, we're making a lot of them better so that they can go back to war and more suffering.'

Over the next three months hundreds were treated, dozens put down. They were eight miles from the front line and although the sound of gunfire became louder as the guns became more powerful, Fred found himself barely taking any notice. As he said to Choppy: 'It's nothing like the terrible noise when I was so near the enemy.'

'I'll tell yer what, Fred: we're bloody lucky. There's all those poor sods up at the front and the worst we have to do is bury horses and shovel shit. I think the army may have forgotten about us,' he added with a smile.

Major Carpenter was away more frequently and only occasionally did Fred have the opportunity to see Caesar; they were precious moments. All continued well until the terrible rains of late 1915 when everywhere became a quagmire. They laboured to move large lengths of the fencing so the horses had new areas, but these were soon turned into mud baths; duckboards disappeared into the morass. Fred could always remember that it was on Boxing Day he began to feel unwell; just a headache and a slight fever at first. Sergeant Hughes said he would have a word with Major Carpenter and maybe a visit to the field hospital a few miles away could be arranged. 'Perhaps it's something you've picked up from the horses. I've heard that can happen,' added the sergeant.

Such a visit never happened as within days a big push

by the German forces caused the horse hospital to be hastily abandoned; moving troops, not caring for horses, became the order. Whilst Major Carpenter arranged for most of the fitter horses to be moved to engineers who needed all possible support in moving war materials, a high number were put down and with all the frantic activity and approaching gunfire others panicked, some leaping over the fence and running free. Fred wondered what fate they would meet.

It was in early February 1916 that Fred found himself attached to a group of engineers. Quite how he had become involved with them, he was uncertain. After a long march from the abandoned horse hospital, he became one of around forty men transported westwards by a dilapidated green omnibus to a point where the rail line ended and several roads met. His headaches were becoming more frequent and some days he found himself shivering and seeing things through a colourless haze.

From Calais, trains carried an ever-increasing volume of war materials; some for road building but essentially guns and vast numbers of shells, near to a town which Fred later learnt was Arras; beyond which the railway had been destroyed months earlier. From that point everything had to be taken by other means to the front line and, after the rains of late 1915 and early 1916, vast areas were a quagmire. It was here that horses were needed to drag the ever-larger guns.

Fred was amazed at the size of field guns which were becoming ever larger; the number of enormous crates packed with shells even more staggering. He saw the ten wagons, heavily covered against the likely rain and large-wheeled to assist their passage through the inevitable mud. Pairs of horses had been prepared and laden with thick ropes for the mighty effort to move the wagons. He felt particularly poorly as he watched the wretched beasts being harnessed to the wagons. His brow was covered in sweat, his legs were weak and the whole scene appeared as if he was looking in at someone else taking part in all the activity. Yet his feelings were more for the bay and piebald pulling his wagon than with himself.

'Get movin',' a voice bellowed. Fred was with two other men walking with the second wagon, some ten yards behind the first. He was the front man walking alongside the horses, encouraging and talking to them from time to time. Two older men were at the rear, one on each side watching the wheels and ready for any major obstacle although Fred did his best to guide the horses around the many holes and large lumps of stone littering the track. Gradually, the way became more difficult, any track petering out. Trees were burnt stumps, hedges but ridges winding their way through a vast area of mud. It was the sergeant with the lead wagon who called a halt and Fred watched as one of the men from that vehicle walked back the short distance.

'The sergeant says we'll have a stop as he wants to take a look ahead. All we can see is mud and it's not possible to know whether that's just on the top or goes deeper. I'm going forward with him to see how far we sink in, but it doesn't look good to me. Pass the word back.' Fred gave each of the horses a pat, telling them that they were taking a short break.

Bobby, the Welsh Borderer, who had carried the message to the vehicle behind turned to Fred as the three of them sat down by the side of the wagon. 'You look pretty bad. Are you all right?'

Fred had to shake his head before he really understood the question. 'Well, I haven't been feeling good for quite a time now, but I guess that goes for a lot of us.'

'Have you seen a medic?'

A twinge of a smile came to Fred's face. 'Well, I was about to when we had to get out from our camp and that was that.'

'I don't know what to call you mate, but when did you last have any leave?'

There was a momentary silence as Fred's eyes slowly focused on the questioner, 'I'm Fred. I haven't had any leave.'

'Well, how long have you been out here then, Fred?' he asked.

'I came over in August 1914, not sure how long ago that is.'

'Christ,' uttered the first. 'You mean you've been here for a year and a half and still not got any time back home. Someone must have forgotten you. Who are you with?'

Fred had some difficulty in working out who he was with; he seemed to have moved around a great deal. He just gave a weak smile. A shout from the front announced everyone was to move off. With a little difficulty Fred got to his feet, placing his left hand against the giant wheel of the wagon for support. The three men took up their positions, following the front wagon which moved a little to the left before starting across the foul stretch of mud. The horses struggled, but did their utmost to carry out the exhausting task demanded of them.

The procession had only gone fifty yards when Fred's world came apart; his head swam, the sky and mud collided and his hearing filled with a loud buzzing. He would have fallen immediately if the calf-deep mud had allowed; as it was he lurched and fell face forwards into the filthy mud.

The following hours were lost to Fred. One of his mates with the wagon saw him pitch forward and bawled out, 'Stop! Stop!' The Welshman reached Fred, extracted his feet from the slime, turned him over and lifted him on the side of the wagon. Charlie, the man on the right side wheel pulled a cloth from his trouser pocket and wiped Fred's face, doing his best to clear his nostrils. By this time the sergeant had arrived. 'He looks in a bad way. We can't all turn back so you and you carry him back. It won't be easy for you, but luckily he's quite a small guy. At least you won't have this bloody mud to go through.'

They got him back to camp two hours later, a period of time to which Fred was completely oblivious. From the camp he was transferred by a small horse-drawn cart to a field hospital a further mile back. It was there, the next day, that Fred regained a semblance of consciousness. His mind was constantly slipping through many scenes; he was drowning one moment, seeing the village pond the next. His gran, Captain Carpenter, Willy and Ruby were there one moment, gone the next. His head was splitting, he felt he was being shaken, loud sounds yet they seemed far away. He lapsed in and out of consciousness.

The activity in the field hospital greatly increased with the arrival of over fifty men, some suffering terrible injury; every available nurse and doctor doing the best they could. Labels were attached to each man, crudely stating the treatment needed. 'Dress left foot', 'Amputate right arm', 'Dead', 'Clean head wound' were all to be seen. Stretcher bearers, nurses, doctors were all at full stretch, and more.

Twenty-five-year-old Doctor William Last, whose time at a London medical school had been foreshortened to meet the needs in France, puzzled over Fred. His breathing was laboured and noisy, pulse weak, heartbeat slightly irregular, and temperature high but fluctuating. He turned to Nurse Susan Hopkins: 'I'm baffled by the state of this man. He is clearly very ill, but I can't diagnose a precise cause. We've heard rumours of gas used by the Germans; I don't know whether he has been exposed to that.'

'Doctor, what do we know about the patient? Where has he come from?' asked the slim, dark-haired nurse.

'I understand he arrived from a camp, carried by two men, but everything is very vague. I've heard about men who become infected simply by being in the trenches; rat and lice infestations, even the soil being contaminated, but he doesn't have any expected rash or skin marking. I'll try to get someone else to give a second opinion.' A second opinion did not help Fred. He drifted in and out of consciousness. On one such occasion he recognised someone was sitting alongside and thought it must be the Reverend Windle.

When thirty-year-old Reverend Charlton Woods had arrived at the field hospital, no one seemed to know what he had come for or how they should treat him. Most were wary of clerics as they seemed to be for officers only, but stories soon filtered through about this man. A lance corporal who had arrived at the field hospital with severe leg injuries told how the Reverend Woods had been in the trenches during severe fighting. He had even heard how he had crawled out in to no man's land to offer what solace he could to three dying men. Thereafter, he was treated with respect.

He sat by Fred. 'Is there anything I can do for you?' he asked. 'Can I contact someone for you?' His broad face was compassionate, lined with feeling for this young man, yet another victim of this war.

Fred focused as best he could on this kind face. 'Would you write a letter for me, please?'

'Of course I will.' He reached into his dark green backpack, searched for a moment and took out writing pad and implement. 'Now who is it to?'

'To my mother.'

After gentle questioning, Charlton Woods obtained name and address. 'Tell me what you want me to say to your mother, Private Smith,' reading the brown label attached to Fred's bed-shirt.

'Tell her I love her and I hope to see her soon. Tell her to give my love to Gran. Oh, and to all my friends... and to Ruby.' He lapsed into a brief silence, whether through exhaustion or to give time for his wishes to be written down was uncertain. 'Please tell her I've loved looking after all the horses.' His silence became longer. 'Sir, do you think God loves horses? Will you pray for them?'

A tone of compassion replied: 'I'm sure the God I believe in loves all living creatures.'

The Reverend Charlton Woods pondered over the letter for a long time. He was not unused to writing letters home for wounded men. He knew how a single phrase would be read and reread a hundred times: each word so important. He finished writing; the author of the letter was asleep. The next day the letter was sent on its way; two nights later, Private Fred Smith died.

FORTY-TWO

May 1916

'He really is a man full of wonderful surprises,' Eleanor said to Arthur after hearing of his meeting with Robert Berry, 'first of all his idea for organising the soldiers' parcels and now this.'

Arthur smiled. 'Well, it was just a casual meeting, but I've invited him to come round with Sammy Hatfield later. It was after I'd called into the school to have a word with David earlier this morning that I met Robert and he told me that he and Sammy believed people must grow more vegetables, especially with the shortages caused by the U-boats. Apparently they have built up a supply of seeds from beans, peas and other vegetables they grew last year and have been into Steepleton and Canchester to buy up as many seeds as possible.'

'So he's not just thought of the idea, then?' interjected Eleanor.

'It would seem not. He wants everyone to give over part of their garden to grow vegetables. He thinks the war will go on for a long time and growing vegetables will help and that in the autumn we can all begin storing seeds. And another thing, you remember my dear that you were talking about the new Summer Time Act coming in this month. Well, Robert says the extra hour of daylight will give us all more time for our gardens. Anyway, I hope it's all right with you, darling, I've asked them both round for eleven o'clock.'

'Of course it is, Arthur. I look forward to hearing more.'

Even as Arthur and Eleanor were discussing the idea, Peter Woods was cycling with all speed towards the village. He knew that once again he carried news that would bring grief; the envelope was all too familiar. It was just after ten o'clock that Arthur and Eleanor having cleared the table, were alerted by a heavy knocking at the door. They found a slightly breathless Peter Woods holding an envelope. 'I'm sorry to bother you, but I don't know what to do.'

'That's all right, Peter,' Eleanor gently reassured him. 'What is it?'

'Well, I have this telegram for Mrs Smith,' he said holding out the buff envelope. An immediate feeling of dread descended upon them.

'Oh, it must be about poor Fred.'

'And we know she's not at home,' grimaced Arthur.

'That's what I mean, sir. I delivered a letter for her on Monday and I know she wasn't at home. But this - I can't just put it through her door.'

Arthur glanced at Eleanor; who gave him an encouraging half smile. 'You're right, of course Peter, we have to get this to her. I expect it's against regulations, but will you leave it with me? I can promise to get it to her as soon as possible.'

'Of course, sir,' Peter immediately agreed, handing the telegram over with some relief. 'I don't need to say anything back at the office. I wish you well sir.' He left the vicarage for his return to Steepleton. His heart, too, was sinking; surely this was bad news about Fred.

As soon as he had gone, Eleanor turned to Arthur. 'We don't know when Liz will next be home.' They recalled that when old Mrs Smith had died, Arthur had written to her other daughter, Mary. After an uncertain start, Liz had enjoyed her sister coming to live with her. Everyone had seen what a difference her sister had made, for the inside of the cottage now appeared spick and span and Major de Maine, the owner of the terrace of cottages, had arranged for the exterior to be redecorated. 'Unrecognisable,' Eleanor had said to Arthur a month after the sisters were united.

Towards the end of 1915, Eleanor and Arthur had been amazed at Liz's news. 'Well, Mary and I have made a decision. We need to do our bit for the war effort and Fred would want me to do that, too. So we've decided to go and work at the munitions factory just beyond a place called Epping. They need lots of workers and we've heard from a lady who's got two spare rooms and we'll stay there.' That had been seven months earlier.

'Eleanor, I need to see Liz as quickly as possible. Jack Mansfield has often said that if I've got a real emergency away from the village to let him know and he'll drive me there. I'm sure he will if he can. I guess it's around sixty miles and it shouldn't be too difficult to find the factory. Liz told me that there were over 3,000 people working there so anyone near Epping should know.'

'That's the best idea, Arthur. You bicycle round to Spinney Farm and I'll go round to Liz's house and collect the letter that Peter delivered on Monday. I know she keeps the key round the back in a pot.'

Fifteen minutes later Arthur arrived at the forecourt to Spinney Farm, spotting young Doris Groves carrying a basket full of washing. 'Oh Doris, can you please tell me where Mr Mansfield is? I need to see him urgently.'

'Ay. Master is indoors as I just saw him coming back from sheep field.' Arthur thanked her and in answer to his knock, was delighted to see Jack Mansfield.

'Why Arthur, it's good to see you,' but realised from Arthur's expression that this was not just a social visit. 'What is it?'

Arthur explained, knowing that the farmer would maintain confidence; they had a high regard for each other. 'Of course I can take you, Arthur. It can only be around fifty miles so we can easily get there and back today. Poor lady, let's just hope it's not the worst news, but from what you've told me it certainly sounds bad. Just give me ten minutes and I'll be ready.'

Fifteen minutes later, Eleanor and Arthur were in the back of Jack Mansfield's Phoenix leaving Rusfield. Eleanor had asked that she and Arthur sit together in the back so they could discuss their approach to Liz Smith; letter and telegram were both safe in her shoulder bag. On her way back from Liz Smith's cottage she had called on Robert Berry and explained they would have to postpone their meeting about vegetable growing. Arthur was much relieved to have Eleanor with him for he knew how much better she was at choosing the best words in any difficult situation.

The day was fine and the journey passed without difficulty. As they went through Braintree around half past twelve, Jack Mansfield thought of the previous occasion when he had driven through this Essex market town taking Abraham to his running success at Crystal Palace. Would he ever see that splendid young man race again?

They had seen a little of Epping Forest and twenty minutes later turned off a minor road to confront a heavily-fenced area, fronted by two imposing iron gates. This was no ordinary estate, as there were two soldiers, both with rifles, one at each gate. Arthur explained the reason for the visit and they were told to wait. The corporal went through a small opening to the left of the main gates and disappeared into the nearby building. After a call through to the main office he reappeared and said he would accompany them to a senior manager.

'I'll come back in an hour to an hour and a half; don't worry if you're longer,' Jack Mansfield said to Eleanor and Arthur. 'One other thing: Liz and Mary Smith are doing a very important job, but I'm sure it's not well paid, so if they want to go back to Rusfield straight away I can easily find someone in the town to drive them back.' He smiled, reversed the car and drove off.

'Come on then, love,' Eleanor said as she turned to her husband. 'This is a wretched task, but it's the least we can do for Liz.' A strong smell had been evident which became even more noticeable as they walked along the wide drive. 'Chemicals of some kind,' Arthur quietly suggested.

As they turned from the well-treed avenue, dozens of buildings, most single level but a cluster with high-pitched roofs, emerged. It was only later they learnt the factory had been built to supply gunpowder in Napoleon's time, but many additions had been made in response to the threat from Germany. Some buildings, heavily marked from a variety of discharged materials, were over a hundred yards long, with the occasional second storey breaking up the grey roofing of the lower levels. The stench became stronger, accompanied by increasing noise; a loud hammering causing the ground to shake. A narrow gauge railway line with small engines ran in many directions, conveying the many materials required in making gunpowder and shells, others to move the completed articles on their first stage to France. Huge grey pipes a few feet above the ground, most with a diameter around two feet, ran between the buildings.

It was now a warm day, but waves of additional heat greeted them as they passed the pipes. Eleanor nudged Arthur and nodded towards an area where hundreds of bicycles were stored. There were workers everywhere, scurrying from building to building, many dressed in long outer garments which Arthur assumed to be protective clothing. There were many women working at a high mound of coal which had been off-loaded from barges arriving via a narrow canal, shovelling it in to barrows. A queue of women waited to take the laden barrows to what must be the source of the steam power generating machinery.

Cranes of all sizes dominated the area to their left, together with trucks, handcarts and a number of metal machines for which Arthur could not even guess a purpose. The smell, the sounds, the steam and all the machinery demonstrated a momentous activity being carried out in this unlikely part of the countryside. Eleanor shuddered; she had never seen anything like it. They had walked in silence until the corporal spoke: 'Take care where you walk, please follow me.' As they went through a door she noticed the thickness of the walls; perhaps to resist explosions. Inside was a red, two-wheeled handcart attached to a larger contraption filled with water; clearly a fire engine, although Arthur doubted its efficiency in an emergency.

They ascended the stone steps to a door bearing the legend that only named officials could enter. The corporal knocked and almost immediately the door was opened to reveal a fifty-year-old man, tall, grey-moustached, wearing a light brown overall. He smiled. 'I'm Colonel Woodfull, senior supervisor of this establishment and I've been given a brief idea of the purpose of your visit. The unusual circumstances cause me to break our normal code of practice and allow you on to the site. It all sounds grim. Please come in.'

Eleanor and Arthur found they were in a room running the whole width of the factory; an enclosed balcony to a vast auditorium. Opposite the door through which they had entered and facing the main part of the factory was a brick wall with a narrow band of glass at eye level. This was around sixty feet wide and two feet high; divided into small sections separated by thick brick columns. They guessed it to be for observation. The loathsome smell, the din, the shaking and steam all filtered into this office; voices had to be raised. There was another man in the room.

The colonel gave his undivided attention as Arthur and Eleanor explained their mission. 'So, in summary we have a poor lady who lives in your village, working here with her sister, and following a letter delivered on Monday, a telegram arrived this morning which you believe contains bad news.' Arthur and Eleanor both nodded. 'You had no way of contacting her quickly other than to come here. I must say, Reverend, that I admire the compassion you and your wife have shown. Major Spottiswoode over there,' he nodded in the direction of the man poring over clusters of papers, 'is checking through our records. We have nearly 6,000 people working at this National Filling Factory on two separate shifts, so let's hope Mrs Smith is here now. Whilst the name Smith is common, I'm sure we shall quickly find the detail, but in the meantime let me show you something. I'm sure you will treat what you see with discretion.' Eleanor felt she could thank Arthur's clerical collar and attire for gaining such a favour. They followed the colonel to the observation point; the scene that greeted them was to remain with them for a long while. Never could they have imagined anything that so awfully represented the jaws of destruction and Eleanor and Arthur later agreed that the word "hell" had immediately come to mind as they looked down on the scene stretching out below.

Arthur now adjudged the building to be nearer 200 yards long, its width well over half that distance. It had a high roof, supported by heavy metal stanchions which broke up the factory floor into aisles; from the high roof dozens of electric lights were suspended; clearly good lighting was needed in this grim building. The entire floor space in this vast interior was covered by identical shells; among them were dozens of workers, overwhelmingly women, checking or making last minute adjustments to these fearsome projectiles. The shells, all pointing upwards, created a huge mouthful of angry teeth; each stood waist high to the workers. Neither Eleanor nor Arthur had any idea of the number of shells, but knew that they could only be measured in thousands, many thousands. They realised why the establishment was called a filling factory. Eleanor's mind was filled with the death and destruction for which these shells were intended. In Germany there must be similar factories from which shells had caused the death of Jammy Carey and other Rusfield lads.

Their thoughts were interrupted by the colonel after his conversation with Major Spottiswoode. 'Well, we now know that the lady you seek is in the cartridge factory. Please come with me.'

Having given their thanks to the major, Eleanor and Arthur followed the colonel and whilst the air outside was still contaminated by chemical smells, both were pleased at getting away from the shell building. Outside, Arthur noticed three cranes controlled by women. 'May I ask, Colonel,' Arthur broke into the silence, 'about those buildings over there? They appear to be built partly underground and almost look like ice houses.' He pointed to five low, dome-shaped structures, windowless and surrounded by a low wall.

'They are where the most dangerous chemicals are made and mixed: nitroglycerin and other hazardous materials. I sometimes wonder what kind of world we have created.' By now the sun was strong, but for Eleanor a cold air of greyness and nightmarish quality was felt. 'The workers have a short break every three hours, that's why you see some out here enjoying what we dare call fresh air.' They saw four young women sitting on the grass who had momentarily taken off their caps which highlighted the unnatural colour of their faces: an orange-yellow. The colonel noted the direction of the visitors' glance. 'I'm afraid that what you see is a result of working with very unpleasant materials. It's been known for a while that working here over a long period can cause the skin to change colour. They are vulgarly called "canary girls". Now we are moving the girls around more in the hope that it reduces the effect and last week we provided small masks which must now be worn when they are mixing these chemicals; I just hope it helps these poor girls who work long and dangerous hours, yet just get on with the job. Without them the war would be lost.'

By now they had reached a heavy green door which gave access to a smaller and lower building than the shell centre they had just left. The colonel held the door open for his visitors then led the way up another set of stone stairs to the observation centre. A younger man, a civilian Arthur assumed, came across as they entered. He was introduced by the colonel as Mr Glover; handshakes were exchanged.

'Mr Glover,' began Colonel Woodfull, 'I won't take up your time by explaining the whole story, but it is imperative that the Reverend Windle sees one of your workers immediately. Briefly, and tragically, he has news for the lady that her son may have been killed. Mrs Elizabeth Smith and, indeed, her sister Miss Mary Smith both work here in the cartridge inspection team. Please bring them up here and we will allow them to be alone with our two guests who have come on this sad mission.'

The supervisor made a note of the names and disappeared. The colonel led the way over to the observation area where the scene was a little less fearsome than the one they had just left; shells were substituted by thousands of small cartridges. Running the length of this building were around thirty continuous rows of tables, on both sides of which hundreds of women were sitting shoulder to shoulder with piles of cartridges, each some five inches long. They were closely examining the cartridges and then placing them upright in a flat holder which had holes to take twenty of them. Eleanor noticed a few women who were carrying the full holders to another series of tables to the left; another worker moved cartridges which had been separately placed on the table into a large wooden box behind where they were sitting. Arthur assumed these were cartridges that had failed examination.

Arthur had turned away, his senses found the scene almost too hard to bear, when the door opened. Dressed in grey overalls, Liz and Mary Smith came in, their looks of total surprise instant. 'Vicar, Mrs Windle, what are you doing here?'

The look of surprise, even of a slight smile in seeing familiar faces, rapidly turned to anxiety. 'It's something bad, isn't it?' The colonel and supervisor had quietly left and Arthur beckoned the sisters to sit down. Eleanor unfastened her bag and took out two envelopes.

'Liz, you must be prepared for bad news. On Monday Peter delivered a letter to your home; today he brought a telegram. Knowing you might not go back to Rusfield for some time, Eleanor and I felt it right to bring them to you. Would you like me to read them to you?'

Liz nodded, her face the colour of chalk. She may not be able to read fluently, but she understood only too well what the letter and telegram might say. 'Please do. Somehow, I knew the poor lad would never come back.'

'Let me read the letter first.' He slid his finger along the top, opening the letter which the Reverend Charlton Woods had written. It described how Fred was ill, but contained the words that Fred had spoken: of how he had loved caring for the army horses and of the love he wanted passed on to his family and friends; they were words written with a great tenderness. Liz shuddered at the mention of her own mother, as Fred had been unaware that his grandmother had died. The letter ended: *Mrs Smith, your son is very ill and, sadly, he may not recover. I will come back to this field hospital in a few days to see how he is and will write again with any further news. Please know that we have talked together and Fred is proud of all that he has done in serving his country in this dreadful war. He is, indeed, a fine young man and you should be very proud of him.*

Arthur found it hard to read the words and had an alarming view of what was to follow. Tears were running down Liz's face, hardly less with the other three. He opened the telegram and read:

Regret to inform you of the death from a disease of Private F. Smith, 2nd Battalion Suffolk Regiment at 29 Field Hospital on 29th April. I express the sympathy and respect of the Army Council.

'Oh Fred, darling Fred, God bless you.' The shocking cry from Liz was so personal, yet Arthur had heard the same cry from Eliza and Sparky Carey, from Ruby Rowe, from young Robert Bacon's father and others. He knew it would be repeated. Liz had asked for God's blessing on Fred, but Arthur had to wonder where God was just now.

'And I haven't seen him since he was a baby. I so wanted to,' sobbed Mary. 'Now mother and Fred are both dead. They could never say goodbye to each other.'

Arthur and Eleanor could only quietly sit by as the sisters shared their terrible family sadness. 'What does it mean, disease?' asked Liz.

'I don't know. But there are so many illnesses caught from being in the trenches. I doubt if we shall ever know, but maybe you will learn more in due course,' Arthur, hand on Liz's shoulder, said.

Liz cuffed away her tears and looked at Arthur. 'Vicar, when mother died you was with us. You said some words; I think they was a psalm and then we all said the Lord's Prayer. Can we do the same now? Somehow that will help draw Fred and mother together, us too.'

'Of course.' Heads were bowed and Arthur remembered the evening when old Mrs Smith had died. 'The Lord is my shepherd, I shall not want…' There, in that office overlooking the weapons of war, a war that had killed a beloved son, they joined in the Lord's Prayer. As he said the much-loved words, he did feel a little of God's presence.

It was Eleanor who spoke next as she looked at Liz. 'Fred was a fine and caring person. We all loved him and will miss him, but you should be very proud of him. Remember, it was your strength and your love that made him such a fine person. Never forget that.'

After a few minutes, Arthur told her of Jack Mansfield's offer to arrange for her a car to take them back to Rusfield. 'That is very kind of Mr Mansfield. Please thank him, but Mary and I will stay here. A lot of the ladies working here have lost sons and husbands, so many of us have the same things to share. Thank you for coming to see me, that's been wonderfully kind, in a few days we shall come home to Rusfield.' Mary nodded; she would do whatever her sister wanted.

When Eleanor and Arthur had got back to the vicarage from the National Filling Factory, they shared an unusually quiet evening with their individual thoughts. Eleanor was a little puzzled: Liz and her sister Mary shared the same family name: Smith. She knew Mary had never married so why had Liz kept her maiden name? Maybe she had just wanted to retain her maiden name when Fred was born; not uncommon in Rusfield when an unmarried woman had given birth. She knew so little of Liz's past and feared for her future. Arthur broke into her thoughts as he quietly stood up and then spoke to her with much love: 'Eleanor, it has been a dreadful day for Liz, but one thing I want to say. I was amazed at the work being done at that factory by women, young and old. I saw the same thing at the military hospital we visited a few weeks ago. And you are right; women are at least equal to men, sometimes more than equal.' He added with a slight smile, 'I'm not going to become an angry suffragette when the war is over, but I will do what I can to get them voting rights.' Eleanor kissed him.

That night in bed, Eleanor and Arthur simply clung to each other.

A week later Liz and Mary Smith made the journey back to Rusfield. Mr Glover said they could return to the factory whenever they wanted. When Liz opened the front door she immediately saw a letter which Peter had delivered the previous day. A thought flashed through her mind: perhaps there had been a mistake and it was someone else who had died. She and Mary quickly walked to Olivia Atkins. After a consoling and lingering embrace, Liz asked Olivia to read the letter. It was from Major Richard Carpenter of the 8th Dragoon Guards. It read:

I deeply regret to have learnt that your son Pte. F. Smith, No. 204491 of the 2nd Battalion Suffolk Regiment died on the night of the 29th instant. He had been ill for some days with an unknown illness, but did not suffer.

His service to the army was of major importance and I and all my men had the highest regard for him. After showing great bravery at the front, I was pleased that he joined my team where he worked tirelessly with army horses, enabling a vital part of the war effort to be carried out. He was hardworking, cheerful and a good colleague. I had the privilege of many conversations with him especially about his abiding love of horses and his happy life in your village.

I and all the staff here and his colleagues deeply sympathise with you in your loss.

Your son always did his duty and has now given his life for his country. We all honour him, and I trust you will feel some consolation in remembering this. I know that many attended his burial; the place marked with a simple cross bearing his name. I am sure his effects will reach you via the Base in due course.

In true sympathy.

FORTY-THREE

August 1916

For months Ruby had watched the buzzard, remembering the time Willy had pointed out the tree four years earlier; this year she had seen a buzzard showing itself on a high branch in April. Four days later she spotted its nest and from then on she saw the buzzard most mornings; Willy would have been able to tell her when it laid its eggs. A further three weeks on, she had observed two buzzards and heard a strange yelping noise as one flew to join the other. She wondered if the cry meant "I'm coming" or was it the one on the nest saying "welcome"? And then, on one glorious summer morning, she could hardly believe her eyes when she saw two young buzzards perched on the branch near the nest.

So much to tell Willy and now he was coming home. It was all so exciting after all the sadness that had gone before. She knew how everyone had been saddened by the news of Fred Smith's death; she had loved him. She had liked him when they had walked home together after the party four years earlier and then felt a sense of wonder as that feeling had grown into love. Now as she lay in bed, she knew that Fred's bed next door would remain empty; each time she walked past the forge she imagined him tending the horses. She had burst into tears of joy when Mrs Smith had told her that Fred had spoken of her in the letter home just before he died. Somehow, watching the buzzards had helped, as she knew Fred loved birds as well.

On this same early August morning, Eleanor was returning from Sidney Jones' butchers, thinking just what she might say at the meeting in the afternoon. Not that she knew the questions and she was only one of four on the answer panel, but she was pleased the Mothers' Union was going from strength to strength. The weekly gathering showed warmth and friendship with a number of women attending who, like Eleanor, did not have children. Eleanor tried to look forward to the meeting, although she would have preferred to stay at home; her headache still troubled her.

As she approached the vicarage she waved to Peter. 'I've delivered your letters, Mrs. Windle,' adding with a smile, 'no exciting stamps on either of them.' Eleanor thanked him and opening the door saw the letters on the hall floor: one for Arthur bearing the official Canchester Cathedral crest and, addressed to both of them, a letter from Arthur's mother. Eleanor admired how Charlotte Windle always wrote in such positive fashion; her lively news with attendances at her branch of the Mothers' Union, art classes and time with friends.

Eleanor thought back to the desperate times the previous year when she had thought Arthur's mother might never be able to escape from the terrible deceit of her husband. She had stayed in Rusfield for over a month, becoming immersed in helping to prepare parcels for the Rusfield men, attending church services and choir practices and enjoying afternoon tea with several kind villagers. She had become particular close to Olivia Atkins and they spent time together with their interest in painting: Olivia with her children's drawings and she with still-life sketches.

But as the village moved into the second half of May, Charlotte Windle announced that it was time she returned home. That afternoon Eleanor, Arthur and Charlotte walked the four miles to Wensfield to Eleanor's parents whom she had met on several previous occasions. Charlotte had found she had much in common with Charles and Georgina Brown, especially a love of books. The next day Arthur and his mother travelled to Dorset with Arthur staying for three days to make sure his mother was settled in. As Eleanor put the letter down, she marvelled at how well the widow was coping. She heard the front door opening and called out to Arthur, 'I'm in the kitchen. You're just in time for a cup of tea.'

'How are you feeling, my love? Is the head still hurting?' Eleanor gave her gentle smile.

'I have something for you,' smiled Arthur, putting a pretty decorated tin on the table. 'Some scones which Violet Rushton has baked and wants us to try. Dare I hope we might have one with our cup of tea?' he asked. 'Incidentally, good news from Violet who told me that the next batch of parcels is ready to go off. Of course, the parcels are smaller now but, as we agreed, it's showing the men we think about them, although I'm sure what is received is very welcome. She also mentioned that she and Robert visited Richford House hospital yesterday. Apparently a number of men have arrived from somewhere near Albert, some in a parlous state.' He paused for a moment. 'Over one hundred of our men now away, it doesn't seem possible.'

'And nine that will never return,' added Eleanor. A slight drop of her shoulders and the sadness on her beautiful face slowly turned into a smile, albeit a slightly forced one. 'Here's your tea, Arthur, and one of Violet's scones. They look delicious. Oh, and there's a very happy letter from your mother.' She sipped her tea and enjoyed the unexpected scone while Arthur read the letter.

'Well, mother seems to be getting on very well. We can look forward to going down to see her next month for a few days, which will be lovely. And, to change subjects for a moment, it's not only the parcels for the troops that are going well. I met

Robert round at Violet's shop and he said several people had given over parts of their garden to growing vegetables.'

'Indeed,' interjected Eleanor, 'Eliza told me that Sammy had persuaded Sparky to give up part of his garden to growing beans and peas, something he'd never done before.'

'And Sparky and Eliza were not alone in doing just that. Robert said he and Sammy are sure the idea will work as long as it means vegetables are cheaper.'

As he finished talking, Arthur ran a kitchen knife along the seam of the larger envelope and pulled out some folded papers. With a smile which Eleanor knew just how to interpret he said, 'Eleanor this is from an old friend of yours, the Very Reverend Edgar Hartley Williamson, Dean of Canchester Cathedral. He says that as the bishop is ill it is his duty to make us, I think he means all the priests in the diocese, aware of certain truths. You might like to read it while I move on to this much longer one.'

Eleanor answered in similar vein: 'I cannot wait to read what he has written. He appears to take every opportunity to thrust his own ideas forward.' As Arthur opened out the two large sheets of paper she read: *The deputy assistant chaplain to the forces has written asking for support in his efforts to counteract the temptations of vice and intemperance presented to soldiers when they are stationed in different parts of this and other countries.* Having read through this brief document she realised that it was a wise and well-intentioned plea, but just how should Arthur go about pursuing it? Was it to be the gist of a sermon, should he mention it to every man in the forces when home on leave; indeed, given the awfulness of being at war, how much a priority should this be?

She took another scone, cut it in half and placed a piece on Arthur's plate. She realised how absorbed Arthur was in the longer document. Finally, he put it down: 'Oh, thank you, how well Violet bakes. I would simply say that this second document is interesting.' He passed it to Eleanor.

The document was entitled: *Two reasons for continuing the war.*

There are still, we find, some persons who do not understand about the war. Perhaps the following remarks may help them.

We are fighting for honour and right and truth: to give in now would be disgraceful after having promised to defend our friends.

It would also be the greatest foolishness. We have might as well as right on our side, as the following facts show in round numbers:

For the right Population

Belgium & Colonies	20 million
France & Colonies	80 million
British Empire	400 million
Russia & Rumania	178 million
Italy & Colonies	37 million
Serbia, Montenegro & Greece	6 million
Japan	35 million
Portugal & Colonies	15 million
United States	100 million
Brazil, Cuba, etc	10 million
Siam	6 million
China	400 million
12 groups of countries (Total)	1287 million

Against us

Germany & Colonies	78 million
Austria	50 million
Bulgaria	4 million
Turkey	30 million
4 groups of countries	162 million

Provided we all pull together and persevere, we with 1,287 million can confidently expect to conquer only 162 million against us. Above all, we trust in God, who is a righteous judge, "If God is for us, who can be against us?"

'Well?' Arthur asked as Eleanor laid the papers down. 'What do you make of that?'

'I really can't make out this man. He must be an intelligent person to have become dean, but I am amazed at what he says and now, what he writes. Does he believe that the people in some of these countries really care what is happening in Europe or, worse still, is he suggesting that if the allies and the central powers continue fighting and killing each other in equal numbers that we will eventually win because we have some men left? He appears to think that God is on our side because we have more.' She gave a gentle shake of her head and let out a faint sigh; whether the cause was her headache or the missive from the dean, Arthur was unsure.

'Don't you think you are a little harsh on him, darling? He means well.'

'But meaning well is not good enough. He needs to think more carefully what his privileged position allows him to write.'

'Well,' replied Arthur, 'I certainly find the communication unhelpful.' He paused for a moment as he stood up. 'But I must leave you for a short while; you should rest. I want to call on Mary and Aubrey Bellamy who are finding life very hard after hearing the sad news about Wilfred. They miss him so much.'

'Bless you for going, Arthur. It doesn't seem possible that two more men have been killed since Wilfred's death and I'm sure they won't be the last.'

Having put on his lightest jacket, Arthur turned to Eleanor, 'I'll be back within the hour. I thought we might go on a little walk later.'

298

'That would be lovely. I just want to write two letters including one to your mother, confirming that we are travelling down on the Tuesday.'

Early on the following Saturday evening, Willy Johnson came striding along Pond Street, kitbag on shoulder and waving to villagers who called out a greeting. Hastening into Meadow Way, it was his youngest sister Eliza who saw him first. She let out a joyful scream and sprinted towards him and threw herself into his arms. Willy gave the eleven-year-old a loving kiss, realising how much she had grown since he was last home. 'Oh Lizzy, it's lovely to see you after so long. Is everyone at home?'

'I'm not sure, Willy. We've all been talking about you; I can hardly believe it. I'm going to tell everyone.'

She ran on, but didn't wait to get indoors before she was announcing that her brother was home. By the time he got to the door, his mother and Ruby were there. With tears in their eyes they took it in turn to engulf him in their arms and smother him with kisses. Smiling broadly, Willy eased away a little. 'It's wonderful to see you.'

It was a fine, balmy evening and for three hours the Johnson family sat in their small back garden, smiling, chatting, telling Willy of what they had been doing since they had last seen him; Judith noticing how little her son spoke of what she knew must be the dark side of his time in the army. When young Robert and David asked him about fighting the Germans he passed it off lightly, simply saying that he had a job to do. Ruby made Willy promise that they could go the next day to see the buzzard which she hoped would be waiting for them in her brother's tree.

The sun shone its best summer warmth as they set out on the track that they had not walked together for two years; Ruby took her brother's hand and led, almost pulling him up the slight hill. She had already plied her brother with many questions about buzzards which he had done his best to answer.

'That's right,' agreed the excited Ruby, 'it was just before Easter I saw the pair of buzzards and the nest had already been built. Oh, it's so exciting, Willy!'

They were now approaching the dark green hedge already covered with berries that edged the field in which Willy's tree stood. Responding to further questions, he explained there was an incubation time of around five weeks and that the pair of buzzards would have mated for life.

'Oh, that's lovely,' his sister interrupted. 'They seemed very fond of each other.' She suddenly stopped as the tree came in sight. 'There's our tree.'

'Let's just go on a little way and then sit and wait. You did very well to see it.' The oak tree was now heavily laden with its ever-darkening green leaves and above its sturdy base only glimpses of branches could be seen. They sat and waited. Willy saw the buzzard first, perched on one of the few bare branches in the lower part of the tree, but he waited.

'There it is!' cried Ruby. He enabled her to describe its position in the tree before saying: 'Oh yes Ruby, I see it. Well spotted.' They continued to sit, waiting; the silence broken by a soaring skylark and their own sporadic talk about the buzzards.

'Oh Willy, I'm so glad you have come home. You won't really have to go away again, will you?'

Willy put his hand on that of his dear sister, 'Yes I will, but I hope it won't be for too long this time.' He loved all his siblings, but Ruby held a special place in his heart. He turned and looked at her; she had become an attractive young woman, her light brown hair framing her fairly plain, but honest and gentle face. He saw tears running down her face.

'Don't worry Ruby, I'll be all right. It won't be long before the war is over and I'll be home for good. I expect I'll be working for Major de Maine again although I know Mr

Mansfield has really taken over. Then we can walk together up this track each day to work, just as we used to.'

The tears increased and sobs broke forth and at the mention of Major de Maine's name he could see her body tremble.

'What is it, Ruby? What's wrong? You can tell me, maybe I can help.'

'Oh Willy, I'm not sure. You won't tell mummy will you, promise?'

'Not if you don't want me to.' He put his arm gently round her shoulders, took out a light-coloured handkerchief and dabbed her cheeks, but the tears continued to roll. 'Come on love, just tell me.'

'Oh Willy, it's awful and I'm so ashamed.' She paused, looked at Willy and realised his supportive look which she had so often known when she was younger. 'You see, it's about Master Lionel.' The picture came to Willy of the de Maine's youngest son. He must be in his early twenties by now, remembered as an arrogant and unpleasant young man.

'So what about Lionel?'

'Well, he makes me do things. Lots of things I don't like.'

'What kind of things? Does he bully you?'

Ruby had turned red; he waited, just giving her a reassuring squeeze round her shoulders. 'Well,' she finally said, 'he feels my titties.' Involuntarily she placed one hand on her ample breasts. 'He makes me take off my dress and puts his hand up here.' She moved her hand to the top of her legs. 'Sometimes he rubs me here as well. It's horrible.' Willy felt he should say something, horrified and deeply shocked though he was.

'But Ruby, if you hated what he was doing, why didn't you stop him?'

'He said that if I didn't let him do these things or if I told anyone, Major de Maine would stop us living in our cottage. Oh, Willy, I've been frightened for so long.'

'Ruby, you mustn't worry. It was wicked and wrong what

he did, but it's not your fault that he's been so bad. When did he begin to do these things?'

'It was a long time ago. Do you remember that time there was a party in Mr Jackson's barn, when we went together with Fred and Racer and all our friends? It was before then.'

Willy's mind went back to the party that had been given to thank all the employees: nearly four and a half years ago. He vaguely remembered how Ruby had asked if Lionel de Maine was going to the party and then when they were there, she had first wanted to go home and then clung to him. 'Did anything else happen?' he asked, trying to keep the rising anxiety out of his voice.

'Sometimes he made me rub his cock. Well, that's what he called it.'

'And Ruby, did all this happen often?'

'Well, it did when he was home, but he's often away for a long time now. But he's still the same. Willy, what should I do?'

Willy was appalled at what his loving sister had told him. He was so angry at himself for not realising how she was suffering over four years previously. He just wanted to hold his sister and beat Lionel up.

'Ruby, I can promise you that nothing like this will ever happen again. I will stop this wicked man ever hurting you. I promise and no one else need ever know.'

'Oh Willy, I knew you would help me. And you really promise you won't tell mummy?'

He smiled the gentlest of smiles and wiped away the drying tears from Ruby's face. 'I promise. Do you remember what we used to say? "It may be wet, it may be dry, but I cut my throat if I tell a lie".' The faintest of smiles appeared on Ruby's face.

Later that day Willy excused himself from the family by saying he wanted to call on Eliza and Sparky Carey and Liz Smith. Hard though he knew such calls would be to make, he had to see the bereaved parents of his great friends. Stories of their friendships and days shared between Willy and their sons somehow brought a little comfort, at least briefly when he visited. Not finding it easy to deceive his parents, he needed to see Lionel de Maine immediately. He must stop this monster from abusing and frightening his precious sister. As he moved swiftly along the track to the manor, he realised that it would be of little use to plead for an end to the abuse. No, he would threaten Lionel de Maine that if he even spoke to Ruby again he would personally beat him up, tell his parents and make his behaviour known throughout Rusfield. But, he thought, Lionel would know that Willy would soon be back in France and he had promised Ruby that others would not know what had transpired. Well, he would lie and say that he had just told Ruby's father who would do the same to Lionel; indeed, perhaps, he should tell him anyway.

It was Mrs de Maine who answered the door, as Florrie had long since moved to join her sister in Canchester and Elsie, the only full-time domestic servant, had Sundays off. A smile broke out on Isabella de Maine's face. 'Why, Willy, how wonderful to see you. I heard you were coming home on leave, how kind of you to call on us.'

Before Willy could say anything, she called: 'Sebastian, come and see who's here: a real surprise. Come in and tell us how you are.' The normally quick-thinking and imaginative Willy found himself nomnplussed by his reception; this was some way off from a confrontation with the son of the manor owners. Willy followed the couple across the hall and into the large lounge. 'I have just made a large pot of tea. Let me get an extra cup and we can share it together,' Isabella said. The tea was poured for him and it was the major who led the conversation, asking how Willy's war was going; Isabella de Maine asked after Willy's personal well-being and his family.

Willy had always thought of his past employer and wife as good people, but he had never seen this friendly and warm side of them. They told him how the single farm under the overall ownership of Jack Mansfield was prospering now that its emphasis was on growing barley and other crops. Willy was thinking of his next move and after some twenty minutes broke into the talk about local farming. He tensed up a little as he said: 'It is so good to see you and how kind of you to have made me so welcome. I would really like to see Lionel, is that possible?'

Major de Maine and his wife may well have been surprised at his request as they had never been aware of any closeness between their youngest son and this fine soldier. 'I'm afraid it's not possible,' answered Isabella de Maine. 'As you know, conscription came in earlier this year and Lionel was called up in April. He spent some time training, but yesterday he reported to his regiment's headquarters and will now be on his way to France. In fact he's now a junior officer with the Suffolks: the same regiment as you. Maybe you will come across each other.'

FORTY-FOUR

August 1916

Tempted at first to tell Major and Mrs de Maine of their son's appalling behaviour, Willy had stopped short; for once with the de Maines it was beyond his ability to keep things a secret. At least with Lionel in France, Ruby was safe for the present. Maybe the best person to speak to was the vicar; he was a discreet man; Willy decided to think about that.

As he turned into Pond Street he virtually bumped into Grace Reynolds, bound for her cottage near the pond. 'Willy, I heard you were home on leave; it's a real joy to see you.'

'Grace, and how splendid to see you.' Grace had always been the most attractive girl at school and all his mates had thought how lucky Racer was to have her as a girlfriend; she really was beautiful. 'How are you and all your family? Are you enjoying teaching?' Willy asked.

'Yes, thank you. Everyone's well, although we had a bit of a scare when young Lily caught measles, but she recovered well enough. And I love teaching; Wensfield School reminds me of our time at Rusfield, but we have our down times as well. I have twins in my class and last month their father was killed in France: so terribly sad.'

Willy nodded; he had seen friends' families devastated by

305

recent deaths. 'And how is Racer or, as I should say to you,' he added with a smile, 'Abraham.'

'Oh, he's fine; at least that's what he wrote in his recent letter. It was wonderful seeing him in March. I know he was worried about Boney and it's terrible about Jammy and Fred. When this terrible war is over we shall all realise how much we miss them. But Willy, you may be just the person who can help. You're home for quite a few days aren't you?'

'For ten more days. What can I do?'

'Well, about two miles out of the village, there's a camp where soldiers are training. Earlier this week, two of them came in to the village and Abraham's father and I were chatting with them. One of them said how hard it must be for the children with their fathers away, especially having time on their hands during the school holiday. One thing led to another and we agreed to get together and have a special day for the children on Wednesday. Most of the soldiers can join us and we are to have some races on the village green and then, would you believe it, kite flying on Bramrose Hill. Apparently, one of the men we were talking to used to run a kite-making club. So Mr Watts is going to let us use the biggest classroom to make the kites and then we are going up Bramrose Hill to fly them. I think there will be a lot of children; can you come?'

Willy smiled. He was sure none of the soldiers would have been able to resist an invitation to help the beautiful Grace; no more could he. 'It sounds great fun. Of course, I'll help. But Grace, I must get back home as we're all going for a walk up the hill now and then back along the stream. Ruby is organising a stick race; I just wonder who will end up in the water!' He kissed her lightly on the cheek. 'It's been wonderful seeing you. I'll pop in tomorrow and you can tell me more about Wednesday's event.'

'Thank you, Willy.' She turned left towards her house, thinking how Willy was always the one who knew the right thing to do. Willy turned right and thought about Grace; what a lovely woman she was and, he felt sure, what a fine teacher: lucky children.

The afternoon walk took Willy's mind back many years when the Sunday family walk had been one of the week's highlights. Now, with Ruby, Rachel, Eliza, Harry, Robert and David in tow, he thought of Frank, now nineteen and in Mesopotamia. Judith and Raymond, hand in hand, walked behind their growing family; their thoughts, too, were on Frank, but rejoicing in seeing Willy again. When the stick race on the slow-moving stream was over, unconvincingly won by David as the sticks were all bunched together, the family walked back through the village. Willy was delighted to hear about the gardening project and had already made up his mind that the next day he would visit Violet Rushton and Robert Berry to thank them for the parcels he had received. He had, of course, been sad to find that none of his closest mates were about; even sadder that he would never see some of them again. But it had been good to see Grace and he looked forward to Wednesday's activity with the children.

'There must be over thirty of them up,' Grace called to Doris as they watched the many coloured kites flying, some high, others fighting to stay aloft. They watched Willy run down the hill to unravel Florrie Edwards' green and blue kite that had become entangled in a hawthorn bush. He soon managed to detach it and, with Florrie, walked a little way up the hill to relaunch it; her tears evaporated.

'Just as well we have plenty of helpers,' Fred Richards laughingly said to Olivia Atkins and Arthur Windle, 'it's certainly no easy job trying to keep them all aloft.'

'I'm so sorry that Eleanor doesn't feel well enough to be with us,' added Olivia, turning to Arthur. 'When I called in earlier this week, her cough still seemed quite bad.'

'Yes, it comes and goes, but she can't seem to really get rid of it.'

Grace had been surprised at how many children had turned up at the school, all carrying a small picnic lunch; Mabel and Jack Mansfield had kindly agreed to provide drinks of home-made lemonade at the school afterwards. Grace, Willy, six soldiers and five other villagers had spent an hour earlier in the morning at the school. On the spaced out desks they had put: a variety of coloured tissue paper, old newspapers, thin wooden sticks, glue, scissors and lots of string, a product of which Violet Rushton had plenty in her shop.

The children came tumbling into the room, abandoning all they had been told about coming into lessons quietly. It was Sergeant Robertson who took over. Other than a shriek from Lucy Palmer who claimed William Jones had jabbed her with his scissors, an incident Grace swiftly put down as an accident, everything went well.

'Well, that looks like the first stage,' Olivia Atkins remarked to Grace. 'I'm not sure how many of them will fly, but we shall see.'

Grace smiled, 'Time for the races now and then picnic lunches. Hopefully, that will give the glue on the kites plenty of time to stick properly.'

'Let's hope they survive as far as Bramrose Hill,' responded Olivia, 'some of them look a little fragile.'

On the village green, it was Willy who led the way in organising races, but it was the soldiers' three-legged race that caused the greatest excitement. The sun continued to shine down on this happy day in the village.

As Willy prepared to move off to fly the kites, he was surprised to see Peter Woods across the green talking to his sister, Ruby. He walked over. 'Peter, how good to see you. Have you come to help?'

Peter, momentarily embarrassed, smiled before replying: 'Ruby told me about the children having a special day and thought I might be able to help. I hope you don't mind me being here?'

'Delighted to have you joining us, Peter; everyone feels you're already part of the village.' Willy could not think of anyone he would prefer to see with his sister, realising Peter had already cycled twelve miles to get back to the village after delivering the post and still had the return to Steepleton. Damage in transporting the kites was slight, easily put right by the strategic use of more glue that David Watts sensibly carried.

'Now most of you have made your kites with one or two friends,' Sergeant Robertson shouted above the excited chatter. 'Stay with your partners, carry your kite carefully and follow me.' He led them off up the hill to an open area. After a few false starts and two of the boys taking a tumble, the kites at least got off the ground. Some flew really well and stayed aloft for far longer than Willy had thought likely and he admired the patience of Sergeant Robertson in helping the children whose kites seemed more adapted to ground activities. After much excited flying of the kites, an increasing number becoming entangled with others, they were collected in with strings safely rolled and placed under the watch of Sergeant Robertson. Grace and Willy then organised a massive game of hide-and-seek for which the scattered bushes and small clumps of thick trees provided excellent hiding places.

At five o'clock, Sergeant Robertson told Grace that the men must move back to their camp, as the next day they were returning to Canchester. It was Willy who co-ordinated the three cheers for the soldiers and all the adults came over to thank them. 'We haven't enjoyed ourselves so much for a long time, have we boys?' the sergeant said turning to his men.

The children waved farewell, kites were gathered up and the slopes of Bramrose Hill returned to their age-old peacefulness. As the soldiers finally disappeared back to their camp, Eliza Carey wondered how many of them would survive the war. She had lost her wonderful son and knew many Rusfield parents would be wondering how many more would be added to the thirteen who had already given their lives. Anguish in the village tightened its hold, even on an outwardly happy day.

FORTY-FIVE

February - March 1917

As he picked up the letter, Willy's hand was shaking from the biting cold. He had been overjoyed to see it in the small batch of mail that had reached the trench that morning, only four days after another Rusfield parcel had arrived. He had put the grey socks on top of the previously sent thick ones, managing somehow to force on his boots; the grey balaclava was an additional protection. He shared the twenty woodbines with Cooper and Rigby, two of the men who always looked at the post, but never received anything. Wearing two pairs of gloves made opening the envelope cumbersome.

Older brother Frank was well and had been transferred to Egypt which, to Willy, sounded a better place to be than Mesopotamia. Robert and David would be leaving school soon and both were likely to work for Mr Mansfield; such a good man, thought Willy. Ruby was well and his mother wrote that her occasional periods of upset had disappeared and her friendship with Peter Woods was flourishing. His mother was sorry that the Tuesday evening choir had been suspended for a few weeks as Eleanor Windle was not well.

When he had been home six months earlier he had asked his parents not to protect him from any grim news and now she wrote that two more Rusfield men had been killed. Willy remembered Walter Groves, a year younger than himself; he thought back to going into Harry Groves' small grocers shop and spending his weekly penny on sweets. Willy also recalled Walter telling him about his parents' silver wedding to which over thirty brothers, sisters, nieces, nephews and cousins had attended; over twenty living in the village. Willy knew how each Rusfield death spread its web of sadness.

He felt that he had been in this trench for ever, although it was only since the turn of the year. Would 1917 be any different to the previous three years? He thought not. Two months after he had returned from Rusfield, the rains had set in and rarely stopped. The Somme, which had continued to see terrible fighting in his absence, had become a sea of mud, the shattered ground over which the men had tried to advance in July and August, a bog. Holes from the incessant gunfire were vast in which men and horses occasionally drowned and attempts to construct paths were useless; to move was as much a fight against the filthy, smelling mud as it was against the enemy.

The trench itself had become increasingly foul, the water filthier and deeper. The stench never left Willy's nostrils and he thought it would remain with him for ever. Willy had seen plenty of rats in the barns at the manor, but never the size of these. They fed on anything thrown away and on human corpses of which there were plenty: British and German. He had watched Buzzer Briggs and his mate, Fugger, put a pole across the trench along which a rat would run. Buzzer would then wait for it to get halfway and hit it with a thick cudgel. Willy had never counted the number of rats killed in this way, although he and the others in the trench admired Buzzer's growing skill.

His mind went back to another grey day in early October when he found himself with a quiet man that he had seen before, but with whom he had not spoken. He had been surprised when this young, fair-haired and pleasant-featured comrade said to him in a winsome, almost apologetic voice: 'I think today's a bit special for me.'

Willy, always quick to pick up clues in another's comments, smiled and asked: 'And why is that? Incidentally I'm Willy Johnson.'

'Oh, and I'm Arthur, Arthur Passmore.' They shook saturated gloves together before the new acquaintance of Willy further responded. 'Well, I think it's my birthday, at least that's what I was told. If that's right, I'm twenty today.' He smiled in a most disarming way before adding: 'Not really the weather for celebrating a birthday is it?'

Willy smiled: 'Well, I'm sorry I haven't got much of a present for you, but at least have one of my fags.'

'Thanks, that's kind. Well, you see I never knew my parents. I was brought up in this place in Hull; it was called a home, but wasn't really like the homes that some of the mates I went to school with told me about. I suppose the nuns did the best they could, but they were never very friendly. The best times were when I went to Park View School as I made some good friends there. Mind you, I never saw any park nearby.' He went on to tell Willy how, after leaving school, he had lodged with the Robinson family who, rather grudgingly, let him join the local Territorial Army and as soon as he reached his eighteenth birthday, the regular army. Soon after that he was in France.

Willy took out his treasured tin and offered another eagerly accepted cigarette. Arthur continued by moving on to his time in France. It was when Arthur went on to talk about an advance into a village in early 1916 that Willy realised it was almost certainly the same place he had been through, and about the same time. It was an abandoned piano that made the link between the two men.

Arthur told of advancing on a deserted Flemish village; abandoned vehicles and human bodies just outnumbering the scores of dead horses. There was not a properly standing house; 'But,' went on Arthur, 'we found this piano. There was this one house, the roof had almost all gone, but more of it remained than with most. A mate and I went in and we could hardly believe our eyes; just inside was this black piano, still standing.' He smiled before continuing, 'I wouldn't say it was in tune, but it sounded all right. I'd learnt to play a few tunes when I was in the home and managed to knock out "Let Me Call You Sweetheart"; I remembered it well enough. It was just one of those magic moments as a dozen guys heard me playing and gathered round. Anyway we sang and then we joined in some other choruses. Of course, we had to move on fairly soon, but I will always remember it.'

Willy had hardly been able to believe what Arthur described. 'But Arthur, I remember going through a terribly destroyed village and seeing a piano in this knocked-about, small house. Did you leave the piano lid up?'

They both laughed, slapping each other on the back. From that moment they became good mates. Willy reflected on a friendship which a couple of fags had started and an abandoned piano cemented.

A few days later, Willy was reflecting on the stupidity, or maybe just ignorance, of the military leadership. Who could these men be that gave some orders; where had their intelligence come from? It was a young lieutenant that passed on the orders: 'We've heard that the Huns across there,' his arm wavered as if uncertain of the exact direction, 'have been reduced to reinforce their line where the Australians are breaking through further west. We're going to give them the bayonet and take over their trench.' Willy knew this was less than a hundred yards away. 'Be ready for 14.00 hours.' It was then midday.

Surely, thought Willy, to advance in the daylight was madness. 'Fix bayonets.' Men struggled to follow this order; young Grimes two down the line from Willy dropped his bayonet and came up spitting out filthy water. Willy was next to Arthur Passmore, but neither had any idea how many men

314

were going over the top; their world was limited to the few in their part of the flooded trench. Yet once Willy had fixed his bayonet, any fear disappeared: the whistle sounded; up the slimy steps and over the muddy top. This was no sustained charge; this was fighting against deep mud, yet suddenly and unexpectedly Willy found his feet on a strand of firmer ground. He knew it was Arthur alongside him as he continued this crazy rush towards the enemy line. Ten yards short of the trench a machine gun from a nearby hillside opened up. He heard Arthur next to him let out a shriek; he was gone. Willy moved on to a near certain death, but was amazed to find himself looking down into the trench with a white-faced lad looking up at him. With a single thrust he drove his bayonet into the youth's chest and with another movement pulled it out. He was aware of others moving into the trench, the line of attacking men had been greater than Willy had realised. The enemy trench was in their hands; the British intelligence had for once been correct.

As dusk fell, Willy crawled back to where the body of his briefly-known friend Arthur lay, dead; his upper body shattered from the cruel chatter of a machine gun. Willy lifted his body, crouched low and made back to the shelter of the overrun trench. Later he scooped out a shallow hole and lay the young soldier down before the shallow grave disappeared in the foul mud. No other would miss this young soldier; no parent, no sibling, seemingly no friends. The next day the news came that the Germans were counter-attacking and a courier arrived ordering the British to retreat. Willy learnt later in the day that over 700 men had been lost in gaining no yards at all. To Willy, the pointless death of Arthur had encapsulated the whole nature of the war; he reflected, too, on the young German soldier he had bayoneted.

That had been in October, now it was February. In the spells away from observation, failed attacks and brief breaks for a hot drink, Willy found his mind returning to other times. Sometimes of imagined life in Rusfield; perhaps, such thoughts protected him from wondering about the unknown future.

Back in January, the temperature had suddenly dropped as the wind moved to the east and within a week the ground had become frozen, in and outside their trench. The sharpest knife could not cut through the smallest loaf, uncovered hands immediately became numb and frostbite common. The endless sound of guns continued, but now the German shells were more deadly in their effect as the solid frozen ground refused to blunt the explosion. Men's faces took on the look of frozen masks, bereft of expression.

He folded the letter, struggled to extract his old tobacco tin and carefully placed it next to other letters. The bitterly cold weather had brought one other change for Willy, one probably denied to the other men in the trench. From the trench there was one direction Willy could always look, upwards. Seeing the sky, his thoughts turned back to his schooldays when Meadowman had trooped them out into the school yard and got them all to look up. 'Is that cumulus, stratus or alto-cumulus?' Peter Meadows would ask them; then back to the classroom to draw the correct formation. Now the endless grey stratus had given way to cirro-cumulus, the icy companion of cold weather. He thought Meadowman would be pleased he had remembered. The clouds were his sole enjoyment of the natural world; nothing grew and he had not seen a bird for weeks. He wondered how the buzzards around Rusfield were managing; wonderful that Ruby still watched their special tree on her way to work.

But then, in late February, something quite unexpected occurred: a voice he heard from along the trench. At first he recognised its familiarity, but could not put a name to its owner. Then he knew: Lionel de Maine. There, just along the trench, was this lieutenant, little older than himself. It was, as Ruby would have said, the tone of "posh people". Under the officer's peaked cap he recognised the saturnine features of the man he most loathed; the creature who had so abused his sister. If it had been possible to move rapidly along the trench he might well have struck him; but lack of space and Willy's own good sense prevailed. To be severely sanctioned, even shot, for striking an officer would be the ultimate foolishness. He would bide his time.

In fact, Willy decided to leave any acknowledgement of recognition to come from Lieutenant Lionel de Maine. After all, thought Willy, well over two years had passed since they last set eyes on each other and even then they only occasionally crossed paths. If he was not recognised then he would wait for an opportune moment for confrontation. During the next three days Willy saw Lionel several times, although the lieutenant spent much of his time in the officers' dugout which provided a modicum of protection from the cold and, at night, room enough to stretch out. On the fourth day Willy thought the lieutenant's eye had roved in his direction, then stopped for a moment, but, perhaps, this was his imagination. Half an hour later he was sure, as the man sought him out and spoke: 'Soldier, I may be wrong but I think we should know each other. It's Willy, isn't it?'

Willy saluted, although he wanted to spit, as he sprang to as accurate an impression of attention as his frozen body would allow. 'Yes sir. I am and I think we know each other through the time I worked for your father.'

Willy was surprised when the young officer stepped forward and, placing his hand on Willy's left shoulder, said: 'God, it's good to see a face from Rusfield in this awful hole. What a place to meet.' He moved his hand from Willy's shoulder, thrust it forward, urging a handshake. Willy had no alternative but to respond. 'I've only been near the front line for a few weeks and this is a bit of a shock. It's pretty grim; how long have you been here?'

Willy was bemused at the apparent friendliness of Lionel;

317

was he totally unaware of what Willy knew? 'Four months, although it seems forever,' responded Willy. He found it hard to intersperse the conversation with "sir" but, he thought the newcomer to the trench did not seem to worry. They went on to talk about Rusfield although Lionel appeared to know few people from the village. The conversation ended with Lionel indicating that the present lull in activity would shortly end.

The next day saw the change. Sergeant Grant, who had arrived at the same time as Lionel, told Willy and the rest of the men in his stretch of the trench that they were all moving to the east where a breakthrough of the German line was planned. Led by Lieutenant de Maine, they were to join a large force. Under cover of darkness they left their unwelcome home of the past weeks and Willy judged they covered around ten miles before stopping under the cover of a dilapidated barn. He felt warmer, or at least less cold, than he had for many weeks; marching was welcome. As dawn broke, the same barren landscape could be seen, but passing through a small, totally destroyed village they were aware of much activity; preparation, thought Willy, although he could only guess at preparation for an attack. It was two hours later that the men reached their destination: a trench which to most looked much the same as the one they had recently left.

Willy had found that in any group of soldiers, someone always emerged in the role of joker; now it was Private Wally Walters. 'Well, the food is certainly much better,' he freely admitted, finishing the bully beef and biscuits. 'Much better than that bloody pea soup with bits of old horse, but I wonder what they are feeding us up for.' He went on to tell the story of the fat German officer which most had heard many times.

The next day the plan was revealed. The trench was a quarter of a mile from the enemy front line which had been constructed to keep at bay allied advances on a railway yard, a major centre for transporting supplies to the Germans. Now, the allied decision had been made that this railway centre must be put out of action, which would only be possible after the forward defence line of the Germans had been overcome. The enemy line was strongly held and so a major assault was necessary. The usual plan was in place: major bombardment to negate the huge barbed-wire defence and to bring havoc to the enemy in their trenches, then a full-scale attack by the British through the destroyed barbed-wire line. The bombardment by the heaviest British guns would start the next day.

Three days later, massive fire from over 300 guns was trained on the German defences, followed by smoke to cover the British advance. All was ready for the attack by almost 8,000 men along a mile front.

The attack was launched at 06.20 hours. It was not easy for Willy to hear orders as two days before, he like all the others, had been ordered to stuff cotton wool in his ears rather than be deafened by the allied guns behind them. The signal to attack was again a whistle. The officers, armed with revolvers, were the first over the top: Willy saw Lionel lead the way without a moment's hesitation; he and the rest of the nearby men followed. The enemy fire increased; despite all efforts to keep the attack unknown to the Germans, it had been anticipated by them and their guns were ready. After what seemed an endless dash, Willy could just make out through the smoke, a gap; for all the British shelling, most of the barbed-wire barricade remained. He sensed the line of men narrowing to get through the gap, but was also aware of men falling as the machine guns sprayed their deadly metal. Men were falling, screaming and there was no way they could go on. Willy felt a sudden pain in his shoulder; it was now hard to hold his gun which was, in any case, useless against the German firepower. Even through his plugged ears, Willy heard the cry of, 'Retreat.' He turned. His hearing impaired and now the smoke reduced his vision, the pain in his shoulder increased. He staggered a further twenty yards before pitching into a shell-hole. Two other men were already there, one who had lost his nerve on the way forward and had gained fortuitous protection, the other screaming as he pitched forward. Through the increasing cloud of pain, Willy wondered whether to immediately attempt to get back to his own trench or to wait. At least the smoke gave minimum cover; to wait in this forlorn hole until darkness with his wound bleeding so profusely was a more dangerous option. Even as his beleaguered mind was attempting to assess the situation, the screaming man looked at him: it was Lieutenant Lionel de Maine, his right leg hanging by a bloody, exposed bone. Willy's mind immediately recalled the order which Lionel himself had given before the attack: 'Don't stop for the wounded as you'll be a sitting target for enemy machine guns.' The thought of Ruby flashed through his mind, yet he could not abandon a fellow soldier.

Go now, he thought. Keeping low, just under the rim of the shell-hole, he gathered up Lionel in his arms, the pain in his shoulder almost unbearable. Nearly 100 yards to go; he staggered, but somehow kept going, unaware of other men trying to get back, of the bodies of those who would never make that trench. Thirty, twenty, ten yards in time that seemed suspended. Just a few yards and a cutting swathe of machine-gun fire hit them both; Lionel's head, exposed in Willy's hold, exploded and Willy felt the agony in his back. He fell, dropping the dead Lionel de Maine.

It was an hour later that a courageous Sergeant Grant who had miraculously got back to the trench unscathed, crawled to the two men. He could see that nothing could help the one, but the other he carried back. Two stretcher bearers took Willy to the emergency dressing station in a hurriedly erected tent.

On an early March morning with the slight promise of spring in the air, Peter Woods cycled past the pond; he could not help succumbing to tears. How many times, he wondered, had he carried telegrams and letters that he knew would shatter lives when opened? The most recent had been a telegram delivered to Major and Mrs de Maine; Peter knew it could only say one thing. Now he carried a letter and a telegram for the Johnsons. He had got to know the family so well, he had grown to love Ruby whom he saw as a wonderfully honest and caring young woman; now he carried this letter which would bring such pain. He knew it concerned Ruby's beloved older brother; if it had been about Frank, its Egyptian origin would have shown.

He turned into Meadow Way and knocked on the cottage door; it was opened by Judith Johnson with Ruby at her shoulder. The immediate smile of happiness on Ruby's face as she saw Peter, changed in an instant when she saw what he was holding.

Later, Ruby showed Peter the letter that had brought instant and terrible grief to her lovely household. It was from Annette Jackson, sister in charge of No 65 Casualty Clearing Station; part of it read: *Your brave son knew that he was dying and retained some consciousness until his last moments. He asked me to say: "Tell mother that all is well as I am passing away peacefully. Give Ruby a special kiss from me."* The official letter which arrived the next day was stark, but carried the same dreadful news.

CHAPTER FORTY-SIX

March – August 1917

Robert Berry mopped his brow, grimaced a little as he stood upright and rested with both hands on his hoe. 'God, Sammy, it just gets worse. It beggars belief that dear old Mrs Rowe has lost her second son. Poor soul. I thought South Africa was bad enough, but this – it's awful.'

Sammy Hatfield looked up from where he was weeding between the rows of peas. 'You're right. First Ernest, now Aubrey. I called in on Mrs Rowe yesterday; she was absolutely broken, bursting into tears as she spoke about both of her lovely daughters-in-law being widowed so young. She kept saying it was all wrong for parents to see their children die; there was just nothing I could say. My heart bled for her.'

'Ay,' agreed his friend, 'it's all right us doing what we can with vegetables, but that doesn't help those who are suffering so much. The deaths just go on. I look up at my flag there,' pointing to the Union Jack fluttering in the gentle breeze, 'and I think of all those boys dying for their country. Last week I saw Eliza Carey chatting with Judith Johnson and Charlotte Groves outside Violet's shop and I realised all three had already lost a son in this bloody war. Well, the Americans have come in and I suppose that's good news. I just wish the news we get from France would give everyone something to cheer about.'

There were certainly no cheers in Rusfield. Each village death was a further hammer blow; everyone knew another family where a loved one had died. The news in early March that Willy Johnson had been killed touched so many people; generations of the family had lived in Rusfield. This strong-featured young man was remembered as the captain of the all-conquering football team and a popular lad; an unlikely person to die on the battlefields of northern Europe. Ruby was in ruins for weeks, first Fred Smith and then her beloved brother to whom she had always looked in awe; now both gone. Her mother thought it was Peter Woods that saved her from total breakdown. They had been fond of each other for several months and on her brother's death, Peter had been wonderfully understanding and supportive. Ruby's regard for Peter was revealed when she showed him the buzzard on its nest; her parents knew he must be very close to her when she let him into the secret of Willy's tree. All too soon followed other deaths, until by the end of May, twenty-five men from the village and other parts of the parish had died; all but two had been through the school. The villagers not only shared in the shock and sorrow of those killed, but trembled at a similar fate for their immediate loved ones.

It was after the service on the second Sunday in June that Grace Reynolds and Doris Groves agreed to an afternoon walk on Bramrose Hill. They had always been neighbours and their friendship had flourished at the village school and for the years they shared work at Spinney Farm. Doris had often been grateful for her friend's steadying influence; Grace envying Doris her greater flamboyance; they remained very close. As they joined the track just beyond Hezekiah Freeman's cottage, they listened to each other's stories of work. However, it was not long before their conversation turned to the cloud hanging over the village.

'When did you last hear from Abraham?' Doris asked.

'Just three weeks ago. He never says much about how he's

getting on, but seems well enough. I'm sure that from all we read and hear, it must be terrible, but I don't think he's allowed to say anything about where he is or what he's doing. Anyway, Abraham's never been one for saying much about himself. But what about Albert?'

Grace noticed the slight pause, suggesting her friend needed to gather her thoughts before replying. 'I worry about him. I don't hear from him very often, it's nearly two months since I last heard and then his letters seem odd.'

'Odd? How do you mean?'

'Well, it's difficult to explain. I know life out there must be terrible, but he sounds so troubled. I know he and Abraham are always different, even for cousins, but Albert does go on a lot about himself and it always sounds as if everything is so bad. I'm sure it must be, but it's not really like the wonderful Albert I used to know.'

Grace stopped and placed her arm round her friend. 'Oh, Doris, I'm sure it will be fine when this terrible war is over. I remember we talked about this, after Abraham and Albert were both home on leave together just over a year ago; Abraham was worried about him then. But, Doris, Albert had an awful injury and he shouldn't really have had to return to France, but that's what's happening in this war. Once he gets back home I'm sure he will be the old happy-go-lucky Albert again.'

'Oh, I hope so, but I've been thinking a lot. Somehow I think Albert doesn't really want me to keep writing. Perhaps he has gone off me even though we were so very close when he was last home. I still like him a lot, but I think it may be best if I gave him the chance to feel we are a little freer of each other. I really think that would be best.'

As they approached the sun-drenched hill where they had played so many times when young, they were silent for a while. 'Let's sit down for a few minutes,' suggested Grace. They stopped in the shade of an oak tree which she and

324

Abraham often sat under, before either of them thought their lives would be interrupted by war. She looked at her friend and saw tears trickling down her pretty face. 'Doris, it's obviously up to you what you do, but don't you think that Albert might be really upset?'

'I just don't know. I'll have to think about it some more; I just think Albert may feel happier if he doesn't think I'm trying to cling to him.' She withdrew a little lace handkerchief from the sleeve of her frock and wiped her tears away. 'Come on, let's race each other up to the top, like we used to!'

They stood up together; Doris still with her confused thoughts, Grace wanting to help, but fearing what Doris might do and how that might affect Albert.

The war clouds continued over the village as they did over the whole of Europe, but there was another tragedy in Rusfield that had nothing to do with the fighting. The vicarage had become a focal point of much sadness; the young and once vivacious Eleanor was severely ill and everyone was worrying about the much-loved wife of their vicar. As Sparky Carey, who had never been known to step inside the church except for baptisms and funerals, said to his old friend Bernie Thomas: 'Whenever I go past the church, I pop in and say a prayer. She is such a lovely lady, the kindest and best I've ever known. I don't know whether I believe in God or not, but surely he will save her. She's so young.' Bernie knew that even the most convinced non-believer in Rusfield would echo the same feelings.

Arthur and Eleanor's love for each other was clear to all. As the villagers agonised over her illness, they marvelled at the way Arthur continued to give so much of himself to others who suffered their own tragedies. His good friend, Frederick Richards, remarked to his wife, Pauline: 'It's as if Arthur's own personal tragedy somehow makes him even more aware of other villagers' suffering.'

On this late July morning, Arthur sat by his beloved's bedside, left hand gently resting on her pale wrist. To Arthur she was as beautiful as ever, but pale, much thinner-faced and, as she slept, he could hear the rasping of her laboured breathing. Arthur had wished a thousand times that he could absorb this dreadful illness; surely there was a cure, but then everything had been tried. He remembered it was in the height of the previous summer that she had returned from a church meeting and gone directly to bed. Her cough had persisted and Betty Hazlett had prescribed a simple medicinal liquid, but when this failed she asked Doctor Christopher to call. The doctor had spoken of his concern, for by this time Eleanor's cough was producing phlegm that showed traces of blood. It had been Jack Mansfield who drove them to Canchester hospital. Stethoscope examination had revealed, all too clearly, a problem with Eleanor's lungs and this was later confirmed by the recently installed x-ray, enabling Mr Wraith, the consultant, to diagnose and track the progression of the disease. Later, he spoke plainly but sensitively to Eleanor and Arthur of his diagnosis: 'Whether you know it as consumption or tuberculosis, I'm afraid that is my convinced diagnosis. It means the lungs are affected, the left most severely.'

'But I thought,' interjected Arthur, 'this illness only happened in crowded cities.'

'It's certainly most common in London and other crowded cities, but there are many local cases. I'm sure there have been others suffering with the same disease in your village.'

By the time Christmas and the New Year had passed, other symptoms that the consultant had foreseen showed their ugly features: Eleanor's breathlessness became more apparent and Arthur had increasing difficulty in persuading her to eat properly. Her tiredness dragged on for days until total exhaustion overtook her body, making movement up and down the vicarage stairs a laboured task. Arthur marvelled that for all her increasing ill-health, Eleanor's spirit never declined; she smiled and showed gratitude for the simplest offering. When the memorial service was held at the end of March for Willy Johnson, Eleanor quietly sat in a side pew and whilst her beautiful voice was silent, she gently mouthed the words.

Arthur made enquiries of Doctor Christopher and gently relayed his thoughts before Eleanor. He was surprised to see Eleanor smile. 'What is it my love?'

'Well, I remember reading that some of these new convalescent establishments had been built in Germany, but the war makes that hard for me to attend. Now we know some of our coastal towns have convalescent homes that have been bombed. It seems the Germans have it in for me.'

But with the coming of early June and east-coast bombing raids something of the past, Eleanor was persuaded to go to a convalescent cottage hospital near Clacton. The Seaspray was close enough to the coast for the rich sea aroma to be present, but after three weeks Eleanor asked Arthur that she be allowed to return home. 'I don't really feel any better and I miss home. I miss friends calling, I miss hearing all that's going on in the village and I miss seeing you all the time. I suppose I'm selfish, but I want to go home.' How much they loved each other. Two days later, the beginning of July, she returned to Rusfield.

As Eleanor's eyes opened now, she smiled at Arthur. 'My love, what news have you for me?' He knew how much she loved to hear all that was going on; she could still be part of Rusfield.

'Well, Violet Rushton tells me that there are over 150 parcels ready to go off, each with a packet of cigarettes, some sweets and a knitted item. Oh, and all the children have made a card, each one with the name of the man to whom the parcel is going. Some of the parcels have been added to by families putting in a few extras to their loved ones; a good idea, rather than sending separate parcels.'

'That's all wonderful news,' gasped Eleanor, her pale face

breaking into a radiant smile. 'Is there news of any of the men away?'

'Susannah told me that Olivia received a letter from Jack yesterday and was hugely relieved to learn he is well. After all the tragedies that Olivia has gone through, to lose Jack would be devastating; he's such a splendid young man. It's hard to remember that he has been away for three years.' He went on to tell Eleanor about the flower arrangement Olivia Atkins had arranged in the pedestal by the altar which he was then asked to describe. This caused Eleanor to smile again when he added at the end of his description: 'I hope I've got the colours right.'

'Don't worry Arthur, while I may not be able to go and check, I can ask mother to look.'

They both looked towards the door as Charlotte Windle came in carrying a small tray, covered with a pretty Chinese-designed cloth, which she placed on the table next to Arthur. 'Ruth brought round a dozen tomatoes yesterday which make a most nutritious soup.' She stooped down and gently kissed Eleanor on the forehead. 'I hope you enjoy it. I've also made some small egg custards. Rachel Fielding was telling me when she brought half a dozen eggs round earlier this morning that her chickens are really doing well. Anyway, if you fancy one, Arthur can go down and get it from the cool box, but they will keep until tomorrow, if not.'

At the beginning of August, Arthur had carried Eleanor downstairs and now she lay on the chaise longue which village choir members, supported by other benefactors, had presented with much love. This followed Eliza Carey, who now came in to help every day, mentioning to Isabella de Maine that the spare bed brought downstairs had not looked very elegant in the conservatory. Only Isabella knew what a generous contribution her brother, Sir Lancelot Prestwish, had made; she knew how highly he regarded Eleanor, since first meeting her some years previously.

Now permanently in the conservatory, Eleanor slept for

increasingly long spells during the day, which partly made up for broken nights when fits of coughing disturbed her sleep. Arthur had been as thrilled as Eleanor with the gift, not only as a most generous sign of people's affection, but to help raise her head in a more upright position; lying flat promoted even more coughing.

As August moved on, the weather dramatically changed. It had been the sunny weather that had given Arthur the idea of moving Eleanor into the conservatory overlooking their lovely garden which several parishioners now helped Arthur to maintain. However, Eleanor insisted on staying there even as the rain fell. With prolonged pauses, she said: 'It's all part of God's world. I don't agree with everything the church says, but I do believe God created the world and that sunshine and rain are both part of that creation.' Lying on the chaise longue, she saw some things more sharply than ever before. 'I love the patterns the rain makes as it runs down the glass, and just now when the rain stopped, two beautiful butterflies came out to celebrate and danced on and around that red dahlia by the patio. Arthur, please look out the butterfly book and show me, I think they were gatekeepers, but I do get them muddled up.'

Arthur made sure that he kept the birdseed container well filled, for although he knew that birds were now finding plenty of seeds in the fields, many did not reject the opportunity of easier feeds in the garden.

'I think butterflies and birds are two of God's most glorious creations, they are so beautiful.' She watched the birds in between her fitful periods of sleep and the visits of friends, who all understood they were rationed to short periods by the caring Arthur. Eleanor was delighted to find that Betty Hazlett who called in almost every day, both as a nurse and a dear friend, shared her love of birds. Eleanor would relate the ones she had seen and together they would watch out for the tits, sparrows and different finches that went to the hanging feeder and the starlings, chaffinches and thrushes that fed mainly on what the other birds dropped. One day she could hardly wait to tell Betty, and later Arthur, that she had seen nine long-tailed tits.

Eleanor knew she was dying. She told Arthur how he must look after himself when she was no longer with him; remarkably she sometimes made a joke of it. 'Don't forget to take your sermon with you when you go on a Sunday and remember to keep feeding the birds.' On another day, she said how they should both remember the life they had had together. 'Even though it's been for fewer years than many share, it's been richer and more wonderful than anyone else could imagine. Arthur, you are a marvellous husband and I do believe in God and I know that we shall never be far apart.' She turned and smiled at him; he leant forward and kissed her. He could hardly bare to hear her speak of dying, but had the sense not to deny something which he knew was near. His mother would stay as long as Arthur wished and she and Arthur took it in turns to sit, sometimes sleep in the armchair in the conservatory; Eleanor often needed a drink or to have her brow mopped. The rains continued with unseasonal flooding in parts of the garden as the days shortened.

It was on 28 August, the night of the great storm, that Eleanor died. Arthur was alongside her when he realised the change in her breathing pattern; an increase even to the usual gasping. He went to her, carrying the gentle light from the all-night burning candle, and held her hand. Suddenly, her breathing stopped; she had passed away. Arthur placed each hand on one of hers, leant forward and kissed her brow. He gazed at her and the tears fell. He whispered words to his wonderful wife, words that thanked her, words that spoke of his all-consuming love, words that would have broken any listener's heart – but there were no listeners. He was alone, yet he knew that Eleanor's presence, in whatever form, would be with him forever. He sat, he held her ever colder hands, he wept. No prayer came to mind; how could he love a God who had taken away the only thing that really mattered? How could such a life be cut so short and end in such pain? When his mother entered the room an hour later for her turn with Eleanor, she found Arthur bent low over his beloved, still clasping her hands, still weeping.

CHAPTER FORTY-SEVEN

September 1917

Arthur knew his misery was shared by all in Rusfield, but this gave him no solace. Everything he touched or saw reminded him of her; these were the things she had touched, that she had seen. He missed everything about her, but most of all he missed her voice: her conversation, her wisdom and her humour. He had visited many who had lost loved ones in the terrible war years, but surely none had ever felt all that he was now experiencing. He had talked to them of God and his love, but where was that now? No comforting verse, no words he had spoken to others gave him a moment's relief. How useless had been all his prayers and those of so many in the village. God had not listened or, worse still, had spurned all intercessions. He had sat in the stillness of Eleanor's garden, and listened; but he heard no voice and he realised his own foolishness when he recalled saying to one who had lost her son: 'Time is a great healer.' How wrong; each day that passed brought greater, not less pain.

His mother was fearful of how Arthur would approach the coming Tuesday, yet hoped he would then be able to put the funeral behind him and move on. She was relieved Hugo Sheridan was taking the service, for as vicar at Wensfield he had married Eleanor and Arthur and was a great friend of Charles and Georgina Brown, Eleanor's grieving parents.

As the day grew nearer, Arthur's distress dipped into depression; he trembled with grief at the thought of Eleanor being laid to rest in the cold ground. The thought even went through his mind that he would not be able to attend, yet in his heart he knew this was an occasion when he and Eleanor needed their spirits to touch.

While the unusually violent storm attending Eleanor's final hours had passed, the rain continued, and late on the first Monday in September, the eve of the funeral, it continued to lash against the conservatory windows. Charlotte Windle had wondered why Arthur sat in this room where the wretchedness of the weather was exaggerated, but he had told her that it was there he felt closest to Eleanor. Charlotte felt desperately tired, but knew she should wait until her son retired for the night. The time moved on slowly, but she now saw that it was already Tuesday. A few minutes later she realised the rain had stopped and the new moon with its weak light was forcing its way through the night clouds.

Arthur stared up at the silvery light, forced a smile and spoke quietly: 'Perhaps the weather is turning. I often used to think that Eleanor could change anything.' He stood and moved towards his mother. She, too, stood and they embraced, not a word was spoken, but love flowed between them: love and great pity.

Arthur followed his mother upstairs; they embraced again on the moonlit landing, neither speaking of the event to follow later that day. Alone in his room he gazed at the empty bed. He had no inclination to go to bed, for sleep was not possible and still fully clothed he sat in the upright Victorian chair. This was Eleanor's favourite chair and he recalled how Aunt Elsie, his mother's sister, had given it to them as a wedding present; but his mind soon returned to Eleanor. 'I always wanted to get married on a snowy day,' he remembered Eleanor saying as they had come out of Wensfield church on that February day to see large snowflakes falling. There had been a little covering of snow as they had been driven to the station to catch the train to Southwold. Their welcome at the Old Ship Hotel had been warm; so many happy days there. Wonderful memories for them and they had returned to the hotel for two more holidays before the war. How much they had enjoyed just wandering along the empty, sandy beach, Eleanor determined to paddle, shrieking with joy when stepping into the icy water. They had walked for miles in the seven days, coming back to the small hotel exhausted, but not too tired to love in a way that Arthur had never thought possible. Only eight years, but amazing years that Arthur realised few others could ever know.

He sat, he may have dozed; it was a little after half past five that he was conscious of a brief bird song from the garden. He wondered why any bird would sing an hour before dawn; Eleanor would have gone to one of many natural history books they had accumulated and sought an answer. Perhaps, it was a sound of joy, simply heralding another day. He stood and realised how stiff his limbs had become. It was hours before the funeral and a splash of his face was all that he felt inclined after pouring the cold water from the blue and white jug bought by Eleanor at Steepleton market.

Carrying the light and treading carefully so as not to wake his mother, he descended to the conservatory. There was a slight lightening of the eastern sky as the hall clock struck. How many dawns had there been; yet no other one like this? He had uttered no prayer that night, hardly any since Eleanor had died, but words spoken by him at the many funerals came unexpectedly to mind. Perhaps it was watching dawn breaking which called to mind the words: "In Christ shall all be made alive", but they meant nothing.

He was uncertain why, but a few minutes later he collected his heavy coat, scribbled a brief note for his mother, unlocked the side door and walked the short distance to the church. The sky, now fully aglow as he approached the ancient wooden door to the porch, promised a fairer day than of late. He knew St Mary's would be open, since with the tragic news of the first Rusfield casualties it had been decided that the church must always be left open; solace might be sought at any time. One objector had warned of church silver being stolen, but Fred Abrahams had retorted that he would rather see something stolen than deny anyone access to God's house. The Methodist chapel also kept its doors permanently open, a decision determined by Arthur's increasingly close friend, the Reverend Reggie Gregg. Eleanor had once said to Arthur that it struck her as strange that it had taken a war for some churches to reverse an age-old habit of locking its doors.

Arthur could hear her gentle voice saying this with just her touch of light mockery. It was a tone she used when she questioned, or indeed criticised the church for what she called its mumbo jumbo: there's so much meaningless tradition that gets in the way of Christianity. Oh, why are there so many things that men have made up; not truths that Christ ever talked about? Arthur knew how she had never said such things with bitterness, but a sadness because much of church tradition conflicted with her simple, but strong faith. What would she want Arthur to do now, what would she gently tell him? He reflected for a moment that her belief, her ideas had touched him; in preparing services he found himself more wary of some of the Old Testament readings, casting aside, or at least seriously questioning, biblical readings that he thought Eleanor would question. But even when critical of the church's teaching, she softened her words by adding: 'Well, anything that helps any one of us to follow Christ's teaching and get nearer to God must be all right. We're all different.'

He stepped round a puddle on the well-trodden path a few yards from the massive oak door. Above the door, the semicircular tympanum, washed and worn by eight centuries of wind and rain so that its once highly-decorated design of the world's creation had deteriorated to a fragile and unadorned outline. Arthur pushed hard and the door eased open with its well-rehearsed scraping sound that no one had resolved. He was glad visitors were welcomed by a light church; the early English windows had been well designed seven centuries previously. The colours on the altar cloth and modest silverware sparkled, the increasingly brilliant arrows of the early morning sun cutting through the window at the east end. Arthur was surprised to find himself in this place he knew so well; what had prompted him to come amid his self-searching grief? Out of habit, as much as meaning, he crossed himself and sat at the end of one of the front dark-stained pews.

One debt he owed his father had been an introduction to some of the classic religious buildings of the land. He remembered the cathedrals at Gloucester, Salisbury and Wells, but most of all the magnificence of King's College where he had been overwhelmed on a visit to Cambridge in his youth. Yet, as he sat quietly in this modest and simple church he felt closer to those who had built it than ever he felt in one of those great edifices. How little it had changed in all the centuries; here people had come in times of disaster and, for some moments, he imagined the poorly-clad villagers coming in and praying during the times of the Black Death, the Great Plague, the threat from Napoleon and moments of personal tragedy. He could hear Eleanor, accompanied by her gentle smile, saying: 'Arthur, just think of all those people who have been in here before you; somehow they found the strength to go on.' At that moment the increasing sunlight caught a flower pedestal bearing white and red chrysanthemums. The pulpit with its intricate workmanship, not a work of significance as Grinling Gibbons might have carved at one of the cathedrals, but which someone had taken much time and skill to achieve. Maybe, he would make time to find out more about St Mary's and write a proper history.

But then his mind stopped wandering and his eye fell on where he knew Eleanor's coffin would rest at midday, and the pain returned. He dipped his head on to his arms resting on the pew in front and slithered forward on to his knees, as much in angst as prayer. Tremors overtook his whole frame, tears his eyes and he gently sobbed. 'Why hast though forsaken me?' were not words he spoke, nor even thought, but was his whole view of God and the world.

He had heard no sound of anyone coming down the aisle, but then a gentle voice: 'Come now, Vicar. Let me pray with you.' He brushed his eyes, blinked, turned and saw dear Liz Smith standing there. Liz, of all people, one whom he never associated with St Mary's, another person whose life had known, indeed still knew deep tragedy.

Shamefaced, he pushed himself up and stood; she right next to him, sorrow inscribed in her haggard features. 'I'm sorry Liz; I didn't know anyone was here.'

She gently spoke, 'Lovely Eleanor: we all weep for her. She was the most kindly woman this village has ever known. On this day of all days, no one will be thinking of anything but her,' and here she paused for a moment before adding, 'and you, Vicar. Come, let us sit down together.'

After a few moments, Arthur realised her hand was resting on his. There were tears in her eyes as well. 'Liz, I'm sorry, but why are you here?'

'In part to pray for dear Eleanor, but there is another reason: you see today is my Fred's birthday. If he hadn't died in this terrible war he would be twenty-one today. Fourth of September, his birthday; the only difference is that today's a Tuesday and he was born on a Friday. They say that Friday's child is loving and giving; that was Fred. No one ever had a better son. Oh yes, he'd never found learning easy, but he was so kind. When Willy Johnson came home on leave after Fred died, he came to see me. Do you know what he said, Vicar?' Arthur gave a slight smile of encouragement, but kept silent.

'He said that Fred was the most loyal friend he ever had. Willy had lots of friends and to say that was wonderful.'

It was now Arthur's turn to place his hand on that of Liz's, 'Bless you Liz. I had no idea it was Fred's birthday. He was a splendid young man. So we really share our sadness today.'

'Indeed we do, but let's also think how we can share the best of memories: mine of Fred and yours of Eleanor. Think of the good things you have enjoyed together: be thankful for those. Vicar, do you remember when you came to see mother in her final moments and then we sat downstairs together with Nurse Hazlett?'

'I do. Your mother was a fine lady.'

'And do you remember when you and Eleanor, oh so kind, came to see me at the munitions factory when Fred died?' Again, Arthur nodded at his clear memory of that day. 'Well, both those times we said the Lord's Prayer together, do you remember that, too?' Another gentle nod and smile.

'Let's join in saying it together now, shall we? Remembering dear Eleanor.'

'And Fred,' he added.

'Yes. Let's think of them being here with us now, at least in spirit. I'm not a church person, but I think there is a God, perhaps he's here right now; five of us together.'

Whilst other villagers were rising from their beds, eating a hurried breakfast, Liz and Arthur said the prayer in a way that he had never known the words before. For a moment he imagined Eleanor's smile displaying approval. They sat quietly for a moment and then, without any prompting rose together. Liz leant forward and gently kissed Arthur's cheek. 'I don't think anyone really dies whilst there is still someone who remembers them with love. I'll be with you when we gather in here in a little while; just remember, so will Eleanor in spirit.'

'And Fred,' he added. Liz turned and left the church. Arthur followed a few minutes later.

CHAPTER FORTY-EIGHT

September 1917

Arthur had been grateful to the bishop for offering Dr Gresham Matthews, the cathedral's principal organist, to play for Eleanor's funeral. However, he courteously declined, for Rita Small was not only a capable musician, but a close friend; she and Eleanor had performed at village concerts and formed the village choir. Arthur knew Rita had listened carefully to Eleanor's wishes and anyone passing St Mary's on the previous Saturday or Sunday afternoon would have heard the organ as she determined to make the chosen music as perfect as she could. Her main worry was that tears would make playing difficult.

By midday on the Tuesday the church was full, although the service not due to start for half an hour. Led by Fred Abrahams and the Reverend Reggie Gregg, pew rows had been closed up and with all the chairs from the Methodist chapel, the normal seating had been doubled. By quarter past twelve there were over three dozen people assembled in and just outside the church porch; a number growing by the minute.

Rita Small had started playing forty minutes before the service; Handel, Bach, Telemann and Purcell all featured prominently, known favourites of Eleanor. Some members of the congregation were more mystified by the organist's improvisation of two tunes: "Dry Those Fair, Those Crystal

Eyes" and "I Dreamt that I Dwelt in Marble Halls". As she played, Rita Small's mind turned back to the village party five years earlier when her dear friend had delighted all by her rendering of both songs. 'They will remind me, and I hope some other people, of a wonderful village evening in peaceful times,' Eleanor had smiled, adding, 'you remember we started that evening with everyone singing "Daisy, Daisy", but I don't think I can expect you to play that.' Led by Eliza Carey, Rebecca Fielding and Olivia Atkins, arrangements of beautiful flowers adorned the church.

Arthur sat with his mother on one side, Eleanor's parents on his right. There were mourners from Steepleton; John Francis had rearranged the bus times to enable many to reach Rusfield. A number of dignitaries from Canchester Cathedral were there and many from Wensfield where Eleanor had grown up. Several had been ready to offer eulogies at the service and Arthur had chosen two friends he knew Eleanor would especially appreciate. They both spoke lovingly of her contribution to the village: Robert Berry of the way Eleanor had inspired the village spirit "in these terrible times of war" and Peter Meadows, having driven from Devon with his wife, who praised the work of Eleanor in setting up the reading room and supporting the school. The readings had been chosen by Eleanor. Charles Brown read his daughter's favourite words from the Sermon on the Mount and Charlotte Windle another passage from St Matthew's Gospel. She had to fight back tears when she reached Christ's words which had been so well heeded by Eleanor: *'I tell you the truth, whatever you did for one of the least of these brothers of mine, you did for me.'* More than once Charlotte Windle cast a sideways glance at her son, worried how he was coping with the service; she prayed that Arthur's earlier words to her were proving true: 'I'm sure that Eleanor will be with me.' So it seemed.

The late summer sun shone as the assembly walked the short distance to the vicarage garden; those closest to Eleanor having been invited to go inside to be with Arthur. He, with his mother nearby, moved a while later from house to garden, acknowledging the kind words spoken to him. He was surprised at some he saw: Dr Christopher and Eleanor's consultant Mr Wraith, Sir Humphrey Watkinson who had driven down from Westminster and Sir Lancelot Prestwish with his sister Isabella de Maine. They spoke, as if with one voice, of the privilege of having known Eleanor and extending their condolences to Arthur. The imposing figure of Peter who did not seem to have changed in the five years since retiring as master of the village school, warmly shook Arthur's hand: 'No words can properly reflect my high regard for Eleanor; she achieved so many good things.'

But when Arthur went towards the colourful herbaceous flower beds that Eleanor had created, he was surprised that approaching him was the Very Reverend Edgar Hartley Williamson, Dean of Canchester Cathedral. Perhaps he recognised a surprised look on Arthur's face for when he reached to shake hands, he said: 'You may be surprised to see me; I fully understand that. I just wish you to know that the prayers of everyone at the cathedral, especially my own, are with you. May I just briefly say something now?'

In his surprise, Arthur could not immediately call to mind how to address his visitor. After a momentary pause he said, 'Dean, how kind of you to come. You are most welcome to Rusfield.'

The dean smiled, an expression Arthur had never seen on his face before. 'Thank you for saying that; I do realise that we have met on very few occasions. I particularly remember the time some five years ago, an occasion that I think back on with some embarrassment and much regret, for which I apologise.'

Arthur mouthed a dismissive sound of this unexpected, but sincere sounding apology. The dean continued: 'I just want you to know that I hold your late wife in very high regard; she was truly a surprising, nay, an amazing lady.' Hard though he tried to conceal it, Arthur's surprise returned to his face. 'You see, she and I exchanged letters, about which I think you may be unaware. She wrote to me twice, both times with exceeding clarity of meaning and some passion; I remember them well.' Whilst Arthur knew nothing of the correspondence, he appreciated only too well how clearly and passionately Eleanor had been able to express herself.

'The first time she wrote was after I published a paper criticising the suffragette movement; she gave me many reasons why women should have the vote. I didn't agree, but I admired her arguments. But it was the second occasion that really, excuse me for using the phrase, took the wind out of my sails.' A slight smile overcame his saturnine features as he explained: 'You may remember that just over a year ago I sent out a document stating reasons why, based on the populations of the allies and the enemy, the war would end in victory for us. The much larger total of allies being given by me as the reason for ultimate victory was dismissed by Mrs Windle as nonsense and anti-Christian. She indicated that I was saying that if the war went on for much longer and the rate of killing was equal on both sides that eventually no peoples from Germany or their supporting nations would be left, whilst the allies would have many millions remaining.'

'I had no idea she had written to you, Dean. But listening to what you have just said sounds very much like her.'

'Well, I thought deeply about what she said and I came to the conclusion that my reasons for giving a victory were foolish and could be conceived as advocating an endless slaughter.' He paused for a moment. 'But I have taken up enough of your time on this very sad day. She was, indeed, an extraordinary woman and I wish I had shown the goodness to apologise to her a while ago.' He reached out to shake hands and slightly turning, added: 'Perhaps, you will allow me to come back to Rusfield, if you are willing to receive me. May God bless you.' He turned and moved away.

Arthur really wanted to go away quietly and ponder what the dean had said. So Eleanor did have a secret from him; what a surprise. He could not believe how many villagers came to give words, necessarily brief, of comfort: all spoke of the kindness of Eleanor. His feeling of her presence became stronger.

Arthur's brief reverie was halted by an immaculately dressed lady in her mid-thirties striding towards him. He could not recall ever seeing her before, but she approached with grave assurance. 'Your Reverence, may I offer you my deepest sympathy. You don't know who I am, but let me introduce myself.' She spoke in what Arthur felt was a slightly affected voice, but with sincerity. 'I am Amelia Payne-Croft and I travelled from Steepleton to pay my respects.'

'Thank you for coming. I'm sorry that I didn't immediately recognise you,' Arthur replied.

'No, we have never met, but I did meet your wife.' Even as she spoke, her name took on a meaning to Arthur. The suffragettes, he realised; she was the leader of the group in Steepleton. 'Well, I was one who advocated determined action to further our cause. Your wife agreed with the cause, but spoke out strongly about any action which might risk harming anyone. I remember well how she addressed our meeting and subsequently wrote, expressing her view most strongly. I didn't agree with her, but I did admire the way she spoke and wrote. I just wanted to pay my respects today and to acknowledge a most principled person. Please accept my deepest sympathy.'

With similar speed and directness to her approach, she took Arthur's hand and moved away. Arthur was as surprised as he had been with the dean's appearance and words. So Eleanor had written to Amelia Payne-Croft as well, a letter that also had a profound effect.

With all the people present, Arthur did not see Harriet and Joseph Bruce leave; it had been surprising they had come. That morning Peter Woods had arrived early, bearing them an official letter. Their son, Tommy Bruce, had been killed at a place of which they had never heard, Passchendaele. His parents, reeling from the terrible news had, nonetheless, wanted to pay their respects to a woman they so admired. Their tragic secret was known only to Peter who was unrecognised by some, not being in his postman's attire. That morning he had carried his dark suit along with the tragic letter for the Bruce family and daily post and changed at the Johnson's cottage. He had been so pleased to see Ruby there and they had parted with a kiss. He felt desperately sad for Tommy's parents, but his grief was overwhelmingly for Eleanor Windle; a lady for whom he could never think highly enough.

The crowd began to disperse, the admiration for Eleanor and the sympathy for Arthur remaining. As Ruby Johnson left, she wondered who else had seen the buzzard high in the elm tree by St Mary's throughout the wake. Willy would have been pleased she had spotted it.

One of the last to leave was Pauline Richards, Abraham's mother. 'I felt I should just mention it, Vicar; Frederick will come with me to the hospital on Friday. He's sure he can get away from work, so you don't need to worry.' Arthur had to think for a moment before he fully understood what she was talking about; of course, the rota for visiting Richford House.

'Please thank Frederick for the kind thought, but no, I will come with you still. Things have to carry on.'

CHAPTER FORTY-NINE

September 1917

Later that evening, Arthur explained to his mother how the day had appeared to him through a haze, as if he had been looking in from a distance. 'I can only hope that everyone who came didn't find me too distant, for that's how I felt. People were so kind and the things they said about Eleanor were so well deserved. Fancy the dean coming!'

'You were wonderful, Arthur. I'm sure everyone knows how hard today has been for you and all the tributes to Eleanor are, of course, so well deserved. I was looking at all the beautiful wreaths and flowers that people brought and there were so many attractive posies made by the children: I'm sure Eleanor would be thrilled.'

'Mother, it may sound strange, but I knew that Eleanor was with me today. As people spoke about her, I could almost see her smile and hear her gentle laugh.'

That night Arthur's sleep was punctuated by spells of despair realising he would never hear or see Eleanor again, and periods of relative peace when he felt Eleanor with him. After breakfast Arthur and his mother sat in the conservatory, drinking a second cup of coffee.

'Arthur, it's not always a good idea for mothers to give advice, as it can easily become gross interference. However, I will risk all,' she smiled, 'by suggesting you try to keep busy. You will find times when you just want to sit quietly on your own. That's fine, but just try to set your mind on all the good things you and Eleanor did together. Oh, and one other thing, Arthur. You'll find that some people will be reluctant to even mention Eleanor's name; that's either because they think you don't want her name spoken or, in some strange way, to protect themselves. Well, if that happens, you may well think it a good idea to bring Eleanor's name into your conversation. It's difficult to understand, but sometimes those who come to support need reassurance themselves. Now that's enough advice. Would you like another cup of coffee?'

Half an hour later, Arthur was trimming a rogue yellow rose branch arching over the front-room window. He realised he would have to devote more time to the garden, previously Eleanor's great joy, when his reverie was broken by the sound of a bicycle pulling up: Peter Woods.

'Good morning Peter, have you nearly finished your morning round?'

'Good morning sir. Yes, I just need to empty the pillar box. Sir, I wasn't sure whether to call on you.' The youthful-looking Peter, left hand holding his bicycle upright, paused. He continued as the vicar's smile sourced encouragement: 'There were an amazing number of people here yesterday and I didn't want to get in the way, but I want to add my sincere sympathy and say how everyone will miss Mrs Windle. She was a very special lady, sir.'

'Thank you Peter, thank you.' He realised Peter had rehearsed his words and how heartfelt they were. 'I feel that just recently I have been out of touch with village matters; is there much news of late?'

Peter did not want to worry the vicar unnecessarily, but knew that he would want to be aware of important matters. 'Well, sir, you may not have heard that Mr and Mrs Bruce's son has been killed.' He saw by the vicar's expression that the news was unknown to him.

'When did this happen, Peter?'

'I'm afraid I had to deliver the letter yesterday morning.'

'I'm so sorry, but thank you for telling me. I must get round to see them this afternoon. Peter, you must find it hard sometimes delivering these dreadful letters and telegrams?'

'Yes sir, I do. A few weeks ago I actually asked about a job at the flour mill, but at the last moment decided not to go ahead. Sometimes it is awful, as I can imagine how dreadful it must be for people when I deliver these letters and telegrams.'

'Yes, it must be wretched for you,' Arthur hesitated, realising the young postman had more he wanted to say.

'Yes, but I shouldn't be thinking about myself, should I?'

'Peter, it would be surprising if you didn't feel the pain sometimes, only a very insensitive person wouldn't feel as you do.' Arthur placed a hand gently on that of Peter's holding the bicycle, 'Everyone in the village respects you and, believe me you do an important job because someone has to deliver these letters and you know the people. I hope you will continue, but I would understand if you decided it was all too much. Nobody would blame you.'

'Thank you, sir, for those kind words. That's really why I have kept going. I wish I could be out fighting with all the lads, but I know that can't be with me being blind in one eye.'

'Peter, it's been good to see you. If it had not been for you, I wouldn't have known to go round to see Mr and Mrs Bruce this afternoon.'

Peter Woods smiled, got on his bicycle and pedalled along to the pillar box at the junction of Bury Way and West Lane to collect letters, many to carry news to men away fighting.

Hoping not to meet anyone on the way, Arthur walked along Sandy Lane and passing Robert Berry's cottage admired the four large tubs outside his cottage, two with tomatoes and two with lettuces. Robert had told him that the "grow more vegetables" scheme was going well now that nearly seventy villagers were taking part. Arthur continued past The Ark after which the road began its slight descent to where cottages became less frequent near the edge of the village.

His mind turned to Harriet and Joseph Bruce whom he knew, although not well. They were regular worshippers at the Methodist chapel and Harriet had been an enthusiastic member of Eleanor's choir. Joseph was a hurdle maker with a large barn at the rear of his cottage where he made the low fences mainly used to retain sheep. He coppiced the ash from Dell Wood and made the bar hurdles using poles trimmed from the ash, splitting them with his billhook and then nailing them together in the form of a five-bar gate. He also made lighter-weight hurdles using coppiced hazel, but Arthur had heard that times were hard for the family as sheep were giving way to arable farming.

His eye took in the pretty thatched cottage, although he noticed the roof needed attention, and saw two young children in the street playing marbles. Arthur knew little about marble games; it was clear that they were thoroughly enjoying themselves although their main joy appeared to be in getting covered in dirt. He approached the one whom he judged to be about five years of age. 'What is your name?' he asked in his kindly manner.

'I'm Ruth and that's Daisy.'

Arthur smiled at these two girls, judging Ruth to be the oldest, and recognised the similar features of the two with their dark hair falling over their grubby, but happy faces. As they returned to their marbles, he knocked on the door, but their attention had not been fully diverted from the visitor. 'They won't hear you, mister; they're in the back garden. You can go through there.' Ruth rushed to the side gate and swung it open, then returned to the game.

Arthur walked along the side path and sure enough Harriet and Joseph Bruce were sitting on the back doorstep. They looked up at the sound of footsteps, Joseph hurriedly standing. Arthur saw the tear-stained and pained face of his wife and noticed that Joseph's left hand was heavily swathed in a bandage.

'Vicar, please forgive the state we're in.' He reached out with his right hand in a warm welcome by which time Harriet Bruce had struggled to her feet. Arthur noticed two more children at the bottom of the narrow, well-maintained garden with the older one pushing the other on a swing fixed to an overhanging branch.

'Will you come inside, Vicar? I can make a cup of tea for you.'

'That's most kind, but no thank you. And with this weather it would seem a shame to go indoors. I can easily sit on this,' Arthur replied, pointing to a low brick wall that edged the small patio. He was pleased that the two grieving parents returned to their earlier seats on the well-scrubbed step and as he sat, said: 'I am so, so sorry to hear about Tommy. Please accept my deepest sympathy. If there is anything I can do in any way to help, you must let me know.'

'Thank you, Vicar. That's most kind of you and we especially appreciate you coming round at this unhappy time for you, too. Mrs Windle was a kind, thoughtful lady and the village will be a much poorer place without her.'

Immediately his wife had finished speaking, Joseph Bruce continued, opening out the sheet of paper which was beside them on the step. 'Yes, it is terrible news, but we will always be very proud of Tommy. Indoors we have some photographs of him when he was home on leave and we'd love to show you these before you go.'

Arthur smiled and nodded his acceptance of this offer. 'We shall miss him terribly, but in this letter his sergeant said Tommy was very brave in attacking an enemy machine-gun post. He also said that Tommy had died instantly and we thank God for that.'

Arthur glanced at Harriet Bruce, head sunk, and saw her

shoulders gently moving as she silently sobbed. He made the quick decision to change the course of conversation. 'I'm sorry to see you have injured your hand. Is it serious?'

Joseph Bruce looked down at the bandaged hand. 'Well, I was stupid enough to cut it when I was splitting some wood. I don't know how many hundreds of poles I've split, but my billhook must have hit a tough knot. Nurse Hazlett has been very caring and she came quickly when Harriet went round to her cottage, stitched it and keeps checking all is well. I'm all right really, but she tells me I must take things carefully for a few days and rest. She thinks I will get attacks of giddiness if I'm not careful and I want to do everything I can to help it heal as quickly as possible. I can't afford to be away from work for long.'

'But you were good enough to come to Eleanor's funeral yesterday.'

Harriet Bruce looked up. 'Well, that was different. We both wanted to be there to pay our respects. We were not going to miss that, whatever happened.'

'That was very kind of you. I appreciate your thoughtfulness and I know Eleanor would be saying the same. Thank you.'

Their conversation was brought to a sudden halt as Ruth, followed immediately by the younger Daisy, came running round the corner towards the grieving adults. 'Daddy, will you tell Daisy that she isn't allowed to have an extra go with her marble just because she's younger than me. I don't think that's fair.'

The parents' features turned to embarrassment. 'I'm so sorry, Vicar. Please excuse the children.' Joseph's face took on an attempted stern look: 'Ruth, I've told you before that you mustn't just burst in and interrupt people when they are talking. Now, say you're sorry.'

Ruth immediately looked humbled, gently took hold of her younger sister's hand in a protective gesture, turned to the adult visitor and said: 'I'm sorry, sir. It was rude of me.' By

350

this time the other two girls had hurried from the bottom of the garden and joined the group on the patio, curious to know what was happening.

'What a lovely family you have,' Arthur offered. 'I've already met Ruth and Daisy, but not your other two daughters.'

'This is Ruby,' Harriet Bruce said, introducing the older girl whom Arthur had seen pushing the swing. The eight-year-old gave a slight curtsey. 'And this is Maud, she's just four.'

'Well, I know you two like playing marbles and I saw you enjoying pushing Maud on the swing,' said Arthur, trying to involve all of the children. 'What other things do you like doing?'

It was Ruby, perhaps feeling her role as the eldest of the four, who answered: 'Well sir, we like going for walks and paddling in the stream. I like reading and I'm helping Daisy and Maud to read.'

'So you all like school, do you?' They all nodded with much enthusiasm.

'And we were hoping to go on the treasure hunt on Saturday, but mummy says she's not sure we can,' chipped in Ruth. 'Father won't be able to go and mummy says she may need to stay with him.'

Arthur vaguely recalled that Grace Reynolds and Reggie Gregg with help from others at the Methodist chapel were organising a family treasure hunt across Bramrose Hill with a succession of clues eventually leading to the manor where Isabella and Sebastian de Maine would provide a drink and an apple.

'But you could go with someone else, couldn't you?' asked Arthur of the disappointed children. It was the next, rather unexpected comment, or rather a question, that would long remain in Arthur's mind.

'Could we go with you, Mr Vicar?' asked Maud, the youngest of the four.

There was a brief pause before Harriet Bruce, with another embarrassed look, answered: 'Maud, you shouldn't ask like that. I'm sorry, Vicar. And I'm sorry that Maud addressed you in that way.'

Arthur smiled. 'I don't mind. I've never been addressed as Mr Vicar before, I rather like it.' In a moment his mother's advice about keeping busy came to him, intermingled with a memory of Eleanor enjoying a village treasure hunt a year or so previously.

'Maud, it was kind of you to ask me. I'm not sure if your parents would agree, but if your mother isn't able to join in on Saturday, I would love to take you. I'm sure we could help each other with the clues.'

The children all broke in to smiles, Maud clapping her hands in sheer joy. 'Vicar, are you sure? That would be very kind,' said Joseph Bruce. 'The children would love that.'

The treasure hunt on the following Saturday, blessed with continuing sunshine, was another happy village day easing, albeit briefly, the sadness and anguish that hovered over Rusfield. So it was that Ruby, Ruth, Daisy and Maud, accompanied by Arthur and his mother, was one of the forty family groups that assembled on the green before setting out for Bramrose Hill. Maud carried the piece of paper bearing the first clue, proudly read to her by Daisy. It was a happy day, long remembered by the villagers, not least by Arthur.

Arthur read one of the lessons at the memorial service for Private Tommy Bruce at the Methodist chapel and, as with every service for a man who died in the war, virtually everyone from the village was present. Over a year earlier, Jack Mansfield of Spinney Farm had been the first of the local employers to grant time off for attending these services; others had followed.

Charlotte Windle divided her time between helping Arthur in the garden and joining in village activities. She took her turn at the reading room when Isabella de Maine was unwell, helped in organising a batch of parcels for the troops and joined Olivia Atkins in preparing sketches for a new children's book. A close bond had grown between the two of them and they increasingly enjoyed each other's company with Charlotte sharing in Olivia's worries about her son Jack and rejoicing in a letter arriving from him. However, in Charlotte Windle's mind it became clear that she must not outstay her time in the village; Arthur must learn to manage on his own. Her return home was arranged for the first Friday in October; it would be almost four months since she had come to Rusfield. Arthur would accompany her back to Dorset, stay overnight and return to take the Sunday service at St Mary's.

Although Charlotte Windle had misgivings about leaving Rusfield, she was delighted to see her own home. She needed to have no worries about the state of the house, for friends had kept a watchful eye on it; Margaret Brentford had arranged flowers in both the small hallway and the lounge. Mother and son separately reflected on how their relationship had become ever closer during the past months. Tears remained in Charlotte's eyes long after Arthur left, caused through his parting gift to her: a ring given to Eleanor by Arthur for her thirtieth birthday. 'Mother, please accept this as a thank you. It was Eleanor's wish that I give it to you.'

The Waterloo-bound train left Sherborne on time and apart from a group of soldiers, there were few passengers. Arthur found himself alone in the carriage with the rain splattering against the window, part concealing the autumn countryside. His mind leapt between loving thoughts of Eleanor and moments of profound depression; she was either with him or totally absent. He, too, had begun to see some of the church's teaching as no more than "mumbo-jumbo", that it concerned itself too little with the fundamental tenets of Christianity. He agreed more and more with Eleanor's seemingly simple but clear view of God as shown through Christ's teaching and example. He continued to be puzzled by prayer, unable to believe that it would cause God to intervene in people's lives and events; to him this was at conflict with free will. His anger at God for taking Eleanor from him had assuaged, for anger had never been the way for Eleanor. He had commenced a letter to the bishop saying that he no longer saw himself fit to continue as a priest, but decided this might be something best discussed with the dean, if he did come to see Arthur.

To Arthur's slight surprise a Buddhist monk entered the carriage at Salisbury, smiling and making a polite comment that he hoped Arthur did not mind him joining him. Arthur judged the middle-aged passenger to be from the Indian continent and whilst he knew little of the Buddhist religion, his saffron robes announced his calling.

After a while the newcomer introduced himself with the comment: 'These are difficult times my friend, are they not?' Arthur agreed that the war was a great test of men's courage and that the suffering at home and abroad seemed never ending.

'Indeed, I think many find it a challenge to our very being; I know I do.'

'But,' replied Arthur, 'perhaps our beliefs, and I know little of your religion, should give us some solace.' Encouraged by the other's gentle smile and nod, Arthur went on; 'I hope you won't mind me asking a question.'

'Of course not, although I cannot promise a helpful answer.'

Arthur struggled for a moment to frame what he found himself wanting to know. 'I'm sure your belief gives you the comfort we have just mentioned, but I find myself very ignorant. Can you tell me something of Buddhism? Please forgive me for being curious.'

'I understand. To explore another's faith is good, for in doing so I am sure one can learn much. I have been fortunate enough to study some aspects of the Christian faith and I think there are some teachings that are common to both of us.'

'I'm sure that is so,' responded Arthur. 'Please go on.'

'One of our most important beliefs is that when one's body dies, that person's mind does not come to an end. Even though our conscious mind ceases, it moves into a deeper level of consciousness. I don't know whether I'm explaining this very well.'

'Indeed, you are. Please tell me more.'

'Everything we do leaves an impression on our mind so one can think of it as a garden with our actions and behaviour rather like sowing seeds in that field. Those seeds or actions can bring further happiness or future suffering. We know this as the law of karma; it's fundamental to our Buddhist morality.' How much like Eleanor, Arthur thought. He could have been describing part of her faith.

They continued to discuss each other's faith and both smiled when they agreed that a religious discussion was an unlikely occurrence on a Saturday morning train. The Buddhist monk, whose name Arthur found embarrassingly difficult to remember, explained that four years previously he had travelled from Ceylon and was now involved in the monastic order in London. It was to Arthur's disappointment when his travelling companion told him that he was leaving the train at Woking.

They said their farewells with much warmth and agreed that life was a journey for truth. 'Perhaps,' said the monk, 'truth or, as you would say God, is so great that no single religion can fully encompass it. I thank you for sharing our search together.'

As the carriage door was closed, Arthur realised what an unexpected fellow traveller had been with him. He smiled to himself when he realised that some would view this as divine intervention; he knew his own unsteady faith could not go that far.

CHAPTER FIFTY

May - August 1918

He was haggard, listless and his six-foot frame had changed from his days as Boney, the fearless goalkeeper and the well-muscled young man who humped bags of grain at the brewery. He was a frightened soldier who trembled at every explosion. Private Albert Jones had lost all heart and cared little whether he survived the war or not. His final link with sanity had been shattered by the letter received two weeks earlier: Doris had ended their relationship.

Having built up huge forces the Germans had launched a massive attack to end the stalemate by punching their way through the Allies' defences before the American troops became established. Albert had been in a British division previously in Flanders which had been moved from the front line to recuperate after a lengthy duty. However, Duchêne, the French commander had overruled the British command and the fatigued troops, now firmly under his charge, became part of his plan of defence in depth. Albert was now one of thousands massed in front line trenches, targeted by great numbers of German guns. The first bombardment had been followed by a poison gas drop affecting many of the men; Albert had at least escaped this additional horror.

It seemed a lifetime ago that he and his friends had gathered in Rusfield, enjoyed a drink together and looked forward to the future; later, his time with the glorious Doris. Had that been before or after he was wounded for the first time? Surely afterwards, those moments had promised so much for the future once the bloody war was over. The leave back home and the discovery that his mate Jammy had been killed in the same explosion had begun his recurring nightmares which he had never previously known. He recalled a second period of leave, taking the younger family members to gather blackberries on Bramrose Hill. A faint smile came to his worn face when he remembered his own brown paper bag splitting open and all the berries spilling; George immediately boasted that he had now got more blackberries than his big brother. But when he had asked Doris to go for a walk over the same hill two days later, she had said she needed to do an extra day's work at Spinney Farm, but he felt it was an excuse. She had seemed reluctant even to hold his hand and their previous passionate embraces were not to be repeated. Albert found that when his parents asked him what France was like, he had to pretend it was not too bad; they just did not understand. He had been pleased to return to France, finding comfort alongside other men who shared this war although he hated every minute of the shelling and the trenches of dead bodies.

It was the companionship, the stories they swapped and the assumed common inevitability of being killed to which he warmed. They joked together and, in moments away from the front, they joined in choruses, often crude ones. There had been the time when writing a letter home Podgy and Heave-ho were nearby writing letters, too. When they had all finished Albert said he would pass them on for the first stage of the journey back to England. As he put them together he noticed that on the back of Podgy's letter was written: *Remember NORWICH*. 'Podgy, you don't come from Norwich,' he said, looking across at the older man.

Podgy let out a great guffaw. 'Of course not, I'm from

Newcastle, that's not why I've written *NORWICH* on the back of the envelope. Don't you know?' He saw Albert's puzzled expression. 'Well, it's what a lot of us write. Annie will know what it means: "Nickers Off Ready When I Come Home".' He laughed again and Albert and Heave-ho joined in.

There might be different mates each time he returned to the front, but mates just the same. They only knew each other for a brief time, but most would willingly have given their lives for one another.

How could his parents, how could anyone back home know what it was like to stand for twenty-four hours up to one's waist in water? The rain was almost as bad as the shells, neither ever stopped. Rats abounded and open excreta had to be chucked out of the trench hoping that some poor devil would spread lime on it; if that did not happen the men would find themselves crawling out through it. The agonies of trench fever and trench foot became more and more common; trench fever gave severe diarrhoea and extreme weakness, and standing in the water all the men feared trench foot. Albert had one mate, Pokey, who had first felt numbness in a foot, then swelling and open sores and eventually gangrene. The toes rotted; the pain had been agonising.

Into 1918 it had got worse. After a rare advance, Albert and some 300 men had found themselves abandoned in a wilderness. The only shelter was shell-holes scattered across a stretch of destroyed and desolate wasteland. No one really knew what was happening, but the order came through that all were to stay in their position. Albert was there for three days; it rained incessantly. On first sheltering in the shell-hole, some five feet deep and thirty feet wide, he found he had three companions: a dead German, a dead horse and one fellow soldier. His new mate's name was Martin, a New Zealand private. When they realised they were likely to be there for longer than made any sense, he and Martin managed to bury the German and the horse in the stinking mud of the sloping shell-hole wall. For themselves they tried to dig cave holes into the side, but within hours their intended shelter had filled in with the slithering mud wall.

To both men the extraordinary thing was that their new sanctuary, and there were other men in similar shell-holes in this surreal area, became known and then accepted by a higher echelon in the military. Each day, minimal rations were brought to them by some poor devil struggling through the sea of mud; they really had no idea where he came from. Each day a two-gallon petrol tin of tea, further wrapped in a small box of straw attempting to keep it warm, had arrived; Albert could still taste the petrol-flavoured tea. This had been accompanied by bread, butter which was often floating in foul water and a tin of bully beef, for which Albert had a makeshift opener. The saving grace for Albert was the company of Martin Grayson who was twenty-four. His grandfather had emigrated to New Zealand as a young man from Camlachie in Glasgow. Albert had found his new mate's accent attractive and gently reassuring as he went on to speak of his time before joining the forces to defend the mother country.

'After a while in Auckland, my grandfather moved near to Christchurch. He married the daughter from another farming family who had left Scotland around the same time. They had three children who worked on either the farm or in the timber industry. The youngest was my father and after working hard he managed to buy a small area of land near a place called Little River. It was there he met my mother and I grew up on this farm where sheep were the main thing. They never told me, but I think they just could not have any more children, so I was the only one.' He smiled, 'And I didn't arrive until mum was nearly forty.'

'Was the farm successful?' asked Albert.

'Well, it was never easy, but dad got by and it slowly prospered and he added more land. I always loved helping dad on the farm and so when I finished at school there was only one thing I wanted to do. My mother had never enjoyed the best of health and by the time dad was sixty he found it quite hard. It was all right then because I was around, but when I left them for this,' he extended his arms, opening out his hands to indicate their location, 'I knew dad would have difficulty. He managed to get old Zeb in to help, but I'm sure they both struggle as Zeb is around the same age as dad. I can't wait to get back home.'

This was the friendship between mates that Albert loved; it was the only good part. The two went on talking about their families and friends back home and the jobs they had done before the war. Albert listened eagerly to Martin's stories about his farm. 'It's a beautiful place,' Martin said with great enthusiasm, 'the rolling hills seem to go on for ever, we have a beautiful stone church and like you I enjoyed my schooldays. And then there's the sea, it's not very far away and we always loved messing about in the water. We even have a railway station that runs in from Lincoln, mainly carrying timber.' Amazing, thought Albert, that his mate had come all the way from the other side of the world to fight in this godforsaken place; for what?

It was the next day whilst they continued to swap memories that a furrow came to Martin's brow when he was talking about the excitement of shearing time. 'There's only one thing that really worries me, Albert.'

'What's that?'

'Well, what will happen to mum and dad if I don't get back? Suppose something happens to me over here, how will they manage?'

They fell into a silence. The incessant gunfire from both sides continued, broken only by the savagely rhythmic sound of less frequent machine-gun fire, but all sounded a good distance away. Here in this filthy shell-hole they felt strangely distanced from the war.

'Martin, your Little River sounds a wonderful place.

Before the war I thought I might go abroad; some guys in our village went off to Canada and what I heard sounded good. I should think New Zealand is just as good.'

'Or better,' smiled Martin.

'I guess so, maybe I should go there when all this is over – if I survive.'

'Albert, I'm sure you would love it. I wonder, I just wonder if you would think of going to work on my dad's farm if anything happens to me?'

On what turned out to be their last day in the shell-hole before they received the order to retreat, Albert found himself promising Martin that if the New Zealander was killed he would go and help his father. He was not sure whether Doris would accompany him; he thought not.

To Albert, the three days in the shell-hole had been an escape; strangely, a period of tranquillity. As soon as he had clambered out and joined in the plodding through the all too familiar mud for what seemed like miles, the trembling and fear returned; every sound from a gun caused another quiver to run through his body; both gunfire and shake became continuous.

He had been one of many who received brief care in the field hospital hastily constructed on a small hillside to escape the worst of the filthy mud and after treatment he was given six days' rest. With body marginally repaired, but his mind in turmoil, Albert had been examined by a young doctor and declared fit to return to duty. More than once he thought of ending his life; it was unfair that in the many attacks on enemy positions he was spared while others fell. Then, as the rains died and the warmth of spring and early summer promised some hope, Doris' letter had arrived. Whatever the confusion of the past months, he had a clear picture of Doris: engaging smile, tumbling hair, a lovely body and their shared times of passion. Now this was over. Perhaps she had found someone else; it did not matter, she had finished with him. All over.

Finding himself huddled in this trench facing the fresh German onslaught, it was probably chance that he found himself next to Mike, an older man, that saved him from tipping right over the edge into madness. Albert realised that this slightly-built, balding man shared the same fears as himself; his trembling at each crash of gunfire and a face that was pale, emaciated and unsmiling. The enemy assault reached such a climax, retreat orders were inevitable.

It was sometime later, how many days Albert had no idea, that he found himself resting in a barn with Mike alongside him. They occasionally talked, each recognising the other's fear. Private Mike Marsden was thirty-nine and had joined the army when conscription had come in. He was a passionate family man with eight children and a wife who suffered badly from asthma; he had hated leaving his small Yorkshire village and family. He, too, had been through terrible times in the Somme and had felt growingly certain of his own forthcoming death.

Soon fresh orders arrived. The Germans had rapidly advanced several miles but, for reasons unknown to the allied command, their battalions had come to a halt. Rumours trickled through that they had run out of ammunition or that the Americans caused an unexpected halt to their advance; all that Albert and Mike knew was that they were ordered back to the front line. It was on the second evening in their hurriedly dug-out trench they were told of a fresh initiative: an attack would take place at 06.30 the following morning. Albert had prepared for so many attacks that he responded automatically: gun cleaned and other weapons checked. His new mate Mike, who was alongside him, offered a hurried prayer. The summer morning was grey and as the time approached, the great roar of allied guns presaged the assault and a dense smokescreen was laid to conceal the attack; a tactic too well known by the Germans. The whistle blew at 06.30 precisely; no scramble up a makeshift ladder from this shallow trench, just the clamber over the top and then the crouching, dipping and weaving run that Albert had adopted so many times. The Germans adopted their normal response with blind fire, but random though it was, Albert saw men dropping on all sides and heard screaming as he ran on and on. Unlike earlier times when massive barbed-wire walls had been erected, there had been no time for such enemy defences. Albert ploughed on, one of a mad, fiendish band of khaki-clad figures; suddenly they were in the enemy makeshift trenches, time had not allowed deep digging. Enemy arms were raised and guns thrown aside: a victory at last.

The sun cut through the clouds and the warmth matched the elation that descended on most of the men; not on Albert. He had survived again. It was the next day when Lieutenant Roebuck was carrying out an inspection that the young officer stopped and pointed at Albert and some men nearby: 'You eight men get back to number two line and report to Sergeant Manning. He's got a job for you.' Turning to the man next to Albert, the Lieutenant added: 'Corporal Brownlow, you're in charge.'

Thirty minutes later, a shock awaited the men. The exhausted-looking Sergeant Manning briefly explained: 'In the last attack one man refused to move. He tried to hide in the trench. A court martial has sentenced him to be executed. Six of you will be in the firing squad, you two,' pointing at Albert and a fair-haired lad who barely looked out of school, 'will guard him until the morning.' The six men paled, this was the worst of all orders; Albert could only feel a little relief that he was not one of them.

A second, more intense shock hit Albert a few minutes later when he and the other selected to act as a guard were marched by the sergeant to the prisoner; it was the shaking figure of Private Mike Marsden, the father of eight from Yorkshire. His prison was but a shell-hole, two privates stood nearby, rifles to the ready. They were to be replaced by Albert and the young private until the execution early the following morning. The condemned man did not look up when the guard change took place.

That night Albert managed to engage his former mate in brief conversations. Although fear gripped every part of his body, Private Marsden understood that he was to die in a few hours. 'My family, my Joyce, what will they do now? I have betrayed them,' he broke down in to pitiful sobbing. That night Albert was more comforter than guard; the other guard sat by in his own world of mental distress.

As the first glimmer of light showed on that July morning the execution party prepared. The six men in the firing squad knew that only two had loaded rifles, the other four with blanks; none would know who fired the fatal shot. But the next shots fired were not from any of these men, but a huge barrage of cannon fire followed by the earth shattering explosion of enemy shells. The Germans had launched a final, desperate assault in this sector of the Front. In this war when life or death frequently hinged on chance, a huge explosion shattered the area. The two guards were killed instantly, the execution party and condemned man either killed or severely injured in the blast which created yet another shell-hole in this pitiless landscape.

In the last week of August, Peter Woods rode in to Rusfield carrying a telegram with the news of the thirty-fourth war death. A month later, Susannah and Sidney Jones received a package which contained a small identity disc bearing the name of their son, his number, rank, regiment and religious denomination.

CHAPTER FIFTY-ONE

August - November 1918

That two old soldiers, Sebastian de Maine and Robert Berry, were the first to seriously discuss the best way to commemorate the village men who had died was unsurprising. The idea spread with increasing intensity in the three drinking houses and George Cooper raised it at the St Mary's church council. A village hall to be built on the land adjacent to the school, recommended by the Mothers' Union, appeared the most favoured idea, although others soon emerged: a memorial garden at the school where the men had spent their young days and a stained-glass window at the west end of St Mary's. A slightly boisterous discussion broke out at The Queens Head for the commemorative garden to be on the village green, not at the school, but Rachel Fielding suggested to her customers that a stone monument with the men's names suitably inscribed be placed near the church.

The morning service on the first Sunday in August fell on the eve of the national Bank Holiday, but in most minds, marked four years since the war had started. Arthur Windle had deliberated long over his sermon and after discussion with the Reverend Reggie Gregg at the Methodist chapel, decided to encourage the establishment of a memorial fund. On that day, which again saw a full church, he started: 'My dear friends, I know there are different ideas how we can best commemorate the brave men who have died whilst serving our King and country, but I would earnestly suggest that we put on one side exactly how this be done; there will be time enough for that when the war is over. There are encouraging signs that the allied armies are gaining, but sadly, before the war ends there will be more men who will die.' Even as he spoke, Arthur could see nods of agreement and when he spoke of starting a collection the nods of approval increased. Arthur knew that his good friend was putting forward the same idea at the Methodist chapel. By the following Sunday £17 13s 6d had been collected and the fund grew.

However, the creation of a memorial fund provoked further anxiety. Thirty-six men with strong Rusfield connections had already died, but a further 182 were still fighting. The families of these men waited in fear; the rest of the village shared in their anxiety.

For Doris Groves, fear was shared with remorse. Ever since Susannah and Sidney Jones had received news of the death of Albert, Doris had never been far from tears. A thousand times she wished she had never written the letter to him months earlier; why had she ever penned those words? She saw it as her own selfishness, her lack of understanding of him being torn from her and his family. She should have listened to her dear friend, Grace, who patiently bore the absence of her beloved Abraham with apparent composure. She knew life was full of "if onlys", but if only she had posted the letter, she might have waited for Peter Woods and retrieved it, but no, she had gone to the postbox as he was emptying it and given the letter to him. Within minutes she had deeply regretted writing of ending their relationship, but by the time she had cycled into Steepleton and found Peter at the post office, the letter had gone to the railway station. Only Grace knew that the next day she had travelled to London where she thought the letter would go; maybe she could recover it. Her enquiries at the Liverpool Street post office took her on the underground train to Baker Street and then the short walk to Regent's Park, but disappointment greeted her. The whole of Regent's Park, which she had once been to on a family outing, was covered in a gigantic structure. She approached two guards who were hovering near the entrance to the park, but when she had asked one about reclaiming her letter, he had burst out laughing. The other, recognising the trembling nature of her question, threw up his hands and said, 'I'm sorry, love. There is no chance. I don't expect you know, but there are two and a half thousand ladies here sorting letters and parcels; they get through thousands each day. I'm sorry.' Tears had clouded her return and had rarely stopped whenever she was on her own. Doris' anguish had not lessened in the four months since writing the letter in May.

In the intervening months, news had come of the deaths of Billy Griggs and Jimmy Thomas whilst Charlie Wayman, still in a London hospital, had lost his left leg and would not be back home for three months. Fred Jackson or Jack Mansfield often drove Charlie's wife, Freda, to Steepleton to visit her husband in London.

It was on a misty day in late September that a remarkable event occurred; soon, and for many years to come, to be known as the "Rusfield miracle", it was nothing less. Peter Woods had no idea of the life-changing nature of one letter he was carrying. He delivered a small package to Jack Mansfield, then called at the Jones' house in Wood Lane but, as usual finding no one at home, decided to deliver it to their butcher's shop in Pond Street. As with all those who had lost a loved one, Peter felt great sympathy; none more than towards Susannah and Sidney Jones. Pulling up outside the shop, he entered to find them as busy as ever; Susannah having just placed some beef and onion pies in the rear oven and Sidney behind the counter. Peter held the door open as Eliza Carey came out, bade her a good morning and took the few steps towards Susannah. 'Good morning,' he addressed her in his cheerful manner, 'just one letter for you.' After her acknowledgement and a greeting from her husband, Peter turned and left. He had seen a slight puzzlement on Susannah's face as she took the letter; had he stayed a minute longer he would have heard her cry out. She had wiped her hands on her apron, opened the envelope, unfolded the letter and almost immediately collapsed on a nearby stool.

'What is it, love?' her husband asked as he came quickly to her.

'It's… it's from Albert. Look,' she said thrusting the letter to him. 'What does it mean? I don't understand.'

Sidney joined his wife in total bewilderment. 'Maybe it's just been long delayed, a letter he wrote months ago.'

'But that can't be. Look at the date: twenty-sixth of August. It doesn't say this year, but it must be.' Together they read:

Dear loving parents,

I'm afraid this letter will be another shock as I haven't written for a long time. A mate of mine, whose name is also Albert, is writing it for me as my right hand and arm are still bandaged. Don't worry, I really am all right and I'm sorry to give you worries again. I don't really know all that has happened, but it won't be long before I'm back home. I can't remember everything and it's difficult to explain in a letter. What is important is to send my love; I think so much about you and Flo, Willy, Henrietta and George. Give them a big hug from me. I was injured by another shell and ended up in hospital again. I'm not sure exactly when. It seems I was there for several weeks before I was moved to this hospital which is near Calais; I can see the sea. The doctor said I needed feeding up and I've put on a lot of weight. Last week my leg came out of plaster and I can walk really well now and won't need my stick in a few days. The doctor said I can go home in about three weeks. I can't wait to see you all. Please remember me to all my friends as well, especially Doris if she ever asks after me. I thought about writing to her but I don't really think she would want a letter from me.

Your loving son Albert

'He's alive,' gasped Susannah. 'So he's been injured again, but he's all right. I can't believe it, but it must be true, mustn't it Sid?'

'Of course it must, my love. I don't know what's happened, but someone must have got things terribly wrong. I suppose with so many being killed, things get mixed up.' He put his one arm round Susannah and both cried; in joy, in wonderful joy. 'I'll make a cup of tea and then let's close the shop for the rest of today. Who would believe it?' The "Rusfield miracle" had been born.

Putting up the closed sign twenty minutes later, Susannah and Sidney decided to make one call before walking home. They had been close to Arthur Windle since he had persuaded Sidney's employers at the brewery to give him some compensation; his efforts had enabled them to buy the shop. On that occasion, six years earlier, Arthur and Eleanor had been surprised when Susannah had thrown her arms round him; he was no less surprised now. Her explanation was confused and even when they were all sitting down in the vicarage kitchen, he did not really understand. Then they showed him the letter. His faith did not embrace a belief that God had intervened in saving their son; why not the others who had died? But he silently thanked God and could feel Eleanor sharing in the joyful news.

Customers had been surprised to find the butchers shut, but by early evening there were few villagers who had not heard the news. Amazement and joy abounded. However, Arthur was not the only one who realised that others in

369

mourning would now cling to a hope which would surely not be repeated; nor was it in Rusfield.

By late October when the news from Europe finally showed victory to be in sight, Private Albert Jones came back to the village. The family rejoicing was constantly interrupted by a succession of friends calling at the cottage in Wood Lane. Albert's return was the source of celebration that the village had not known for years. He did not have the strong look of the man who had gone to war, but anyone with him in the trenches six months earlier would have been surprised at the rebirth from his terribly haggard, torn look. He walked with a slight limp and his right hand, the one that Nurse Betty Hazlett had treated two and half years previously, was improving.

Three days home and he had still not seen Doris Groves. He had thought many times about calling on her, but had not plucked up the necessary courage; he little knew that she had the same failing. However, on the fourth afternoon, she was passing the Jones' cottage on her way back from Spinney Farm when she saw Albert in the garden looking at the vegetables; facing away from her. She wondered how her trembling legs carried her towards him and, still three yards away, Albert suddenly became aware of a slight sound and turned. Neither needed to worry about apologies or regrets, for they simply threw their arms round each other. They hugged, they kissed, they held each other for what thirteen-year-old Henrietta, who happened to be looking out of her bedroom window, later described as: 'For ever. I thought you were never going to let go.' Hand in hand they went round to the rear garden and into the kitchen. Any misgivings Susannah may have previously had about the dark-haired and certainly attractive twenty-year-old Doris, disappeared when she saw the joy on her son's face. To her, nothing but his happiness mattered.

Susannah had put the potatoes to one side, rapidly poured cups of tea and put out on a best plate some chocolate-chip biscuits baked the previous evening. She later admitted to bad manners to her husband: 'I was so overcome by their happiness, I forgot to invite them into the front room.' Sidney had always admired his wife's understanding of people, so he was not surprised that half an hour after the reunion, she turned the conversation from recent village happenings by saying: 'There's still nearly three hours of daylight left, why don't you two go for a walk? It'll do you good, Albert; you know what Nurse Hazlett said about making sure you exercised each day.'

Doris and Albert were delighted at the suggestion and, a few minutes later, hand in hand, the couple turned left from the cottage, passing the pond to begin the slight ascent to Bramrose Hill. They chatted away happily until Doris suddenly stopped. 'Do you remember when we walked up here over two years ago, and it suddenly came on to rain? We can't have been far from here and we sheltered in that old barn. Let's see if it's still there.' She knew it was, as several times she had walked this way in the months following the arrival of the fateful letter to Albert's parents, gone into the barn and wept tears for Albert and her own subsequent foolishness. Albert, less certain of the way, soon picked up the pace as he recognised the faint path to the left and followed. There was the barn.

They later admitted to each other that they knew what would happen next. 'It's just the same,' exclaimed Doris as they stood just inside the barn, dark, save for the shafts of light from the open door. There were the bales of straw that had been stored for a need long forgotten, the lofty timbers and an earthen floor protected from the ravages of weather by the centuries-old roof. Doris moved to Albert and put her arms round him, clasping him to her anticipating body. 'Oh Albert, I do love you, so much. Forgive me for that letter, I never meant it. I just missed you so much.'

'And I love you, Doris. I have thought about you so often: wanting you so much.' They kissed, their lips and tongues touching, feeling, knowing of the other's love. 'I'm sorry if

I've changed. I know I become easily upset and have a long way to get completely better, but I love you more than ever.'

'Albert, I know you have had a terrible time, but that's all over. You haven't really changed and I'll help you get completely well again.' Even as she consoled him, her hands had unbuttoned his coat. They embraced again, their kisses more passionate. She slipped off her dark green cloak and laid it on the loose straw that had become separated from the main bales. 'Albert come, take me. Please.'

Swiftly, though with some fumbling, they undressed each other, unaware of any slight chill in the air. Both were completely naked. They embraced; Albert feeling her hardened nipples against his chest, she his stiff manhood against her as yet unfulfilled body. She detached herself from him for a moment and made a slight cushion under the spread-eagled cloak with their other clothes. She lay down, moved her legs apart and held up her arms. 'Come.'

As Albert entered her and moved in unison with the woman he had loved for so long, his mind emptied of the terrors of war; replaced with a passion, a deep love which overrode all else. He could feel every part of her body against his own; her hold on him tightened and her nails dug into his back as she uttered a cry and shivered in an all-consuming fervour. A moment later he, too, climaxed.

As they left that place, the sky was peacefully darkening with the approaching twilight. Albert's mind and body felt strangely, yet wonderfully repaired; Doris could feel part of him within her. She had no fears; she knew they would be together for ever.

At the end of October, Charlotte Windle travelled to Rusfield. Over the past months she had increased the length between visits, still wanting to reassure herself that Arthur was coping with the loss of Eleanor, but not wanting to fuss over him. The late autumn weather had changed with the shortening of the days and she and Arthur could hear the rain tapping against the window as they sat in the comfortable lounge; empty coffee cups on nearby resting places.

'Arthur, the story of Albert Jones is obviously a remarkable one. You told me in your letters about the terrible time that he had; of being trapped in the shell-hole with the New Zealand man and then being a guard to the man awaiting execution and the explosion. But that doesn't explain why Albert was declared dead. Do you know what happened?'

Arthur crossed one leg over the other, sat forward and gently smiled. 'Mother, it's an amazing story. Albert, bless him, hasn't always been forthcoming, but I think we can work out what happened.' His mother nodded and sat back. 'It's one of the bravest stories that will come out of this terrible war which at last seems to be nearing an end.' He settled back in his chair, fingertips together in Dürer style.

'We can't even begin to imagine the terrible time he had in 1917 and the first half of this year. It was an experience that no one should ever have to go through and it's not surprising his mental state was shattered by what happened. You have mentioned how he was trapped in the shell-hole with the New Zealand man; well he told me last week that he had written to the lad's father to see if there was any news of his son. I even had the feeling that Albert might like to go to New Zealand.

'But it was a little later that events took an even more incredible turn. When he was ordered to be one of two guards the night before the execution, he was appalled.' He paused, even telling the story was distressing. 'Believe it or not, and it is incredible, Albert felt so much for the older man that he offered to change places with him. There was a change of guard duties and a different sergeant took over late that evening, so the only person other than Albert and the poor soldier waiting execution who knew of the swap was his fellow guard. Albert said that soldier was so frightened that he hardly knew what was going on. He certainly didn't try to do anything about Albert and the other man swapping places.

373

'Albert and the condemned man exchanged identity discs; you may have heard how the soldiers have to wear a small disc which bears their name and other details. I can't even begin to imagine the scene when early the next morning Albert was led out by the man who had taken his place, along with the sergeant and the men to carry out his execution. My God, it must have been like something from hell. But at that moment a heavy bombardment from the Germans began. Albert said he thinks a shell must have landed very near, but his first clear memory was being in a hospital near Calais.'

'So what do you, or rather Albert, think had happened?' Charlotte asked.

'We shall almost certainly never know the whole story, but when I asked Albert, he could only imagine that the men he had been with had either been injured or killed by the shell. He said his mind was full of fearful images before the shell fell, but he thinks he had already been slightly separated from the rest awaiting the order to fire. When he was talking to me, he broke down when he went on to say that he vaguely remembered a post to which he was about to be tied. I didn't press him, of course, but a while later he added that he couldn't separate in his mind what had actually happened and what he imagined in his frequent nightmares. The poor man; his suffering has been unbelievable.'

'And what a brave, brave man,' Charlotte Windle added.

Arthur sat up a little more before adding, 'And Albert has told his father that when the war is over he is going to seek out the wife of the man with whom he changed places. That soldier's disc would have been with Albert so probably his wife would have been told he was injured. However, since the disc with Albert's details was sent home, he assumes the man must have been killed. If he is dead Albert wants to tell his wife what a brave man he had been. Can you imagine that? Albert, as you say, is an incredibly brave and wonderful young man.'

CHAPTER FIFTY-TWO

November 1918 - April 1919

To Lance Corporal Jack Atkins advancing beyond Festubert in northern France, Corporal Abraham Richards over 120 miles to the south-east in Reims and millions of other fighting men, the end came as something of a surprise; relief, but so long had they been fighting that peace seemed beyond any horizon.

The guns became silent and the shells stopped killing, but Arthur Windle knew lives would remain scarred for generations. He thought back to the death of the first Rusfield man, Copper Chambers; hardly a month had passed since then without a further fatality. The tentacles of war had reached so many in the village. But when St Mary's bells were rung on Monday, 11 November by Fred Richards, Alfred Reynolds and Jack Groves, who refused to let his increasing breathlessness prevent him from what he called 'my final but greatest ring of all', there was much rejoicing, albeit tempered by a profound sorrow for those grieving. After several unofficial discussions it was agreed that a more immediate celebration be held, although the major one must wait until the men returned home. This "muted celebration" as Arthur thought of it, would be held on the village green; November weather was unpredictable, but the scene for so many past village events saw no opposition. Fred Jackson's offer of his largest barn

375

was held in reserve. The kitchens at The Queens Head and The Ark became centres for baking with more refreshments prepared in many cottages and the larger kitchens of Henrietta Jackson, Isabella de Maine and Mabel Mansfield. The food was kept overnight in the storeroom behind Violet Rushton's shop where so many soldiers' parcels had been prepared. The Union Jack, flown in Robert Berry's garden for many years, was proudly carried by the veteran of an earlier war to the green. Chairs had been carried from the Methodist chapel to the school, then only requiring a short journey to the green. The school closed and work in and around the village stopped for the day.

As Olivia Atkins joined Pauline Richards to lay coloured paper on the tables where the children would sit for tea, she gave a weak smile to her friend, saying: 'Have you heard from Abraham recently?'

'I had a letter just a month ago and he made it sound as if all was well; but you know Abraham, always one to understate dangers and difficulties. What about you?'

'I haven't heard from Jack for six weeks, but he sounded all right then. I wonder when they will all come home. It said in the newspaper that it could be well into next year before they are all back.' Having clipped the paper to the tables, they laid out the designs which the children in the youngest classes had made at school. There was now an army of helpers rushing to get everything ready for the start at noon; early preparations in the open air had been delayed as long as possible. It was cool but the sky remained clear of rain clouds.

The children carried Union Jacks that they had made and attached to small sticks; races organised by Grace Reynolds, Reggie Gregg and three of his chapel members helped build up appetites. The array of food, a tribute to all who had been faced with the shortages, surprised everyone. Arthur started the celebration with a prayer of thanksgiving, followed by two verses of the national anthem led by the choir which had been formed by Eleanor, with Sammy Hatfield on accordion and Bernie Thomas on his ancient fiddle. Two hours later, as everyone left the green after many helpers had cleared everything away, all agreed it had been a memorable day. The many families with men still abroad had celebrated with slightly muted feelings, those who had lost love ones concealed their thoughts or quietly stayed away.

On the following afternoon, Arthur sat in the vicarage kitchen finalising the next Sunday's service. When he and Reggie Gregg had met at the manse the day after the armistice, they had agreed the main thanksgiving and remembrance service be held when the men had returned from abroad, but immediate services to mark the armistice should be held at both church and chapel.

Arthur and the Methodist minister had become close friends and as he sat thinking about the service, Arthur reflected on their times together over the past months. Many of the doubts which had torn holes in his faith remained, but he still felt at one with Eleanor's central beliefs that there was a God and the teaching and example of Christ were the essence of the Christian faith. His occasional meetings with the Very Reverend Edgar Hartley Williamson could hardly be described as building a warm friendship, but a mutual understanding had developed and Arthur had been persuaded by the dean to continue his priesthood. Arthur decided that he should not forego his allegiance to St Mary's and the Rusfield community until the war was over.

It was his conversations with his Methodist friend that had really swayed him to stay within the ministry. Whilst he was close to many villagers, it was only with Reggie Gregg that he felt able to expose his doubts and critically examine his faith. His colleague knew that Arthur's sense of loss when Eleanor died was of the most profound depth, and marvelled at the selfless way in which Arthur continued to serve the community; to Reggie this was a wonderful act of Christianity. 'Arthur, I too have doubts, serious ones. I've wrestled with some of the same doubts you have mentioned: how on Christ's earth can we ask a God whom we believe to be powerful enough to intervene in a war, when that same God has allowed it to happen in the first place? I can only think that we were given the intelligence to ask such questions and that one day, I don't know how or when, I may understand such things.'

Arthur had found these conversations encouraging, at least preventing him from a rejection of God's presence in the world, even if he was certain of little else. More than once the words of the Buddhist monk with whom he had briefly travelled went through his mind: 'Truth or, as you would say God, is so great that no single religion can fully encompass it.'

The services on the following day were attended by full congregations; tears of joy and sadness shared the occasions at both places of worship.

'I read over a month ago that things would soon get back to normal, now the bloody war is over,' Sammy Hatfield remarked to Bernie Thomas, together drinking in the New Year at The Ark. 'I don't think things will ever be the same again.'

'I was talking with Olivia Atkins a couple of days ago and she is still waiting for her son Jack. Still, I'd better say it: here's to 1919,' Bernie toasted, gnarled hand lovingly holding his pint glass. 'It must be better than the past few years. Olivia told me that the last time Jack was home for Christmas was 1913. Can you believe it, over five years ago?'

The army of Rusfield men had begun to trickle home. Frank Boulton and Harry Grainger were the first back; Frank with a badly damaged leg sustained from fighting two days before the armistice, and Harry missing two fingers from a rogue grenade. By Christmas thirty more were back in Rusfield and the homecoming continued.

Pauline and Frederick Richards heard in late December

that Abraham was in an infantry base depot near Calais waiting for an available boat. His letter revealed that he was well and as he put it: *When I think about all that's happened I'm just lucky to be alive.* He went on to say that like all the volunteers at the beginning of the war, he was being given some preferential treatment regarding the timing of his return.

Wives, parents, brothers, sisters and sweethearts all waited; some, like the Richards family, received notice of their man's homecoming; Gwendoline Edwards and others were amazed that when answering a knock at the door they found their man standing there. Men arrived home in uniform with steel helmet and greatcoat; some loved ones almost unrecognisable from the eager volunteers of a few years earlier. Most found that mother or wife had ensured civilian clothes were waiting, but some which had last been worn years earlier, showed much slack in the fitting. When Jack Atkins finally came home in late January he, like so many battle-scarred soldiers, found the whole idea of peace bewildering; thoughts were a mixture of horrors experienced and friends who did not return. Loved ones needed all their sensitivity to cope with their man's return. Fathers who had fervently looked forward to seeing their children after such a long absence found their loving advances barely returned; Harry Grainger broke down in tears, exclaiming to his wife Mildred: 'Ruby doesn't seem to care about me. She thinks I'm just a visitor.' Daniel Reynolds wanted to be out in the open air even in the coldest weather.

Arthur Windle and Reggie Gregg tried to keep up with families when men returned, carefully avoiding interference, but aware that only time and the patience of entire families could heal the separation and horrors of the time away. Some men eased back into civilian life with apparent ease; Abraham Richards was one, it was as if he had hardly been away, yet his parents realised that he might just be more successful in hiding his memories. Arthur wondered if one of the saving graces for Abraham was that within a few days he recommenced running.

At first on gentle runs, but as health improved so distance and speed took over. He soon returned to being the well-known figure running through and well beyond Rusfield. However, he like other returning men, declined to talk of war activities and Arthur perceived traces of guilt in some that they had survived and not their mates.

Arthur made it known that the vicarage door was open each morning from ten o'clock for anyone who wanted to drop in for a chat and a cup of tea or coffee; some villagers called during the next weeks, but rarely any of the war veterans. His heart continued to bleed for Eleanor; she would have known the best way forward with the returning soldiers. She would have charmed them, listened and given support. He was surprised to find that he now prayed more often for help. His old habit, was it no more than that he wondered, of spending a quiet time in his dressing room before retiring, became more frequent. His appeal for forgiveness of his own sins was frequently on his lips. This was never more so than with the approach of an appointment, he could not think of a better word, in early February.

Ten days after his return to Rusfield, Jack Atkins received a letter from Patricia Bagshott that her parents would love him to stay in Ealing for a few days. In spite of prolonged absence, their correspondence and two short spells together had enhanced their love and letters between them spoke of a life together. Three days before his departure to Ealing, Jack had been surprised when his mother said to him: 'Jack, there's something I need to tell you, something really important.' Jack looked at his loving mother, as beautiful and caring as ever, but faltering even in the few words she had just spoken.

'Jack, please trust me. It won't be easy for me to tell you and it will be even harder for you to hear, but please remember that I love you dearly and always will.' Jack was further surprised to see a tear forming in his mother's eye. He wondered what it was she wanted to tell him; perhaps about her childhood and the disastrous fire that had killed her parents at the family home in Coventry when she had been eighteen, later moving to Rusfield. The thought even flashed through his mind that she had met someone and was going to tell him of a marriage arrangement, but why should she be so fearful of telling him? He would have rejoiced in anything that would bring his mother happiness.

'I have invited Arthur Windle round tomorrow evening to join us; you will see why later.' She walked across to her son, leant down and gently kissed him. He knew the kiss was a sign to ask no more for the moment.

The following evening Olivia and her son were ready to receive Arthur Windle. A blazing fire warmed the small, comfortable room; several of her own drawings added to its attractiveness. It was Jack who answered the knock just before six o'clock and welcomed the Rusfield vicar. As he took the visitor's coat and his mother and the vicar greeted one another, Jack felt a slight tension between them. Jack offered drinks, but these were politely declined as the two older people sat down; both failing to relax in the armchairs. It was Olivia who spoke first.

'Jack, my dear, you must be wondering what it's all about. I have something to tell you which I should have told you many years ago. I kept putting it off and then intended to tell you when you became eighteen. Again, I delayed and then the war came and you were away for so long. I'm sorry I've been a coward and can only ask for your forgiveness.'

Jack gave a gentle smile, just wanting his mother to tell him whatever this was all about. He determined not to interrupt her. 'It's a long story and there's no easy way to tell you. It's about me and your father.' Jack's mind flashed to the only evidence he had seen of his father: Edward Atkins' headstone in the Rusfield graveyard relating his death on 23 October 1894. But in the next few seconds Jack was to receive his first major shock from his mother: 'Jack, your father was not whom you think it was. I have to confess that your father was not Edward whom I had married.' Jack's look was a mixture of surprise and slight anger.

'But Mother...' he cut short what he was about to say, remembering the promise to himself that he would not interrupt.

'Jack, you know I came to Rusfield in 1890 when I was eighteen and worked at Spinney Farm and two summers later I was married. Edward was handsome and when we first met he was amusing and I loved him. What I've never told you was that he could be very cruel. We were quite poor, but we could manage. I earned a little money in odd jobs and Edward's modest money, mainly from hedging and ditching, was only seasonal work. I didn't know when we got married that Edward drank a lot. I knew he occasionally spent time in The George, but he had kept the full extent from me; or maybe I was just too stupid or in love to see. He began to drink more and we just didn't have enough money. Thinking back, I realise Eliza Carey tried to warn me, but I hadn't paid any attention. Jack, I'm not just blaming the man you thought was your father, a lot of it was my fault. Things got worse and some evenings he came home very drunk and then he'd hit me and force himself on me. It was awful.'

Jack found himself having to say something, 'Mother, I had no idea. Why didn't you ever tell me? You should have left him if things were so bad?' He reached out and gently placed his hand on her knee.

'Jack, I had nowhere to go. I hadn't any money and by this time my grandmother had died; I didn't have any other relatives and didn't know anyone in Rusfield well enough to tell them what was happening. I know all this sounds as if I'm making excuses for what happened later; maybe I am.'

'But didn't other people, you mentioned Eliza, see what was happening?' Jack could not easily believe what his lovely mother was telling him, yet he knew she was not lying.

'Edward was clever. He would always punch me so the bruises were covered. In any case I felt too ashamed, because I knew I was failing to make our marriage work. Once he did punch my face and threw a saucer which cut my forehead, but I pretended that I'd had a bad fall and people seemed to believe me. Things just got worse and some evenings I'd wrap up and go for long walks hoping that by my return he would have got home and fallen asleep. That often happened, but sometimes he'd got home first and locked the door and I had to stay outside in the log shed.' She stopped for a while and Jack knew she was approaching the climax of her story.

'One evening, Arthur,' she briefly gestured in his direction, 'came round to see me. Somehow he'd heard that all was not well and had come to see if he could speak with Edward. But he had gone off to The George particularly early that evening as he'd just received his pay. I was desperate. I liked Arthur. I'd got to know him a little since he'd come to Rusfield and when his wife died after they had been married such a short time, lots of us had tried to help him. Well, that's the evening no one else knows about, until now. It's no excuse, but I was in a really bad state from all that had happened and Arthur was desperately unhappy since Florence had died. We realised each other's despair and reached out to each other for comfort: somehow our feelings spiralled out of control and we made love. Arthur is really your father.'

Tears overcame Olivia, but Jack failed to notice them; the room was spinning round, he felt his world was coming apart. He tried to focus on the man whom he had just learnt was his father, but could only see a blurred figure. It was the Reverend Arthur Windle who spoke next, hesitantly.

'Jack, I was the one to blame, just me. Your mother was in a terrible state and I caused things to happen, things that I have felt ashamed of a million times over. I was the priest, I had come round to offer my support and I abused my office. Your mother was guiltless, blame me.'

'That's not true, Arthur. We were both young, we had the normal passions of young people and they had been stifled: mine through the abuse of Edward, yours through your wife's death. For a brief time we each held one who cared, and we were completely carried away.'

Jack turned and looked at Arthur Windle. 'But how do you know he's my father?'

'Jack, Edward and I had not been together for weeks; after that evening I managed to keep away from him. He preferred hitting me more than anything else.'

'But didn't he know you were pregnant?'

'I pretended my sickness was food poisoning. And remember he was killed in that thunderstorm only three months later. I was frightened. I would have told him, but that never happened.'

'So you were pleased when your husband was killed in that thunderstorm?' Jack regretted saying this as soon as the words were said.

'No, I wasn't pleased. How can anyone be pleased at someone being killed in such a terrible way? But our love for each other had died a long while before.'

'So why didn't you two marry then?'

'We talked about it, Jack,' Arthur replied slowly. 'We talked about it a lot. Your mother knew that if it became known that I was the father, it would later be hard for you. She worried about that a lot. I know your mother was thrilled when you were born and her love rightly turned to you. We still talked together, but always made it look as if it was just between priest and parishioner. I wanted to be known as your father, but we had made a vow to each other. As you grew up and became the son I had always wanted I begged your mother to marry me, but she said no.'

'Jack, you've got to understand,' interjected his mother, 'that such a confession would have ruined Arthur. He would have had to leave the church, certainly Rusfield, and he was a

384

good man. No, I couldn't. But my real sin was in not telling you a long time ago.'

The fire crackled and a log tumbled forward, otherwise the room was silent. Olivia had known it was going to be hard to tell Jack; she had not realised how hard. Olivia and Arthur were not surprised when Jack stood up; they were delighted when he stooped down, placed an arm round his mother's shoulders and kissed the top of her head. He, too, had tears in his eyes.

'Mother, I'm hardly able to believe what you've just told me. I don't know what I feel and I wish you had told me a long time ago. I'll just have to think about everything I've heard.' He paused for several seconds. 'I remember you said earlier that whatever you told me, you loved me. I love you, too.' He added: 'Neither of you will tell anyone else, will you?' Both Olivia and Arthur nodded their agreement.

When Arthur left the West Lane cottage a short while later, he wondered if Jack would ever really think of him as his father.

As she retired to bed, Olivia's heart went out to her son, but she was relieved that Jack now knew the long-kept secret; she would never regret his conception at a time when two injured people's compassion became a momentary loving union. She briefly thought of the one other person who knew the secret, but knew it would be safe.

Jack was confused as to what he should think; he knew he must accept what he had just been told, but he wondered if he could ever see the Rusfield vicar in his new role.

The soldiers continued to come home; there was talk of little else in the village. Relationships disrupted by their years away took time to rebuild; some were never the same, but in the passing months so many villagers gave support that much healing took place. Sebastian and Isabella de Maine opened their home each Friday morning for men returning from the war to call in, talk with one another and enjoy a cup of tea together. The walk to the manor was pleasant and sharing time, often with friends they had not seen for years, was good; some could not bring themselves to go. The memorial fund continued to grow, as did discussions about the best way to commemorate the Rusfield men who had died. More immediately, the memorial service filled many minds. Arthur, Reggie Gregg and those on both committees were determined to make it a village service where people from church and chapel would join easily with those who had no allegiance to either. Sunday, 27 April was chosen, the Sunday after Easter, commemorating the resurrection, an occasion thought by both Arthur and Reggie Gregg to be appropriate; to those who had no place for church anniversaries, it was the Sunday following St George's Day.

St Mary's overflowed with villagers; whichever way people looked they saw a soldier, now with his family. There was a single red flower on a table near the altar for each man who had given his life, arranged by the loving hands of Eliza Carey and Liz Smith who had both lost sons. Reggie Gregg read out the names of the thirty-nine men; Frederick Richards from St Mary's and Bertram Jackson from the chapel read the lessons. Returning from Devon, Peter Meadows, who had known virtually every one of the men during his time as headmaster, spoke words that were heartbreaking, not least to himself. Liz Smith still had tears of pride in her eyes for words that he had said to her before the service, when they both talked of her only son, Fred Smith. 'Liz, I remember Fred in the school football team, but I also remember how we needed matching shirts for that all-conquering team. We collected together enough shirts, but they were of different colours. It was you who dyed them our chosen colour, green, and ironed them.'

Arthur began his sermon: 'This tragic episode in the history of our village started with some of our young men walking in to Steepleton to join the Territorial Army. To them and all the others who later joined our armed forces we offer our praise. To those who never returned we give our gratitude; they will always be remembered in Rusfield. To those of you whose husbands, sons, brothers or friends never returned we give our love.'

Everyone went away with their own thoughts and memories. As Jack Atkins and Patricia Bagshott walked away hand in hand, with Olivia and the three other members of Patricia's family close behind, Jack was determined to tell his fiancée of his new-found father. He had wrestled hard with the recently discovered truth, endlessly talking it over with his mother, now finding that his own feelings towards Patricia helped him to understand a little more of the evening in the family cottage many years earlier.

EPILOGUE

1919 and Beyond

On the first day of September, Mrs Richards stood watching the children line up before going into Rusfield School. 'It's nice to see you, Miss,' smiled Margaret Robinson on the teacher's first day at her school.

'You should say "Mrs Richards", Marjorie,' corrected her eleven-year-old sister, Martha. 'Grace is married now.' Grace had excitedly looked forward to having her new class since deciding to move from Wensfield School. The change had not been without tears as she had loved her first teaching position, but being in her own village was a new adventure.

Arthur Windle would be a little later arriving at the school for the assembly to which he had been invited on this first day of term; forty-five minutes being allowed to register and settle in the new children. Meanwhile, Arthur walked into the rear garden of the vicarage which, with a little help from David Johnson, he managed to maintain. He cut a cream rose and took it across to the churchyard where he placed it on Eleanor's grave, near to the door into St Mary's; 28 August 1917, two years since she had died. He missed her as much as ever, but knew she was close by him. Some confetti from the previous Saturday had blown across her grave and Arthur smiled. Eleanor would have loved all the weddings that had taken place at St Mary's in the past few months, the scene for so much joy and hope. Dear Ruby Johnson, distraught by the deaths of Fred Smith and her loving brother Willy, but now much loved by Peter Woods, still postman in the village: no longer the herald of war deaths. Married two days earlier, Arthur was sure their future was bright.

And all the other weddings earlier in the year: Doris Groves and Albert Jones had been the first and Arthur had been astonished at the way Albert's mental wounds had been lessened by the caring Doris. Albert and Arthur had spent much time together and the younger man had told Arthur how he had travelled to the small village in Yorkshire and called on Nellie Marsden. His visit had revealed that her husband, Mike, had been killed, the letter from his sergeant stating that he *died instantly in an explosion.* She had been grateful that Albert told her of her husband's bravery; Albert relieved that no accusation of cowardice had ever been suggested in official letters. Nellie had told Albert that her parents were now living with her and together they were coping well with the large family.

Two weeks earlier, Doris, proudly cradled seven-week-old James, whilst Albert told Arthur they were emigrating to New Zealand in a year's time when their son would be old enough for the long journey. Albert had corresponded much with Robert Grayson and his wife. They admitted to struggling on their farm near Little River and how they could certainly offer plenty of work to Albert along with a cottage for his family. Sadly, his son Martin had been killed two months before the end of the war. In one of the letters home, Martin had told his parents about the time he spent with a young Englishman in a shell-hole and how they had talked about the farm.

Weddings of young men returning from the war had been expected, but the marriage of Violet Rushton and Robert Berry was a surprise, one that delighted the many who knew them. They now lived above Violet's shop, the storeroom where the soldiers' parcels had been prepared having been pleasantly converted into a well-appointed additional room. Violet had happily agreed to the transfer of her husband's treasured Union Jack from Sandy Lane to their garden overlooking the village green.

On a beautiful mid-July day, Abraham Richards and Grace Reynolds had married. As he now stood alone in the churchyard, Arthur pictured the large numbers that had cheered as the couple stepped out of the church. The village youngsters, who had followed every race that their hero won, had joined the many guests for the joyous occasion. The wedding feast had been in Jack Mansfield's barn, beautifully decorated by their many friends. As Grace had told Doris, 'Abraham and I want it to be there because that's where we fell in love at that Easter-time party seven years ago.' She added, with her engaging smile: 'Although, I suppose we should really have held it in the infants' classroom as I liked Abraham when I saw him there on my first day at school!' Abraham was now assistant manager at Spinney Farm where one of the attractive cottages was enjoyed by the young couple as their first home.

To Arthur, the most wonderful of all weddings had taken place not in Rusfield, but at St Peter's in Ealing. Jack had married Patricia with both Arthur and Olivia recognised as parents of the groom. Arthur would forever be indebted to Jack for his courage in speaking to the congregation at St Mary's, following his own confession. After Arthur had moved down from the pulpit to speak to the many present, Jack, grasping his mother's hand, had walked forward and the three had joined hands together. Jack had spoken of his pride in his parents, Olivia and Arthur. Arthur thought back to how he had expected the admission to be greeted with anger and much criticism, but had found only surprise and love. When they saw each other now, Olivia and Arthur no longer had to hide behind the disguise of priest and parishioner; they were dear friends and the proud parents of a splendid son. Arthur had seen Patricia earlier in the morning walking from the cottage vacated by Robert Berry; now the home for the young couple. Jack had recently taken over as manager of the bakery in Steepleton and hoped to own the flourishing business one day.

Before moving off to the school, Arthur sat for a few minutes in the quietness of St Mary's. He was still uncertain of his own future. Some of the church's utterances still found no favour with him, but he felt much more certain of a God whose presence was never far away. He now shared Eleanor's love for the Sermon on the Mount and understood Christ's love shown in his suffering on the cross. He rejoiced in a firmer foundation for his own faith.

After the knowledge of him being Jack's father had not lessened the villagers' regard for him, he realised how much he wanted to stay in the village. He had again met with the dean who had indicated his support and promised to encourage the new bishop to reconsider the intended reprimand and Arthur's removal from Rusfield. A final decision was awaited. Before leaving Eleanor's grave, Arthur looked across the age-old churchyard and noticed a buzzard sitting in its favoured tree by the village green.

Now, as he sat on the slightly raised podium and looked out at the children enthusiastically singing their morning hymn, he felt the village to be in good hands. He was sure any decline in the school numbers over the next year or so, would soon be put right.

The following Saturday, Abraham, Jack and Albert met at The George, the first time for many weeks. Turning to his life-long friend, Jack put down his glass and asked: 'Well Racer, another championship race won last month, so what about the Olympics next year? Antwerp isn't it?'

Abraham with a slight smile replied: 'Well, I hope so, I

managed to equal the best time I did before the war, but I need to do better than that. I can only hope to be there.'

'Oh, you'll be there,' responded Boney. 'All Rusfield will be cheering you on, including Fred, Willy and Jammy.'

'Well, I can hardly let them down.'

ACKNOWLEDGEMENTS

Whilst any errors rest with the author, he particularly acknowledges the help of:

Jennie, my wife, who supported me from the outset

Jane Bennett, my daughter, whose help in every aspect of the book was a major driving force.

Naomi, Alice and Hannah of Troubador Publishing Ltd.

Charlotte Fausset, whose drawing of the village brings Rusfield further alive.

John Temperton of United Kingdom Athletics

British Postal Museum & Archive

Royal Gunpowder Mills, Waltham Abbey

Author contact: regrettoinformyou1914@gmail.com